Route of the *Demeter*
Route of the *Czarina Catherine*
Orient Express (Paris to Varna)

RUSSIA
BUKHOVINA
Carpathian Mountains
TRANSYLVANIA
MOLDAVIA
Galatz
RIA-HUNGARY
ROMANIA
River Danube
Varna
BULGARIA
TURKEY
Dardanelles
Sea of Marmara
GREECE
BLACK SE
Czari
Cather
TURKEY

PRAISE FOR

The Secret Diaries of Charlotte Brontë

GREAT GROUP READ 2009
—Women's National Book Association

"For fans of biographical tales and romance, Syrie's story of Charlotte offers it all: longing and yearning, struggle and success, the searing pain of immeasurable loss, and the happiness of a love that came unbidden and unsought. I did not want this story to end."

—Jane Austen's World

"The story is impeccably researched, the language authentic feeling, and James has imagined a story that most Brontë fans will enjoy thoroughly. In some ways, her tale of Charlotte's life almost seems like an undiscovered plot from one of Brontë's own works."

—BookNAround

"5 STARS. An excellent combination of truth and conjecture that is a gratifying and magnetizing read! I have had the wonderful pleasure of reading Syrie James's first book, *The Lost Memoirs of Jane Austen*, and in both books I find myself very impressed by the author's extensive research and knowledge. . . . I felt she captured an accurate and distinct voice and personality for both Jane Austen and Charlotte Brontë. . . . I dearly hope she continues to write more in this vein, I love her reverent and precise representation of these beloved authors. In addition, her graceful storytelling is seamless and entertaining. I highly recommend this novel."

—Austenesque Reviews

"Syrie James first showcased her research prowess with her novel *The Lost Memoirs of Jane Austen,* and the skill has come in handy again in *The Secret Diaries of Charlotte Brontë*. Although framed as Brontë's confessional journal, James easily takes the biography of Brontë and sketches it into a work of art. . . . The availability of specific, passionate details is what gives the book its main pull. . . . Syrie manages to weave the dysfunction of the family into the journal in quite a touching manner. . . . A can't-miss novel for Brontë fans and historical fiction buffs alike."

—*Sacramento Book Review*

"James adapts Brontë's voice, telling Brontë's story as though it came straight from the great writer. Living with an alcoholic, drug-addicted brother and a deeply eccentric father, Brontë—and her sisters—still managed to write some of the most famous novels of their time. With *The Secret Diaries of Charlotte Brontë*, James offers a satisfying—if partly imagined—history of the real-life experiences that inspired Brontë's classic novels."

—*BookPage*

PRAISE FOR

The Lost Memoirs of Jane Austen

THE INTERNATIONAL BESTSELLING NOVEL

"Syrie James . . . is a fine storyteller, with a sensitive ear for the Austenian voice and a clear passion for research. The result is a thoughtful, immensely touching romance that does justice to its subject and will delight anyone who feels, as Syrie James does, that Jane Austen couldn't possibly have written with such insight without having had a great romance of her own."

—*Jane Austen's Regency World*

"There are not enough accolades I could use to recommend this book. . . . I read it thinking all the while it was a newly discovered memoir of the famous writer. That is how good the writing is. . . . It is a love affair equal to anything Jane Austen wrote. . . . Thank you, Syrie James."

—*News Review* (Oregon)

"Suspense builds and it's a tribute to the world James creates that readers will anxiously root for Jane to find true love and wealth even though we know it never happened. Deserves frontrunner status in the . . . field of Austen fan-fiction and film."

—*Kirkus Reviews*

"Most interesting is the way James creates a life story for Austen that illuminates how her themes and plots may have developed. . . . [T]he reader blindly pulls for the heroine and her dreams of love, hoping against history that Austen might yet enjoy the satisfactions of romance. . . . James's novel offers a deeper understanding of what Austen's life might have been like."

—*Los Angeles Times*

By Syrie James

Dracula, My Love

The Secret Journals of Mina Harker

A Novel

SYRIE JAMES

AVON

An Imprint of HarperCollins*Publishers*

This book is a work of fiction. The characters, incidents, and dialogue are drawn from the author's imagination and are not to be construed as real. Any resemblance to actual events or persons, living or dead, is entirely coincidental.

HarperCollins books may be purchased for educational, business, or sales promotional use. For information please write: Special Markets Department, HarperCollins Publishers, 10 East 53rd Street, New York, NY 10022.

FIRST AVON PAPERBACK EDITION PUBLISHED 2010.

Designed by Diahann Sturge
Maps designed by John Del Gaizo

Library of Congress Cataloging-in-Publication Data
James, Syrie.
Dracula my love : the secret journals of Mina Harker : a novel / Syrie James. — 1st ed.
p. cm.
ISBN 978-0-06-192303-6 (pbk. : acid-free paper)
1. Young women—Fiction. 2. Dracula, Count (Fictitious character)—Fiction. 3. Vampires—Fiction. I. Title.
PS3610.A457D73 2010
813'.6—dc22 2010003346

10 11 12 13 14 OV/RRD 10 9 8 7 6 5 4 3 2 1

For my son Ryan Michael James, who piqued my interest in vampires, and who is a wizard in his own right.

And in memory of my brilliant, beloved father, Morton Michael Astrahan, who used to thrill me with his bedtime stories, which always ended with a cliffhanger . . . and who encouraged me to follow my dreams.

ACKNOWLEDGMENTS

With undying gratitude to Bram Stoker, whose *Dracula* has become the stuff of legend and whose work has inspired a whole new genre of fiction. A grateful thank-you to my agent, Tamar Rydzinski, for insisting that I figure out a way to retell *Dracula* from Mina's point of view; this book would not exist without you. Thanks to my son Ryan, for introducing me to the magic and wonder of vampires years ago, and for all the insightful notes and comments along the way.

I am indebted to Leslie Klinger for his detailed work *The New Annotated Dracula,* which became my Bible, and to Fred Saberhagen's *The Dracula Tape,* which redeemed Dracula by cleverly revealing the truth behind many of his past misdeeds.

A loving thank-you to my husband Bill, for enduring my obsession with all things Dracula with such good humor and grace, and for his thrilling and ecstatic response upon reading the first draft. Thanks to my mother-in-law, Mary James, who kept a very romantic journal of her own, and whose love of books and reading has been an inspiration in so many ways. To Lucia Macro, Esi Sogah, Christine Maddalena, and the entire team at HarperCollins, who work so hard every day, and who sparked to this project when it was little more than a wisp of vapor on the page.

And most importantly, a heartfelt thank you to all my readers. Researching, plotting, imagining, and writing this novel has been one of the greatest adventures of my life. I hope you have as much fun reading it as I had in composing it. Enjoy the ride!

Europe 1890

N
S
E
W
NORTH SEA
Demeter
Whitby
ENGLAND
London
Exeter
Amsterdam
HOLLAND
Hamburg
PRUSSIA
RUSSIA
0 250 500 Miles
0 250 500 Kilometers
BUKHOVINA
Carpathian Mountains
Paris
Orient Express
Vienna
TRANSYLVANIA
MOLDAVIA
FRANCE
Buda-Pesth
Galatz
AUSTRIA-HUNGARY
ROMANIA
River Danube
Varna
Czarina Catherine
BULGARIA
BLACK SEA
SPAIN
MEDITERRANEAN SEA
TURKEY
Dardanelles
Sea of Marmara
GREECE
TURKEY
Strait of Gibraltar
Route of the *Demeter*
Route of the *Czarina Catherine*
Orient Express (Paris to Varna)

Dracula's Transylvania

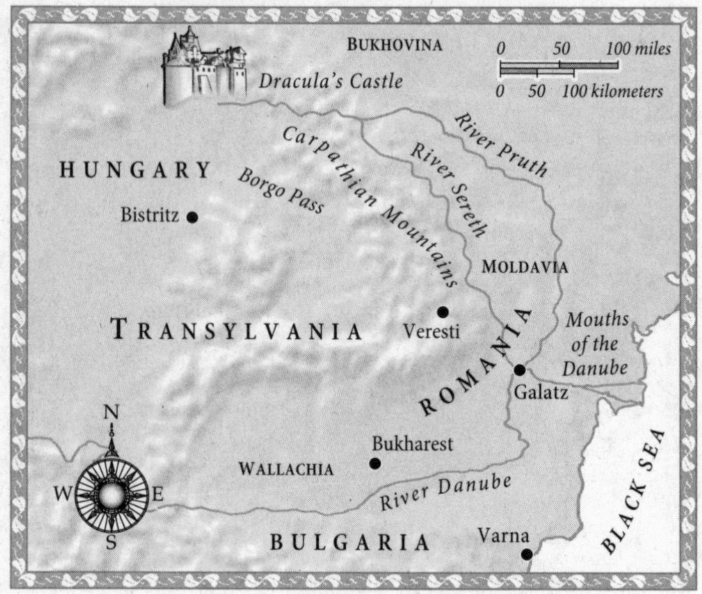

Mina Harker's England

PROLOGUE

1897

IT HAS BEEN SEVEN LONG YEARS SINCE THE FIRST NIGHT HE came to my chamber, seven long years since the string of haunting, incredible, and perilous events occurred—events which I am certain no one else will believe, even though we took care to make a written record of it. It is those transcripts of our journals—mine, and the other's—which I look at from time to time, to remind myself that it all really happened and that I did not merely dream it.

Now and then, when I spy a white mist gathering in the garden below, when a shadow crosses a wall at night, or when I see dust motes swirling in a beam of moonlight, I still find myself jumping in expectation and alarm. Jonathan will press my hand and catch my eye with a silent, reassuring look, as if to let me know that he understands, that we are safe. But when he turns back to his reading by the fire, my heart continues to hammer in my chest, and I am overcome not only by the sense of apprehension that Jonathan knows I feel, but by something else as well . . . by longing.

Yes, longing.

The record I kept—the journal I so carefully wrote in shorthand, and then typed for the others to read—was not the entire truth; not *my* truth. Some thoughts and experiences are too intimate for others' eyes; some desires are too shocking to admit, even to one's self. Were I to reveal all to Jonathan, I know I would lose him for ever, as surely as I would lose for ever the good opinion of all society.

I know what my husband wants—what all men want. For a woman—single or married—to be loved and respected, she must be innocent: entirely pure of mind, body, and soul. And so I once was, until *he* came into my life. At times, I feared him. At other times, I despised him. And yet, even knowing what he was and what he wanted, I could not help but love him.

I will never forget the magic of being held in his embrace, the compelling magnetism of his eyes as he gazed at me, or how it felt to whirl about the dance floor in his arms. I still shiver with delight when I recall the dizzying sensation of travelling with him at the speed of light, and the way his slightest touch could make me gasp with unimagined pleasure and desire. But the most wondrous times were the hours upon hours of conversation, stolen moments in which we revealed our most private selves to each other, and discovered all that we held in common.

I loved him. I loved him passionately, profoundly, from the very depths of my being, and with every beating of my heart. There was a time when I might have gladly given up this human life to be with him for ever.

And yet . . .

All these years, the truth of what happened has weighed heavily on my mind, taking the pleasure out of ordinary things, stealing my appetite, and banishing sleep. I find I cannot carry the guilty burden within me any longer. I must put it all down on paper, never to be seen by others' eyes, but certain that only in the writing will I at last be free to let it go.

ONE

When I first stepped off the train at Whitby on that bright July afternoon in 1890, I had no inkling that my life, and the lives of everyone I knew and loved, would soon be subjected to the gravest of dangers from which we—those of us who survived—would emerge for ever altered. When my foot touched the station platform that day, I was not overcome by a sudden chill, nor did I have an uncanny premonition of the unthinkable events to come. There was, in fact, nothing to indicate that this holiday at the sea-side would be any different from all those pleasant sojourns that had come before it.

I was two-and-twenty years old. I had, after four happy years, just quit my position as a school-teacher in preparation for my upcoming marriage. Although I was deeply concerned about my fiancé, Jonathan Harker, who had not yet returned from a business trip to Transylvania, I was filled with delight at the prospect of spending the next month or two in a beautiful place with my best friend in the world, where we could talk together freely and build our castles in the air.

I caught sight of Lucy standing on the platform, looking lovelier than ever in her white lawn frock, her dark curls peeking out demurely from beneath her stylish, flowered hat, as she searched for me through the crowd. Our eyes met, and her face lit up.

"Mina!" Lucy cried, and we raced into each other's arms.

"How I have missed you!" I replied, hugging her. "It seems as if a year has passed since we last saw each other, instead of months. So much has happened in the meantime."

"I feel the same. Last spring, we were both single women. And now—"

"—we are both engaged!" We smiled happily and embraced again.

Lucy Westenra and I had been best friends ever since the day we met at Upton Hall School when I was fourteen years old and she was twelve. Despite the fact that we came from very different backgrounds—Lucy had loving, wealthy parents who doted on her, while I had never known my parents and was only receiving a quality education courtesy of a grant—we became inseparable. We were a study in contrasts: I was a rosy-cheeked, green-eyed blonde of medium height who others seemed to consider attractive; whereas Lucy was an astonishing beauty, with a perfect, petite figure, bright blue eyes, an ivory complexion, and a crown of stunning dark brown curls. Lucy loved to ride and play ball and tennis, whereas I had always been far happier with my nose in a book; yet we found common ground in other things.

All through our school years, we slept together, played together, studied together, took long walks together, laughed and cried together, and told all our secrets to each other. As I had had no real home to return to when school was out of session, I had often—and gratefully—spent many holidays with Lucy's family, either at their home in London or in the country, or at whatever fashionable sea-side resort had taken Mrs. Westenra's fancy at the time. When I later became a teacher at the same school, our friendship continued unabated; when Lucy graduated and returned to London with her widowed mother, we kept in constant touch through letters and regular visits.

"Where is your mother?" I asked now, glancing about for Mrs. Westenra.

"She is back at our rooms, resting. What do you think of my new walking dress and hat? Mamma insists that this is the latest thing to wear at the sea-side, but she has made such a fuss that I have become quite bored with it."

I assured Lucy that her dress was lovely, and that the only reason she found fashion tiresome was that she had never gone in want of it. "If you had only four frocks and two suits to your name as I do, Lucy, you might find yourself suddenly coveting the very garments that you now disdain."

"What you may lack in quantity, Mina dear, you make up for in quality, for you always look very sweet and becoming. I love your summer frock! Shall we go? I have a cab waiting. Tell the porter to bring your luggage out front. Wait until you see this place. Whitby is a wonder!"

Indeed, as we drove away from the station, I marvelled at the lovely view out the open window of the carriage. A gentle breeze carried the salty tang of the sea, and squawking seagulls circled overhead. Immediately below us, the River Esk cut a path between two sloping green valleys, flowing past a busy harbour on its way to the sea. A vivid blue sky and puffy white clouds made a lovely contrast to the red-roofed houses of the old town, which were all packed in, one on top of the other, along the steep hillside. "What a charming town!"

"Isn't it? I was so pleased that Mamma decided to go some

place new this summer. I had grown quite fed up with Brighton and Sidmouth."

"It was so kind of you to invite me to join you again." I took one of Lucy's gloved hands in my own and squeezed it affectionately. "Now that I have left teaching and given up my room at the school for good, I do not know where else I would have gone this summer."

"I would not dream of spending this holiday with any one else, Mina dear. We will have such fun! They say there are lovely walks all about, and you can hire boats and go out on the river."

"Oh! I have always loved to go rowing."

"And look across the river: do you see that long trail of steps curving upwards? Apparently it leads all the way up to the church and that ruined abbey on the hill top. I am simply dying to explore, but ever since we arrived yesterday, Mamma has been too tired to leave the lodging-house, and she did not want to attempt to climb the hill. Now that you are here, we can take long strolls together and see everything."

"Is your mother ill?"

"No. At least, I do not think so. She just seems to fatigue easily of late, and steep climbs leave her short of breath. I am hoping the sea air will do her good. Now," Lucy added excitedly, "what do you think of my engagement ring?" She removed a glove and thrust her hand at me.

I caught my breath as I studied the delicate gold band set with pearls that adorned her slender finger. "It is beautiful, Lucy."

"Let me see yours."

"I do not yet have an engagement ring," I admitted. "But just before Jonathan left on his trip overseas, he learned that his examinations were successful. He is a clerk no longer, but a full-blown solicitor! He promised to buy me a ring as soon as he returns."

"Did you at least exchange locks of hair?"

"Of course! We keep the locks in little envelopes for now."

"Arthur and I keep ours in matching gold lockets; his hangs from his watch-chain. I do not wear my locket often, however, ever since he gave me *this*." With a happy smile, Lucy fingered the black velvet ribbon around her throat, which was ornamented with a diamond buckle.

"I have been admiring your neckband ever since I got off the train. It is truly exquisite."

"The diamond buckle was Arthur's mother's. I love it so much, I hardly ever take it off, except when I sleep."

We drove up to a nice, rambling old house in the Royal Crescent, run by the widow of a sea captain, where Lucy and her mother had taken rooms. I had my luggage delivered upstairs to the chamber that Lucy and I were to share. As Mrs. Westenra was still napping, and it was too early for dinner, the two of us grabbed our hats and parasols and set out to explore Whitby.

"What news do you have of Jonathan?" Lucy asked, as we strolled out along the North Terrace, enjoying the sea-view and the pleasant summer breeze. "Have you received another letter?"

I heaved a perturbed sigh. "I have not heard from him for a whole month. I am very worried, actually."

"A month is not such a long time between letters."

"It is for Jonathan."

For the past five years, Jonathan had been apprenticed as a solicitor's clerk in Exeter to a dear friend of his family, Mr. Peter Hawkins, the same man who had financed his education. In late April, Mr. Hawkins had sent Jonathan as his representative to the Eastern European country of Transylvania, to meet with a nobleman named Count Dracula, on whose behalf they had conducted a real-estate transaction. Jonathan had been excited to go, as he had yearned to travel, but had never had the means to leave the country before.

"All these years, Jonathan and I have written to each other

with great regularity, sometimes as often as twice a week. When he first set out on this trip, I received great newsy letters about his crossing, about all the sights he was seeing, the people he was meeting, and the new foods he was tasting. Suddenly, all communication ceased. I had no idea if he had reached Transylvania, and thought some evil might have befallen him. I obtained Count Dracula's address from Mr. Hawkins, and wrote to Jonathan there. At last, I received a note—but it was brief and hurried, not like Jonathan at all, with no mention of the letter I had sent—just a few lines, saying that his work there was nearly done and that he would be starting for home in a few days. I wrote back immediately, informing him of my travel plans, so that he could write to me here at Whitby. But now *another* month has gone by without a reply. What could have happened to him?"

"Perhaps he stayed longer in Transylvania than expected, or decided to see the sights on his way home."

"If so, why has he not written? Why did he not answer my last letter?"

"Mail often goes astray, Mina, and it can take *ages* to arrive when it comes from another country. Believe me: Jonathan is fine. You will hear from him any day now. He would not want you to worry. He would want you to enjoy your holiday."

I sighed again. "I suppose you are right."

We descended a steep flight of steps leading down to the pier, and proceeded on past the fish-market, where fishermen and their wives were stationed at the bows of their anchored boats, hawking the last of the day's catch to a few plainly dressed bargain-hunters. The air was filled with the sounds of squealing seabirds, lapping water, and sails whipping in the breeze; and it was so alive with the salty tang of the sea and the smells of fresh fish and musty hemp that I could almost taste them.

"How I love the sea-side," I exclaimed, reinvigorated by the happy cacophony of sights, sounds, and scents about us. "Now:

you must tell me everything, Lucy. How is your Mr. Holmwood? Or should I say: the future Lord Godalming?"

"Oh! Arthur is such a dear. He promised to come to Whitby soon for a visit. I do miss him so when we are apart."

"Have you set your wedding date yet?"

"No, but Mamma is pressing for us to be married very soon, perhaps as early as September. I must admit—I hope I *can* admit this to you, Mina—September seems *awfully* soon. It is only two months since I accepted Arthur's proposal. I am still not used to the idea that I am actually going to be *married*."

I glanced at Lucy in surprise. "In your letters, you said you were head-over-heels in love with Arthur, and thrilled about your engagement."

"I am! I *do* love Arthur. He is so tall and handsome, and has such lovely, curly hair. We have so much in common, and Mamma simply adores him. I know he is the perfect man for me, and I am very happy."

We had crossed the bridge over the river, which was the only way to reach the East Cliff. At the other side, we began our ascent up another, very long flight of steps—the ones Lucy had pointed out from the carriage—which wound up the slope in a delicate curve from the town to the ruined abbey and church above.

"If you are happy, Lucy," I said as we climbed, "then why do you look so troubled?"

"*Do* I look troubled?" Lucy's brow furrowed in that sweet, puckered look I had come to know so well. "I do not mean to! It is only that I get a little sad when I realise this will be our last holiday together, Mina, just you and I, and that very soon, I will no longer be thought of as an eligible young lady but as a sober, old, *married woman.* I did so enjoy the thrill of being young and admired and wanted by so many different men! To think all that is over, and I am not yet twenty years old!"

I took in the woebegone expression on Lucy's lovely face and restrained the urge to laugh. "Dear, dear Lucy," I said, taking her arm in mine, "I would like to sympathise, but I am afraid I never experienced the *thrill* that you speak of. I have only ever had one suitor: Jonathan. It is not every girl who receives marriage proposals from *three different men* in the same day."

Lucy shook her head in bemusement. "I still reel in disbelief every time I recall that day! I tell you, it never rains but it pours. I never had a single proposal before the twenty-fourth of May—at least not a real proposal—for you cannot count the time that William Russell hid a ring in my slice of iced cake when we were nine years old, or the day Richard Spencer kissed me in the field behind Upton Hall School and asked me to promise to marry him. I was just a girl then, and they were silly young boys. I have had loads of men admiring me ever since I moved home to London, but no one came close to asking the question; and then suddenly *three proposals* at once!"

Lucy had written to me with the particulars of that extraordinary day. Dr. John Seward, an excellent young physician, had stopped by in the morning, declared his love, and asked for her hand. He was followed by another suitor—a wealthy American from Texas named Mr. Quincey P. Morris, who was close friends with both Dr. Seward and Mr. Holmwood—who made the same earnest request just after lunch. Lucy, overwhelmed by regret, had been obliged to explain that she must refuse their offers because she was in love with another man. That very same afternoon, Arthur Holmwood had managed to find a quiet moment to make his own sweet declaration, which Lucy had accepted with enthusiasm.

"It must have been a wonderful feeling," I said, "to discover that you were adored by so many good, noble, and worthy men."

"It *was* wonderful—and yet it was too, too awful at the same time. How Dr. Seward and Mr. Morris could have determined that they were in love with me, I really cannot say; for every time they came to call, I was obliged to sit by like a dumb animal, smile a little school-girl smile, and blush modestly at every word they spoke, while Mamma did most of the talking. Sometimes I just wanted to scream with frustration, for it was all so silly. Yet I liked them all, and there we were, alone at last, and each man was pouring out his heart and soul to me. Then I had to send two of them away, hats in hand, to know that they were passing quite out of my life for ever! I burst into tears when I saw the expression on Dr. Seward's face, for he looked so downcast and broken-hearted. When I told Mr. Morris there was someone else, he said, in that charming Texas accent of his, 'Little girl, your honesty and pluck have made me a friend, and that's rarer than a lover.' He said lots of brave and noble things about his 'rival,' not even knowing it was Arthur—his closest friend. Then—did I tell you in my letter what Mr. Morris asked me to do before leaving?"

"Yes! He asked you to kiss him, to help soften the blow, I suppose—and you did it!" We paused part-way up the steps to catch our breath, and I glanced at her. "I admit, I was a little surprised."

"Why?"

"Lucy, you cannot go around kissing every man who asks for your hand, just because you feel sorry for him!"

"It was just one kiss. Oh, Mina! Why can't they let a girl marry three men, or as many as want her, and save all this trouble?"

I laughed out loud and took Lucy in my arms. "You silly goose. Marrying three men? The very idea!"

"I felt so bad that I had to make two of them so unhappy."

"I would not waste another minute worrying about Dr. Seward and Mr. Morris if I were you," I said, as we resumed our climb. "They will recover from their disappointment in time, and find other young women who will worship the ground they walk on."

"I hope so, for I believe everyone deserves to feel the kind of happiness that I have found with Arthur and that you have with Jonathan."

"So do I. To be a wife—to be *Jonathan's* wife—to spend our lives together, to help him with his work, to become a mother—it is all I could ever want."

Lucy went quiet for a moment, and then said: "Mina: did you always feel that way?

"What way?"

"I know you and Jonathan have been friends for ever—but you did not regard him as a suitor until recently. Did you ever think of another man, before Jonathan?"

"No. Never."

"Never? Surely, in the time since I left Upton Hall, there must have been *some* boy or man that you liked, and who liked you back—someone of whom you have never spoken?"

"If there had been, you would know about it, Lucy. I have always told you everything."

"That will not do. A girl must keep a *few* secrets." Lucy batted her eyelashes playfully. Then she laughed, and added: "I hope you know I am teasing, Mina. I have kept no secrets from you, either—*or* from Arthur. Mamma says honesty and respect are the most important things in a marriage, even more important than love, and I agree—don't you?"

"I do. Jonathan and I abhor secrecy and concealments. We made a solemn pact, long ago, that we would always be completely open with each other—a promise we believe is particularly important now that we are to become husband and wife."

"That is just as it should be."

We had reached the top of the steps now, and strolled past the Church of St. Mary's, a fortresslike stone building with a stout tower and crenellated roof-top, whose sturdy exterior seemed ideally designed to survive the onslaughts of the stormy North Sea weather. Our explorations took us now to the adjoining ruins of Whitby Abbey—a gaunt, imposing, and most noble ruin of immense size, situated on sprawling green lawns, and surrounded by fields dotted with sheep. We could not help but stare in wonder at its beauty, taking in the grand, roofless nave, the soaring south transept, and the delicate lancets of the east end of the former abbey church.

"There is a wonderful legend about this abbey, that I read about before I came," I said. "They claim that on certain summer afternoons, when the sun strikes the northern part of the choir at a particular angle, a lady in white can be seen in one of the windows."

"A lady in white? Who can it be?"

"Some believe it is the ghost of St. Hilda—the Saxon princess who founded the abbey as a monastery in the sixth century—seeking revenge from the Vikings who sacked her great edifice."

"A ghost!" Lucy cried with a laugh. "Do you believe in ghosts?"

"Of course not. No doubt the 'vision' is just a reflection caused by the sun's beams."

"Well, I prefer the legend. It is far more romantic."

We left the abbey and headed back past the church, emerging into a wide-open area between the church and the cliff, which was full of weathered tombstones. "Good gracious," I said. "What an immense churchyard—and what a view!"

Indeed, the graveyard surrounding the church was very large and well situated. Resting dramatically atop the high cliff, it overlooked the town and harbour on one side and the sea on the other—and it seemed to be a popular place. A good two dozen people were strolling along the series of paths that criss-crossed the churchyard, or sitting on the benches beside the walks, gazing at the view and enjoying the breeze.

The view drew us like a magnet. We strode directly towards

the eminence, where we found an iron bench, painted green, and situated close to the cliff's edge. We sat down. The seat afforded a magnificent, panoramic view of the town and harbour below us, the endless sparkling sea, the sea-walls, two lighthouses, and the long stretches of sandy beach all the way up to the bay, to where the headland stretched out into the sea. Beside us, two artists worked at their easels; behind us, sheep and lambs bleated in the fields; I heard a clatter of donkey's hooves up the paved road below, and the murmur of conversation of the passers-by; but otherwise, all was peaceful and utterly serene.

"I think this is the nicest spot in Whitby," I declared.

"I could not agree more," returned Lucy, "and this is the best seat in the whole place. I hereby claim it as our very own."

"I believe," I said with a happy smile, "that I shall come up here quite often, to read or to write."

Had I known, then, of the events which would occur at this very spot, which would so disastrously alter Lucy's fate, and so dramatically and inexorably influence mine, I would have turned around and insisted that we leave Whitby at once. At least—I like to think that I would have had the courage to do so. But how can one imagine the unimaginable? Particularly when it all began so innocently?

❧

On my first night in Whitby, Lucy began walking in her sleep.

The evening had been pleasant enough. After our walk, Lucy and I had returned to the house at the Royal Crescent, where we had enjoyed an early dinner with Mrs. Westenra. That good lady was in excellent spirits and welcomed me heartily. Afterwards, while Lucy and her mother went out to pay some duty calls on acquaintances in the area, I sneaked away to the East Cliff again on my own, where I spent a lovely hour sitting on "our bench" and writing in my journal.

That night, however, not long after Lucy and I retired to our room and fell asleep, I was awakened by a rustling sound. It was a warm night, and we had left the shutters and window open. As I sleepily opened my eyes, in the glow of moonlight illuminating the chamber, I perceived that Lucy had risen from her bed and was dressing herself.

"Lucy? What is wrong? Why are you up?"

My friend did not answer but continued buttoning up her petticoat. Her eyes were wide and staring, with a sort of vacant look; now she took a skirt from the wardrobe and began to step into it.

"Lucy!" I rose and padded barefoot across the room to her. "Why are you getting dressed?" Again, there was no answer; Lucy did not appear even to be aware of my presence. All at once, I understood what was happening.

I had witnessed this peculiar behaviour on Lucy's part on several previous occasions, years earlier, when we were at school. One snowy night, she had risen from our bed and walked outside, barefoot and in her nightdress; thankfully, a servant had found her before she froze to death, warmed her by the fire, and brought her back to bed. Another time, Lucy had dressed herself in her best coat and hat and walked down-stairs to the kitchen, where she had consumed a large slice of apple-pie and a glass of milk before she was discovered. The next morning, she had only a vague memory of these incidents, or none at all.

"Lucy, dear," I said now, as I put my hands on her shoulders and gazed into her vacant eyes, "it is the middle of the night. You must go back to bed. Let me help you undress."

To my relief, she did not fight me. At the sound of my voice, or perhaps it was the touch of my hands, her intention entirely disappeared, and she calmly yielded herself to my ministrations. I managed to undress her, put her nightdress back on, and get her back to bed, all without waking her.

At breakfast the next morning, Lucy was her usual, sunny self, chattering away as if nothing out of the ordinary had occurred the night before. With a little laugh, I told Lucy and her mother about what had happened.

"Sleep-walking?" Lucy replied with a surprised laugh of her own, as she spread butter and jam on her toast. "It has been quite a long while since I did *that*."

Mrs. Westenra did not find the news as amusing as we did. "Oh dear," said she, her pale forehead furrowing with concern as she played with the string of pearls around her neck. "I have always been worried about that old habit of yours, Lucy. To think that it should come back now, of all times, when we are at this strange, new place."

Mrs. Westenra was a petite but full-figured woman of five-and-forty. It was easy to see where her daughter had gotten her beauty, for they both possessed the same attractive features, the same deep blue eyes, dark, curly hair, and smooth, ivory complexion. Turning to me, Mrs. Westenra added, "She inherited this tendency from her father. Edward used to get up in the night and dress himself and go out if I did not wake him in time to stop him. One night in town, a bobby found him wandering about in St. James's Park in his best Sunday suit. Another time, in the country, he took all his gear down to the river at two o'clock in the morning and went fishing."

Lucy laughed. "I remember that. Silly Papa." Then her smile fled, and she grew misty-eyed as she sipped her cocoa. "Oh, how I miss him."

"Your father was a wonderful man," I agreed.

Mrs. Westenra shook her head sadly. "I never thought I would be left alone like this. I thought surely I would go first. Dear, dear Edward." Her eyes suddenly filled with tears, and she reached across the table and took Lucy's hand. "Thank goodness Lucy has been at home with me this past year and a half. How I shall get on after she is married, I do not know."

Lucy put her other hand atop her mother's, meeting her gaze. "Mamma, you will do just fine. Arthur and I will not live far away, and we shall come to visit you so often, you will hardly know I am gone."

Mrs. Westenra dabbed at her eyes with her napkin. "I hope so, my dearest. I am very happy for you, Lucy, and I hope *you* will be happy, too."

The two women shared a loving smile. I felt a warm glow of affection for them both—and at the same time, despite myself—a little pang of envy. It was one of my greatest sorrows in life that I had never known the joys of a mother's or father's love. The dark stigma of my past had been a source of mortification to me ever since I had learned of it as a child, and I still blushed with shame every time I thought of it.

"Now let us talk about the wedding," said Mrs. Westenra, recovering her spirits as she took a dainty bite of her scrambled eggs. "I think you and Arthur should be married as soon as possible."

"What is the rush, Mamma? Long engagements are very common. Even you and Papa waited a year before you married, did you not?"

"Yes, but our circumstances were very different. Your father was struggling to start a new banking business, and he wanted it running smoothly before we wed. Arthur does not have any such financial constraints. He is very wealthy. As the only son, he will one day inherit Ring Manor and all of his father's estates and holdings. There is no reason on earth for you to wait." Mrs. Westenra spoke with such urgency, I sensed there might be some other reason behind her desire to see Lucy quickly wed; but she only added: "In any case, September is a lovely month for a wedding."

"Well, I will wait and see what Arthur says when he arrives," Lucy said sweetly.

"What about you, Mina?" Mrs. Westenra enquired. "When and where are you and Jonathan to wed? Have you made plans?"

I hesitated, then said solemnly, "We had talked about marrying in Exeter in late summer—something very simple, of course—but now I do not know." I told her about Jonathan's business trip to Transylvania, how late he was in returning, and how long it had been since I had heard from him. "There is something about his last letter that does not satisfy me. It is his writing, and yet it does not read like him."

"Have you written to his employer?" asked Mrs. Westenra.

"I have. Mr. Hawkins has not heard a word either."

Lucy and her mother tried their best to allay my fears, but under the circumstances, there was little they could say. After breakfast, Lucy proposed a walk up to the East Cliff again. Her mother, who seemed winded just in walking from dining-room to sitting-room, begged us to excuse her. Before Lucy and I could go out, however, Mrs. Westenra took me aside privately and said, in a low, anxious tone:

"Mina: I did not want to say anything in front of Lucy, but I am very worried about her."

"Why are you worried?"

"It is this old habit of sleep-walking of hers. It can be a very dangerous thing. Say nothing to her of this; but you must promise me to keep an eye on her, and to lock the door of your room every night, so she cannot get out."

I gave Mrs. Westenra my solemn promise, firm in the belief that I could protect Lucy from all harm. Oh! How very wrong I turned out to be!

THAT AFTERNOON, LUCY AND I RETURNED TO THE CHURCHYARD atop the East Cliff, where we chatted with a gnarled, former sailor called Mr. Swales, who said he was nearly a hundred years old. He and his two elderly cronies were so charmed by the sight of Lucy that they took seats next to her just moments after we sat down on our favourite bench. Lucy posed thoughtful questions about their adventures at sea with the Greenland fishing fleet, and their glory days during the battle of Waterloo.

I was more interested in the subject of local legends; but when I turned the conversation in that direction, old Mr. Swales insisted that all those tales about the White Lady in the abbey window and so forth were stuff and nonsense.

"They be just fool-talk for day-trippers and the like," the elderly man scoffed. "Don't ye pay them no mind, miss. If ye like tales, howsoever, I'll tell ye some good 'uns that be true."

He went on to relate several colourful stories about the town and churchyard. Lucy became upset when he pointed out that the stone slab at our feet, upon which our favourite seat rested, was the grave of a man who had committed suicide. Mr. Swales assured her that he had sat there himself off and on for more than twenty years, and it had done him no harm.

When we returned to our lodging-house, our landlady, Mrs. Abernathy, said there was a letter waiting for me. My heart leapt in excitement. I recognised the hand at once: it was from Jonathan's employer, Mr. Peter Hawkins. Unable to wait until we reached our chamber, I ripped open the envelope at once. To my relief, I saw that the dear old man had enclosed a letter he had received from Jonathan.

"You see?" Lucy cried, straining for a peek at the enclosed missive as I glanced over it. "I told you Jonathan would write. What does he say?"

My heart sank. It was Jonathan's handwriting; but I had longed for reassuring words and an explanation for his long silence. Instead, the enclosed letter to his employer was a shattering disappointment:

Castle Dracula—19 June, 1890

My Dear Sir:

I write to report to you that I have satisfactorily completed the business errand upon which I was engaged, and intend to start for home to-morrow, but will probably stop for a holiday somewhere on the way.

I remain, yours faithfully,
J. Harker

"One line," I said quietly, as I passed the letter to Lucy. "One line only. It is very unlike Jonathan."

"How so? He wrote to Mr. Hawkins, not you; I think it quite succinct and business-like."

"That is just it. Mr. Hawkins is more like a father to Jonathan than a business associate. We have both known him ever since we were children. Jonathan would never address the old man in such a business-like tone."

"Perhaps he was in a hurry. And look: he says he plans to stop for a holiday on the way home."

"Even if Jonathan did stop somewhere, he should have arrived long before this. And why did he write to Mr. Hawkins, but not to me? I sent him my address here in Whitby." A sudden fear gripped my stomach, and so assailed my senses that I was obliged to sink into a near-by chair. "Do you think it possible—could Jonathan have met another woman while on his journey? Is that the reason for his silence?"

"Another woman?" Lucy cried, aghast. "Never! Jonathan is as faithful as you, Mina Murray. He is very much in love with you, and you are the two most loyal people I have ever met. He would never look twice at another woman, I assure you."

"Do you really think so?"

"I *know* so. You *will marry Jonathan*, Mina. I am sure there is some simple reason for his silence, and you will learn it in good time. He will come home to you, I promise."

NEARLY A FORTNIGHT PASSED WITH NO FURTHER NEWS FROM Jonathan, keeping me in a state of suspense that was really quite dreadful. Lucy heard from Arthur, however. To her disappointment, he was obliged to postpone his visit, as his father had been taken ill—which meant postponing our plans to go rowing up the river, something we had been eagerly looking forward to.

Adding to this anxiety, Lucy continued to sleep-walk from time to time. In each instance, I was awakened by her moving about the room, determinedly seeking a way out. I now slept with the key securely tied to my wrist. Despite all this, we enjoyed our days together, which were spent strolling through the town or up to the East Cliff, or taking long walks to the charming near-by villages. Although we took care to wear our hats, Mrs. Westenra remarked with satisfaction that Lucy's once-pale cheeks were now taking on a becoming rosy hue.

On the 6th of August, the weather changed. The sun was hidden behind thick clouds, the sea tumbled over the sandy flats with a roar, and everything was shrouded in a deep grey mist.

"We be in for a storm, my deary, and a big 'un, mark my words," said old Mr. Swales, as he joined me on my seat in the churchyard that afternoon. He was a dear old man, but that day, as he rambled on, he seemed entirely fixated on the subject of death. Staring out to sea, he said in an ominous tone: "May be it's in that wind out over the sea that's bringin' with it loss and wreck, and sore distress, and sad hearts . . . Look! It sounds, and looks, and tastes, and smells like death!"

His words unnerved me. Although I know he meant no harm, I was glad when he left. For a while, I wrote in my journal, and watched the fishing-boats scurrying back to safety in the harbour. My attention was soon caught by a ship out at sea. It was a sizeable vessel, heading westward towards our coast with all sails set, but it was knocking about in the queerest way, as if changing direction with every puff of wind.

When the coastguardsman ambled by with his spy-glass, he stopped to talk with me, all the time looking at the same ship. "She's a Russian, by the look of her," he said, "but she doesn't know her mind a bit, and is steered mighty strangely. It's as if she sees the storm coming but can't decide whether to run up north, or put in here."

The next day was again cold and grey, and the strange schooner was still there, gently rolling on the undulating sea, its sails idly flapping. That evening after tea, Lucy and I returned to the cliff-top to join a large assemblage that was curiously watching the ship, as well as the approach of sunset—a sight so beautiful, with its masses of clouds in every shade of sunset colour from red to purple, violet, pink, green, yellow, and gold—it seemed impossible to believe that bad weather could be imminent.

By evening, however, the air grew uncannily still. At midnight, when Lucy and I were safely tucked in our beds, a faint, hollow booming came from over the sea, and the tempest broke in sudden earnest. Rain poured down in a fury, clattering against the roof, the window-panes, and the chimney-pots. Every peal of thunder sounded like a distant gun and made me jump. I was too agitated to sleep, and for many an hour, I heard Lucy tossing and turning in her own bed. At last, I fell into a fitful slumber, and I had a strange dream.

Perhaps I have a very active imagination; perhaps it is in my blood; but I have a propensity to dream very vividly—and I have dreamt every single night, all night long, ever since I was a little child. At any moment when I awake, I can recall the dream I was just experiencing in perfect detail, and it always takes me some minutes to reassure myself that it was not real. Sometimes, my dreams are silly, sweet, and tangled fantasies incorporating bits and pieces of the day I have just been through; at other times they are nightmares, frightening manifestations of my darkest fears; but on occasion they have proven to be portents or signs, showing me what my future holds.

On this night, I dreamt that I was back in my chamber at school—only it was not the school where I had lived and worked—it was a place I did not recognise. In the dead of night, in the glow of a brilliant moon, I wandered down a long, cold passageway in search of something—I knew not what. Outside, a fierce wind blew through the tree tops, making the eaves of the building creak and groan, and casting frightening shadows on the walls. The floor boards felt icy beneath my bare feet, and I shivered in my thin nightdress. I wanted to return to the warmth and safety of my bed, but I could not; I could only move forward, one step at a time, compelled onward by some force I could not name.

All at once, a deep, soft voice came out of the darkness: "My love!"

Was it Jonathan calling? Was he here, at last? "Where are you, Jonathan?" I cried, as I ran down the long, endlessly twisting corridor, past many closed doors.

"My love!" I heard again.

I suddenly realised it was not Jonathan at all but a voice I had never heard before. I flew breathlessly around a corner, only to lurch to an abrupt halt as a door opened just ahead of me. From that door issued a tall, dark figure. Was it was man or beast? I could not be certain. In the shadowy passage, I could not perceive the being's features; just two gleaming, red eyes—a sight which made me gasp in alarm.

He—or it—approached and stopped before me, uttering words in a soft tone that sent a chill up my spine, yet at the same time were both captivating and strangely compelling:

"I am coming for you."

TWO

I AWOKE WITH A START, MY HEART POUNDING, TO HEAR THE storm still raging outside. The dream had felt very real; the image of the dark, faceless figure remained vivid in my mind. Who was he—or it? Why did he call me *My love?* Why was he coming for me? This contemplation was interrupted when I heard movement in the room. I struck a match and discovered Lucy sitting on her bed in her nightdress, pulling on her boots. I lit the lamp and went to her.

"Lucy: dearest. You must go back to bed."

"No," she replied, pushing me away emphatically in her sleep. "I must go. He is coming for me."

A wave of apprehension washed over me. Had not I just heard those same words in my dream? "Who is coming?"

"I must go!" was her only response, as she began to tie her shoe-laces.

It took some doing to convince Lucy that, under no circumstances would I permit her to leave the room. She did not wake, but continued to be restless all night, rising yet again to dress herself. How strange, I thought—when I managed to get her back to bed once more, and settled beneath the bedclothes myself—was it possible that Lucy and I had had the very same dream?

"I NEVER REMEMBER ANYTHING I DREAM," LUCY SAID WITH A shrug the next morning, when I asked her about it. "It took me ages to fall asleep, but when I did, I slept like a log."

I let out a great yawn, exhausted by the night's proceedings; but since Lucy looked so bright and happy as she opened the shutters to let in the early-morning light, I decided to make no mention of them.

"What a horrible storm!" Lucy went on. "Thank goodness it is over now."

"Old Mr. Swales was so full of doom and gloom yesterday about this tempest. I hope all the fishing-boats survived intact."

"Let us go down and see."

We dressed quickly, skipped breakfast, and hastened outside. The early-morning air was crisp, fresh, and clear, and the newly risen sun peeked out here and there between billowing clouds. As we hurried down the street, I felt a sudden chill, and the oddest sensation came over me. I saw Lucy shiver, and said, "Are you cold?"

"No," she replied, "but I just had a funny feeling—as if someone was watching us."

"I had the same feeling!" We looked quickly around us. The buildings along the street were all cast in shadows, but the street itself was empty except for us and two other souls, who were marching briskly in our direction, towards the West Cliff.

"I do not see anything," Lucy said.

"I think the storm has set our nerves on edge." Sharing a little shudder and a laugh, we took each other's arms and hurried down to the harbour.

The sea was still dark and awash in angry-looking, foam-crested waves. There were only a few people about, and they were all chattering excitedly. All the fishing-boats appeared to be securely moored to their docks; however, a large sailing ship—the same strange, foundering ship, I realised, which had aroused such curiosity in the days before—had beached itself across the way, by the pier jutting under the East Cliff. It now stood tilted on the sand and gravel at a perilous angle, its sails in shreds, and some of its top hamper crashed to pieces across the deck and sands below.

"Such a beautiful ship!" I cried in dismay. "What a shame!" I turned to a red-bearded, weathered-faced man standing near-by, and asked, "What happened? Do you know?"

"I do," replied the man solemnly, as he puffed at his pipe. "I saw it all late last night. They say it's a Russian ship called the *Demeter.* The coastguard saw her coming in, all shrouded by mist and fog, and signalled her to reduce sail in the face of her danger, but got nary a response. She kept wavering this way and that, like there was no hand at the wheel. Then the storm broke with a great roar, and she was lost from sight for a time. Suddenly the wind shifted, and there she was again. By some miracle the schooner made straight into the harbour, rushing in with such speed that I knew she must fetch up somewhere. Indeed, she ran in as soft and sleek as a seal flappin' under an ice-floe, then rammed up on the sand heap with a great concussion. When the coastguard boarded the vessel, then it was that the great horror met their eyes."

"What great horror?" Lucy asked fearfully.

"That ship was steered by a dead man," he replied, his eyes widening under his bushy eyebrows.

"A dead man?" I repeated. "How can that be?"

"There lies the mystery, missy: for the entire crew is missing, and they found the captain's corpse lashed to the helm, swinging horribly to and fro, his dead hands clutching a crucifix."

"Oh!" Lucy and I cried together, in stunned alarm.

"The only survivor, it appears, was a dog."

"A dog?" I repeated, surprised.

He nodded. "Just as the vessel touched shore, a huge dog leapt off the bow onto the sand, made straight for the cliff, and disappeared. Neither hide nor hair of it has been seen since. It must be a fierce brute, too; for it seems to have fought and killed a local dog—a half-bred mastiff that was found in the roadway opposite to its master's yard, with its throat torn away and its belly slit open, as if with a savage claw."

"Oh!" Lucy cried again.

I was inclined to stay and hear more, but this tale so distressed Lucy that she insisted we return to the Royal Crescent at once. Later, as she picked at her breakfast, Lucy said with a frown, "We were having such a lovely holiday, and now that horrible ship has to appear—with a—*with a dead man at the wheel!* I shudder just to think of it."

Mrs. Westenra, who was not feeling too well herself, suggested that Lucy spend a quiet day with her to calm her nerves. "You have received a shock, my dear, that is all. In a few days, you will have forgotten all about it."

I, too, was unnerved by the eerie appearance of the beached ship, but I had no desire to let it ruin my holiday, or to spend the day cooped up inside. Although the morning had grown quite overcast, it still promised to be a nice day, and I felt a strong compulsion to go up to my favourite seat on the East Cliff to read and write. I quickly checked my appearance in the looking-glass, smoothing out my simple skirt and jacket of amethyst piqué, straightening the jabot of my white blouse, and ensuring that my blonde hair was tidily secured beneath my straw hat. Satisfied that

I appeared presentable, I took a book and my journal, hugged my companions good-bye, and headed out, filled with a strange, inward anticipation that I could not explain.

The wind was blowing briskly as I traversed the churchyard, past the widely dispersed gravestones washed clean by the night's rain. I inhaled deeply, finding pleasure in the mingled scents of wet gravel, stone, earth, and grass. For some reason, for the second time that morning, I was possessed by the strange feeling that I was being watched; but as I glanced around, I could again perceive nothing out of the ordinary.

People of all ages and descriptions were strolling about as usual, chatting and smiling. Were it not for the multitude of mud puddles which had gathered in the low spots along the path edges, there would be nothing to indicate that a storm of the most spectacular nature had blown through only the night before, much less a storm which had violently driven in a ship populated by ghosts.

I was pleased to see that my preferred bench was empty. I sat down and revelled in the beauty of the scene below me. Sunlight danced on the ever-shifting, dark blue sea, and the waves crashed up in great, foaming, white crests against the beaches, sea-walls, and distant headlands. I thought about Jonathan; I prayed that he was safe, and had not been crossing the stormy sea the night before.

Just as I took out my fountain-pen and was about to begin my journal entry, the wind suddenly and unceremoniously picked up and took off with my hat. One moment, my bonnet was secured to my head; the next, it was airborne and rolling away in frantic circles across the pathway.

I leapt up in dismay and dashed after my retreating bonnet. Despite my most earnest attempts to retrieve it, however, it maddeningly remained just a few inches out of my reach. It was making a bee-line for the most dangerous section of the cliff—

that part where the sustaining bank had fallen away, and some of the flat tombstones actually projected out over the sands far below. I stopped a few feet from the cliff edge, certain that my hat was lost to me; for it would be only seconds now before it rashly flung itself out into open space and sailed to its doom below in the depths of the sea.

Suddenly, a tall form rushed past me and grabbed my hat at the very brink of the cliff, just as it was about to hurl itself into oblivion. I had never seen a human being move with such speed; but then, with calm assurance and a pantherlike grace, the gentleman returned to my side and presented me with his spoils.

"Is this your hat, miss?" he enquired in a deep, rich voice, enlivened by a very slight, indistinct foreign accent.

I stared at him, suddenly speechless. He was a young gentleman—not much older than thirty, I thought. He was tall, thin, and extremely attractive, with a handsome nose, perfectly white teeth, and a jet-black moustache that matched his hair. As he smiled down at me, I was captivated by the force of his dark blue eyes, which were at once intense and compelling. He was impeccably dressed in a knee-length black frock coat, black tie, vest, and trousers, and a crisp white shirt, which were perfectly tailored to fit his fine figure, and whose materials and workmanship immediately announced his wealthy status. His complexion glowed with good health; his entire face and form, in fact, so embodied the very model of masculine beauty and charm that for a breathless moment, I wondered if I had conjured him from my imagination.

As our gazes met, an expression crossed his face which I had never before seen directed at me—not even by Jonathan. It was an expression of such immediate, profound, and undisguised interest, it caused my heart to flutter.

"Thank you, sir," I said, when at last I found my voice. "I am very much obliged to you."

"I am pleased to have been of service." His gentle accent, I decided, was of European origin, yet his English was perfect. He bowed, briefly removing his black top hat, still staring at me intently with those fascinating eyes, as if taken aback by the force of unexpected feelings.

I knew I should not engage in further conversation with him. He was a stranger, and I was a single woman, engaged to another, and here without a chaperone. Only one proper course of action was open to me, and I was well aware of it: I must curtsey silently and be on my way. And yet . . . I could not bring myself to do it. Instead, I studied the straw bonnet in my hands, a simple affair, unadorned except for a white ribbon and a small cluster of flowers, and said:

"You were very brave, sir, to—to rush so close to the cliff edge like that, just for a hat. It was quite dangerous."

He seemed to collect himself and gave me a warm smile. "It appeared to be an article that you wished very much to rescue. I did not think of the danger."

There was, I decided (darting another glance in his direction) an inexplicable hint of "danger" in everything about him, which made him seem at once exotic and mysterious—but which, I told myself, had more to do with the fact that he was *so very attractive* that I could not take my eyes off him, than it did with anything particular about the man himself.

"It is not an expensive hat by any means, as you can see," I replied, "but I have had it a long while, and I have grown attached to it. And it is all the more valuable, in that it—it is the only hat I have with me." *Good Lord,* I thought, *why was I babbling on like an idiot about my hat?*

"Ah," he said, as we started back in the direction from which I had come, "then I take it you do not live in Whitby?"

"No. I have been here but a fortnight. I am on holiday with a friend and her mother."

"I am a visitor here as well. I arrived in Whitby only yesterday."

"Where are you from, sir?"

He looked at me, then replied: "Austria."

"I have seen pictures of Austria, and from all accounts, it is a lovely country."

"It is indeed; but this is also a lovely place, is it not? There is such a marvellous view from these cliffs. The sea is so beautiful, so restless, and so endless. I never tire of looking at it. We do not have such sights back home."

"I have always loved the sea-side, at any time of year. Although, if you arrived in Whitby only yesterday, you must have found last night's storm a rather rude welcoming."

"The storm—yes. It *was* fearsome." As we passed a cliff-side artist who was painting the broken ship on the sands below, the gentleman paused briefly to admire the work. "Your perspective is very interesting," he told the painter, "and your choice of colours is very pleasing to the eye."

The artist acknowledged the compliment with a smile and a nod. Just then, I noticed my errant hat-pin lying on the gravel pathway by the bench where I had been sitting. I quickly retrieved it and stopped to refasten my hat.

"Are these yours as well?" the gentleman asked, referring to my book and journal, which were lying on the path a few feet away, their pages fluttering in the breeze.

"Yes, they are."

He retrieved them. As he dusted off my journal, his attention was drawn to the open page and the loops, squiggles, and other strange symbols inscribed there. I was a little embarrassed that a stranger's eye had fallen on my private diary, but at the same time relieved by the unusual method I had employed in writing it.

"Forgive me," he said, "if I enquire too freely, but is this written in some new form of shorthand—or as I think you call it—stenography?"

"It is," I replied, surprised that he was familiar with this abbreviated, symbolic writing method.

"A fascinating system, is it not—as old as the Acropolis stone from Ancient Greece. The way it allows one to write with increased speed and brevity, as quickly as people speak."

"Yes, and at the same time it achieves total privacy, for it makes that writing unintelligible to most others—which is ideal for keeping a diary."

He smiled. "I am familiar with a number of methods, but this one I do not recognise."

"It is called Gregg's shorthand. It was published two years ago, and is not yet commonly employed. I have only just learned the art, so that I might be able to—" I hesitated. To go on with my thought would, I feared, put an abrupt end to a pleasant conversation I truly wished to continue; but the truth could not be avoided. He had a right to know, at once, that I was betrothed to another. "I learned stenography," I went on, "so that I might be of some help to my fiancé in his work. He is a solicitor, you see. I hope to be able to take down what he says, and then transcribe it for him on the typewriter."

At this admission, the gentleman's smile briefly faded; but he quickly recovered his aplomb and said, "So you are adept with a typewriter as well as stenography? These are very unusual skills. Your fiancé is a lucky man to have so learned, so devoted, and so beautiful a companion. A very lucky man indeed."

My cheeks grew warm, not only from his words of praise but from the admiration in his eyes as he spoke them. "Thank you, sir, but I feel that I am the lucky one. Jonathan is a good man."

He did not comment on that but only paused and glanced about us, saying, "He is not here with you, I presume, as you said you travelled with a friend and her mother?"

"He is on a business trip overseas and has not yet returned."

"I see. In the meantime, you are quite at leisure, yes?" Before

I could reply, he added, "I have not yet had an opportunity to explore the area. The ruined abbey looks most intriguing. Would you do me the honour of joining me on a tour about the grounds?"

As he looked down at me, my heart began to pound in a strange, frenzied cadence. We had been conversing a few minutes only, yet there was something about this man, *about his eyes,* that was so mesmerising, I could hardly bear to tear my gaze from his. I could not deny it: I was very attracted to him, and he seemed to be attracted to me. Oh! I thought: these new-found feelings which were coursing through me—although undeniably thrilling—were wrong; *very wrong, indeed.*

He must have read my thoughts on my face, for he said: "There is nothing improper about our walking and talking together. We are simply two modern people, conversing in broad daylight, and there are plenty of others about."

I opened my mouth to decline—but instead I heard myself say, "I would be delighted to accompany you," and before I knew it, I was falling in step with him along the gravel path.

"I could not help but notice the title of your book." He nodded towards the tome I was carrying. "*On the Origin of Species.* A most interesting choice."

"Are you familiar with it?"

"I am indeed. It is a seminal work in scientific literature."

"I find Darwin's theory of evolution most interesting. The idea that populations evolve over the course of generations, through a process of natural selection—"

"—And that only the *fittest* survive—"

"—And *form new species*—"

"Yes!" he returned, with animation. "The ideas have been around long before Charles Darwin published his book; some have traced the concept as far back as Aristotle. But Darwin's theories have at last brought it to the attention of the general public."

"The book has aroused such heated debate!"

"Which is not surprising. Darwin's theory has called into question the validity of many long-held religious doctrines—"

"—Such as Creationism—"

"—And the much-cherished hierarchy of man over beast."

"I suppose it does come as a great shock to some," I said with a smile, "to consider that humans are no longer the undisputed crown of creation."

"Indeed, yes. We are merely another link in a great chain." He returned my smile, adding: "Your taste in reading intrigues me. I would have expected a young lady like yourself to be more interested in popular novels than the theories of evolution."

"Oh, but I *do* love novels! I have read nearly everything by Dickens, George Eliot, and Jane Austen, and I must have read Charlotte Brontë's *Jane Eyre* a dozen times."

"I, too, have enjoyed the work of these authors. Do you read poetry as well?"

"I do. In fact, I believe there is a scene in Scott's *Marmion* that was set right here, at Whitby Abbey."

"Yes: a nun was walled up alive for breaking her vows."

"Exactly! Scott wrote with such verve, did he not?"

"And such a wonderful use of language: 'Oh, what a tangled web we weave—' "

We finished the quotation together: "—'when first we practice to deceive!' "

We shared a laugh. As we talked on, discussing our favorite works by Shakespeare, Wordsworth, and Byron, a little thrill raced up my spine. I could not recall the last time I had had such an interesting conversation with a man—or with any other person, for that matter. Lucy had never been a great reader; the other teachers at school had generally been too tired and overworked to read for pleasure in their spare time; and although Jonathan had been well schooled in literature and greatly enjoyed reading, he now mainly perused newspapers, magazines, and law journals.

We were approaching St. Mary's. "What an interesting church," my companion said, as he swerved towards a side-path leading away from it. "It more resembles a castle or citadel than a house of God."

"Have you had an opportunity to go inside the church, sir? It is very different from the exterior, and quite beautiful."

"It is such a fine day, I would much rather remain outdoors, if you have no objection."

I said that I did not; and as we walked on towards the abbey, he commented: "You seem very young to have had such a wide-ranging exposure to literature. Did you do all this reading at school?"

"I did. I was fortunate enough to attend a school with an excellent library. I later taught at the same institution. What about you? Were you educated here in England?"

"No. This is the first time I have visited your country."

"The first time? That is remarkable, sir, for your English is excellent—perfect, in fact."

"I have been studying your tongue for a long time now, and have had several teachers . . . but I know that I still require improvement." He smiled modestly, and added: "You said just now that you are a school-teacher. Do you enjoy it?"

"I love it! Or—I did. I think teaching a most noble profession. I was obliged to resign my position just before coming to Whitby, for the school is just outside London, and Jonathan lives and works in Exeter. I cried when I had to say good-bye to my pupils and my friends among the teaching staff, for they had all become very dear to me."

"Let us hope that you can find a similar post in Exeter, where you will be equally as happy."

"Oh no! That would never do. Jonathan does not like the idea of my working after we are married—that is, except for any small duties I can perform to help with his business."

He regarded me with open surprise. "This is a very old-fashioned idea, for such a modern young lady."

"Is it? I do not think so, sir. In any case, I have never really thought of myself as modern."

"And yet you are," he said, with an admiring smile. "You are intelligent, well-read, and well educated. You have a profession. You have achieved financial independence. You have mastered some of the newest inventions and skills. And you have, I assume, made your choice of husband entirely of your own free will?"

"I have," I replied with a laugh.

"Furthermore, you have proven that you are willing daringly to defy certain established social conventions." At this, he made a silent gesture, which included himself, myself, and the abbey grounds, which we were passing through together. As I laughed again, he went on: "I would think that to-day's New Woman would give great thought to what *she* wants after marriage, and not just to what society dictates, or what her husband expects."

"Sir: although I may appear to be an advocate of the New Woman's ideals, I have reached my situation in life more by necessity than design. All my life, until I began teaching, I was dependent on the charity of others for my education and subsistence. I worked for a living because I was obliged to support myself, although I did grow to love it. I admit: I cringe a bit when I think that, in future, I shall have to ask my husband for every penny for even the smallest purchase. But Jonathan is rather fixed in his habits and has a rigid sense of propriety. I look forward to being his wife, to managing our home, and—" (I added with a blush) "—to having a family. I want to make him happy."

A dark look crossed his countenance, and he fell silent for a moment, looking away. "Well. As I said before: he is a very lucky man."

Just then, the church bells tolled the hour of one o'clock. I gave a sudden gasp. "Oh! I am so sorry. I forgot the time. I promised to meet my friends for luncheon at one—and now I am late."

"I, too, have some place I must be."

I held out my gloved hand to him. "It was a pleasure to meet you, sir. I very much enjoyed our conversation."

"As did I, Miss—?"

"Murray."

"Good day, Miss Murray." He took my hand in his, brought it to his lips, and kissed it. I shivered. Was that shiver induced by the pressure of his grip and the brief touch of his lips—which felt strangely cool, despite the fabric of my glove, which separated his flesh from mine? Or was that shiver the product of the confluence of emotions which continued to course through me? "I hope we will meet again," he said, releasing my hand with a bow.

"Good day." I hurried to the steps and started down, permitting myself only one brief, backwards glance. He was watching me. As our gazes touched, he smiled and bowed again.

It was only when I reached our lodgings at the Royal Crescent that I realised I had never asked him his name.

ALL THROUGHOUT THAT AFTERNOON AND EVENING, I COULD NOT stop thinking about my encounter with the gentleman in the churchyard, an event I recalled with both pleasure and guilt. I did not breathe a word about it to Lucy—and I had always told Lucy everything.

Why this strange need for secrecy? I asked myself, as I lay in my bed that night in the darkness. Our encounter had been entirely proper. Why was I unwilling to record it in my journal or share it with my best friend? Perhaps, I thought, it was because in the course of my conversation with the gentleman that day, I had felt more excited, more alive, and more intellectually stimulated, than in any dialogue I had shared with Jonathan in years. How could I admit that to any one—even to myself? Such thoughts and feelings were wrong, very wrong, and entirely disloyal to Jonathan.

As for Lucy: she was so beautiful, and men were generally so bewitched by her, that I often felt invisible when in her presence. Yet in *this gentleman's presence*—(oh! Why had I not asked for his name?)—*I* had felt beautiful; *I* had felt bewitching. It was ludicrous, I knew; I was engaged to be married, and so was Lucy. Yet somehow, I wished to keep the experience to myself.

IN THE DAYS THAT FOLLOWED, AS LUCY AND I WANDERED ALONG the sunny cliffs and through the town, I found myself actively searching the crowd for the gentleman I had met in the churchyard. Every time I caught sight of a tall, well-dressed man in black, I would turn in silent anticipation, only to find myself repeatedly disappointed. Where had he disappeared to? Whitby was a small place, and yet there was no sign of him anywhere.

Then a thought occurred to me: why on earth would a man as wealthy, well-informed, and breath-takingly handsome as he, waste a moment on a former school-teacher like myself, who had made it abundantly clear that she was unavailable? Surely, I decided, he was only being polite when he had asked me to walk with him that day, and when he had said he hoped we would meet again. The intense interest I had sensed from him was, no doubt, only a projection of my *own* interest in him. With a sigh, I resigned myself to the fact that our chance meeting was to be a one-time occurrence—*which is just as it ought to be*, I reprimanded myself sternly.

On the 10th of August, two days after the *Demeter* had so tragically beached itself on the Whitby shore, Lucy and I ventured out early to our favourite seat on the cliff, to watch the funeral cortège of the ship's poor sea captain. The townspeople turned out in full force to honour the dead man. Lucy and I were both saddened by the proceedings and unnerved by the bizarre circumstances which lay behind them—particularly when I shared with her the details of the extraordinary account about the Russian ship in the local newspaper.

"The article says that the only cargo on board the *Demeter* was a set of fifty boxes of earth, which were unloaded and dispatched by a consignment company on the day of its arrival," I explained.

"What unusual cargo!" Lucy replied. "What could any one want with fifty boxes of earth?"

"It is very peculiar, indeed. But far more strange—and terrifying—was the addendum to the captain's log, which was discovered hidden in a bottle in the dead captain's pocket."

"What did it say?"

"He wrote that ten days out at sea, a member of the crew was found missing. A strange man was spotted on board, but no stowaways were found. Then, one by one, the sailors began to disappear, until only the first mate and the captain were left. By this time, the mate had gone stark raving mad with fear. He told the captain—" (here I read aloud from the account in the *Daily Graph*)—" '*It* is here; I know it, now. On the watch last night I saw it, like a man, tall and thin, and ghastly pale. It was in the bows, and looking out. I crept behind It, and gave It my knife; but the knife went through It, empty as the air!'

"The mate went down to the hold to search the boxes they were carrying on board. He came back up like a shot, screaming in terror that only the sea could save them, and he threw himself overboard! Now only the captain alone remained to sail the ship. He first determined that the mate was a madman, and that it was the mate himself who had killed all the crew; but the next day, the captain says he saw *It*—or *Him*. In terror, he lashed himself and his crucifix to the wheel, to—in his own words—'baffle this fiend or monster,' and stay with his ship to the end."

Lucy's face went deadly white as she listened. "What did the captain mean—to 'baffle this fiend or monster'? Who, or what, did he see? Who killed all those men?"

I shook my head. "It is a mystery. No one knows what became of the great dog, either. It must have wandered onto the moors and still be hiding there in terror, for now it has no master. Added to all this is the terrible tragedy of what happened to old Mr. Swales last night."

The elderly sailor, who had entertained us so recently with his tales of Whitby's past, had been found dead early that morning on our very own bench, with a broken neck and a look of fear and horror frozen on his face. "The poor, dear, old man!" Lucy said. "Do you think the doctors are right—that he fell back in some sort of fright?"

"It is possible. He *was* very old—nearly a hundred, he said. Perhaps he saw Death with his own dying eyes."

"To think that it happened right here, on our very own seat," Lucy replied with a shudder. "It is too, too distressing."

I DECIDED TO TAKE LUCY ON A LONG WALK TO ROBIN HOOD'S BAY that afternoon, hoping to so tire her out, that she would have no inclination for sleep-walking. It was a lovely day. We made our way there in gay spirits, and enjoyed a capital tea in a sweet, little, old-fashioned inn, sitting at a table by a bow-window with a marvellous view of the seaweed-covered rocks of the strand. We took our time walking home, with many stoppages to rest.

"I have been thinking over what Arthur wrote in his last letter,"

Lucy remarked as we ambled along a path crossing a verdant field. "It was so sweet and endearing, the way he expressed his love for me and laid out all his plans for our wedding and our future. Perhaps Mamma is right, and we *should* be married this autumn."

"I think that would make her very happy."

"Arthur has offered to purchase a special license," Lucy went on, her eyes shining, "so that we can be married at a beautiful old church in his parish and have our reception at Ring Manor. All the men will wear morning coats, and I will carry orange blossoms. I mean to have ever so many bridesmaids! Will you be my maid of honour, Mina?"

"Of course I will!" We stopped to embrace, an encounter which caught the attention of a group of cows, who nosed towards us with unexpected speed and gave us quite a fright.

"I hope you do not mind," Lucy said, as we ran on down the path, laughing, "that I will be married before you—even though you were engaged first and are older than I."

"I do not mind at all, Lucy. I am happy for you!"

"I have not forgotten our promise about the mystery of the Wedding Night," Lucy added. "That whoever gets married first must reveal *everything* to the other!"

We both giggled at that, as colour rose to our cheeks. "You are not obligated to tell me *absolutely* everything, Lucy. Some things, I think, are meant to be private."

"We shall see about that. I must admit, I am very curious! Meanwhile, Mamma says my wedding dress will be fashioned of white silk in the newest style, and trimmed in the finest white lace. What about you? Who will make your wedding dress?"

"I cannot afford anything new. I will probably just wear my best dress."

"Your best dress? Do you mean the black silk?" Lucy cried, aghast.

"Yes. I made it myself, and I think it very pretty. I took great care with the embroidery. Jonathan always compliments me when I wear it."

"But black! Mina, black is for mourning!"

"Black is also very practical. Women often marry in black."

"I do not care. I will not hear of you wearing black at your wedding, Mina. White has been *the* colour of choice for half a century, ever since Queen Victoria wore white lace to marry Prince Albert."

"Yes, but women still wear all sorts of different colours on their wedding-day."

"*Godey's Lady's Book* insists that white is the most fitting hue. It is an emblem of the purity and innocence of girlhood, and the unsullied heart she now yields to the chosen one. Have you not heard the poem?"

"What poem?"

Lucy recited:

Married in white, you will have chosen all right.
Married in grey, you will go far away.
Married in black, you will wish yourself back.
Married in red, you will wish yourself dead.
Married in blue, you will always be true.
Married in pearl, you will live in a whirl.
Married in green, ashamed to be seen.
Married in yellow, ashamed of the fellow.
Married in brown, you will live out of town.
Married in pink, your spirits will sink.

I laughed. "That is just silly superstition."

"It is not. *Some* things, I believe, are meant to be taken very seriously; and the colour of your bridal dress is so important. Do you remember Sarah Collins from school? *She* married in *grey: you will go far away.* Well! Two months later, she and her husband emigrated to America! And our dear friend, Kate Reed? She wore *green—ashamed to be seen*—and ever since her husband lost all his money in that bad business scheme, she has been so mortified by their reduced circumstances that we never hear from her!"

"Those are just coincidences, Lucy. I am sure I can marry in any colour I like and be very happy."

Lucy shook her head, unconvinced. "*Married in black, you will wish yourself back.*"

"*Wish yourself back?* What does that even mean?"

"Perhaps it means that you will travel a great distance from home and be unable to return, no matter how hard you wish it. Oh! I would be devastated if you were to move far away, Mina! It is hard enough that you will be living in Exeter, where I suppose I shall only be able to see you a few times a year." She turned to me with the most grave expression in her blue eyes, imploring: "Please promise me that you will not marry in black, Mina, or you will be sorry all the rest of your days."

She looked so earnest that I could not bear to disappoint her. "I will see what my budget allows, dearest. If I do have a white dress made, it will have to be a very simple one, which I can wear again on a regular basis."

This cheered her up somewhat. All the rest of the way back to Whitby, Lucy chatted on excitedly about her wedding plans, her honeymoon trip, the new dresses and hats she would be requiring, the arrangement of her furniture in her new house, and etc. While I was very happy for her, all this talk about marriage and future domestic arrangements caused me a little pang of envy and sadness—for I still had no idea where Jonathan was.

THAT VERY NIGHT, THE HORRORS BEGAN.

THREE

LUCY AND I WERE SO TIRED FROM OUR LONG WALK THAT we crept off to our chamber as soon as decorum allowed. Minutes later, Lucy was slumbering peacefully in her bed, and I gratefully laid my head on my pillow just minutes after closing my journal.

Did I fall asleep and dream—or did I imagine it, fully wakened? I cannot be sure; all I remember is that the tall figure with the red eyes from my earlier dream appeared again in my mind, and his voice called to me out of the darkness in a tone that was both adamant and softly entrancing:

"My darling: you will soon be mine."

I awoke with a gasp, my heart pounding. Why did I continue to have that dream—if a dream it was? What did the words mean? Whose "darling" was I?

I had no idea what time it was. The room was very dark and eerily quiet. I suddenly realised, to my dismay, that I could not hear the sounds of Lucy's gentle respiration. I found a match and struck it—and a sense of dread came over me. Lucy's bed was empty! Worse yet, the key to our chamber was resting in the lock, instead of in its place about my wrist.

I leapt from my bed and made a mad dash through the house, but Lucy was nowhere to be found. Moreover, the hall-door leading to the outside was no longer locked, as it had been when we retired. Breathlessly, I returned to our chamber, put on my shoes, and for propriety's sake, fastened a big, heavy shawl about my shoulders with a large safety pin. A quick glance through Lucy's clothing revealed that her dressing-gown and all of her dresses were still in their places—which meant that she must have walked out into the night clad only in her thin white nightdress! Horrified, I hurried out into the street to search for her.

I flew down the Crescent and along the North Terrace, looking in every direction for a glimpse of a slight figure dressed in white. It was a cool, windy night, and I shivered as I ran. The moon was bright and full, blinking in and out of view between heavy, driving black clouds. At the edge of the West Cliff, I strained my eyes to look across the harbour, worrying that Lucy might have gone up to the bench we liked to frequent, in the churchyard on the other side.

At first, everything around St. Mary's Church was obscured in shadow, and I could perceive nothing. Then, just as the bells in the church tower struck a single, echoing toll, a shaft of moonlight illuminated the church and churchyard, and I glimpsed the very sight I had been fearing: a figure, clad in snowy white, was half-reclining on our favourite seat, and another figure—very dark—was bending over it.

Overwhelmed by an ever-growing fear, I raced down the steps to the pier. The town was deadly silent, not a soul in view, as I flew along past the fish-market and across the bridge, then started up the seemingly interminable flight of steps to the church. It was a great distance, perhaps a mile in all, and although I ran as fast as my feet would carry me, it took me quite some time to cover it. As I neared the top of the steps, I was gasping for breath and had a painful stitch in my side, but I pressed on. At last, in the dim glow of the silvery moonlight, I once more caught sight of the dark-haired, reclining figure on the seat across the way. It *was* Lucy! To my horror, a long, black—something—was still bending over her.

"Lucy! Lucy!" I cried.

There came no answer. I started in terror as the dark figure behind her straightened, and a pair of gleaming red eyes stared back at me. What was it? Man or beast? And those red eyes! They were just like the eyes of the figure I had seen in my dream! Was the being real, or only a figment of my fear and imagination?

My heart pounded in dread as I passed by the church, where I lost sight of Lucy for a moment. Why, I wondered, was that *thing*—if it was real—hovering over Lucy? What was Lucy doing there? Did she go to him—or it—willingly? Did he overpower her? Was Lucy awake or asleep? Or—dear God—was she dead?

I raced across the empty churchyard. By the time I reached Lucy's side, the mysterious figure had vanished. Lucy was barefoot and leaning back over the iron bench, her eyes closed, her long raven curls spilling out behind her. Her lips were curved in a half smile, and she was taking in long, dreamy, languorous breaths. I sighed with relief; she was alive! And she was clearly asleep. I looked around, terrified that the red-eyed phantom might reappear at any instant, but all was dark and silent around us.

Lucy started shivering in her sleep. I quickly wrapped my shawl around her and used my safety pin to fasten it at her throat—an action which, to my dismay, must have inadvertently pricked her—for she put her hand to her throat and moaned. I sat down beside her, took off my shoes, put them on her feet, and then gently tried to wake her. It took some doing; in the end, I had to call her name several times and forcibly shake her to bring her round.

"Mina?" Lucy said softly, when she finally opened her eyes and looked at me with a drowsy smile. "What is it? Why have you wakened me?"

I strained to keep my voice even so as not to frighten her. "Dearest: you have been sleep-walking again."

"Have I? How funny." Lucy yawned and stretched as she glanced about, and then said in surprise, "Where are we? Is this the churchyard?"

"It is, my sweet."

"Oh!" She looked confused for a moment; and then—although her mind must have been somewhat appalled at finding herself in a graveyard in the middle of the night, wearing nothing but her nightdress—she only smiled prettily, trembled a little, put her arms around me, and said: "Did I truly walk all the way up here, alone?"

"I am afraid you did. Lucy: I saw someone with you. Do you remember anything?"

"No; nothing, since I went to bed," she replied, sounding a little frightened now. "Who did you see?"

"I do not know. It was from a distance away; it was very dark. Perhaps I imagined it."

"I remember nothing," she repeated, her brow furrowing, "except that—I was having a dream. It is all so foggy; you know I never remember my dreams. I only recall that I was walking along a path. I heard a dog barking, and then I saw—" Suddenly she stopped speaking, as a far-away look came into her blue eyes.

"What did you see?"

Lucy remained silent for a long moment; then she shook her head and said abruptly: "Now it is gone. I cannot remember."

I sensed that Lucy recalled more than she was admitting. However, this was neither the time nor the place to ask about it; the specter of the dark, red-eyed figure still filled me with apprehension. "Come. We must get you back to the house at once." Lucy rose obediently and allowed me to lead her. When we started down the gravel path, she saw me wince as the sharp stones cut into my bare feet.

"Wait," Lucy said. "Why am I wearing your shoes? You must take them back."

"No! There is no time. We must get home, and quickly. What if someone were to catch sight of us, walking barefoot and unclad in a churchyard in the dead of night? What would they think?"

The notion seemed to alarm Lucy. She did not press the point but hurried on. All the way home, my heart pounded with fear and dread that we would be seen, or—far worse—would again encounter the mysterious being from the churchyard; but fortunately, we reached our room without meeting any one and securely locked the door behind us.

After washing our feet, we knelt by my bed to pray, to thank God for delivering us home in safety. As we rose, Lucy took me in her arms and said, "Thank you for coming to look for me, Mina."

We hugged each other tightly. "I hate to think what would have happened if you had awakened in that dark churchyard all alone."

"Yes," was her abrupt reply. As she pulled out of my embrace, I thought I glimpsed a secretive, mysterious look briefly flit across her face. What was she not telling me? I longed to ask her about it, but I did not have the nerve. After all, I had my own guilty secret, did I not—about the man I had met in the churchyard?

"I am happy you are safe now. But I *would* like to know how you got the key to our room off my wrist, without waking me!"

Lucy shrugged and said simply, "I am sorry. I cannot remember."

I stood quietly while Lucy bound the key to my wrist once more with a ribbon, making sure to tie very tight knots this time. We crawled into our beds, and all was quiet for a long while as I shivered beneath the counterpane, too agitated to sleep. I assumed Lucy had dropped off; but then her voice came out of the darkness.

"Mina: will you do me a favour?"

"Anything, my dear."

"Will you promise not to say a word about this to any one? Not even Mamma?"

I hesitated. I understood, of course, what Lucy was concerned about. Should such a story leak out, her reputation might suffer injury; not on account of her sleep-walking, but from the impropriety of her appearing unclad at night in the churchyard, a story which would undoubtedly become distorted by gossiping tongues. "Do you not think your mother, at least, ought to know?"

"No. Mamma has not been very well of late. I would not want to give her any more cause to worry. Think how she would fret were she to become privy to all this! And she is not the most discreet individual. She and Arthur are very close. I would simply die if Mamma were to disclose this to him."

"All right, then. I will say nothing. We will pretend it never happened."

Lucy slept late that morning. When I woke her at eleven, she looked rather pale; overnight, her skin had somehow lost any trace of the lovely, rosy hue with which it had been formerly imbued by the summer sun. Despite this, she awoke in excellent spirits, with a sparkle in her eyes and a little, self-satisfied smile on her face.

I could not account for these curious changes at the time—although I later came to understand them far too well. I was merely grateful that our adventure in the night had not harmed her but had instead apparently benefited her somehow. Perhaps, I thought, she has just awakened from a very pleasant dream.

As I was getting dressed, however, and Lucy was brushing her hair before the looking-glass, I noticed something which filled me with regret.

"Lucy! What is that on your throat?"

"What do you mean?" she asked, drawing back her cloud of dark hair and turning her head this way and that, as she studied her reflection.

"On the side of your neck, there: what are those two marks?" They were two little red points, like pin-pricks; and just below, a crimson drop of dried blood stood out in sharp relief against the snowy white collar of her nightdress.

"I have no idea. They were not there yesterday."

"Oh dear!" I cried, distressed. "It is my fault. Last night, when I pinned my shawl around you, I must have accidentally pierced your skin. I am so sorry! Does it hurt very much?"

Lucy laughed and patted me on the shoulder. "I do not even feel it. It is nothing, truly."

"I hope it will not leave a scar; the marks *are* very tiny."

"Do not concern yourself so. I am sure they will heal very quickly. The collar of my day gown will no doubt hide them, but just in case—" Lucy buckled her black velvet band around her throat, obscuring the marks from view. "There. Now no one will ever know a thing about them."

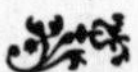

IT WAS A PERFECT DAY FOR A PICNIC. LUCY AND I WALKED BY the cliff-path to Mulgrave Woods, where Mrs. Westenra (who drove by the road) met us at the gate with our lunch basket. We spread a blanket on the soft grass beneath a huge tree and enjoyed the repast that our landlady had prepared for us.

As Lucy and her mother chatted amiably about wedding plans, my own thoughts drifted: at first, to the nagging fear that still haunted me about the figure from my dream—the figure that I had spied the night before in the churchyard. Had it been real—or was my mind simply playing tricks on me? If it was a man, why was he leaning over Lucy in that strange manner? Where had he disappeared to? I could not help recalling the stories I had read in the newspaper only two years before, about Jack the Ripper. He had preyed on young women in London in the dark of night. Was Jack the Ripper—or someone like him—on the loose in Whitby? The notion sent a shudder of terror spilling through me.

Perhaps, I thought, I should go to the authorities; but then I remembered my vow to Lucy, to say nothing of the event to any one. There was no point, I decided, in mentioning a circumstance so mortifying, and part of which *might* have been imagined, particularly when no harm had come to Lucy. However, in the future, I would have to make *absolutely certain* that Lucy could never get out of our room at night.

I shook off these silent musings, determined to enjoy the beauty of the day and the company of my companions. I joined in their spirited conversation, arguing amiably about the ideal colour for Lucy's bridesmaids' dresses, and the best food and beverages to serve at her reception. In a sense of fun, Lucy and I made a variety of outrageously inappropriate suggestions, which prompted a burst of hilarity all around.

After some time thus pleasantly engaged, I thought of Jonathan, and how much I missed him. I pictured Jonathan's handsome face in my mind: the carefully groomed brown hair, the high forehead, full cheeks, dark brown eyes, and well-proportioned nose and mouth, all set with that dear, resolute expression that I had come to know so well. The image made me sigh, for I could not help but think how absolutely happy I *would* have been at that moment if *he* had been there with me.

All at once, the face in my mind was replaced by the image of a different person entirely: that of the tall, handsome gentleman I had met three days earlier in the churchyard. With the face, came the same thought: how happy I would have been had *he* been there with me. The idea made me blush with guilt. Mina! I chided myself. Why do you think of him? You do not even know him—and you are promised to Jonathan! Yet at the same time, I could not help but wish that I might see him at least one more time.

My wish came true that very evening.

After dinner, Lucy and I strolled out to the West Cliff Pavilion, where a large crowd of happy summer visitors gathered nightly to enjoy the promenade concerts and dancing. I wore my evening dress of midnight blue silk, and Lucy looked radiant in her beaded, rose-coloured satin gown, with her curly hair framing her face, and that lovely black velvet band against her ivory throat.

We had ventured to the pavilion on three previous evenings, and each time had been delighted by the music and the swirl of the dancers, which we had viewed from a vantage point outside the brightly lit pavilion.

On this occasion, darkness had just fallen as we took up our customary position on the terrace, standing near one of the pavilion's many tall, open doors. I had often thought it very inconsistent that in our rigid society, which did not allow men and women to so much as touch in public, dancing was deemed to be entirely acceptable. In fact, it had long since been a courtship ritual. Even the waltz, which allowed partners to hold each other closely, was now extremely popular. I was grateful for this trend, as dancing was one of my favourite pursuits; but I had resigned myself to being an observer this season.

I smiled, listening, as the music spilled out into the warm night air. Lucy, on the other hand, was restless. She kept tapping her toe and moving ever closer to the door, until we were soon standing just inside.

"Lucy," I admonished, trying to draw her back, "come away."

"No." Lucy pulled her hand from mine. "I am tired of always standing outside. Oh! The dancers look so beautiful, do they not?"

A pair of young gentlemen, noticing our entrance, broke from their party and immediately strode up to us. They both had eyes only for Lucy.

"I believe you are new here, miss," the first young gentleman said, smiling eagerly at Lucy.

"Would you care to dance?" the second gentleman asked quickly, to the dismay of the first.

Lucy beamed. Sensing that she was about to reply in the affirmative, I interjected: "Thank you kindly sir, but I am afraid my friend must decline, as she is engaged to be married. We both are."

The pair of youths frowned and bowed, excusing themselves as they quickly departed.

"Oh!" Lucy cried with a vexed and regretful sigh, as she watched her would-be suitors stride away. "Did you *have* to say that?"

"Of course I did."

"But why? Dancing is a perfectly respectable activity! You and I have danced our feet off every summer at every sea-side resort we have ever visited!"

"Yes, but that was in the past. If I did not tell them, Lucy, it would be like a little lie; it would raise certain unfair expectations. Before you know it, those young men would be asking you to walk out with them."

"Well, I could tell them *then.* You will think me a horrid flirt, Mina; but this is my last chance! After this summer, I will be old and married and settled down for life. I will never again be able to dance with a score of beaus at a summer pavilion. And oh, how I would *love* to dance! The music is so splendid, it is all I can do to keep my feet still."

"Arthur is the only man you should be dancing with now—and I should dance with no one but Jonathan."

"But Arthur and Jonathan are not here! Oh! I *do* love Arthur. I do not know what I have ever done to deserve him. But it is so unfair! How dreadfully dull it is to be engaged when your lover is not present. I might as well be living in a convent. Sometimes I wish I were free again!"

I was about to offer a recrimination to Lucy's sentiment when a sudden, shocking feeling came over me. I realised that I agreed with her. Even if Jonathan had been present, in truth he was a bit shy when it came to dancing, always claiming that he had two left feet. How nice it would be, I thought—*sometimes*—to be free again; to be allowed, if only for an hour or two, to converse with—and dance with—any man I liked. My cheeks flamed at this heresy. It was so unworthy of me! Yet I could not deny that there was truth to it.

At that moment, my eye was drawn to a figure across the crowded room. I gave a little gasp. It was the tall, handsome gentleman I had met in the churchyard! He was standing at the edge of the dancers, dressed as before in his finely tailored black frock coat—and he was staring fixedly—at me. Even from this distance away, I felt the heat of his penetrating gaze boring into mine, as if I were the only other person in the room.

He began heading at once in my direction. My heart began to pound. I had not as yet spoken a word about him to Lucy; but now I had no choice.

"Lucy," I said quickly, "I met a gentleman the other day."

"What?"

"I met a man when I was walking on the cliff a few days ago—a very nice man."

"You met a man? Why did you not tell me? Who is he? What is his name?"

"I do not know, but he appears to be crossing the room just now, to speak to us."

Lucy followed my gaze. "Is that him? The handsome, black-haired gentleman?" she murmured in breathless wonder.

I nodded silently. It had been three days since I had last seen him, and he was—if possible—even more handsome than I had remembered.

An odd look suddenly crossed Lucy's face, and she went quiet for a moment, staring at him as he moved purposefully towards us through the crowd. "I wonder if I have seen him around town? He—" Then she shook her head with a puzzled giggle, and said under her breath: "No; I could never forget such a face. He is absolutely gorgeous!"

The gentleman stopped before us, removed his hat, and bowed, his eyes never leaving my face. "Good evening, ladies."

At the sound of the man's deep, gently accented foreign voice, Lucy started and stared at him again, as if taken aback. I darted a curious glance in her direction. What did her reaction mean? The gentleman, on the other hand, seemed barely aware of Lucy's presence, so focused was his attention on me.

"Good evening, sir," I replied, struggling to keep my voice even, despite the loud pounding in my chest. "It is nice to see you again."

"It is a great pleasure to see you again, Miss Murray. You look very beautiful this evening. That is a lovely gown."

"Thank you, sir." I felt my cheeks grow warm under his admiring scrutiny, the kind of look that I was accustomed to seeing directed at Lucy rather than myself.

"The dresses you ladies wear in the evening here—I far prefer them to that new fashion you wear by day, all buttoned up—" (he made a face, and motioned to his throat) "—with the collars up to here."

I laughed. "The fashion is not all that new, sir. But I agree: at times it can be suffocating—particularly in the heat of summer."

He now glanced at Lucy as if for the first time, and then darted an enquiring look in my direction. I added: "You find me at a disadvantage, sir. I would like to introduce you to my friend, but I am unacquainted with your name."

"Can that be so? Please forgive me. I have been remiss. Allow me to introduce myself: I am Maximilian Wagner, of Salzburg." He bowed again and held out his hand to me.

The touch of his hand sent a tingle up my spine; as before, his fingers felt strangely cool through my thin kid glove. "How do you do, Mr. Wagner? May I present my dearest friend, Miss Westenra?"

"Miss Westenra: Miss Murray has spoken of you. I am very pleased to meet you."

Lucy, who had been staring at him all this time, seemed to give herself a little mental shake; she now returned his smile and placed her gloved hand in his. "The pleasure is mine, sir." Turning so that Mr. Wagner could not see, Lucy directed a very comical face at me, urgently conveying her silent astonishment and satisfaction with the man's handsome manners and appearance. It was all I could do not to laugh in response.

The music came to a brief halt, and some of the dancing couples disbanded. A good-looking swain rushed up to Lucy and said, "May I have the next dance, miss?"

Lucy instantly put her hand in his and said, "I would be delighted, sir." Glancing back at me with a parting wink, she added, "I will see you later, Mina."

The musicians began to play the first strains of one of my favourite waltzes, Strauss's *Tales from the Vienna Woods.* Mr. Wagner held out his arm to me. "Will you do me the honour of dancing with me, Miss Murray?"

I knew I ought to reply, *I should not, sir;* but with his intense, deep blue eyes holding mine, and my heart hammering in my ears, I could not pronounce the words, any more than I could prevent myself from silently taking the arm he offered. Mr. Wagner led me onto the dance floor. As if in a trance, I faced him, and we moved into waltz position. He drew me gently to him, until my body was only inches from his. The touch of his right hand against my shoulder blade, the feel of his hard shoulder muscle beneath my left hand, and the firm grip of his other hand in mine made my blood course hot and thick through my veins.

The music began in earnest, and we began to dance. He moved with remarkable fluidity and grace, but with a slightly different style than that to which I was accustomed; an older form, I thought, or a Viennese custom perhaps. It took me a few moments to adjust and accommodate—or perhaps he adjusted to accommodate me—I could not be certain. In no time, however, we were whirling about the room, his movements in such perfect harmony with my own that I felt as if I had never, until that moment, truly comprehended what it meant to waltz. A rush of pleasure rippled through me; my thoughts scattered; the soaring, rhythmic melody carried me away; I felt as if I were floating. For a long while I simply gave myself up to the enjoyment of the wonderful music and the feeling of being in his arms, never wanting it to end.

His deep voice broke into my reverie. "You are a wonderful dancer, Miss Murray."

"Thank you, but I am only as good as the partner who leads me—and you are most accomplished, sir."

"I have had many years of practice. I would venture to guess that you have, as well."

"I taught dance and music at school."

"Are those required courses for young English girls?"

"They are—along with deportment and all the usual subjects."

"Reading, writing, and arithmetic?"

"And sometimes French or Italian."

"Ah? Parlez-vous français, mademoiselle?"

"Oui, monsieur; un peu.[1] I am afraid I speak no German, however."

"*Das ist doch kein Problem, Fräulein*—this is no great loss. We do not need German to converse. I far prefer your language, in any case." We shared a smile as he spun me around in time to the music, adding: "Is it true, what I read? That the waltz was considered somewhat disreputable in this country for many years?"

"It was indeed, sir. It might be still, had not young Victoria asked the future Prince Albert to dance a waltz with her before they were married."

"In that case, I find myself most indebted to your Queen."

I laughed. We continued dancing in silence, an activity which neither of us seemed to wish to give up, as one song blended into the next and the next. I was surprised to note that, despite the heat in the crowded room, and the level of our exertion, not a drop of perspiration ever marked Mr. Wagner's brow, and he never grew out of breath; whereas after an hour on the dance floor, I was very warm, winded, and in desperate need of refreshment.

Apparently noticing my discomfort, at the next break in the music, Mr. Wagner said, "Would you like to step outside on the terrace for a few minutes, Miss Murray? And may I get you something to drink?"

"That would be lovely. Thank you." As we moved towards the door, I searched the room for Lucy. I found her to be the centre of attention of a sizeable group of men, with whom she was laughing

1 "Do you speak French, Miss?" "Yes, sir; a little."

and chatting happily. I smiled at this, as Mr. Wagner brought me a cup of punch. "Are you not having any?" I asked.

"I am not fond of punch. Shall we?"

We ventured out to the terrace, where we took seats beside each other on a low stone wall overlooking the sea, and I gratefully sipped my beverage. The fresh sea-breeze felt invigorating, yet the magical spell of the past hour still warmed my blood. Below us, the dark waves crashed and rolled up onto the beach; above us, bright stars twinkled in an inky sky; and all around us filtered the lively music from the pavilion.

"May I say again, Miss Murray, what a delightful dancer you are. I cannot recall when I have ever passed a more enjoyable hour on a dance floor."

"Nor I, sir. You said you have had many years of practice. Where did you learn to dance?"

"In school, as you did," he replied smoothly. "The waltz has a long history in Austria, starting from the days of the Court in Vienna in the late seventeenth century. For the last two hundred years, people from the country-side to the city have all gone 'dancing mad,' as they say."

"I can see why. Some of the most beautiful music in the world has originated in Austria. *Tales from the Vienna Woods* is my favourite, and I also love *The Blue Danube.*"

"I, too, am fond of the music by Strauss, both Junior and Senior."

"Do you like Joseph Haydn?" I enquired.

"Haydn was a very accomplished composer and an interesting man. He taught Beethoven, and was good friends with Mozart; he could tell a fine joke and put away a great quantity of ale."

I let out a surprised laugh. "I was referring to Haydn's music. You speak as if you knew him."

He laughed in return. "I have—read a great deal about him. And enjoyed hearing his music, of course." He changed the subject, adding quickly: "Your friend, I believe she called you Mina. Is that short for something?"

"Wilhelmina."

"A good Dutch or German name; and yet Murray, I think, is Scottish. Did your parents hail from that country?"

I felt my cheeks grow warm, and I averted my gaze—embarrassed, as always, whenever the subject of my parentage came up. "I do not know where my parents came from exactly. I never knew them. I think—I believe they came from London."

"I see."

"What about your parents, sir? Do they reside in Austria?"

"No. They both passed on many years ago."

"I am sorry."

"Do not be sorry. Death is a part of life. It is nothing to regret and nothing to fear."

"You say that so calmly and matter-of-factly: as if you were discussing the weather. Do you truly not fear death?"

"Not at all."

"You are religious, then? A man of the church?"

"Definitely not."

"Well, I wish I could feel as you do. But—I do not like to think about death. Let us talk of something else. Such as: what brings you to Whitby, Mr. Wagner? Business or pleasure?"

"Both, in fact."

"What business are you engaged in?"

"I am a landowner in my own country. I am considering the acquisition of some property in England."

"Where? In Whitby?"

"I am keeping an open mind. I enjoy the peace and quiet of the country, and small towns such as this—but in general, I prefer the *hustle and bustle,* I think you call it, of a great city like London."

"So do I. London is so alive! There is so much to see and do. I love to walk up Piccadilly. Have you climbed up the dome of St. Paul's, and seen Westminster Abbey and Parliament?"

"Not yet."

"Oh! But you must! If you find a house in London, will you make your home there, or will it be a holiday residence?"

"We shall see. I have, for some time, desired a change of scene—and your great country is truly the centre of the world." He lifted his eyes to mine. "Now that I have . . . seen it . . . I think it quite possible that I *shall* move here permanently." He gazed at me with such intensity that a heat rose to my face, and I had to force myself to look away.

"I hope you will be happy with whatever choice you make." A small silence fell as I stared at the distant moon. A sudden stab of guilt pierced through me. What was I doing, dancing and talking the night away with Mr. Wagner, while the man to whom I was promised was missing—perhaps ill, or in danger? I stood, all at once feeling quite ashamed of myself. "It is getting late, sir. I had best find Lucy now and return to our lodgings. Thank you for a lovely evening."

He rose with undisguised regret. "I have enjoyed your company, Miss Murray. May I have the honour of escorting you and your friend home?"

"Thank you, but our house is just up the road, and—" *And,* I thought, it would never do, if Mrs. Westenra or our landlady, Mrs. Abernathy, were to observe us returning at this late hour in the company of a strange, handsome gentleman. Knowing the physical reaction I always experienced at his touch, I did not trust myself to put my hand in his; so I only dipped my head and curtseyed, as I said: "Good-night, Mr. Wagner."

He bowed. "Good-night, Miss Murray. Pleasant dreams."

His deep voice seemed to echo through me as I hurried off to the pavilion, where I was obliged to issue some very stern threats to pry Lucy away from her latest dancing partner. With a sigh, she finally issued her good-bye and allowed me to lead her outside. As we headed in the direction of our lodgings, Lucy twirled about in the street, clasping her hands to her chest in delight, and uttering breathlessly:

"Oh! What an evening! I danced with six different partners, Mina. Six! At one point, I had at least twelve different men who all wanted to dance with me at the same time. They were all so sweet and earnest and attentive. But I admit: none were half as handsome as your Mr. Wagner!"

"He is not *my* Mr. Wagner," I returned, my cheeks reddening.

"Oh, but I think he is." Lucy took my arm and went on: "Your Mr. Wagner is the most attractive man I have ever seen! I used to think Arthur was handsome; but now he seems quite plain to me in comparison."

"Lucy: I agree that Mr. Wagner is good-looking, but that is not the most important quality in a man."

"Of course not! Mr. Wagner is also a brilliant dancer. All the women were looking at him—he was the best man on the dance floor. I would have died for a chance to waltz with him if you had not monopolised him all evening."

"I did no such thing—"

"Mr. Wagner also has exquisite manners, and such a lovely accent. It is so funny; when I first heard him speak, his voice sounded strangely familiar, and I thought: have we met before? Then I had to laugh, for that is quite impossible. I would surely remember it were I to have ever met a man like *him!* What a find you have made, Mina!"

"Please—I have made no *find.* Mr. Wagner is a friend, and nothing more."

Lucy giggled. "*You* may consider him as a friend, my dear, but he is entirely besotted by you!"

The heat in my cheeks spread to my entire face now. "That is not true."

"Mina: are you blind? Did you not see the look in Mr. Wagner's eyes as he crossed the room to you, or when he held you in his arms? I watched you while you were dancing. He made no attempt to disguise it. Mark my words: Mr. Wagner loves you—or is *falling in love* with you. I should know. I have had any number of men look at me in precisely that manner, and three of them went on to propose."

"Lucy, you must not tell me this. It is not right. It *cannot be*!"

"But it *is*! I assume—since you so freely tell everyone about *my* engaged status—that you informed Mr. Wagner about Jonathan?"

"Of course! At the very first opportunity, on the day we met."

"Hmm. He is not a man to give up lightly, then. He must hope that somehow he can win your favour and steal you away."

"If he does, he is mistaken. I have never given Mr. Wagner the slightest indication that I—" I broke off, unable to finish.

"Mina, do not look so mortified. Just because we are engaged, it does not mean we are *dead*! We can still *look* and *appreciate* other men, can we not? We can still dance with them at a sea-side pavilion, without fear of reprisal! If Mr. Wagner believes that you are more interested than you really are—well, I am quite sure you did not *mean* to lead him on." With an impish grin, Lucy added: "I must admit, though: I am almost sorry that you are engaged to Jonathan, for I think Mr. Wagner would be a wonderful catch."

"Oh! You are too, too wicked!" I cried; but I could not prevent myself from joining in Lucy's burst of laughter. When I at last regained a measure of self-control, I said soberly, "You know nothing about Mr. Wagner—and I do not either, really. I am honoured to be engaged to Jonathan. He is my closest friend in the world, other than you, dearest; and I love him—and I miss him."

"I know you do. I love and miss Arthur. And I have no doubt we will both be married by October."

We reached our lodgings. I stopped by the front steps, lowering my voice. "That being the case, Lucy: I hope it goes without saying, that we had best not mention anything about to-night's *activities* to your mother—or to Arthur and Jonathan, when we see them next."

Lucy touched her finger to her lips with a little gleam in her eyes. "I will take our secret to the grave."

FOUR

THAT NIGHT, ALTHOUGH LUCY INSISTED SHE WAS FAR TOO knackered after all that dancing to do any sleep-walking, I locked our door and secured the key to my wrist as usual. Lucy fell asleep at once, and appeared so restful that I did not expect any more trouble. My hopes for a quiet night were dashed, however. My mind was too full of thoughts of Mr. Wagner, and my flagrantly inappropriate behaviour that evening, for easy slumber; and when I did at last drift off, I was wakened twice by Lucy, trying impatiently to get out. Each time, she seemed annoyed to find our door locked, and it was all I could do to get her to return to bed.

Lucy made the most unexpected remark the next day, as we were coming home for dinner. We had spent the afternoon at our seat on the East Cliff, a spot which I had worried might feel a little different—even eerie—to us, since I had found Lucy in such a compromising position there only two nights before. However, she now seemed to be even more addicted to the place than I.

Indeed, it was only with the greatest reluctance that she allowed herself to be dragged home at meal-times.

We had just reached the top of the steps up from the West Pier, and paused to take in the view behind us. The sun was very low in the sky, casting a beautiful rosy glow over the church and the abbey on the distant, opposite cliff. Studying this, an odd, far-away look came into Lucy's eyes, and she said in a dreamy tone: "His red eyes again! They are just the same."

I stared at her, taken aback. It was the first time I had heard Lucy mention "red eyes"—the eyes I had seen twice in my dreams and once on the cliff-top, hovering over Lucy on that horrible night. Her expression was so strange that I followed her gaze. She was staring across the harbour, to the East Cliff—and her gaze seemed fixed on the very seat which we had vacated not long before. I could just make out a dark figure, now seated there alone—and I gave a startled gasp, for despite the great distance, it seemed as if the stranger did have red eyes, like burning flames. A second later, the illusion was gone, as if the effect had been caused by the red glow of the setting sun.

"Lucy, what did you mean just now?"

Lucy blinked distractedly, as if coming out of a day-dream. "What?"

"You said something about a man with red eyes."

"Did I?" She let out a peculiar laugh and shook her head. "I have no idea why I said that."

I did not believe her; but she would not say another word about it.

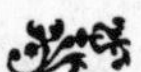

No matter how hard I tried, I could not stop thinking about Mr. Wagner. All day long, my thoughts kept drifting back to the conversations we had shared, and to the way it had felt to be held in his arms as we waltzed across the dance floor.

That night, after Lucy was in bed and fast asleep—knowing full well that I was acting scandalously—I locked her in and sneaked away to the pavilion, hoping to see him again. To my disappointment, although I waited a long while, Mr. Wagner did not appear. As I had no wish to dance with any one else, I left and strolled for a while along the West Cliff, under a bright and beautiful moon.

As I returned to our lodging-house, I looked up and was surprised to see Lucy, fast asleep, with her head leaning against the side of our open window. Seated beside her on the window-sill was what appeared to be a large, black bird. How odd, I thought. One did not often see birds at night, especially in the summer—except for nocturnal species, like owls—but I was not particularly alarmed. By the time I ran upstairs, unlocked, and entered the room, the creature was gone.

"Lucy? Are you all right?" I enquired; for she was crawling into bed, pale-faced, breathing languorously, and holding her hand protectively to her throat, as if she were cold. She did not respond. I tucked her in lovingly; but even in her sleep, I sensed that she was fretting about something, and I wondered what it was.

The next morning at breakfast, Lucy was unusually tired and looked more pale than ever. As she picked at her meal, the landlady brought over a letter, which had just arrived. Lucy's face brightened when she saw that it was from Arthur.

"Arthur says his father is much better," Lucy announced quietly after glancing over the missive. "He says he will be able to come visit in a week or two, and he hopes we will be married very soon."

"How wonderful," replied her mother. Sudden tears came into Mrs. Westenra's eyes, which she insisted were tears of happiness. Later, however, when Lucy was taking an afternoon nap, and

Mrs. Westenra and I were taking tea in the sitting-room, she revealed the truth behind her feelings on the matter.

"Lucy is my only child, you know," said that good lady, as she sank back in her easy chair with a sigh, "and we have always been very close. I am grieved to lose her as my very own—to think that she will soon be a man's wife, and that she will no longer need me as much as she always has—and yet, I am relieved and grateful that she is soon to have someone else to protect her."

"I am certain she will still come to you often and regularly for advice and counsel, Mrs. Westenra," I replied with a warm smile. "I believe that even the best husband in the world could never be a replacement for a mother."

At this, Mrs. Westenra stifled a great sob, and fresh tears rolled down her face.

"Oh! Ma'am, what is it?" I cried, chagrined. "Have I said something to upset you?"

It took her some moments to compose herself. "It is not your fault, my dear," she said as she dabbed at her eyes with her linen handkerchief. "There is something you do not know—something I have told no one." She hesitated. "If I share this with you, you must promise not to tell Lucy; I do not wish to worry her."

"I promise," I replied, thinking how strange it was to find myself the keeper of secrets for both mother and daughter; and moreover, to be hiding a secret of my own.

"You may have perceived that I have been unwell of late."

"I have noticed that you tire very easily."

"It is my heart. It is growing weaker. The doctor said that I have, at most, a few months to live."

"A few months?" I cried.

Mrs. Westenra nodded sadly. "Even now, he said, at any time, a sudden shock could kill me. That is why I have stayed in so quietly most of the time ever since we arrived here."

"Oh! Mrs. Westenra, I am so, so sorry." I grieved for her, and for Lucy, who would surely be very bereft when her mother was gone. "Is there anything I can do for you? Any way I can help, or make you more comfortable?"

She smiled sweetly and took my hands in hers. "Just promise me, when I am gone, to be as good a friend to Lucy as you have always been in the past."

"I will." I kissed her on the cheek. "You may count on me for that."

As the week wore on, to my dismay, it was not Mrs. Westenra's health which caused me the greatest concern, but Lucy's. Lucy lost her appetite and became increasingly pale, tired, and languid, and there was a drawn, haggard look under her eyes that I did not understand. Her mother was equally stymied, insisting that Lucy was not and had never been anaemic. When I asked Lucy about her strange symptoms and declining health, she claimed to be just as puzzled as I.

The days were bright and sunny, but I did not spy Mr. Wagner anywhere on my walks. Despite this, I resisted the urge to steal out to the pavilion at night, instead staying in to watch over Lucy. I took care that our room was always securely locked so that she could not wander; yet I awoke twice to find her sitting in a faint at the open window.

"Dearest," I said, as I helped her back to bed one night after finding her in this weakened and senseless state, "what were you doing at the window? You are so pale. I should call a doctor."

At this, she came instantly awake, and cried, "No! I will see no doctor. What could *he* do?" Then she laughed—a strange, eerie laugh—followed by a determined effort to pinch colour back into her cheeks. "You see? I am fine. Perfectly fine."

Her behaviour was so odd, it greatly worried me—a worry

which grew to alarm when I tucked her in and caught sight of the tiny wounds on Lucy's throat, which she always took care to cover up by day. "Lucy, the marks on your throat—the ones I caused by that unlucky prick of the pin—they have not yet healed. They are still open and red, and they appear to be even larger than before."

"I told you, they do not bother me," she said, covering the marks with her hand. "Now leave me be. I need to sleep."

"If they are not better in a few days," I insisted, "I *shall* call a doctor."

❧

THE NEXT MORNING, LUCY WAS PARTICULARLY TIRED AND PALE and refused to leave her bed. Although I did not like to leave her, she insisted that I go out on my own and enjoy the day and let her continue to sleep. Taking a magazine, I headed off, intending to spend a few hours reading up on the East Cliff. The sky was grey and cloudy, and as I passed the fish-market and approached the bridge, I was deep in my own introspection, when a familiar voice broke into my thoughts.

"Miss Murray?"

I looked up to find Mr. Wagner standing just a few feet away, near the steps leading to the bridge. My heart, as always, began to beat in a rapid frenzy at the sight of him. He looked particularly dashing, with a fashionable straw hat angled atop his dark head. "Mr. Wagner."

"It is a fine morning."

"Do you think so? It is a bit overcast for my taste, but at least I perceive no threat of rain."

"A good thing, as I have just this minute hired a boat."

"You have hired a boat?" I repeated in surprise.

"Yes: the blue one, just there." He pointed to a sweet little skiff, which was anchored by the bridge near-by. "Have you had an opportunity to go out on the river?"

"I have not. Lucy and I have desired to try it, ever since we arrived in Whitby—but now she is not in good enough health for such an outing."

"I am sorry to hear it. She would have made delightful company. But as she is not present—would I be remiss in offering to escort *you* on a little water excursion? I have heard that there is a charming spot to visit, about a mile up the river."

It was a tempting offer, and I briefly considered it. But how could I? With deep regret, I said: "I appreciate the invitation, sir, but I am afraid that decorum prevents me from accepting."

"Decorum?"

"I enjoyed dancing with you, sir—very much—but that was in a pavilion full of people. To go out on the river, unaccompanied by a chaperone—it would be unthinkable."

"Unthinkable?" A smile played about his lips as he glanced at the few strangers passing by, who were paying us no heed; then he looked back at me. "Do you really mind so much, Miss Murray, about what people would think? Who will know or care if you spend a few hours on the river to-day—with or without a chaperone? Why not throw caution to the wind, just this once?"

I could not help but laugh. I thought: Mina Murray, you have spent two-and-twenty years living a quiet, sheltered life, always behaving with the utmost propriety. Who *will* know or care? Lucy had told me to enjoy the day. Follow Lucy's advice! Enjoy your last summer at the sea-side before settling down for life!

"You are right, sir. I *should* throw caution to the wind every now and again. I would be delighted to go boating with you."

He smiled and held out his hand. I took it, a thrill surging through me at his touch. As he led me down the steps to the skiff and assisted me on board, I pushed all guilty thoughts from my mind, and allowed myself a twinge of excitement. It was perfectly acceptable, I told myself, to act a little rashly and impetuously on occasion: to step outside one's carefully drawn bounds and experience a bit of adventure. Jonathan would never know; and it *was* just a boat ride.

I took a seat at one end of the boat, while Mr. Wagner sat facing me and did the honours with the oars—a task which appeared to be entirely effortless for him. In short order, we were away from the dock and gliding up the river.

"You handle this boat as if it were nothing, Mr. Wagner."

"It only appears that way because I am rowing with the tide."

I took off my glove and dangled my hand in the cool water, catching sight of my own dappled form in the rippling surface. For some odd reason, I noticed, Mr. Wagner did not seem to be reflected there. How odd, I thought; it must be a trick of the light.

"I see you have *Lippincott's Monthly Magazine* with you," he said, as we made steady progress up the river. "Is that the July issue?"

"It is. How is it that you are familiar with *Lippincott's*?"

"I am a regular subscriber to the new London edition. It is one of many English periodicals I have sent to me, to improve my command of your language and to keep abreast of the latest and best in literature. Did you read Arthur Conan Doyle's story in February's edition?"

"*The Sign of Four?* Yes! It was most engaging. This issue has a new story by Oscar Wilde, called *The Picture of Dorian Gray,* about a man who makes a wish to stay young for ever—and then it comes true. Have you read it?"

"I have. I left home before my own copy could arrive, but I bought one at a newsstand yesterday. Did you like the tale?"

"No; not at all. I found it shocking, at times horrifying, and very crude—but all the same, I could not put it down. I have read it twice already!"

Mr. Wagner laughed. "It is an interesting concept, is it not—the idea of never aging? Would it appeal to you, to be rich, beautiful, and eternally young?"

"I think everyone has a desire for perennial youth," I admitted, "but in the end, this is a *Faustian,* cautionary tale, about vanity and frivolity, and the dangers of trying to interfere with the basic laws of life and death. When I really think about it, I would not wish to be young for ever."

"No? And why not?"

"Because I would be obliged to watch everyone I loved grow old and die."

"What if that were not the case? What if there was one person whom you loved deeply, with whom you could live on for ever, under the same terms?"

I hesitated, then said: "Perhaps then it would prove agreeable, as long as it did not involve selling my soul to the Devil. But until I meet a sorcerer who can put both me and Jonathan under the same spell with impunity, I will be happy to age gracefully like any other mortal."

I suddenly caught myself, wishing that I had not mentioned Jonathan; even though my comment was honest, surely it was awkward to talk about one's fiancé, while out on the river with another man. Mr. Wagner, however, did not seem to notice any awkwardness, and said: "I believe you said your fiancé was away on a business trip. Have you heard from him?"

"No." I frowned, all my worry returning with sudden force. "I expect a letter every day, but he has not written in quite some time."

"I am sorry. Where did you say he went?"

"Transylvania."

"I know it well."

"Do you? What is it like?"

"The country-side is very beautiful. Mountains, forests, and quaint little towns, with here and there an old castle perched on a hilltop. But it is far too quiet and isolated for me. Tell me—what is your fiancé's name again?"

"Jonathan."

"Where did he go in Transylvania?"

"Bistritz was the closest town. The client he went to see lives in a castle near some sort of mountain pass—the Borgo, I think."

"The Borgo Pass? Well! Surely this explains everything."

"Does it? How?"

"The Borgo Pass is in the extreme east of Transylvania, in the midst of the Carpathian Mountains, on the border of Bukovina. It is on the very frontier: one of the wildest and least known portions of Europe, very sparsely populated, with few good maps to be had. Even the most seasoned traveller would have difficulty navigating its twisting highways." In an ominous tone, he added: "I would venture to guess that he became lost for a time, and then was waylaid by *gipsies*."

"Gipsies?" I repeated in alarm.

"Many a victim has found him or herself a willing captive of a Szgany camp-fire for weeks on end," he said, his eyes twinkling, "unable to leave—like the king in *One Thousand and One Nights*—for fear of missing the next installment in their nightly tales."

I laughed at his gentle teasing. "That might explain it, sir, if you or I were the missing party; but Jonathan has a very practical nature. Although he enjoys literature, he is far more enamoured of architecture and history."

"Architecture and history, you say? Well, then: Buda-Pesth is a fascinating city, not to mention Vienna, and the City of Light. Has Jonathan been to Paris before?"

"Never."

"You see? A man who enjoys travel, and who loves architecture and history, could lose himself in any one of those cities for months. Why, it can take half a year just to see the collection in the Louvre, alone."

I nodded. However, the cheerful mood he had induced soon evaporated, and we both fell silent. I knew in my heart that there was no good explanation for Jonathan's absence, and I think he sensed that, for me, it was no longer a joking matter.

A silence fell as we glided on, passing a stretch of idyllically beautiful country-side. He took me to a lovely spot called Cock-mill Creek, where we disembarked and strolled for a while along the river-bank. When Mr. Wagner asked if I would like anything to eat, I admitted that I was very hungry. We stopped at a little inn at Glen Esk, where we were shown to a table on the veranda overlooking the river, and I ordered a sandwich and a lemonade. To my surprise, Mr. Wagner did not order any food or drink himself.

"Forgive me, but I dined earlier, and I have an engagement this evening which promises to include a large and memorable dinner. I would rather not ruin my appetite."

We sat quietly for a while as I ate my lunch, listening to the murmur of the near-by river, which blended delightfully with the buzzing of insects and the twittering of birds. It was still cloudy, but a slight breeze, redolent with the fragrance of summer blooms, pleasantly stirred the leaves of the trees in the surrounding groves.

"This is a beautiful place," I said. "Thank you for bringing me here."

"It is my pleasure."

When I glanced at him now, and caught the full weight of his expression as he watched me—his eyes were so sincere, admiring, and full of interest—I suddenly felt that I could tell him anything, as if I knew with the utmost certainty that he held only my best interests at heart.

"The other night at the pavilion, Mr. Wagner, you asked about my parents."

He nodded, waiting.

"I am an orphan. I was left on the steps of a London orphanage when I was just a year old. I was dressed in rags and wrapped in an old blanket, pinned with a crude note that said my name was Wilhelmina Murray, and would they please care for me."

"From what little you said, I had guessed as much."

"I spent all my childhood at the orphanage. That is where I met Jonathan. He was the son of the widowed cook, and they lived in rooms on the top floor. For years, we regarded each other as the brother and sister we never had. His father's best friend, Mr. Peter Hawkins, paid for Jonathan's education, sending him to an excellent school when he was twelve. My own education would never have progressed beyond the three years of compulsory elementary education had our institution not become the recipient of a generous grant. I was sent to a boarding-school on the outskirts of London. Jonathan and I became avid correspondents, and saw each other whenever we both happened to visit his mother at the orphanage at the same time. Sadly, she passed away last autumn. It was when Jonathan and I met again at her funeral that we discovered our feelings for each other had grown and changed."

My thoughts drifted briefly to that day, when Jonathan had asked me to marry him: it was three days after his mother's service, and we were walking through a London park. He had stopped beneath a large tree, and said, "Wilhelmina, I have never known a girl I love as much you. I think we were meant to be together. Do you feel the same? Will you be my wife?" I had said yes happily, and kissed him: our first kiss. We had grown even closer since then, as we planned out our future together; and everything had, of course, been very proper and chaste between us.

"A nice story with a happy ending," Mr. Wagner was saying now, "and yet you seemed reluctant to share it. Why?"

"I have not told you everything." Taking a deep breath, I went on: "As a little girl, I used to dream about my mother and father. I imagined that they were the king and queen of a distant land, and as the future heir to the throne, I had been hidden away for my own protection. I knew it was a fairy tale, of course, but it pleased me for a time to believe it. Later, I told myself that my parents were just a poor English couple who could not afford to keep me, but that they would come for me one day. Needless to say, no one ever came. When I was eight years old, I overheard the servants at the orphanage gossiping. One of them said—" I felt a heat of mortification rise to my cheeks. "She said my mother was a housemaid who—who became with child—and was dismissed from her post."

"Was that true?"

"Apparently so. She did not mention my mother's name and did not seem to know what had become of her; but somehow she was very well apprised of this fact. Ever since I learned it, I have felt so ashamed."

"Why? Because your mother conceived you out of wedlock?"

"Yes! To grow up knowing that my own mother fell so scandalously from grace—it is a fact that has haunted me all my life."

"It is a sad fate, indeed, to grow up without parents, and sadder still to feel shame with regard to the circumstances of one's birth. But truly, Miss Murray, this is not such a dreadful tale. We all are victims of some kind of past misfortune, and clearly you have not been permanently scarred by yours. Look at you now: a beautiful young woman, finely educated, and about to be married."

"Please do not think that I am ungrateful. I give thanks every day for all that I have."

"I merely wish to help set your mind at ease about something over which you had no control. I think you have come out far ahead of most. In fact, I am quite envious of you."

"Envious of me? Why? I am a poor orphan, with barely a penny to my name. Whereas you, sir—you are wealthy, you travel the world, you have everything a person could want."

A cloud seemed to wash over his countenance at my last remark. "No, Miss Murray, it is *you* who has everything a person could want: the one, true source of happiness on this earth."

"What is that?" I asked, in puzzlement.

"You have found the person with whom you wish to share all the days of your life." His eyes lifted to mine and settled there, and he added, his voice soft and deep, "I have been searching for such a person for . . . a very long time."

Under his gaze, I found it hard to breathe. "You will find her one day," I managed.

"Yes," he returned quietly, his eyes never leaving mine, "I believe I shall."

OUR RETURN TRIP DOWN THE RIVER WAS AS SERENE AND PEACEful as that which had preceded it, and when we parted ways, I thanked Mr. Wagner earnestly for arranging the expedition.

"I will be at the pavilion to-night," he said, as he kissed my gloved hand. "Will you join me?"

I gave him no definite answer but turned and ran home, awash in a fresh wave of guilt. Our conversation that day had reminded me of how much I missed Jonathan. I felt a deep pang of longing for him. One day soon, I hoped, I would hear from Jonathan, and go to him—but once I did that—once I left Whitby—I knew I would never see Mr. Wagner again. The thought brought anguished tears to my eyes. Oh! What was I to do with all these improper feelings, for a man I should not be seeing and could never have?

All evening, I could think of nothing but the night before me, and the fact that Mr. Wagner would be waiting for me at the pavilion. A line from *The Picture of Dorian Gray* kept running through my head—a line which, I thought, might have been written by the Devil himself:

> *"The only way to get rid of a temptation is to yield to it. Resist it, and your soul grows sick with longing for the things it has forbidden to itself."*

As I dined with Lucy and her mother, I felt sick with anxiety, and had to keep reminding myself to stay true to the lie I had told them—that I had spent the day reading and writing in the churchyard.

Mrs. Westenra, apparently sensing my distress, reached across the table to squeeze my hand and said, "Do not worry, my dear. You will see him soon."

"See who?" I replied, alarmed and confused for a moment, thinking that she had somehow found out about Mr. Wagner and my secret desire to meet him that night.

"Why, Jonathan, of course."

"Oh yes, I hope so," I responded quickly.

I felt Lucy's eyes on me throughout the meal but could not bring myself to look at her.

The moment Lucy fell asleep, I rose and put on my blue evening dress. I was so distracted that I nearly forgot to lock the door to our room and secure the key inside my glove.

I hurried out into the night, flushed with nervous anticipation. I entered the pavilion and eagerly scanned the crowd. At first, I saw no sign of him, and my spirits wavered; but then he appeared as if by magic at my elbow and silently offered me his arm. Our eyes met; I moved onto the dance floor and into his arms; the music began; and once again, I was transported into what seemed like another world.

We danced together for hours. Later, as we strolled outside

with the music filtering around us, Mr. Wagner drew me into his arms again, and we waltzed under the stars. He twirled me to a spot that was out of view of the other people on the terrace, then stopped and drew me even closer, until my body touched his, and his face was only inches from mine. As we stood in heated silence in each other's arms, my heart began to pound so loudly, I felt certain that despite the layers of our clothing, he could detect its beat against his chest.

His gaze fell to my lips, and then lower, to my throat, which lay exposed to his view. A sudden, fiery look came into his eyes, like a hunger that must be assuaged. My head began to swim; I caught and held my breath; for I felt a similar desire. At that moment, I wanted, needed, more than anything in the world, for Mr. Wagner to kiss me.

A sudden, hard look came into his eyes, as if he was summoning every bit of strength he possessed to resist this temptation, and he roughly pushed me away.

Just then, a sharp peal of laughter pierced the darkness. The sound, which emanated from a pair of night strollers walking by, brought me back to my senses.

"Go!" Mr. Wagner said, averting his eyes, apparently struggling to regain control of himself. "Now! Before I—"

I murmured an abrupt good-night and darted away. Tears stung my eyes as I raced home, my heart hammering with shame. *If he had not stopped us,* I thought, *I would have kissed him.* What was I doing? What kind of woman was I, to act so shamefully? I knew I must put an end to this . . . but I did not know how.

AS I STEALTHILY ENTERED OUR CHAMBER AND RELOCKED THE door, I heard Lucy's accusing voice out of the darkness:

"Where have you been?"

I lit a lamp. Lucy was lying in bed, staring at me. Was she awake or asleep? I could not tell. "I was taking a night walk," I replied quickly. "I often do so."

As I began to undress, Lucy sat up, her blue eyes—luminous against the strange pallor of her face—still fixed on me. "It must have been a very long walk. I awoke earlier, and you were gone. I was frightened."

"I'm sorry."

"Why are you so flushed and perspiring?"

"I saw someone in the shadows as I returned, so I ran."

"I do not believe you. You went up to the pavilion, didn't you? You danced with Mr. Wagner!"

My cheeks burned. "I did no such thing."

"You are a terrible liar, Mina. Look at you blushing! You can speak freely with me. If any one can understand that temptation, believe me, it is I."

"I do not know what you mean."

"Have it your way." Lucy drew up her knees and hugged them to her chest, smiling. "Mina: do you recall *that night*? The night you found me in the churchyard, fast asleep?"

"How could I forget it?"

"It has been coming back to me, slowly. I remember bits and pieces of my dream now. I felt compelled to go up to that very spot, although I did not know why. I passed over the bridge, and I went up the steps. I heard dogs howling—and then music—beautiful music. And then—" A half-dreamy expression settled on Lucy's face, and she ran her fingers across the bedclothes with a motion as gentle as a caress. "Everything is a jumble, and then I have a vague memory of something long and dark with red eyes."

"Red eyes?"

"The next thing I remember is a strange singing in my ears. Then it seemed as if my soul left my body and floated up into the air. I only came back to myself when you began shaking me."

Just then, there came a strange sound from outside the window. Lucy leapt up and pulled aside the blind. I was startled to observe a large, black-winged creature flitting near-by in whirling circles against the moonlight.

"What is that?" I said. "A great bird?"

"It is a bat."

I had seen bats before, but this creature was bigger and blacker than most, with immense, flapping wings. Once or twice, the creature flew in quite close to the window, and—perhaps I fancied it—I seemed to feel its tiny, piercing eyes fasten on me; then it darted away rapidly to the east.

The dreamy look on Lucy's face vanished, replaced by a sort of wanton expression which I had never witnessed before. She lay back down on the bed and let out an uncanny laugh—a laugh that made me shudder.

"Lucy: why did you laugh like that?"

"Don't you know, Mina dearest?" Lucy said, directing her sultry gaze at me. Then she turned her back to me and seemed to fall instantly asleep.

Everything changed the very next morning.

FIVE

Shortly after breakfast, I went out on my own to a stationer's shop a few blocks away to buy ink for my fountain-pen. After I completed my transaction and stepped out into the street, I ran into Mr. Wagner.

"Good morning," he said with a smile.

"Mr. Wagner." My spirits lifted at the sight of him; and yet I could not bring myself to smile.

"Is anything wrong?"

Yes, I thought; *this is wrong. These feelings that I have for you—and that you have for me.* Aloud, I said: "I am greatly worried about my friends. Neither of them is very well."

"I am sorry to hear it. Is there anything I can do?"

"I do not think so; unless you know the name of a good doctor in Whitby."

"I would be happy to make some enquiries in that regard."

"That would be most kind, sir."

Just then, a stout, red-cheeked woman stepped out of the nearby post office, with several letters in her hand. Catching sight of me with a surprised gasp, she called out: "Miss Murray!"

"Oh dear," I said quietly.

"Who is it?" asked Mr. Wagner.

"My landlady, Mrs. Abernathy—a very garrulous woman."

Whenever I had been with Mr. Wagner in the past, other than the time I introduced him to Lucy at the pavilion, I had not run into any one I knew. Now, Mrs. Abernathy marched up and stopped before us, a look of immense curiosity on her face as she stared at Mr. Wagner.

"Well, well, Miss Murray!" she said heartily. "Who might your handsome friend be?"

Mr. Wagner returned her intense gaze, and said in a soft, deep tone: "No one in particular, madam."

Mrs. Abernathy stood as if transfixed for a moment, her jaw dropping in puzzlement; then she abruptly turned to me, as if she had forgotten all about him, and said, "This just arrived for you, Miss Murray. Good day." Placing a letter in my hand, she turned and hurried away before I could thank her.

"Oh!" I said happily.

"Is it from Jonathan?" Mr. Wagner asked.

"No. It is from his employer; but perhaps he has sent on another letter from Jonathan." I quickly opened the envelope. It contained a brief cover note from Mr. Hawkins, and, as hoped, another letter—but when I saw the return address, I cried out in alarm.

"What is it?"

"The letter he forwarded—it is postmarked from a hospital in Buda-Pesth; and the handwriting—I do not know it." I ripped it open and hurriedly scanned the first few lines of the missive within:

Hospital of St. Joseph and Ste. Mary
Buda-Pesth
12 August, 1890

Dear Madam–

I write by desire of Mr. Jonathan Harker, who is himself not strong enough to write, though progressing well, thanks to God and St. Joseph and Ste. Mary. He has been under our care for nearly six weeks, suffering from a violent brain fever. He wishes me to convey his love–

This news, so long anticipated with equal parts hope and dread, so filled me with agony and relief that I burst into tears.

Mr. Wagner looked on with concern as I struggled to compose myself. "Is he—?"

"Oh! Sir," I cried in between sobs, "Jonathan is found! He is in hospital in Buda-Pesth!"

"I hope he is well, and safe?"

"I do not know. I must go home at once and finish the letter. Please excuse me—"

"Wait. Miss Murray: you are too distraught. Please allow me to be of assistance. I will escort you home."

"No! I am sorry, but—thank you for—good-bye, sir. Good-bye!"

"Good-bye?" he repeated, startled. His eyes narrowed, as a dark look crossed his countenance—a look which caused a sudden rush of apprehension to dart up my spine.

I made no further reply; choking back a sob, I ran off, clutching the letter. Although I did not look back, I felt the heat of Mr. Wagner's gaze on me the whole length of the street, and long after I had turned the corner and passed from his view.

When I reached our lodging-house in the Crescent, I went straight to the sitting-room and flung myself into a chair by the window, where I dried my eyes and set to reading through the rest of the letter. Lucy and her mother, who had been chatting in the otherwise empty room, observed my distress and immediately rushed to my side, drew up chairs, and peppered me with anxious questions. I explained that the letter was about Jonathan and implored them to wait for me to finish. The letter was several pages long; when I had ascertained its contents, which at last released me from that uncertainty under which I had been suffering for so long, I began to cry afresh.

"What is it, Mina?" Lucy said. "Is Jonathan all right?"

"He is ill," I replied, in between sobs. "That is why he did not write. All this time, he has been in hospital in Buda-Pesth, suffering from brain fever!"

"Brain fever?" cried Mrs. Westenra in alarm. "Oh dear, that is very serious."

I nodded, wiping away tears. "The letter is from a nurse called Sister Agatha, who has been caring for him. She says he appears to have had some fearful shock. She says—" Reading aloud from the letter, I went on: "'In his delirium his ravings have been dreadful; of wolves and poison and blood; of ghosts and demons; and I fear to say of what. Be careful with him always that there may be nothing to excite him of this kind for a long time to come; the traces of such an illness as his do not lightly die away.'"

"Wolves and blood and demons!" Lucy repeated. "How frightful! I wonder what could have caused such imaginings?"

"They do not seem to know. Apparently he came in the train from Klausenburg, and arrived in a violent, delusional state. The sister says she would have written sooner, but they were unable to ascertain Jonathan's name or where he came from until recently. He is apparently doing better now and is well cared for, but she says he will need to rest for some weeks yet."

"Well, this is good news," Mrs. Westenra said, patting my knee. "At last, you know where he is, and that he is safe."

"Yes. But how strange that he had this letter sent to Mr. Hawkins, and not directly to me. I wrote to Jonathan in Transylvania, and gave him my address here in Whitby. He must have never received those letters. He says he needs money to help pay for his treatment—and dear Mr. Hawkins, in *his* letter, says he is forwarding him a sum. Oh! To think of Jonathan all alone, in a hospital in Buda-Pesth! I should go to him at once!"

"Yes, you must," Lucy agreed.

When I glanced at Lucy, however, my resolve wavered. Although she was in good spirits—a charade I believe she maintained for her mother's sake—she was still very pale and drawn-looking, and I could not forget the two strange marks at her throat, which (although covered by her collar and her velvet band) I knew had not yet healed. "How can I go?" I said, shaking my head. "You are not well yourself, Lucy. We do not know the cause of your malaise, and you are still prone to sleep-walking. I should stay here and look after you."

"You will do no such thing," said Lucy.

"I will keep an eye on Lucy," said her mother. "We can share a room from now on, if need be."

I sighed. Mrs. Westenra suffered from a delicate health condition herself. It seemed that everyone I loved most in the world was ill, and I felt torn. "Are you certain that you can do without me?" I said dubiously.

"Mina: your place is with your fiancé," Lucy insisted, "and my place is with *mine*. Have you forgotten? Arthur is coming to join us in a day or two! He will take care of me, should I need taking care of. I think I have just been pining away for missing him, and I shall feel right as rain again as soon as he is here."

This reminder somewhat alleviated my concerns, for I knew Mr. Holmwood to be a most devoted and capable man. One other thought, however, struck me: that in leaving, I would be saying good-bye for ever to Mr. Wagner. In all probability, I would never see him again. The thought pained me greatly, but there was nothing I could do about it.

"I shall go to Jonathan, then—the sooner the better," I resolved. "I will help nurse him if I can, and bring him home."

"Is Buda-Pesth very far away?" Lucy asked.

"Yes. It is in Hungary," I replied. "Thankfully, I have a little money saved up—it was to help pay for our wedding, but—Mrs. Westenra, do you have any idea how much such a journey will cost? Jonathan did not share with me the particulars of his travel arrangements, and I have never been out of the country before."

"Do not worry, my dear," said Mrs. Westenra kindly. "Lucy and I have been to the Continent several times, and are familiar with all the ins and outs. The crossing is very easily made, and the European trains are not terribly expensive. As for the cost: I will be happy to help."

"Mrs. Westenra, you are too kind; but I cannot allow you to do that."

"I must insist. You say Mr. Hawkins has sent money to the sanatorium where Jonathan is staying, but it cannot be inexpensive—and he has been there how many weeks already? Even if you could afford the journey over, in a very short time you might find yourselves entirely penniless in one of the farthest corners of Eastern Europe—and I will not have that."

I started to protest again, but Mrs. Westenra went on:

"Consider it a wedding gift in advance, Mina. For years, you and Jonathan have both worked very hard for little pay. Lucy is about to marry a very rich man. My husband left me a comfortable income—and if I cannot use a little bit of it to help a dear friend in need, then what is it for?"

She gave me a silent, meaningful look, which I took to be a

reminder of her secret admission to me, with regard to her heart condition. I understood what she would not say aloud: that she was not long for this earth, and—not needing the money herself—she wanted to share some of it with me.

"Thank you," I acquiesced quietly. "You are very generous."

We agreed that I should leave first thing the next morning, and set to work mapping out my journey. I sent a telegram to the hospital in Buda-Pesth, informing Jonathan of my plans, and spent the rest of the day packing up my belongings. As I had left school for good in July, I had brought everything I owned in the world with me to Whitby. For greater ease of travel, I decided that I ought to keep my things to a minimum on this voyage and carry only two bags, with one change of dress. I arranged to have my trunk sent on to Exeter, in care of Mr. Hawkins, so that it would be waiting for me upon my return.

THAT NIGHT, I WAS TOO FILLED WITH ANXIETY TO SLEEP. THE farthest I had ever travelled was to Cornwall with Lucy and her parents, one summer long ago. I had always dreamed of seeing more of the world; but to see it under these circumstances—it was dreadful! I knew I should be too worried about Jonathan to give much thought to my surroundings.

My eyes filled with tears the next morning as I said good-bye to Mrs. Westenra while waiting for the coach to arrive. I worried that this might be the last time I would see her. "I am so grateful for all your help," I said, embracing her warmly. "You have always been so good to me. I will miss you."

"You will be far too busy and happy to miss me," Mrs. Westenra replied with an affectionate smile. "Now go to your future husband. Give him my love."

Lucy and I said our good-byes at the Whitby railway station, issuing heartfelt promises to write frequently and share every bit of news.

"Take care of yourself, dearest," I said, as we exchanged hugs and kisses. "I know that you are keeping up a good front for your mother, but if you are not well by to-morrow, promise me that you will see a doctor."

"I promise. Give my best to Jonathan. Tell him to get well soon."

"I will. Kiss Arthur for me. I love you," I said, hugging her again, just before I boarded the train.

"I love you too," Lucy said, blowing me another kiss in the air. "Good-bye!"

Long after I took my seat by the window, I saw Lucy standing on the platform, waving at me, making funny faces, and smiling her beautiful smile, until the train pulled away.

THE NORTH EASTERN RAILWAY DELIVERED ME TO SCARBOROUGH, where I changed trains and rode on to Kingston on Hull. From there, I boarded a boat bound for Germany. It was my first ocean crossing, and at first I found it exciting. What a merry place a steamer is, as it prepares for a voyage! The packet deck was astir with passengers, both male and female, many of them richly dressed in sumptuous cloaks, flowered bonnets, and dark silk dresses which seemed far too fine for the circumstances.

As the ship coasted out of the harbour, I stood at the rail, delighting in the feel of the fresh sea-breeze against my cheeks and the view of the heaving channel waves. Once we struck out into the open water, however, I was overcome by sea-sickness, and hurried down into the cabin.

I understand that meals were served above—lunch, dinner,

breakfast—but I did not care; I spent the remainder of the voyage below, growing increasingly ill as the day and night drew on, and as the sea roughened. It seemed an endless voyage, covering some 370 miles from port to port; the groans of the other passengers filled my ears, along with their fevered prayers that we would reach shore in safety.

At last, a calm fell upon us, and I heard the stewardess pronounce the words I longed to hear: "We are in port."

We docked at Hamburg. I recall very little of the remainder of the journey, except that it was long and tiring, required a frequent change of trains, and I heard a great many different languages spoken along the way. I caught a few hours of sleep whenever I could but made no overnight stops, determined to reach Jonathan expeditiously and with as little expense as possible. We passed through some beautiful country-side, and what looked to be some very interesting towns, their names becoming longer and more unpronounceable as we journeyed eastward.

As I dozed in my seat, my thoughts were primarily occupied with my concerns for Jonathan. I was vexed by another thing as well: I could not help but feel regret for the abrupt manner in which I had parted from Mr. Wagner. He had seemed so startled and upset when I said good-bye. Even knowing that our association must and should end, I had hoped to be afforded an opportunity to express my gratitude for his—his friendship—and my best wishes for his continued health and happiness, on the day that I was obliged to leave Whitby. Instead, I had left without seeing him again. Not knowing where he lodged, I had not even been able to send him any word of my plans.

It is all for the best, I told myself, as the gentle movements of the train rocked me ever closer to the edge of sleep. *You are going to Jonathan: to the man you love and are to marry. He needs you. You must think only of him now.*

DURING THAT ENDLESS TRAIN RIDE, I HAD ONE VIVID DREAM which I will never forget.

The dream began most beautifully. I was in the bride's room at a church—where, I could not say—and it was my wedding-day. Lucy, looking lovelier than ever in her bridesmaid's gown of pale blue silk, was helping me to dress. I stood before a looking-glass, gazing in wonder at the reflection pictured there.

"Mina, you look positively radiant!" Lucy enthused.

I did look radiant. My hair was swept up elegantly, and held in place by pearl-studded pins. I was dressed in a splendid wedding-gown of pure white silk, with magnificent puffed sleeves, long, beaded cuffs, and a tightly fitted bodice trimmed with white lace and beads.

"I *told you* white was your colour," Lucy added with a triumphant smile.

My three other best friends from school were there, wearing similar bridesmaids' dresses, all fussing about me to make certain that everything was ready and in place.

Mrs. Westenra removed the string of pearls that always hung about her throat and offered them to me. "I want you to wear these to-day, my dear, for good luck," she said, smiling. "I wore them at my own wedding these many years ago, and Edward and I were so very happy together."

With gratitude, I allowed Mrs. Westenra to fasten her pearls around my neck.

"It is time!" Lucy cried, kissing me on the cheek, as she and the other girls draped my long, diaphanous wedding veil over my head and face.

Our friend Kate Reed, whom I had known and loved since I first started school, placed a fragrant bouquet of orange blossoms into my arms. "Go, my friend," she said happily, "and be married!"

As I entered the church (a grand, majestic house of worship), I heard the music playing, and found Mr. Hawkins—the closest I had ever known to a father—waiting for me at the door, a warm smile on his crinkly face. I was about to take his arm and lead the procession up the aisle, with my bridesmaids following behind us; but then I had a sudden, daring thought: why follow tradition? I was a modern, New Woman, was I not? Why not be different, and break the mold?

Turning to Lucy and my bridesmaids, I said softly, "You girls go first. I will make my entrance last, in your wake."

Lucy's eyes widened in surprise; then she whispered, "How lovely, Mina! You will be the grand finale, and call all the attention to yourself. I believe I shall do the same at my wedding."

Accordingly, Lucy and the other girls made their way up the aisle, two and two. As I followed on Mr. Hawkins's arm, I felt a burst of happiness; for through the nearly transparent veil, I saw that all my favourite, former pupils and fellow-teachers were there, and they were all smiling and craning their necks to look at me. Jonathan's dear mother—although dead for a year—was sitting among the congregants, which pleased me greatly, and did not strike me as the slightest bit odd. The clergyman stood at the altar, which was decorated with enormous bouquets of flowers. Jonathan waited beside him, along with his best man: strangely, it was Lucy's Arthur Holmwood, whom Jonathan had only met once before. Both men looked tall and dapper in dark blue morning coats and pale grey trousers, with their hair neatly combed and serious expressions on their faces.

At the clergyman's prompting, Mr. Hawkins gave me over to Jonathan. I took his arm and we both knelt at the communion rails. The clergyman performed the ceremony, at first speaking rapidly in a language I did not understand. Then, suddenly, he was speaking in English about the Judgment Day, "when the secrets of all hearts shall be disclosed," asking if there was any one who had any objection to the union. To my dismay, I heard a deep, familiar voice cry out:

"I have an objection."

A communal gasp went through the congregation; I turned to find Mr. Wagner standing a few yards away in the centre of the aisle.

"What do you mean by this, sir?" Jonathan cried. "Who are you?"

Mr. Wagner strode up to me and lifted my veil, uncovering my face. "You cannot marry this man," he said urgently. *"You are mine."*

I awoke as I always did, startled and gasping for breath, stunned by the sudden shock of being thrust from one vivid reality into another. I was trembling so hard, and was so greatly unnerved, that I was unable to sleep any more that night, or the next day. I arrived at the station in Buda-Pesth so exhausted, I could take no more than a passing notice of the massive, ancient buildings around me, as a cab delivered me out of the city and into the hills beyond.

The Hospital of Saint Joseph and Saint Mary was a massive old building surrounded by spacious grounds. I had some difficulty at first in making my errand understood by the elderly nun at the reception desk, for she spoke not a word of English. At last, she made it clear through gestures that she wished me to write my name on a piece of paper. She disappeared for a few minutes, then returned with a tiny, robust nurse in a starched black habit, who rushed up to me and, taking both my hands in hers, cried out in thickly accented English:

"Miss Murray! At last! I am so happy you are here. I am Sister Agatha, who wrote to you. I received your telegram, and Mr. Harker is expecting you."

She gave some direction in her own tongue to the receptionist, which I deduced had something to do with the disposition of my luggage, and then beckoned me to follow her.

"Your poor, dear man was given into my care, because I speak English," Sister Agatha said, as she led me through a pair of heavy, wooden doors, to a wide stone staircase, and up two long flights of stairs. "My mother was from London, and I spent part of my childhood there, so I have a natural affinity for people from your country. Mr. Harker has told me all about you. He said you are shortly to be his wife. I can only say, all blessings to you both! He is such a sweet and gentle man, he has won all our hearts."

"How is he, sister?" I asked urgently, as we walked. "You said he had some kind of fearful shock. Is he recovering?"

"He is, but slowly. When he first came here—ach!—he raved of such dreadful things, I have never heard the like of it."

"You said in your letter that he spoke of—of wolves and demons and blood. What exactly did he say in his delirium?"

Sister Agatha shook her head and crossed herself. "The ravings of the sick are the secrets of God, my dear. If a nurse through her vocation should hear them, she must respect that trust. But I can tell you this: his fear was not about anything which he has done wrong himself, but of great and terrible things he has seen, which are beyond the treatment of mortal hands. When he arrived, the doctor diagnosed him as a lunatic, and would have immediately sent him to an asylum had I not pleaded with him to reconsider. I saw something in Mr. Harker's eyes, and heard something in his voice, that told me: this man is not insane, he is merely ill and frightened, and needs a safe, quiet place to rest. The doctor, thanks be to God, came to a similar conclusion, only he calls it brain fever. It has taken many weeks of treatment, but Mr. Harker has at last come round to himself—or a version of himself, at least."

"A version of himself?" I repeated apprehensively.

"He is still very weak—too weak to stand—and easily excitable. You will see. You must be careful what you say to him."

We emerged onto an upper floor. Our footsteps echoed as we progressed down a long, dark corridor, whose stark grey walls opened onto a succession of patient's rooms, where I glimpsed two other nurses busily at work.

"I am a great reader, and we were discussing English literature one day," Sister Agatha went on. "He mentioned that he had enjoyed the works of Dickens when he was in school. Thinking to do him a kindness, I borrowed a copy of *A Christmas Carol* in English, and sat down to read to him. I had never heard the story myself, and he had no memory of it. He listened quietly, until we came to a part about a door-knocker and a locomotive and the loud ringing of bells, and I don't know what—during which he became increasingly agitated. Then there came a bit about a clanking of chains, and a ghost passing through a door—and suddenly Mr. Harker grabbed the book from my hands and hurled it across the room, shouting, 'Enough! I cannot listen any more! Pray, throw that foul book away!' "

Sister Agatha crossed herself again, clicking her tongue in distress. "It was my fault. I heard him raving all those weeks on end about ghosts and demons; I would never have read him that book had I known what it was about." She stopped outside a closed door and heaved a sigh. "I believe it has been many months since you last saw him?"

"Yes."

"Then you should prepare yourself, miss, for a shock. We have not allowed him a razor since he came; but this morning he insisted that we shave him, for your coming. Still, you may find him much changed."

A sense of dread came over me, but I fought it back, struggling to get ready for whatever lay beyond that door. *He is here,* I reminded myself. *He is alive and safe, and you love him.*

Sister Agatha opened the door, and I preceded her into the room. My eyes flew immediately to the bed, and to the man who lay sleeping there beneath a grey blanket. My breath caught in my throat, and my eyes filled with sudden tears. There was no mistaking that it was Jonathan; but Sister Agatha was right; oh, how he had changed! His brown hair, which he had always kept so carefully trimmed and groomed, now fell in long, straggly locks across his ears and forehead. His face, once so ruddy, full-cheeked, and handsome, was gaunt and ghastly pale.

"Mr. Harker?" Sister Agatha prompted gently. "Miss Murray is here."

Jonathan opened his eyes. Upon catching sight of me, a weak smile spread across his ravaged countenance, and he whispered, "Mina? Mina . . . Thank God you have come."

He reached out a thin hand to me. I took it and kissed it, my heart full and aching, as tears rolled down my cheeks. "Dearest Jonathan. How glad I am to see you. I have worried about you so."

"Do not worry, my love," he replied, with quiet affection. "I am getting better, and will progress even faster now that you are here." There was little conviction in his voice, however, and no resolve in his eyes as he spoke. All that quiet dignity, which I had always so admired in him, had vanished completely from his face; he was like a very wreck of himself.

"I will leave you two alone together for a few minutes," Sister Agatha said, after helping Jonathan to sit up in bed and propping him with pillows. "If you need me, I will be sitting just outside the door."

After she left the room (leaving the door slightly ajar), I pulled up a chair to the bedside and took Jonathan's hand in mine again. There was so much I longed to ask him, but he looked so tired and frail, I was afraid to say anything that might upset him. "Did you get my letters?" I said at last.

"What letters?"

"The ones I sent to you in Transylvania."

"You wrote to me there?" he replied, astonished.

"Yes, twice. I had not heard from you in so long. I did not even know if you had safely arrived. I asked Mr. Hawkins for the address."

"What address? Where did you send them?"

"To Castle Dracula." I saw him visibly start at this pronouncement. "Did I do wrong? Was that not where you were staying in Transylvania?"

"It *is* where I was staying," he replied with a sudden grim, angry look. "I should have guessed it. I never saw your letters, Mina. *He* must have kept them."

"Who?"

"The Count." He practically spit the words out, with such venom that it alarmed me; then he fell silent and seemed lost in thought, as the angry look on his countenance changed to something else entirely, a sort of confusion laced with fear.

"Jonathan: what happened?"

He fell silent again and looked away, his mouth set in a determined line. Shaking his head, and sounding very tired, he finally said, "These past few months, they are like a grey, murky quagmire. Whenever I try to think about it, my head spins round, and I do not know if it was all real, or if I dreamed it. They say I have had brain fever, Mina. Do you know what that means?"

"It means that you have been very ill. That you have suffered a great shock of some kind, which has affected your brain."

"It means that *I went mad.*"

"Jonathan, no! Do not think like that."

"It is the truth. Brain fever, by definition, is madness. When I try to remember what happened, I know it cannot be so; therefore, I must have gone mad. All these weeks, even when I found myself safe in this bed, tended by these good nurses, the memories have continued to haunt me. I cannot think about it, Mina—or talk about it—or I fear I shall go mad again."

"I understand, my dearest," I replied, leaning down to kiss his thin cheek. "I shall never ask about it again, I promise."

He looked so grateful—whether it was for my promise, or for my kiss, or both, I could not be certain—but I now pressed my lips to his lips and held them there for a long moment.

When the kiss ended, his hands came up to cradle my face just inches from his, and he said softly, "Oh, Mina, dearest Mina. How I love you."

"I love you, too."

"Thinking of you, planning for our future, that is the only thing that has kept me alive through all this. I have missed you so. I want to be married as soon as possible. Would that suit you?"

The question caught me off guard. A fluttering began in the pit of my stomach, and I sat back in my chair, my heart pounding in sudden surprise. "Do you mean—be married here, in Buda-Pesth?"

"Yes."

"But you are so ill, and you are still confined to bed."

"I know. But—I have given this a great deal of thought, dearest, ever since the sister brought me your telegram, and I knew you were coming. They tell me I will be here for some weeks yet. Mr. Hawkins sent me some money, but it is not enough to pay for a long hotel stay for you, Mina, or for a separate room here. For propriety's sake, we ought to marry at once. That way, you can share my room. Sister Agatha said she can summon the chaplain of the British legation, who could no doubt perform the ceremony as early as to-morrow."

"To-morrow?"

A profound sense of disappointment enveloped me. I saw the logic in what he was saying, of course; I had had the same thoughts about cost and propriety and such, on my journey over. Even old Mr. Hawkins had suggested, in his letter, that it might not be a bad thing if we were married out here. However, I had not expected it to happen quite so soon; and when I had pictured the ceremony in my mind—not my rapturous dream on the train, but in my actual, waking imagination—I had seen it taking place in a quaint, old church, with Jonathan standing at my side. I had never conceived that my wedding might take place in a hospital room, at the bedside of a man who was as yet too frail and sickly to stand.

"I realise," Jonathan said, "that the circumstances are not what you would have wished for in a wedding, but—"

"No; no, you are quite right. We should not wait." I forced a smile and gave Jonathan the most loving look I could muster. "I will be happy to marry you, Jonathan Harker, whenever you think best."

I spent that night in an empty room graciously provided for me by the sisters. When Jonathan woke the next morning, I told him that the arrangements for our wedding were being made.

He smiled and said, "Dear, would you get me my coat? I have need of it."

I thought it an odd request for a bedridden man, but I asked Sister Agatha to bring me the coat. She soon returned saying, "Here are all his things."

"All his things?" I glanced in surprise at the items as she set them on the bed. They comprised but one suit of clothes and a note-book.

"This is everything he had with him when he arrived," she answered, before leaving the room.

Jonathan had left home with a trunk full of clothing, including his best suit and hat, which were missing; his pocketbook was also gone, along with whatever money it may have contained, and the photograph of me that I knew he always carried with him. What,

I wondered, had become of it all? I had promised, however, that I would not ask; and so I stood in silence as Jonathan reached into his coat-pocket and pulled from it a tiny box. With a gentle smile, he offered the box to me.

"I know how much you wanted a wedding ring, dear, and I did not want you to be married without one. So I sent Sister Agatha out on a little errand the day before you arrived. I hope you like it."

Astonished, I opened the little box. Nestled inside the blue velvet interior was a solid gold wedding ring, engraved with an elegant pattern. "Oh! It is beautiful! But Jonathan—however could you afford such a thing? Tell me you did not spend the money Mr. Harker sent you for your hospital stay, to buy this ring!"

"I did not," he replied, with a mysterious smile. "I had another source. Thank goodness I had the sense to ask for your ring size months ago. Please, try it on."

I did so; it was a perfect fit, and looked lovely on my hand. "I see that you do not wish to tell me of your 'source'—and as this is a gift, I will leave it be. Thank you so much, my dearest, for thinking of this. It means all the world to me." I bent and kissed him, then removed the ring and returned it to the box. "Keep it for now, until the ceremony." As I picked up his coat and other garments, intending to place them on a near-by chair, my eye fell on the note-book, which lay beside him on the bed. "Is this your journal?" I asked.

"Yes."

I knew that Jonathan had intended to keep a stenographic record of his trip to Transylvania, to practice and perfect the art of shorthand, just as I had done during my stay in Whitby. It suddenly occurred to me that the answers to all his troubles might lie on the pages within. Did I dare ask him to let me look at it?

He must have read my thoughts, for his face fell, and he said quietly: "Forgive me; would you mind—I would like to be alone for a moment."

I went to the window, where I stood gazing out at the trees and landscaped grounds below in silence, quite upset with myself; for I had not wished to cause him any distress. At length, he called me back.

Holding the note-book, he said, in deadly earnest, "Wilhelmina"—(it was the first time he had addressed me by that formal name, since the day he asked me to marry him)—"My account of what happened to me in Transylvania is here, in this book. I wrote it all down in shorthand, as we discussed; but I think now that it may just be the account of a madman. I never want to look at these pages again. I want to take up my life here and now, with our marriage. But—you know how I feel about the bond of trust between husband and wife. I want no secrets or concealments between us. In that spirit of honesty, I want you to take this book." So saying, he placed the note-book in my hands. "Keep it. You have my full permission to read it, if you will—but do not tell me, and let us never mention it again—unless, one day, some solemn duty should command me to go back to the bitter hours, asleep or awake, sane or mad, that are recorded here." So saying, he fell back on his pillow, exhausted.

"I will honour your wish, my dearest," I promised. "I will put the book away, and I will not read it now—if ever. We will concentrate on your getting well." Later, I wrapped the note-book in white paper, tied it with a ribbon, and sealed it over with sealing-wax, so that it could serve as an outward and visible sign of our trust.

❧

We were married that afternoon. The ceremony was brief and solemn. Fortunately, of the two dresses I had brought with me, one was my best dress—the embroidered black silk—which I had always intended to wear at my wedding. It was odd, I thought, as I glanced in the mirror to arrange my hair; but Lucy's worried interpretation of the wedding poem had come true. Against her wishes, I was marrying in black—and I was indeed far away from home, "wishing myself back."

I donned my black kid gloves; Sister Klara—another good, kind soul—found me a veil; and dear Sister Agatha brought me a small bouquet of multicoloured flowers, which she had gathered in the garden. The two nurses stood up with us as witnesses. Jonathan woke from his nap just as all was in readiness. I helped him to sit up in bed, leaning against the pillows, and took my place at his bedside.

As the chaplain moved into position before us, I could not help but glance at our grim surroundings with a little pang. Jonathan reached out and squeezed my hand, regret in his eyes. "I know this is not the wedding you dreamed of, Mina, but I hope to make it up to you some day."

"I am marrying *you*, my dear; that is all that matters," I replied sincerely.

I was aware of the grave responsibilities I was undertaking: I was to be Jonathan's wife. I would be his, and only his, for the rest of my life. It was what I wanted, and I was happy. Yet, as the chaplain performed the service, I found my thoughts drifting to another place and time—to the dance floor of the pavilion at Whitby—and to the blissful hours I had spent there in Mr. Wagner's arms. I recalled how alive I had felt in his company and the way I had felt as the object of his admiring gaze. What, I wondered, would it be like to stand beside him at the altar—to be *his* bride? These thoughts caused me such a paroxysm of guilt that my throat closed and my face became flushed with heat.

I broke from my reverie to hear the clergyman saying, "Will you, Jonathan Harker, take this woman to be your lawfully wedded wife, from this day forward, to have and to hold for all the days of your life, until death do you part?"

"I will," Jonathan replied, in a firm, strong voice.

When it came my turn to answer that question, although I replied with a willing heart, even those two small words seemed to choke me. We were pronounced man and wife; Jonathan drew me down into his embrace with his poor, weak hands, and kissed me: a long, sweet kiss.

After the chaplain and sisters left, my new husband took my hand in his and kissed it, saying: "This is the first time I have taken *my wife's* hand—and it is the dearest thing in all the world. I would go through all the past again to win this hand, if need be."

Finding my voice again, I assured him that I was the happiest woman in all the world.

That same day, I wrote a long letter to Lucy, for I knew that she would be anxious to hear all that had happened since we parted at the railway station at Whitby. I poured out my heart with regard to Jonathan's state of health, gave her all the details of our wedding, and expressed my sincere wish that she would be very happy in her own upcoming marriage.

The sisters brought a cot into Jonathan's room, and that is where I slept that night, and every night for two weeks thereafter. I fully understood that my *Wedding Night*—that Night of Nights which had always been touted as such a great and wondrous mystery—would have to wait until Jonathan had recovered his health, and we could leave this hallowed place, where the good sisters checked on him so conscientiously all day and night.

For two weeks, I served as Jonathan's nurse and companion. I shaved him every morning, and arranged to have a barber come to the hospital one afternoon to cut his hair. One day, while he napped, I took a carriage into Buda-Pesth. What a marvellous city it was, different from London in so many ways, with so many unusual sights and smells! I loved its immense castle and its old, imposing buildings, many of which had beautiful spired domes. I enjoyed strolling through the tree-lined squares, and across the bridges over the Danube connecting the cities of Buda and Pesth. The Széchenyi Chain Bridge, suspended above the water by a great chain rather than cables, was particularly impressive, with its four colossal stone lions at the ends.

I made only that one visit, however, preferring to stay at Jonathan's side, where I dedicated myself to ensuring that he ate properly, keeping his spirits up, and making sure he steadily regained his strength. He began with short walks down the hall, progressing to strolls out in a wheeled chair, until that day when he could, at last, walk about the grounds under his own power.

When the doctor released him, we said our tearful good-byes to all the dear sisters, thanking them profusely for all they had done. Jonathan mapped out a different and more expeditious route for our return journey than the one I had taken in getting there, which involved riding the Orient Express to Paris, where he insisted that we stop for several nights. I found Paris to be a wondrous and romantic city, even more beautiful than Buda-Pesth. As we strolled the wide boulevards together hand in hand, visiting the museums, dining in cafés, and taking in the sights, I thought I was in heaven.

Jonathan found us a tiny, clean room a few blocks from the Seine, and it was there, more than two weeks after our wedding, that we had our first true wedding night. The only intimacy we had previously shared, beyond holding hands, had been kisses. I believe—although I did not ask him—that Jonathan was as inexperienced as I, and we were both nervous. He seemed to feel the weight of my expectations, and I did all I could to relieve his anxiety. When he came to bed and gravely took me in his arms, I silently commanded myself to relax and gave myself to him willingly.

Afterwards, as I rolled to my side and listened to the sounds of his even breathing from the pillow beside me, I felt a great pang of disappointment.

I could not help thinking of that night, some three weeks previously, when I had stood on the terrace of the Whitby pavilion, in Mr. Wagner's arms. As he had gazed down at me, his lips just inches from mine, my heart had pounded with wild abandon. I had been filled with desire. My encounter with my husband, however, had been very different. It had begun very sweetly, but—dare I admit it?—it was over much too quickly and was devoid of the pleasurable physical feeling that I had hoped for. Jonathan, on the other hand, seemed perfectly satisfied—elated, in fact—and highly pleased with himself.

Was this all I could ever hope to expect from my marriage-bed? I wondered. Was the act of married love truly something that only men could enjoy, and women must endure?

SIX

When Jonathan and I arrived at Exeter on the 14th of September, Mr. Peter Hawkins was waiting for us with a carriage.

"My dear children." He exchanged kisses with me on the cheek and shook Jonathan's hand heartily as we took seats opposite him inside the conveyance, after our luggage was placed on board. "Please forgive me for not meeting you on the platform. I have been suffering from an attack of gout these many weeks, and it is difficult to get about."

"It is so good to see you, Mr. Hawkins," I said with great affection. "I am sorry you have not been feeling well."

"Do not worry about me, it is only an old man's complaint; let me take a look at *you*. Mina, you are as beautiful as ever. Jonathan, you are a bit on the thin side, and a little more pale than usual, but not too bad, considering. I must say, I am very pleased—nay, relieved—to see you both home again, safe and sound."

"We are glad to be back, sir," Jonathan replied. "Thank you again for all you did for us while we were in Buda-Pesth."

"It was the very least I could do, my boy. I promised your dear father on his death-bed that I would look after you and your mother. Until now, I thought I had done my best in that regard."

"You have done so, sir. You have been like a father to me, and I will always be grateful."

Mr. Hawkins frowned, the lines in his face deepening as he smoothed back his thinning white hair with a freckled hand. "I did not do right, it seems, in sending you to Transylvania. I have been so deeply worried these past few months, wondering: what is taking so long? What on earth could have gone wrong? I am sorry you became ill, Jonathan. That Sister Something-or-Other at the hospital was particularly vague about it all, and you did not tell me much in your own letter. Is it true that you suffered a mental breakdown of some sort?"

"It is true, sir."

Mr. Hawkins shook his head, very upset. "I am at a loss. I have known you all your life, Jonathan. You are a strong, sensible young man. When faced with a difficulty, you have always kept your head. You are not the sort to have a breakdown. What happened to you over there?"

Jonathan hesitated, an anxious, pained look on his face. "I would rather not speak of it, sir."

I took his hand and squeezed it, hoping to convey my silent sympathy and support.

Mr. Hawkins leaned forward in his seat, his hands resting on his cane. "Son: you went overseas on business for me. Had I been feeling better, I would have made the trip myself. I feel completely responsible. Count Dracula wrote a very gracious letter to me, expressing perfect satisfaction with the arrangements we had made on his behalf and complimenting *you* on your presentation of them. He said nothing of your being ill. Nothing at all. In fact, he—"

"Please, speak of this no more!" Jonathan blurted out, a sort of wild, confused look in his eyes as he yanked his hand from mine. "I am sorry, sir, if you feel that I have let you down; dismiss me if you wish; I would not blame you. But I have fought long and hard to recover my sense of well-being, and I cannot revisit the source of my discomfort. I cannot!"

Mr. Hawkins's face fell. "Forgive me. I will not ask again, son." He sank back heavily against his seat and lapsed into a grieved silence for the better part of the journey.

JONATHAN AND I HAD ANTICIPATED THAT FOR OUR FIRST FEW months of wedded life, we would live in the tiny flat which he had occupied during his six-year tenure in Exeter. Eventually, we hoped to move into something larger, although still humble, according to our income. However, fate had something very different in store for us.

"I would not think of you and Mina staying in those two dark, depressing little rooms of yours, Jonathan," Mr. Hawkins said, as his carriage drew up in front of his house. "You are a married couple now. You must stay here with me."

Mr. Hawkins owned a big, old, beautiful, three-storeyed house on a lovely, tree-shaded street not far from the cathedral close. The house had a large, airy drawing-room, an oak-panelled library, a commodious and well-outfitted kitchen, a sitting-room on every floor, and a great many bedrooms. Each and every room had been lovingly and tastefully furnished. I was familiar with the place, having spent a memorable week there the previous Christmas as Mr. Hawkins's guest, when Jonathan and I had been newly engaged.

Now, Mr. Hawkins had prepared a very nice suite of rooms for the two of us up on the first floor. As Jonathan and I unpacked, we found that our generous host had provided many thoughtful touches, including a vase of pretty flowers on our sitting-room table, and a pair of matching silk dressing-gowns that he'd had made especially for us.

The cook prepared a delicious dinner in honour of our return. The three of us spent a good two hours at table, where the conversation flowed smoothly and amiably. It was like a return to old times: to the countless occasions over the years when Mr. Hawkins had visited Jonathan and his mother at the orphanage in London, or at her little flat after she retired, and we had gathered around her kitchen table for one of her wonderful meals.

After dinner, as the three of us relaxed over a superb bottle of wine, Mr. Hawkins raised his glass and said: "My dears, I want to drink to your health and prosperity, and congratulate you on your marriage. I wish you all the greatest happiness."

"Thank you," Jonathan replied. "May I drink to your health, as well, sir; and please allow me to express our deepest gratitude for your hospitality."

"I trust you found your rooms comfortable?"

"Very much so, sir."

"And you, Mina? Do the arrangements suit you? Do you like this old house?"

"Oh, yes sir!" I returned with feeling. "It is a beautiful home. I have loved it since the first moment I saw it."

"I am glad. My wife Nora felt the same way. The day we saw it, she said: 'Peter, I must have this place. I cannot imagine living anywhere else.' So I bought it for her, and we spent many happy years here before she passed away." He gave a little sigh and seemed lost in thought for a moment.

"Let me assure you, sir," Jonathan said, "that we will not impose on you for long. As soon as I am settled back in at work, we will find a place of our own."

"If that is your wish, I will not try to stop you," Mr. Hawkins responded, with a little frown. "You are newly wed. No doubt you would prefer to be alone together somewhere, rather than to live with a sick, old man like me."

"Sir!" Jonathan began, but Mr. Hawkins stopped him with a wave of his hand.

"It is entirely understandable. I am sure I would wish the same thing, were I in your shoes. But before you go looking elsewhere, allow me to at least attempt to persuade you otherwise." He took a sip of his wine, and continued: "It has always been my dearest wish that you two would marry one day. Now, as you settle down in life together, I would like to do something to make your lives a little easier. As you know, our only child, our darling boy Roger, did not live past his fourth birthday. Nora has been gone these many years. You two are all I have left. I have, with love and pride, seen you both grow up, and I consider you as my own flesh and blood. I have watched you, Jonathan, mature in your work over the past five years, into a man of great dedication and integrity, and I know you will make a very fine solicitor. As such, I want you to know that I have drawn up the paperwork to make you a partner in the firm, and in my will I have left you this house, and everything I possess."

Jonathan and I were both stunned speechless for a long moment. "Sir," Jonathan managed at last, rising to his feet, "that is—I—thank you, sir. Thank you so much. I do not know what to say."

"Thank you will do just fine, son," Mr. Hawkins returned with smile.

As he and Jonathan shook hands, tears came into my eyes; then I leapt to my feet and Mr. Hawkins and I exchanged an embrace as I thanked him, and we all started laughing and crying at the same time.

When we had recovered a bit and resumed our seats at the table, Mr. Hawkins said, "There is one last thing to discuss. I may have ten years left in me, or ten minutes; only the good Lord knows about that. As I said, if I were you, I might not think it the most desirable thing in the world to live here with me. But as this place is to be yours one day, it seems a shame for you to go anywhere else. This house is far too large for one person—ever since Nora passed on, the walls have seemed to echo with a sort of hollow emptiness—and it needs a mistress. Mina, I would give you full sway with the staff. You can run the place any way you like. You can both have all the privacy you want, as I generally retire early. And think of it this way: if you make your home here with me, you will give great pleasure and satisfaction to a lonely old man."

"Oh! Mr. Hawkins," I said.

Jonathan and I exchanged a look, silently conveying our joint agreement with regard to this generous offer; and as he took my hand beneath the table, he said: "Sir, I think I speak for both of us when I say: we accept with the utmost gratitude."

We were so very, very happy that first evening. I had "my Jonathan" back—or so it seemed; we were settled in a lovely place with a man who was as dear to us as a father; and we had a measure of privacy at last. After dinner, we retired to the drawing-room, where Jonathan and Mr. Hawkins encouraged me to play the piano for them. Although I was somewhat out of practice, I soon found my fingers, and passed an enjoyable hour entertaining them with some of our favourite tunes.

At length, we said our good-nights and retired to our room. I was about to begin preparing for bed when I was struck by a sudden compulsion to open the French doors and walk out onto the balcony. There was a bright moon, and the sky twinkled with stars. I stood at the rail, taking in the glory of the dark heavens, and inhaling deeply of the crisp coolness which invigorated my lungs.

"What are you doing out here?" Jonathan asked softly as he joined me on the balcony.

"I just wanted a little air. It is a beautiful night."

Jonathan wrapped his arms around me from behind and pulled me close. "It is beautiful because you are here with me."

I placed my arms lovingly over his and leaned back against him, drawing pleasure from his solid warmth. We stood in contented silence for a moment, listening to the chirp of the crickets, and gazing out at the tree-studded garden and the line of rooftops beyond, which were enveloped in ghostly darkness.

"Mina, you have made me so happy."

"I am happy too, my dearest."

"I have dreamt of this day for so many, long years."

"Years? Surely it has not been years, dearest. We were only engaged last autumn."

"Yes, but I have been wanting to ask you to marry me ever since I was seven years old."

"Seven?" I repeated in surprise.

"And I have been imagining you here with me in Exeter ever since I began my apprenticeship at age sixteen."

"Have you? I had no idea. You never said so."

"We were such good friends. I was not sure if you shared my feelings. I was afraid if I told you how I felt about you, it would change things; that it might drive you away."

"That could never happen, my love."

"Oh, Mina!" he said, his lips against my hair. "I want to forget everything that has happened these past few months. I want only to move forward, to dedicate myself to my work, and to loving you." Gently, he turned me around to face him; my arms wove up around his neck as he looked down at me with earnest affection. "I want to have children, Mina—lots of them, and soon. Do you?"

"You know I do. I have always longed to have a family of my own. And I want all of them to look like you."

"Only the boys," he replied with a smile. "The girls must all have your beauty. We will have the best-looking family at church on Sunday—we will take up an entire pew—and then we will return home for roast beef and pudding and read to the children by the fire. How does that sound?"

"It sounds perfect, my dearest."

"I love you, Mina."

"And I love you."

We shared a heartfelt, affectionate kiss. I was filled with happiness at that moment: firm in the belief that all was well, that Jonathan would very soon be fully recovered from his long illness, and that life would go on as smoothly and delightfully as we imagined it.

Suddenly, a sharp rustling sound from a near-by tree startled us, ending our kiss. We pulled apart to see a large black bat flapping away across the dark sky to the north.

"What was that?" Jonathan said, alarmed.

"I think it was a bat."

"I cannot recall ever seeing a bat in Exeter before."

"I saw them quite frequently at Whitby." I was overcome by an ominous feeling. "It is cold. Let us go in."

The appearance of the bat inexplicably left us in a strange, quiet mood. Our talk and our kiss had been so warm and tender, that I had anticipated—hoped—that Jonathan would make love to me. Although our love-making always left me with an aching need that I could not quite define, I had learned to appreciate the act for the feeling of intimate closeness it engendered between me and my husband. That night, however, it was not to be. From the look on Jonathan's face as we undressed and crawled into bed, I deduced that his fears had returned. With a pang of worry and disappointment, I kissed him softly, then laid my head on my pillow and said good-night.

Jonathan soon fell into a restless sleep. Although I was exhausted from our long day of travel, the newness of our surroundings, combined with my concerns for my husband, conspired to keep sleep at bay. It seemed that I had just drifted off at last when I heard Jonathan cry out:

"No! No! You monster! You monster!"

I awakened to find Jonathan senseless and clutching his pillow, crying, "What on earth is in that bag? Set it free! Set it free!"

I knew he was suffering from one of the nightmares which had plagued him during his hospital stay and had continued during our honeymoon. I reached out gently in the darkness to touch his face, which was damp with perspiration. "Jonathan. Wake up. It is all right. It is just a dream."

He awoke and lay trembling beside me. "My God," he cried, his voice hoarse and filled with terror, "that horrible bag! Will I never forget?"

I knew better than to ask what "horrible bag" he was talking about. Instead, I put my arms around him and said soothingly, "It was not real, dearest. But I am here, and I am real. Hold me." I felt Jonathan's body tremble as he held me tightly and buried his face in my shoulder.

"Mina. Dearest Mina. Promise me you will always love me, and that you will never leave me."

"I will always love you, my darling, and I will never leave you," I replied, kissing him.

It took me a long while to coax him into a relaxed state, so that we could both fall back to sleep.

WE SPENT THE NEXT FEW DAYS SETTLING IN. ALTHOUGH JONATHAN continued to have nightmares, he seemed to be himself by day. I had breakfast with him and Mr. Hawkins every morning, and they both came home for luncheon. Since Mr. Hawkins had not been feeling well of late, he had not taken on any new work in quite some time. Even so, they were busy at the office all day, for Jonathan had been away a long time, and as a new partner in the firm, he had much to learn.

While the men were gone, I took time to become acquainted with the housekeeping staff. I spoke with the cook about meal-planning—a subject of which I had had little experience. I unpacked the trunk I had sent on from Whitby, which contained the rest of my clothes, my books, and my typewriter. I had two new dresses made, and I took some delightful walks around Exeter and the near-by cathedral close.

Sometimes on my solitary walks, or while I was unpacking, or ironing, or trying to concentrate on a book, I found myself humming *Tales from the Vienna Woods,* the tune that Mr. Wagner and I had danced to on that first evening at the pavilion. I would catch myself, as with an involuntary blush, I recalled the nights I had so recklessly rushed off to meet him there and the other times we had spent together. The memories caused my heart to flutter. Where was Mr. Wagner now? I wondered. Had he bought property in England? Did he decide to stay in the country, or did he return to Austria? I missed the talks we used to have, and I found myself conducting long, imaginary conversations with him in my mind.

I could not deny that I missed him. Those ten days in Whitby, after Mr. Wagner and I met, had been one of the most exciting times of my life. I knew that my behaviour there had been improper; but I did not regret any of it. It was in the past; it was over; but the memories were there for me to bring out and smile at whenever I chose, before putting them safely away where they belonged.

I adored living in Mr. Hawkins's beautiful old house. From the windows in our bedroom and the drawing-room, I could see the rows of great, leafy elms standing out majestically against the old yellow stone of the cathedral. With the windows open, I could hear the cathedral bells toll the hours, and the delightful cawing and chattering of the rooks overhead cheered me all day long.

In short order, though, I became restless. I had enjoyed my leisure time in Whitby, when my days had held no greater responsibilities than the decisions of where and how long to walk, what time to dine, and which books to read. However, I was on holiday no longer. I was accustomed to the regimented schedule of a school-teacher. I asked Jonathan one morning if I might help with his work, or if there was anything that he needed transcribed on the typewriter; but he said no, not at present.

I hungered for something meaningful to do. I longed for my days to have more import, as well as some impact on others. Mr. Wagner's words came back to haunt me: "I would think that today's New Woman would give great thought to what she wants after marriage, and not just to what society dictates, or what her husband expects."

What was a woman to do, I wondered, if she found the role of dutiful wife and home-maker insufficiently fulfilling?

After Mr. Hawkins retired that evening, as Jonathan and I were reading and working by the fire in our sitting-room, I said:

"Jonathan: there is a matter I wish to discuss with you."

"What is it, dear?" he said, without glancing up from the legal documents he was reviewing.

"Mr. Hawkins has a very fine instrument down-stairs. What would you think if I gave piano lessons a few hours a week?"

Jonathan looked up from his papers now in surprise. "Piano lessons? Are you joking?"

"I am perfectly serious. I used to teach music at school. I miss my students, and I miss teaching. It would give me something useful to do with my time."

"Mina," he replied patiently, "it is understandable that you miss school. You were at that institution for more than half of your life. But these feelings will pass. I am certain that, in time, you will find plenty of things with which to occupy yourself."

"What kinds of things?"

"I don't know. What do other new brides do?"

"I suppose they spend their time decorating and furnishing their new house. But this house is already beautifully decorated and fully furnished—and in any case, it is still Mr. Hawkins's house, not ours."

"Are you not busy overseeing the staff?"

"The staff runs the house very efficiently without my interference."

"Then find a women's group to join. Or take up needlework. You used to enjoy that, did you not?"

"Needlework?" I repeated with a grimace. "I may have taught girls how to embroider at school, but I never liked it. It is only something women do when they have nothing better to do. I hoped you might require my help at the office, but as it seems you do not—"

"I can see that you are distressed about this, Mina. But we have only been married a few weeks, and in Exeter but a few days. Give yourself a chance to settle in and become accustomed to our new life here. One day, if we are blessed with children, you will have plenty to do, and you will not be giving any thought to teaching other people's children or working in my office."

"But Jonathan, that is in the future. I am talking about my life now."

"And *now*, you are a married woman. Married women do not work outside the home. That sort of thing is just not done."

"I understand your feelings on this matter, dear. I am only asking to teach a few hours a week, *inside* the home. It would make me very happy."

He slapped his papers down on a near-by table and glowered

at me impatiently. "I make a perfectly respectable living, Mina. What would people think if you started teaching? That I was unable to provide for us? That I required your help to make ends meet? That would be mortifying—particularly when we are living here, at no real expense!"

"Do you really care so much what people would think, Jonathan?" The moment the phrase left my mouth, I recognised its source: Mr. Wagner had asked me the very same thing, the morning before our boat ride.

"Yes, I care very much!" Jonathan cried. "I am a partner in Hawkins and Harker now. I meet with new clients every day. I must prove myself worthy of the responsibilities which have been bestowed on me. Should I—should *we*—make any mis-steps, people will talk, and it will affect the business!"

I felt bad now. Jonathan had worked himself up into such a state of anxiety that I feared it might bring on a relapse of his former condition. "I am sorry," I said quickly. "I had not thought of it affecting your business. We will, of course, do as you think best."

❧

THAT NIGHT, I HAD A STRANGE DREAM ABOUT LUCY.

I had been worried about her for quite some time. I had written to Lucy from Buda-Pesth, and had sent another note informing her that we would soon be on our way home. However, despite Lucy's promise to correspond, I had not heard from her since the day I left Whitby—and she had been unwell at the time. I had told myself not to be concerned; after all, she had her mother and Arthur to watch over her. I had been out of the country for many weeks, and as Lucy herself had so often reminded me, mail does often go astray, particularly when it is sent overseas. Still, I had a vague feeling that something was very wrong.

My dream only increased my worries. In the dream, I looked up from my bed to find the blinds open on our French doors and a ghostly figure peering in at me through the darkness. It was Lucy! She was standing out on the balcony, clad only in her white nightdress, with her raven hair tumbling about her. She smiled and beckoned to me with a finger. I rose, opened the doors, and stepped outside.

Suddenly, the landscape changed. I was not on my balcony, but back at Whitby, at the base of the steps to the East Cliff. Lucy laughed merrily, turned, and ran up the stairs. I knew, somehow, that she was running into danger; that the terrifying, dark figure with the red eyes was awaiting her atop the cliff.

"Stop, Lucy! Stop!" I called after her, but she paid no heed.

I raced after Lucy, but she remained well ahead of me. The harder I ran, the longer the flight of steps became, stretching endlessly upwards and upwards until I thought they would never end. Suddenly, another figure appeared beside me: it was Lucy's tall, handsome, curly-haired fiancé, Arthur Holmwood.

"Lucy!" he shouted. "Where are you going?"

"Arthur? What are you doing here?" Lucy replied, pausing briefly to look back at him with a wanton and contemptuous smile. "Go home, Arthur. It is too late. You are not wanted any more." She turned and ran on.

Mr. Holmwood's face fell. "Lucy!" he uttered in the most woe-begone of voices. "Darling! Come back!"

"She does not know what she is saying, Mr. Holmwood. She is walking in her sleep. We must stop her!"

Mr. Holmwood and I dashed up the stairs together, at last arriving at the summit, to find Lucy standing not twenty feet away with her back to us. We hurried up behind her. She began to laugh—a strange, eerie sound, like the tinkling of glass when struck—a laugh that sent a chill up my spine. I reached out to touch her shoulder. To my horror, as Lucy turned around to face us, her countenance distorted into something demon-like and full of rage. Her eyes were blazing red orbs which seemed to throw out sparks of hell-fire, and her brow was as wrinkled as the coils of Medusa's snake. Clawing at us through the air, she let out a fierce, diabolical hiss, like a panther or cobra about to strike.

I snapped awake in terror, clutching at the bed-clothes, and stifling the urge to scream. Oh! Horrid, horrid dream! Why did my unconscious mind torment me with such an absurd, frightening vision? What on earth could have provoked it?

Even long after waking, the nightmare was difficult to banish from my thoughts. I could not get over the notion that something was very wrong with Lucy. Determined to re-establish contact with her, I sat down that very morning and wrote a long letter, apprising Lucy of our return to Exeter and all the latest news. No sooner had I posted it, than a letter arrived from Lucy herself.

I caught up the envelope with relief, smiling at the sight of Lucy's familiar scrawl. My relief was mitigated, however, when I noticed that her letter had been postmarked a month previously—a few days after my departure from Whitby—and that it had originally been sent to Buda-Pesth, then forwarded here. I took out the two folded sheets within and read them avidly. Lucy said she was feeling fine and fit again—that she had "an appetite like a cormorant" (a large, voracious seabird), was sleeping well, and had quite given up walking in her sleep. Arthur was with her; they were rowing, riding, and playing tennis; even her mother was feeling better.

The letter briefly raised my spirits—until I read the postscript: "P.P.S.—We are to be married on 28 September."

I glanced at the calendar. It was now the 18th of September! Lucy's letter, I reminded myself, was very old indeed. Was Lucy truly to be married only *ten days hence?* If so, why had I not received an invitation? She knew how to reach me in Exeter. If I was to be Lucy's maid of honour, surely I should have heard from her again by now, with the details of the ceremony and reception.

I knew that Lucy and her mother had planned to return to Hillingham, their home in London, for the last week of August. Were they in fact in London now? Could it be that Lucy had become ill again?

That same evening, a great calamity occurred which temporarily pushed all thoughts of Lucy and her wedding from my mind.

SEVEN

IT ALL HAPPENED SO SUDDENLY. SHORTLY BEFORE DINNER, Mr. Hawkins said he had a bad headache, and begged to be excused. Jonathan and I kissed him good-night, and he retired early. Later, as my husband and I were preparing for bed ourselves, we heard a scream from Mr. Hawkins's room. We ran into the hall and found the maid sobbing in Mr. Hawkins's doorway.

"I brung the master 'is bed-time medicine, like always, but the poor old gentleman's lying there as cold as ice, and 'e won't wake up!"

The doctor said it was probably an aneurism in his brain, and that it had killed him instantly. Oh! Such a kind gentleman—admired by all for his good temper and generous nature—and now he was gone! Mr. Hawkins's unexpected death was a severe blow to everyone in the household. We heard the staff crying all the next day as Jonathan and I huddled in the drawing-room together, shedding our own stunned tears.

"It is so unfair," I said sorrowfully. "I thought to enjoy Mr. Hawkins's company for many years to come."

"As did I," Jonathan replied, wiping his sad eyes with a nervous hand. "How am I to get on without him, Mina? I relied on him for so many things. All my life, he was my father, my mentor, and my friend. He has left me a fortune, which to people of our modest upbringing is wealth beyond dreams—and you know I am grateful. But at the same time—"

"At the same time, what, dearest?"

"I left England in April as a newly promoted solicitor, and now, suddenly, the entire firm is in my hands. I do not know if I can handle such an immense responsibility."

"You can handle it, my dearest," I said, taking his hand. "Mr. Hawkins would not have made you a partner if he did not feel you were worthy of the title. He believed in you. I believe in you. Now all you need to do is to believe in yourself and take one day at a time."

Mr. Hawkins had left in his will that he was to be buried in the grave with his father, at a cemetery not far from central London. Accordingly, Jonathan made all the necessary arrangements. I wrote to Lucy, telling her our sad news. We took the train up to town on the 21st of September, arriving very late. The funeral was held the next morning. I wore my best black dress, the same one I had worn on my wedding-day, and Jonathan had a new black suit quickly made. Since Mr. Hawkins had no relations at all, Jonathan was the chief mourner. There were only a handful of other people there besides ourselves and the servants.

As Jonathan and I stood hand in hand during the simple, graveside service, tearfully saying our last good-byes to the man we felt was our best and dearest friend, I suddenly felt wistful for Jonathan's departed mother, whom I had also loved, and for the parents I had never known.

"Jonathan," I said, after the service was over and the few attendees had gone, "do you realise that the last time we were in London together, it was also for a funeral?"

He nodded sadly. "I was thinking about Mother myself."

"I used to love visiting her at the orphanage. She was always in such good spirits, and the way she could cook up a meal from nothing, in no time!"

"The orphanage is only about a mile away," Jonathan pointed out. Neither of us had been there for several years, since his mother retired. "Would you like to visit the place, for old time's sake?"

I admitted that I would. We covered the distance in half an hour. As we stood outside the tall, aging building, regarding the flight of worn stone steps leading up to the front door, I could not help but think of the pitiful circumstances of my own arrival there some one-and-twenty years before.

"Come on," Jonathan said, smiling for the first time that day, "let us go in and say hello to our old friend the administrator, Mr. Bradley Howell."

When we rang the bell and were admitted inside, however, we learned that the establishment was under new management. In fact, there were very few people there whom we recognised; and of course, all the children we had known while living under that roof had all grown up and moved on long ago. When we explained who we were and asked if we might take a quick look round, permission was granted.

We poked our heads into the kitchen, one of our favourite spots to congregate when Jonathan's mother ran the ship; but we did not know a soul, and as the staff was in the midst of serving luncheon, we hurried on.

"It feels so odd," I whispered to Jonathan, as we slowly made our way along the familiar, dark corridor on the ground floor, "to be back in these same old halls and to find myself a stranger."

He nodded. "I spent far more time down here with you and the other children than I did in our rooms upstairs with Mother."

"Do you remember the time we stole all the bonbons from Mr. Howell's desk, and then hid in the cupboard under the stairs and devoured every single one of them?" I asked.

"I was so sick, I could not look at another sweet for months!"

We shared a few additional memories of antics we had got up to in our youth, which made us laugh. As we passed by the dining-hall, we heard the loud hum of conversation from within, amidst a steady clatter of forks and spoons. We took turns peeking in through the small window in the door, where I caught sight of fifty or more children seated at long tables, eating their noonday meal. Seeing their pale little faces and their assortment of ill-fitting garments reminded me of myself at that age, and gave me a little pang.

Suddenly a small boy, perhaps eight years old, dashed up the passage with a flustered expression, aiming for the dining-hall door. As Jonathan and I stood aside to let him pass, he paused and glanced up at us with wide eyes. "Are you here to adopt somebody?" he asked hopefully.

"Sorry, young man," Jonathan said kindly. "We are just visiting. We used to live here ourselves as children."

The boy took in the shiny new shoes and new suit Jonathan was wearing, and then lingered on his beautiful, red cashmere scarf. "You must be doing all right now! That's my favorite colour: red."

"Is it?" Jonathan said. I knew that the scarf had been a gift from Mr. Hawkins years before, and that Jonathan had long treasured it; but without a second thought, he said, "It's yours," as he wrapped the scarf around the little boy's neck.

The boy gasped with wordless delight; then emotion seemed to overcome him, and he pushed open the door and disappeared into the dining-hall.

I took Jonathan's hand and squeezed it as we proceeded down the hall. "That was very sweet and generous of you."

Jonathan only shrugged. "I wish I could give every one of them a home, and parents who loved them."

We had just reached the foyer when an old woman in a white cap and apron happened by. I recognised her at once as a servant I had never liked: she was the one I had overhead gossiping about my mother when I was just seven years of age. Upon seeing us, the old woman stopped and cried out, "Well bless my soul, if it isn't Miss Mina an' Master Jonathan. Haven't seen the likes of you two in many a year."

"Hello, Mrs. Pringle," I returned politely. "How are you?"

"Same as ever, just older an' ornerier. How are you two getting on?"

"Fine, thank you ma'am," Jonathan replied. "In fact, we are married now."

"Are you, then? Good for you. Your mum would have liked that." She glanced at me now and went quiet for a moment, as if trying to recall something long forgotten.

"Well, ma'am," Jonathan said with a smile, "it was good to see you again. Good day." He took my arm, and we were about to head for the door, when the old woman blurted:

"Did you ever get that envelope, Miss Mina?"

I turned to her in surprise. "What envelope?"

"Why, the envelope what was left for you when you was a girl."

Jonathan and I exchanged a look, and I said: "I received no envelope, Mrs. Pringle. How do you know of it?"

"Why, I was here the day it arrived. A young woman put it into my own hands, on the doorstep. So pale and sickly she was, I remember thinking: she's not long for this world. She'd writ your name on it, and made me promise to deliver it to the head of the orphanage and to say he was not to give it to you until you reached eighteen years of age."

My heart began to pound. "When was this?"

"You might have been six or seven at the time, as I recall."

"Who left the letter? Was it my mother? What did the letter say?"

The old woman lowered her eyes now, with a surreptitious look that told me she had read the letter, before delivering it to the institution's director—if she *had*, indeed, ever delivered it. "I could not say, ma'am. Strange that Mr. Howell never sent it to you, after you come of age. I suppose he just forgot."

I was stunned and excited by this news. It was the first piece of information I had ever heard about my mother since that remark about her indiscreet behaviour which had so traumatised me as a child. But I was saddened, too, to hear that she had been sickly. We said good-bye to Mrs. Pringle and went in search of the new director of the establishment, a bewhiskered, preoccupied man who said he knew nothing about any letter addressed to me but would be happy to forward the envelope should he ever come across it. I gave him my address in Exeter, and we departed.

"Oh, Jonathan!" I cried, as we strode down the street. "Can you imagine it? A letter to me—perhaps from my own mother!"

"I hope he finds it; but I would not get your hopes up, my dear. It may have been discarded long ago."

"Even so. Just to know that she was thinking of me when I was six or seven; that she *wanted* to communicate with me; it makes me feel better somehow."

It was by then the middle of the afternoon. Over lunch at a café, we indulged in more happy childhood memories. Jonathan suggested that we help the orphanage by making a donation from his newly inherited funds, and I agreed. We tried to decide what to do with the few hours we had left in London before we had to catch our train. I wanted to call on Lucy and her mother, both to say hello and to reassure myself that all was well with them; but Jonathan insisted that we did not have time, since Hillingham was on the opposite side of town.

We took a bus instead to Hyde Park Corner, and then walked down Piccadilly, an activity we had always enjoyed. With my arm linked in Jonathan's, we strolled along the busy street, looking at all the people, the shops, and the fashionable residences. Outside Giuliano's jewellery shop at 115 Piccadilly, I noticed a beautiful girl in a big cart-wheel hat, sitting in a new and expensively built open carriage. I was idly wondering who she was—no doubt an important customer, I thought, waiting for a piece of fine jewellery to be delivered—when I felt Jonathan clutch my arm so tightly that it made me wince.

Under his breath, he said: "My God!"

"What is it?"

"Look!" Jonathan cried, his face now very pale, and his eyes bulging in mingled terror and amazement.

I followed his gaze. He was staring at a man who stood nearby, turned partially away from us, his attention intently focused on the pretty girl in the carriage. As I looked at the man, a strange feeling came over me: my skin felt clammy, my heart began to race, and I began to shiver. The man—who was tall and thin, dressed all in black, and had black hair and a black moustache—bore an uncanny resemblance to Mr. Wagner! But I knew *it could not be he;* for this man looked to be at least fifty years old—a good twenty years older than the man I was acquainted with. He had a short, pointed beard, and his face looked hard and cruel.

"Do you see who it is?" Jonathan said in horror, still gripping my arm anxiously.

I struggled to remain calm. "No, dear. I don't know him. Who is it?"

"It is the man himself!"

I had no idea who Jonathan meant, but his answer both shocked and frightened me, for he seemed to be talking not to me, but to himself—and he was very greatly terrified. I do believe that if I had not been there to support him, he would have sunk down to the ground. Now a clerk came out of the jewellery shop and handed a small parcel to the lady in the carriage, and she drove off. The strange man quickly hailed a hansom, hopped in, and followed in the same direction.

Jonathan stared at the departing cab and said in great agitation, still as if to himself: "I believe it is the Count, but he has *grown young*. My God, if this be so! Oh, my God! If I only knew! If I only knew!"

"You must be mistaken, my dear." My heart pounded in alarm. I understood that Jonathan thought this man was the same Count Dracula he had visited in Transylvania; but his words made no sense to me. How could a man grow young? I feared to ask him any questions, however, lest it cause a return of the brain fever which had so weakened him before; so I remained silent and drew Jonathan away quietly.

He did not say another word but allowed me to lead him, walking on as if dazed until we reached the Green Park, where we sat down on a shady bench. Jonathan closed his eyes and leaned against me, still holding my hand tightly. After a few minutes, I felt his grip relax, and I realised he had fallen asleep.

As I sat there, cradling Jonathan's head with my shoulder and listening to the breeze stir the trees overhead, my heart continued to race. Who was the strange man we had seen? Why did he look so much like Mr. Wagner? I would have guessed him to be that gentleman's father, had Mr. Wagner not said that his parents were dead. What, I wondered, was behind Jonathan's violent reaction to the man? If only I could ask him! But I dared not, for fear I would do more harm than good.

OUR HOME-COMING THAT NIGHT WAS SAD IN EVERY WAY. THE house felt strange and empty without that dear soul, Mr. Hawkins, who had been so good to us; Jonathan was still pale and dizzy, under a slight relapse of his malady; and a telegram was awaiting me, sent from London the day before, with the most devastating news:

LONDON 21 SEPTEMBER 1890

MRS. MINA HARKER

YOU WILL BE GRIEVED TO HEAR THAT MRS. WESTENRA DIED FIVE DAYS AGO AND THAT LUCY DIED THE DAY BEFORE YESTERDAY. THEY WERE BOTH BURIED TO-DAY.

ABRAHAM VAN HELSING

I read the words once, twice, three times, hoping that it was some mistake. When the full meaning of the dreadful message made its final impact, my legs buckled beneath me; I dropped onto the sofa in shock and let out an anguished cry.

"What is it?" Jonathan asked, as he darted to my side. "What is wrong?"

"Oh, what a wealth of sorrow in just a few words!" I said brokenly, as I handed him the telegram.

He read it, then sank down beside me, stunned. "Mrs. Westenra? And Miss Lucy? *They are both dead?"*

Tears sprang into my eyes. "How is it possible? I knew that Mrs. Westenra was ailing; still, I had hoped she might recover. I will dearly miss her. But Lucy! Poor, dear Lucy! My dearest, most beloved friend. Her birthday was next week! She was not yet twenty years old!"

"I am so sorry, Mina," Jonathan said softly, as he took my hand. "She was a lovely girl, and I know how much you loved her."

"She sounded so well and happy in her last letter," I sobbed. "How could she be dead? What on earth happened?"

"Perhaps some kind of accident befell her."

"If so, who is this Mr. Van Helsing? Why has *he* written to me? For such important news, why did I not hear from Lucy's fiancé, Mr. Holmwood?"

"He may have been too upset to write," Jonathan mused. "Van Helsing must be their solicitor. It could be that you are mentioned in Lucy's will."

"Lucy never bothered to write a will, I am sure of it. Oh! To be taken so young, less than two weeks before her wedding, when she was so full of life and promise! And poor Mr. Holmwood, to have lost such sweetness out of *his* life!" A sudden thought occurred to me, and I choked back another sob. "Jonathan, do you realise: while you and I were attending Mr. Hawkins's funeral this morning and visiting the orphanage, Lucy and her mother were both already dead and buried. Gone, gone—never to return!"

I wept as if my heart would break. Jonathan pulled me into his arms and held me, stroking my hair silently; but there is little any one can say or do to ease the shock and pain of the loss of a best friend.

Before we went to bed, I wrote to Mr. Holmwood, expressing my deepest condolences and seeking more information about the tragedies that had befallen my friends.

It seemed that our grief and troubles were never-ending; for that night, Jonathan was again beset by bad dreams.

"No! Keep your hands off me! Get away, you wicked harpies!" he cried in his sleep, as his hands clutched one side of his throat, as if to protect himself from some invisible harm.

I woke him gently, as I had done every night since we had been married. "Jonathan," I said softly, as he lay trembling beside me, "this has been going on such a long time. I know I said I would never ask—"

"Then don't ask now," he replied raggedly. Closing his eyes, he turned away.

I lay awake into the wee hours, puzzling over the strange turn our lives had taken over the past month. Lucy, Mrs. Westenra, and Mr. Hawkins, all dead and buried; Jonathan and I married, with a house of our own; my husband a solicitor, newly wealthy, and the master of his own business; yet beset by mental attacks and frequent, horrible nightmares. So much tragedy, so many changes, and all of it so sudden—it seemed impossible to believe.

Jonathan went off to work the next morning in a determined frame of mind, as if relieved to have the responsibility of his position to take his mind off the other, terrible things; but I was worried about him. Clearly, he was not well. Did his nightmares threaten an impending return of his brain fever? If so, what could I do to help him if he refused to talk about it?

It was then that I remembered the statement he had made on the morning before our wedding. He had said that I was free to read the journal he had kept during his stay in Transylvania as long as I did not talk to him about it.

Well then, I decided: the time had come.

As soon as the front door shut behind him, I ran upstairs to our bedroom and locked the door. From a cupboard, I retrieved the parcel that I had sealed with wax in Buda-Pesth, and unwrapped it. Drawing up a chair to the window, I sat down with Jonathan's foreign journal and began to read.

EIGHT

IT WAS SLOW GOING AT FIRST, AS MY SHORTHAND WAS RUSTY from disuse; but I was soon poring through Jonathan's scrawled pages with ease. Nothing, however, could have prepared me for its shocking and truly frightening contents.

The document began harmlessly enough, with a long and detailed account of Jonathan's travel experiences in Austria and Hungary, and a picturesque description of the Transylvanian country-side. Upon his arrival at his hotel in Bistritz, a very cordial letter was awaiting him:

My Friend—

Welcome to the Carpathians. I am anxiously expecting you. Sleep well to-night. At three tomorrow the diligence[2] *will start for Bukovina; a place on it is kept for you. At the Borgo Pass my carriage*

---

2 Public stagecoach.

will await you and will bring you to me. I trust that your journey from London has been a happy one, and that you will enjoy your stay in my beautiful land.

Your friend,
Dracula

Jonathan was surprised when the landlord at the hotel tried to persuade him not to continue on his journey. To his further consternation, the man's wife, somewhat hysterical, went down on her knees and implored him not to go, crying, "Do you know what you are going to?"

When Jonathan insisted that he had business to conduct at Castle Dracula, and could not very well leave without completing it, the woman dried her tears and placed her own rosary and crucifix around Jonathan's neck, telling him to wear it "for his mother's sake."

Jonathan thought their behaviour extremely odd, until he boarded the public coach the next morning and observed the local peasants eyeing him with pity and uttering strange words that he translated to mean "were-wolf" and "vampire." As the coach took him deeper and deeper into the Carpathian Mountains, Jonathan became increasingly uneasy. His fellow passengers, with fearful looks but not a word of explanation, all began giving him crucifixes and other charms against evil, such as garlic and sprigs of wild rose and mountain ash. What kind of man was he visiting, Jonathan wondered, that everyone was so afraid for him?

Late that night, on a lonely winding of the Borgo Pass, the public coach was met as promised by a calèche[3] and four coal-black horses, sent from Castle Dracula to fetch Jonathan—an arrival which prompted a chorus of screams from the peasants and

---

3 A light, horse-drawn vehicle seating two to four passengers, with a seat for a driver on a splashboard.

a universal crossing of themselves. One of Jonathan's companions whispered to another: *"Denn die Todten reiten schnell."* ("For the dead travel fast.")

I paused in my reading, the hair on the back of my neck standing up on end, for I recognised that phrase. It was a line from Gottfried Burger's poem "Lenore," the dark, horrific tale of a young woman who is taken on a wild horseback ride to a graveyard by her fiancé's animated corpse, and then drawn down into his coffin to her death!

With equal parts fascination and dread, I picked up Jonathan's journal and continued to read:

The carriage was driven by a strange, tall man with an iron grip, a long, brown beard, and a great black hat which shrouded his face. In excellent German, he commanded Jonathan to board his vehicle. Frightened, but with little alternative, Jonathan did as he was directed. The calèche took off, moving at incredible speed. The journey to the castle became more and more harrowing, for the horses began straining and rearing, terrified by the cries of howling wolves. The driver stopped and soothed the horses by petting them and whispering in their ears. Later, to Jonathan's amazement, when the carriage was surrounded by a huge pack of angry wolves, the driver stepped down into the road, and with a great sweep of his arm, uttered an imperious command which caused the beasts to fall back and disappear! This was all so strange and uncanny that Jonathan was afraid to speak or move.

When the carriage finally arrived and dropped Jonathan in pitch-darkness on the doorstep of what he perceived to be an immense, old castle, he was left alone for quite some time. Doubts and fears invaded his mind. What sort of grim adventure had he embarked on? At last, to the sound of rattling chains and the clanking of massive bolts, the great door opened, and he met his host.

"I am Dracula," intoned the tall, thin, elderly Count, shaking

Jonathan's hand with a strength that made him wince and a grip that felt as cold as ice. "I bid you welcome, Mr. Harker, to my house. Enter freely and of your own will!"

The Count was very pale, his skin nearly the same shade as his white hair and moustache. He was a well-educated, charming, and hospitable gentleman, who spoke English with a skill and ease that Jonathan found surprising for a man who claimed that he had never been to England. The castle was ancient and many parts of it seemed forbidding, lit only by antique lamps whose flames threw long, quivering shadows against its stone walls and long, dark passages. To Jonathan's relief and delight, however, his own accommodations proved to be both comfortable and beautifully and expensively furnished, if centuries old. He found a delicious supper awaiting him, laid out on an elegant, solid gold table service. Count Dracula did not join him, insisting that he had already dined.

The next day, Jonathan took stock of his surroundings. The castle was extremely isolated, surrounded by jagged mountains, and situated on a high precipice above a forested valley. He was left on his own for a long period of time during the day, as Count Dracula preferred to interact by night.

Jonathan soon discovered a beautifully furnished and very complete library, containing hundreds of thousands of volumes and a great many periodicals in a variety of languages, a vast number of which were in English. The Count joined him there.

"These companions," Count Dracula said, referring to his books, "have been good friends to me for some years past. Through them, I have come to know your great England; and to know her is to love her. I long to go through the crowded streets of your mighty London, to be in the midst of the whirl and rush of humanity, to share its life, its change, its death, and all that makes it what it is."

Jonathan completed the business matter which had brought

him to Transylvania, explaining the details of the property his firm had purchased on Count Dracula's behalf: a large, old, isolated mansion called Carfax on the outskirts of London, which the Count intended to occupy. After the legal documents were signed and prepared for posting, Dracula peppered Jonathan with questions about both the estate and England's business and shipping practices. Over the next few nights, the two men shared many long, congenial conversations on a wide variety of subjects, which kept them up until daybreak.

Although the Count was charming and courteous, this strange, nocturnal existence began to tell on Jonathan, and a series of discoveries made him feel ill-at-ease. Despite the evidence of wealth on display, Jonathan could find no sign of a single servant in the place. It seemed that the Count had been preparing all his meals—meals of which the Count never partook—and Jonathan was now certain that it was the Count himself who, in disguise, had driven the coach that brought him there. Other than the library and Jonathan's guest quarters, most of the doors in the castle were locked and forbidden to him, and Count Dracula warned him never to fall asleep anywhere in the castle except his own room.

One day, as Jonathan was shaving, he felt a hand on his shoulder and heard the Count say, "Good morning." Jonathan started in confusion and amazement, because Count Dracula—although he was standing immediately behind him—was not reflected in his shaving mirror! There was no mistaking it; the Count cast no reflection at all! Jonathan was so startled that he accidentally cut himself. The Count, upon seeing Jonathan's face, lunged at his throat with a sort of demoniac fury, drawing back only when his hand touched the string of beads which held the crucifix Jonathan was wearing. This made an instant change in him. The fury in the Count's eyes then passed away so quickly that Jonathan could hardly believe it had ever been there.

"Take care how you cut yourself," the Count said calmly. "It is more dangerous than you think in this country." He seized Jonathan's shaving glass. "And this is the wretched thing that has done the mischief. It is a foul bauble of man's vanity. Away with it!" He opened the heavy window with one wrench of his hand and flung the glass out the window, where it shattered on the stones of the courtyard far below.

What was the meaning behind such odd behaviour? Jonathan wondered. He now began to question everything. Why did the Count never eat or drink in front of him? If he was the coachman, what strange powers did he possess over the horses and the wolves? Why were all the people at Bistritz and on the coach so terribly afraid for Jonathan? What was the meaning of the crucifixes, the garlic, and the sprigs of wild rose and mountain ash they had given him?

Jonathan became truly anxious when, after a brief investigation of the castle, he found all the exterior doors locked and bolted. In no place save from the castle windows was there an available exit. Was he being held a prisoner? Did Count Dracula mean him harm? Or was Jonathan only being deceived by his own fears? He resolved to keep his suspicions to himself, keep his eyes and ears open, and prepare to leave as soon as possible. However, Count Dracula insisted that Jonathan stay in Transylvania for another month, and urged him to write a letter home explaining the delay. Jonathan, feeling obligated to his employer to please the Count, reluctantly complied.

One night, while peering out a window of the castle, Jonathan observed a most shocking sight: he saw Count Dracula emerge from one of the lower windows and crawl down the sheer face of the castle wall in lizard fashion. Jonathan could not believe his eyes. The old man was actually crawling *head down* above that dreadful abyss, his fingers and toes clinging to the stony outcroppings, before disappearing through a hole which led to a walkway far below. What manner of man was this, Jonathan wondered in terror, who could or would leave a building in such a fashion? Or what manner of creature was it, in the semblance of man?

Jonathan determined to explore the castle further, and to seek a way out—but all the doors in the castle, other than the library and his own room, were still locked to him. At last, at the end of a long, dark passage, one locked door gave way upon great force. He found himself in a dusty but comfortably furnished parlour, which he deduced had been occupied by the ladies in Dracula's family in days gone by. The dreadful loneliness of the place chilled his heart. He soon felt overwhelmed by exhaustion and, ignoring the count's warning, he lay down on a couch and fell asleep.

The events that followed were like some horrific dream, and yet they felt startlingly real. Three beautiful, voluptuous young women suddenly appeared in the room before him—ladies by their dress and manner—with red lips and brilliant white teeth. Two were dark-haired, and the other was fair. They approached Jonathan, laughing and whispering. They made him feel uneasy, yet at the same time (he wrote with shame) he was filled with a wicked, burning desire that they would kiss him.

"Go on!" said one dark-haired beauty lasciviously to the blonde. "You are first, and we shall follow."

"He is young and strong," added another in a sultry tone. "There are kisses for us all."

The fair-haired woman, the most beautiful of them all, bent over Jonathan, licking her lips coquettishly. Her breath was honey-sweet, and Jonathan tingled with ecstasy and desire as she placed her lips against his neck. He waited in an agony of anticipation as he felt two sharp teeth pausing at his throat. Suddenly, Dracula swept into the chamber with a roar, grabbed the fair woman by the neck, and hurled her across the room. His eyes blazing like red furies, he cried:

"How dare you touch him, any of you? How dare you cast eyes

on him when I had forbidden it? Back, I tell you all! This man belongs to me!"

Jonathan remained paralysed with fright. The women's hard, fiendish laughter rang through the room, as the fair girl taunted the Count, "You yourself never loved; you never love!"

"Yes, I too can love," the Count replied, in a sudden, soft whisper. "You yourselves can tell it from the past." He ordered the women to leave.

"Are we to have nothing to-night?" said one of the women, disappointed.

For answer, Dracula offered them a bag which he had brought with him, which moved as though there were some living thing within it. To Jonathan's horror, he thought he heard a low wail come from inside the bag, as if it contained a small, half-smothered child! The terrible women snatched up the bag with glee, and then—to Jonathan's utter terror and astonishment—all three suddenly disappeared! They seemed to fade out of the room, their corporeal forms and the dreadful bag vanishing into the rays of the moonlight, as Jonathan lapsed into unconsciousness.

I paused in my reading, my pulse pounding. Dear God! So this was the horrible bag which Jonathan had cried out about in such terror in his sleep! A bag containing a half-smothered child! And those horrible, phantom women—who could they be? I read on:

Jonathan later awoke in his own bed, overwhelmed by horror. What had just happened to him? Was it real or a dream? Why did the Count say, "This man belongs to me"? Had those women intended to kiss him, or to use those sharp teeth he had felt at his throat? Did they intend to devour whatever was inside that awful bag? And how could they have *disappeared* before his very eyes? Could it be that he was going mad? Or was he mad already?

A few days later, on 19 May, the Count coerced Jonathan into writing three post-dated letters, the first two saying that his work was done and he was about to start for home, and the third saying that he had already left the castle and safely arrived at Bistritz.

"The posts are few and uncertain," Count Dracula said suavely, "and writing these letters now will ensure ease of mind to your friends."

Jonathan deduced in horror that the Count—concerned that Jonathan knew too much and might prove a threat to his plans—only meant to keep Jonathan alive long enough to learn everything he could about England before moving there. Then he intended to kill him. The letters would serve as proof that Jonathan had departed the castle unharmed. The last of the letters was dated 29 June. Jonathan took this as a sign of the span of his life.

Jonathan felt like a rat caught in a trap. Desperate to escape, Jonathan wrote two more secret letters, and passed them through the bars of his window to a group of gipsies encamped in the castle courtyard below. To Jonathan's dismay, Dracula intercepted the letters and opened them. Upon discovering that one was from Jonathan to Mr. Hawkins, Dracula apologised and urged Jonathan to redirect a new envelope and seal it within. The second letter was unsigned and written in shorthand, so Dracula burned it.

Weeks passed. Jonathan remained a prisoner. He hid his journal, but many of his personal belongings disappeared, including his best suit of clothes and all his notes and papers. The band of Szgany gipsies returned to the castle, and for some reason unloaded several wagons full of large wooden boxes. In the days that followed, Jonathan heard the sounds of men working with spades somewhere far below, as if digging in the earth in the depths of the castle.

Late one night, Jonathan witnessed the Count crawl down the castle wall again. This time, to Jonathan's shock, the Count was dressed in Jonathan's missing suit of clothes, and he was carrying the same bag he had earlier given to those three terrible women. There could be no doubt as to the nature of his murderous quest!

Jonathan sat doggedly by the window for a long time, watching for his return. At length, Jonathan became mesmerised by floating motes of dust, which danced in the moonlight. He realised, to his alarm, that he was being hynotised! The dust motes magically materialised into the forms of the three women who had tried to seduce him. Jonathan ran screaming from the place, seeking safety in his room.

A few hours later, to Jonathan's horror, he heard something stirring from Dracula's room below. He heard something like a sharp wail, which was quickly suppressed, followed by deep, awful silence. Jonathan wept in anguish for the child that, he presumed, had been kidnapped and murdered. Soon after, a distraught woman appeared in the courtyard below, beating her hands against the castle door in torment and crying: "Monster, give me my child!"

From high overhead, Jonathan heard the voice of the Count, calling out in a harsh, metallic whisper, which seemed to be answered from far and wide by the howling of wolves. In minutes, a pack of wolves poured into the courtyard. There was no cry from the woman, but she disappeared from Jonathan's sight, as if devoured entirely.

When dawn broke, Jonathan resolved that he must shake off his fears and take action. He did not often see the Count during the day; perhaps that was when he slept. Jonathan knew that the window far below him—the one from which he had seen the Count emerge twice before, in lizard fashion—was the Count's own, locked room. Somehow, he must gain entrance to it. If an old man could crawl down that sheer castle wall, Jonathan decided, why couldn't he? Better to risk his own life trying to escape than to remain helpless in the Count's power.

Jonathan removed his boots and scaled the rough castle wall—a dangerous, terrifying feat—and made it into the Count's chamber. To his surprise, the room contained only dust-covered furniture and a great heap of gold coins that were more than three hundred years old. Jonathan followed a dark, winding stairway down to a tunnel-like passage. This led to an old chapel where, to his astonishment, he discovered fifty long, wooden boxes lined with newly dug earth. Inside one of the boxes lay the Count, apparently asleep! Terrified, Jonathan made a hasty retreat.

On the night of 29 June—the date of Jonathan's last letter—Dracula announced with apparent sincerity: "To-morrow, my friend, we must part. You return to your beautiful England, I to some work which may have such an end that we never meet. Your letter home has been dispatched; to-morrow I shall not be here, but all shall be ready for your journey." The Szgany, Dracula explained, had some work to complete the next morning on his behalf; after that, they would make ready his carriage and convey Jonathan to the Borgo Pass, to meet the diligence to Bistritz.

Jonathan, suspicious, asked if he could leave immediately, insisting that he would happily leave behind his baggage if allowed to walk away on his own. Dracula expressed concern but acquiesced and opened the front door. To Jonathan's terror and dismay, a pack of snarling wolves impeded his departure. Later, safely locked in his room once more, Jonathan overheard a voice he thought might be the Count's, telling the three terrible women, "Your time has not yet come. Wait. Have patience. To-morrow night is yours!"

Terrified, Jonathan determined that he must escape or die. The next morning he scaled the castle wall again and went down to the old chapel, where he found Dracula asleep in a box of earth as before. This time—impossibly—the Count appeared to be much younger than before! His hair and moustache were not white, but iron-grey; his pale skin was a healthy pink; and blood trickled from the corners of his mouth. How could this be? What did it mean? Had he just eaten that woman's child?

Horrified, Jonathan grabbed a shovel, intending to kill him;

but the Count—as if in a trance—turned his head at the last second with a hateful glare, and the blow glanced harmlessly off his forehead. Terrified that the Count might rise and murder him, Jonathan fled the chapel. He heard the gipsies arriving—no doubt to escort the Count on the first leg of his journey to England. There was no way on earth, Jonathan determined, that he would be left alone in that castle with those sisters from Hell! He would scale the castle wall farther than he had yet attempted, taking nothing but the clothes on his back, his journal, and a few pieces of Dracula's gold. He would make his escape that very day!

He penned one last, desperate line: "Good-bye, all! Mina!"

And there the journal ended.

I HARDLY KNEW WHAT TO MAKE OF MY HUSBAND'S JOURNAL. It was such a terrible record that it left me perplexed and in tears. As soon as I had finished reading, I went back and re-read certain passages again, hoping that I had misinterpreted some of the shorthand symbols; but I had not. Oh! How my poor dear must have suffered! No wonder he arrived at the hospital in Buda-Pesth raving about demons and wolves, and ghosts and blood!

Was there any truth in the account, I wondered, or was it all a figment of Jonathan's imagination? Did Jonathan get his brain fever, and then write all those strange and horrible things? Or had he some cause for part of it? Jonathan had always been—as Mr. Hawkins had pointed out—the most sensible, calm, level-headed individual I had ever known. He was not the sort to have wild imaginings . . . which made the contents of his journal all the more confusing and upsetting.

I turned back to the beginning, to the part where Jonathan had overheard the peasants talking about were-wolves and vampires. I had read of vampires before, in poetry and literature; but they were just fictitious creatures, common to the folk-tales and superstitions of Eastern Europe. Jonathan had never mentioned the terms again in the whole length of his journal; and yet his descriptions of events raised many disturbing questions in my mind. Jonathan said that those three awful women at the castle had vanished before his eyes, and then had re-materialised out of the dust particles in the air! Had he imagined the women entirely, or was he merely deluded about that part? If the women did exist, what was their relationship with Count Dracula? Were they trying to seduce Jonathan—or did they mean him some greater harm? What about the creatures in the bag; were they truly children Dracula had brought to the women as treats—to be *eaten?*

How, I wondered, was such pure evil even conceivable?

As for that fearful, elderly Count, with his cruel manners and strange, loathsome habits, I had so many questions, I hardly knew where to begin—but I knew equally as well that I could not open the subject to Jonathan.

Oh! How quickly everything changed, just a few short days after that! Sometimes I wonder: would we have been better off if we had never learned the truth?

It was a quarter past eight when I heard the sound of familiar footsteps on the front walk, announcing Jonathan's return. I thrust his journal back into the cupboard and went down to greet him, pasting a smile on my face and behaving as normally as I could. The cook had prepared supper, but I had little appetite.

We retired early. After his long day, Jonathan fell asleep at once. I was far too distressed to sleep. I could not stop thinking about that man we had seen in London. Jonathan had seemed quite certain that he was the Count. What if he was right? There was a thread of continuity in it, after all: Count Dracula *was* preparing to come to London. By Jonathan's description, however, Dracula was an old, pale, white-haired man . . . and the man we saw had black hair and a ruddy complexion. *A man could not grow young—could he?* He *could,* however, disguise himself with a wig and make-up—as Dracula apparently had done the night he posed as the coachman—and perhaps again on that last day, when Jonathan had found him asleep in his tomb-like box, with his lips dripping blood. Who or what had the Count feasted on? If Jonathan had not escaped, would Dracula have murdered him?

With a shudder, I thought: if the man we saw in Piccadilly *was* Count Dracula—and if he is indeed the monster my husband described—think what havoc he could wreak in this city, among the teeming millions! The words Jonathan had spoken on our wedding-day, with regard to his journal, came back to me: "Let us never mention it again—unless, one day, some solemn duty should command me to go back to the bitter hours, asleep or awake, sane or mad, that are recorded here."

It seemed that there might indeed be *solemn duty* one day soon. If that duty should come, I decided, we must not shrink from it. We must be prepared.

The moment Jonathan left for work the next morning, I got out my typewriter and began to transcribe his journal. It took the better part of the day; but when I had finished with his pages, I found the journal that I had begun at Whitby, and wrote it out on the typewriter as well. Jonathan was working late, so I continued typing far into the evening with fierce determination. When at last I had finished, I laid the typewritten pages in my work-basket with exhausted satisfaction. Now, I thought, we would be ready for other eyes, should it be required.

Naturally, I mentioned nothing about my day's activity at supper that night.

"I have some business in Lauceston to-morrow," Jonathan told me, as he absently took a bite of his roast beef and sipped his wine. "I will be obliged to stay the night."

"Oh?" I replied, disappointed. "I will miss you. Do you realise: this will be the first time that we have been parted since our marriage?"

"I am sorry, but it cannot be helped. It is only one night, dear. I will be back the day after to-morrow—rather late, I expect."

When we kissed good-bye early the next morning, Jonathan told me he loved me, and held me very tightly; but I sensed that his thoughts were elsewhere, as they had been ever since I had been reunited with him in Buda-Pesth. Oh! I thought, as I watched him walk off down the lane, I do hope the dear fellow will take care of himself and that nothing will occur to upset him.

Then I sank down into a chair and had a good, long cry.

A LETTER CAME BY THAT MORNING'S POST FROM ABRAHAM VAN Helsing, the man who had sent me the telegram about Lucy a few days before:

London, 24 September 1890
(Confidence)

Dear Madam—

I pray you to pardon my writing, in that I am so far friend as that I sent you sad news of Miss Lucy Westenra's death. By the kindness of Lord Godalming, I am empowered to read her letters and papers, for I am deeply concerned about certain matters vitally important. In them I find some letters from you, which show how great friends you were and how you love her. Oh, Madam Mina, by that love, I implore you, help me. It is for other's good that I ask—to redress great wrong, and to lift much and terrible troubles—that may be more great than you can know. May it be that I see you? You can trust me. I am friend of Dr. John Seward and of Lord Godalming (that was Arthur of Miss Lucy). I must keep it private for the present from all. I should come to Exeter to see you at once if you tell me I am privilege to come, and where and when. I implore your pardon, madam. I have read your letters to poor Lucy, and know how good you are and how your husband suffer; so I pray you, if it may be, enlighten him not, lest it may harm. Again your pardon, and forgive me.

Van Helsing

From this letter, I understood two important things: that Mr. Holmwood's father had died, since Arthur had inherited his title as Lord Godalming (no wonder, with so much sorrow, the man had neglected to write to me upon Lucy's death!); and that this Abraham Van Helsing was requesting my help. I had no idea at the time who Van Helsing was, but from his name and the rather awkward wording of his letter I took him to be a foreigner, perhaps from the Netherlands. As he claimed to be a friend of Lord Godalming and Dr. John Seward (one of the other men who had proposed to Lucy), I was most anxious to meet him.

What "great wrong" and "terrible troubles" did he speak of? I wondered. Did it have something to do with Lucy's death? Would I, at last, learn something about what had happened to her? I immediately sent off a telegram, asking Van Helsing to catch the next possible train to Exeter that very day.

It was half-past two o'clock when I heard the knock at the front door. I waited in great suspense in the drawing-room. A few minutes later, the door opened.

"Dr. Van Helsing," announced our housemaid, Mary, as she curtseyed and withdrew.

I rose and beheld my visitor as he approached me. He was a strongly built, broad-chested man of medium height and weight, who looked to be in his late fifties or early sixties. His greying hair, shot through with strands of fading red, was neatly combed, and he had big, bushy eyebrows over a broad forehead. He had a good face, clean-shaven, with a large, resolute mouth, and big, dark blue eyes that gleamed with both compassion and intelligence. Indeed, the very poise of his head struck me at once as indicative of thought and power.

"Mrs. Harker, is it not?" he enquired in a thick, Dutch accent.

I bowed my assent, my heart beating with eager expectation. "And you are Dr. Van Helsing?" At his nod, I added: "I am afraid my husband is out of town, or I am sure he would have been pleased to meet you, Doctor."

"It is you who I have come to see, Mrs. Harker; that is, if you were once Mina Murray, and a friend of that poor dear child Lucy Westenra."

"I am she. Sir, I loved Lucy with all my heart. You could have no better claim on me than to say that you were a friend and helper of Lucy Westenra." I held out my hand, which he took with a courtly bow.

"Thank you, but even so I must introduce myself, Madam Mina, for I know that I am a complete stranger to you."

It was the first time that I had ever been addressed as "Madam Mina," a rather quaint but wonderful appellation, I thought. As soon as were both seated in chairs opposite each other, he went on: "I believe you know Dr. John Seward, yes?"

I knew that Dr. Seward had been in love with Lucy, and that he had once proposed to her; but since I was uncertain as to whether or not this fact was common knowledge, I only replied: "I have never met Dr. Seward, sir; but I know he was a friend of Lucy's. She spoke very highly of him."

"Indeed, Dr. Seward is an excellent young man and a physician of great devotion. Some years past, he was my student and I his mentor. We remain good friends ever since. I am a scientist and a metaphysician. I make my specialty the brain, and also I have much experience in the study of obscure diseases. It was for this reason that Dr. Seward ask me to come over and look at Miss Lucy."

"She was ill, then?" I said, as a great sadness came over me.

"She was."

"I feared as much. Lucy was ill when I left her at Whitby. It was as if she was wasting away for no apparent reason. When she wrote to me a few days later, however, she said she had fully recovered and was returning to her mother's house in London the next day. The news of her death came as such a shock, I thought that perhaps she had met with an accident of some kind."

"No; I fear what happened to Miss Lucy was no accident," he replied grimly.

"What did she suffer from, Dr. Van Helsing? Why did she die?"

"Ah! That is the great mystery, Madam Mina. It is that very question which brings me to you."

"Me?"

"Yes. Although Miss Lucy die at Hillingham in London, I have deep suspicion that the root of her ailment begins at Whitby. As I mention in my letter, I have read what you wrote to Miss Lucy, so I know you were with her at Whitby. Will you help me, Madam Mina? Will you tell me what you know?"

Despite his quaint, stilted manner of speaking, the eagerness in his voice and the shrewdness in his eyes projected a commanding intelligence. "If it is at all in my power to help you, Doctor, I will certainly try. But first, you must tell me what happened to her."

He heaved a deep sigh. "The events which surround Miss Lucy's death are complicated and most disturbing. Are you certain you wish to hear them?"

"I do, sir. I have been so anxious ever since I received your telegram. I cannot rest until I know."

"Well, in brief, then: in London, Miss Lucy again she suffer from condition you so well describe as 'wasting away.' Dr. Seward attended her. In his worry, he wrote to me in Amsterdam, asking me to come. And so I go to London to consult on the case. For days on end, Miss Lucy—so sweet, so lovely—she is ghastly pale and demonstrate all signs of severe blood loss, but with no discernible medical explanation, and she have dreams that frighten her which she cannot remember. We try everything; we confine her to her bed, we transfuse her with new blood, but each time, by the next morning she is nearly bloodless again, and her breathing is painful to see and hear. Then one night, a wolf escape from the London Zoo—"

"A wolf!"

He nodded solemnly. "The beast break through a window of her bedroom, giving Lucy's mother—who slept beside her—a fatal heart attack."

"Oh! Is that how Mrs. Westenra died? How awful!"

"It was indeed a strange and tragic event. That the mother had a heart condition, we knew; but the daughter—I had hoped to save her. Despite my most earnest efforts, however, Miss Lucy grew steadily weaker; and—alas!—ultimately her heart and breathing cease, and she die."

"Oh!" I said again. Tears stung my eyes, and I wept for my two dear friends who had meant so much to me.

Dr. Van Helsing sat silently, offering me his handkerchief and allowing me this moment of grief, until I had regained some measure of control over myself. At length, he said: "I am sorry to be the bearer of such sad news, Madam Mina, but I felt I had to see you. All throughout Miss Lucy's illness, I have suspicions—deep suspicions—about what might lie behind it; but I could not verify, nor am I at liberty to reveal. After reading Miss Lucy's diary, however, I am convinced it all started at Whitby."

"Lucy kept a diary?" I said in surprise, drying my tears. "I never saw her write in one."

"It was begun after you left, Madam Mina. By Miss Lucy's admission, it was in imitation of you. Now: in her diary, she trace by inference certain things to a sleep-walking incident in which she claims that you rescued her. I therefore come to you, with hope that you will ease my perplexity and tell me all of it that you can remember."

"I can tell you, I think, all about it."

"Can you? Then you have good memory for facts and details?"

"I think so, Doctor; but far better than that—I wrote it all down at the time."

"Oh, Madam Mina!" He looked surprised and thrilled. "May I see this writing? I would be so grateful."

I retrieved my journal and showed it to him. "I kept a diary during my stay in Whitby, where I made a record of my thoughts and everything—" (thinking of Mr. Wagner, I quickly amended) "nearly everything—that occurred there, including all the details of the sleep-walking incident you referred to, and all the times that I found Lucy ill or in distress."

Dr. Van Helsing's face fell as he stared at my note-book full of scribbles. "Alas! I know not the shorthand. Will you do me the honour of reading it to me?"

"I would be happy to, Doctor; but you can read it yourself if you prefer. I have written it all out on the typewriter." I took the typewritten copy from my work-basket and handed it to him.

"Oh, you so clever woman! You are so skilled, so adept at many things, and you have such foresight. May I read it now? I may want to ask you some things when I have finished."

"By all means. Read it over whilst I order lunch; and then you can ask me questions whilst we eat."

Dr. Van Helsing settled himself in his chair and became absorbed in the papers. I went to see to lunch primarily to avoid disturbing him, for the cook already had the matter well in hand. I then quietly slipped upstairs for a little while, where I paced up and down the hall with mounting anxiety. What would he think of my little document? I wondered. Would it shed any light on what had happened to poor Lucy? And, the thing that perplexed me most of all: what could be so complicated and mysterious about the illness of a nineteen-year-old girl, that it would baffle a man of Dr. Van Helsing's apparently vast knowledge and experience?

When I had given him sufficient time to peruse the document, I came back down-stairs in a state of nervous anticipation. I found him pacing up and down the drawing-room, his face lit up with excitement.

"Oh, Madam Mina," he said, rushing up and taking me by both hands, "how can I say what I owe to you? This paper is as sunshine. You record these daily happenings in such excellent detail, with so much feeling, which breathes out truth in every line. It is everything I could have hoped for!"

"It will be helpful, then?"

"Infinitely so! Already, it answers many questions. It opens a gate to me. A light pours through which dazzles me much; and yet clouds and darkness are not far behind."

I could not help but smile at his eccentric way with words. I had never before heard any one speak as he did. "Is there anything else you wish to ask about those weeks in Whitby, Doctor?"

"At present, no; the document speaks for itself." He then added very solemnly, "I am grateful to you, Madam Mina. If ever Abraham Van Helsing can do anything for you or yours, I trust you will let me know. It will be an honour and a pleasure if I may serve you as a friend." He went on to praise what he called my "sweet and noble nature" at some length, and in a manner which I told him was far too praiseworthy, then ended by saying: "Your husband—is he quite well and hearty? All that fever you spoke of in your letters, is it gone?"

I sighed. "I think he *was* almost recovered, Doctor, but he has been greatly upset by Mr. Hawkins's death."

"Oh, yes. I am so sorry."

"Then, when we were in London last week, he had a sort of shock which made things worse."

"A shock, so soon after brain fever! That is too bad. What happened?"

"He thought he saw someone he recognised. It made him recall something frightening and terrible, something which I believe may have led to his brain fever in the first place."

Dr. Van Helsing's eyes widened, and he said animatedly, "This occured in London? *Who* did he see? *What* did he recall?"

Once again, tears sprang into my eyes. The horror which Jonathan had experienced in Transylvania, the mystery of his journal, and the fear that had been brooding over me ever since I had read it, all came over me in a sudden tumult of emotion. "Oh! Dr. Van Helsing, I am afraid to tell you. If you only knew what my poor Jonathan has suffered! But—you said earlier that you specialize in the brain. I implore you: if I have been in any way of assistance to you to-day, can you find it in your heart to help my husband? Can you make him well again?"

Dr. Van Helsing took my hands in his and reassured me, in a kind and sympathetic tone, that he was absolutely certain Jonathan's sufferings were within the range of his study and experience. He promised he would do everything he could to help my husband. "But you look too pale and overwrought to continue. We will talk no more of this until we have eaten."

Over lunch, Dr. Van Helsing purposefully turned the conversation to other things, and in time I became composed again.

He would not say much about himself except that he lived alone in Amsterdam and travelled often. His life seemed to be a very lonely one, so devoted to work that he had little time for friendships or relationships.

Later, after we returned to the drawing-room and sat down, Dr. Van Helsing turned to me and said kindly: "Now tell me all about your Jonathan."

"Doctor," I said, after some hesitation, "what I have to tell you is so strange that I fear you will laugh and think me a weak fool—and Jonathan a madman."

"Oh my dear, if you only know how strange is the matter regarding which I am here, it is you who would laugh. I make no study of the ordinary things in life. It is the extraordinary things, the things that make one doubt if they be mad or sane, which interest me. I have learned not to think little of any one's belief, but to keep an open mind."

"Thank you, sir!" I cried, greatly relieved. I pondered a moment and then added, "Since you found my own journal to be so enlightening, perhaps—rather than my telling you about Jonathan's troubles—it would be better for you to read about them instead."

"Read about them? Do you mean to say—did your husband also keep a journal?"

"He did. It is an account of all that happened when he was abroad. It is longer than mine, but I have typewritten it all out. You must read it for yourself, and then tell me what you think."

He accepted the papers gratefully and with undisguised excitement, promising to read them that very evening. "I will stay in Exeter to-night, Madam Mina, and we will talk again to-morrow. I would like to see your husband then, if I may."

Dr. Van Helsing then kissed my hand and went away.

I SPENT THE REMAINDER OF THE AFTERNOON IN A STATE OF FRENzied concern and absent-mindedness, alternating between periods of hope and self-chastisement.

At half-past six that evening, a letter was hand-delivered to the house, which immediately raised my spirits:

Exeter–25 September, 6 o'clock

Dear Madam Mina–

I have read your husband's so wonderful diary. You may sleep without doubt. Strange and terrible as it is, it is true! I will pledge my life on it. It may be worse for others; but for him and you there is no dread. He is a noble fellow; and let me tell you from experience of men, that one who would do as he did in going down that wall and to that room–ay, and going a second time–is not one to be injured in permanence by a shock. His brain and his heart are all right; this I swear, before I have even seen him; so be at rest. I shall have much to ask him of other things. I am blessed that to-day I come to see you, for I have learn all at once so much that again I am dazzle–dazzle more than ever, and I must think.

Yours the most faithful,
Abraham Van Helsing

Moments after this letter arrived, I received a wire from Jonathan, saying that his business was concluded and he was returning earlier than expected—that very night, in fact. Elated, I dashed off a note to Dr. Van Helsing, inviting him to breakfast the next morning.

It was half-past ten when Jonathan walked through the front door. I flew into his arms. "Dearest, I have such news! Wait until you hear!"

"What is it? My goodness, Mina, you look very excited. What has happened?"

"Come into the dining-room," I said, taking him by the hand. "I have supper ready, and I will tell you all about it."

While we supped, I told Jonathan about Dr. Van Helsing's visit, beginning with what had happened to Lucy. He listened with quiet compassion, expressing his sorrow over Lucy's death and sharing my puzzlement as to its cause. He became alarmed, however, when I came to the part about his diary.

"You read it?" he cried, his fork clattering to his plate. "But why? I thought we agreed—"

"You said that I should only read it if some solemn duty should command it. That hour has come, my dearest. When you saw that man in Piccadilly, you reacted so violently, and with such fear, that I knew I had to act; I had to understand what you had gone through."

"Dear God. I was hoping it would never come to this." He ran his fingers through his brown hair in great agitation. "What you must think of me! Go on: say it. You think I am mad."

"Far from it. What I think, Jonathan, is that you are perfectly sane, and a very brave man—and Dr. Van Helsing thinks the same."

"Dr. Van Helsing? Do you mean you told *him* about my journal?"

"I did more than tell him. I copied it all out on the typewriter and gave it to him, along with my own journal. Look! Here is the letter Dr. Van Helsing sent me this very evening. He says it is all true!"

Dumbfounded, Jonathan took the good doctor's letter, his eyes widening in astonishment as he read it. Then, as if unable to comprehend the news it imparted, he read through it a second time, murmuring in amazement: "It is true . . . all true." With a triumphant shout, Jonathan leapt to his feet, sending his chair crashing to the floor. "My God! This is incredible! You have no idea what this means to me."

He paced up and down the room in excitement, clutching the letter in his hand. "It was the doubt that knocked me over, Mina: the terrible doubt as to the reality of the whole thing. I felt impotent and in the dark. I did not know who or what to trust, not even the evidence of my own senses. So I just tried to put it behind me and throw myself into my work, into what had hitherto been the groove of my life. But the groove no longer availed me, for I now mistrusted myself."

"I understand, dearest."

"No; you cannot possibly understand—not truly. You cannot know what it is to doubt everything, even yourself." At this, he drew me up from my seat and wrapped me in his arms. "Oh! Mina, Mina; thank you for this. I feel like a new man. I have been ill, but the illness was only my own self-doubt. I am cured, and for that, I have you to thank!"

We embraced again, laughing. I had not seen Jonathan so happy or confident since the day he had left on his journey abroad, so many months ago. Our giddy mood soon waned, however, as the reality of what we were facing began to sink in.

"If it is all true," said Jonathan, as he shook his head in rising horror, "then what kind of creature have I, in my ignorance, helped to transfer to London?"

NINE

Jonathan met Dr. Van Helsing at his hotel early the next morning and brought him to the house. They arrived so deeply engrossed in conversation, one would never have guessed that they had only just met; it seemed as though they had been friends for years.

"So you think it was Count Dracula that I saw in Piccadilly?" Jonathan said, as we three sat down at the dining-table and helped ourselves to eggs and kippers.

"It is highly likely," Dr. Van Helsing replied.

"But if it *was* him, then he has *grown young*! How is that possible? And what about everything else I saw at the castle? How can it be?"

"The answers to these questions are not so simple, Mr. Harker. I have read the diaries you both with so much honesty and detail have written. You are clever. You reason well. I must ask: after all you see and experience, have you any idea—any suspicion—of the kind of being with which we deal?"

Jonathan glanced briefly at me, then shook his head. "Not really, Doctor."

"When I read Jonathan's diary, I thought—I wondered—" I began, then stopped myself, colouring.

"You wondered what, Madam Mina?"

"Nothing; it is too far-fetched, too ridiculous."

"Ah," Dr. Van Helsing replied with a sigh, "it is the fault of your science, that it wants to explain all; that is why you react thus. Yet we see around us every day the growth of beliefs which think themselves new but which are very old. Tell me, do either of you believe in hypnotism?"

"Hypnotism?" repeated Jonathan. "I never used to; but I suppose I do now, after reading about the work of Jean-Martin Charcot."

"Yes," I concurred. "Charcot's reports are fascinating. He proved that, with his mind, he could read into the very soul of the patients he influenced."

"You are satisfied, then, that hypnotism is possible—a verified science?" We both nodded, and Dr. Van Helsing went on, "From this, I think you must also believe that the reading of thought is possible?"

"I do not know about that," Jonathan said.

"And what about corporeal transference? Materialisation?"

"See here, doctor," Jonathan said, frowning, "I know you said everything that happened to me in Transylvania was true—and it has lifted a load off my mind to think that I did not conjure it up in some fit of madness—but I still do not see how it was all possible; and I do not understand what you are you getting at."

"That is because you think like a solicitor, my young friend. You admire facts: if something you can understand, then that thing *is*. I am saying that there are things which you *cannot understand*, and yet *which are*. Galileo, he grasped the truth about the earth and the heavens, and for this he was found guilty of heresy. Indeed, there are things done to-day in electrical science which would have been deemed unholy by the very men who discovered electricity—who would themselves not so long before have been burned as wizards! Do you know all the mystery of life and death? Can you tell me how the Indian fakir can die and be buried, and his grave sealed and corn sowed upon it, and years later men can dig up the coffin and find the Indian not dead, but that he rise up and walk amongst them?"

"That defies explanation, Doctor," Jonathan said, "if indeed it ever happened."

"Oh, it happened! Many times it has been verified." Setting down his coffee-cup, Dr. Van Helsing looked at us across the table, his eyes gleaming. "Madam Mina: how would you define faith?"

"Faith? I once heard that faith is the faculty which enables us to believe things which we think to be untrue."

"Yes, Madam, precisely! For what I am to tell you now, you must both have this kind of faith. Did you know that men, in all ages and places, believe there are some few beings who live on always and for ever? That there are some men and women who cannot die?"

"I have read such superstitions," I said slowly.

"*Is it superstition?*" Dr. Van Helsing responded. "I admit that I, too, have been sceptic. I have read the teachings and records of the past, which offer their theories and proofs. But I could not believe all that I read; not until I see it with my own eyes. To-day, we are faced with a great puzzle, an enigma—yes? There is still much to learn and discover; but you have seen a part of it, Mr. Harker, in Transylvania; you, Madam Mina, have seen another part at Whitby; and Dr. Seward and I have made further witness with Miss Lucy, in her illness and death."

"With Lucy?" I replied, confused.

"What does Lucy's death have to do with what I went through in Transylvania?" Jonathan asked.

"It has everything to do with it. You know the answer, I think. You are both familiar with the lore of Eastern Europe, are you not? You refer to it in the early pages of your journal, Mr. Harker, but the concept is so alarming that you forget. And you, Madam Mina: you saw Miss Lucy grow pale and weak from loss of blood. You saw the two small, red marks upon her throat—marks which Dr. Seward and I also were alarmed to see, in the days before her death."

"Do you mean the pin-pricks I made, which—" I began; but even as the words left my mouth, the truth came over me in a great rush. It was as if my mind had taken in everything I had seen and read and been told, and at last put it all together like the pieces of some terrible jigsaw puzzle. My entire body tingled with horror, as I cried, "Oh! They were never pin-pricks, were they, Doctor? Those marks on Lucy's throat, they were made by a—by a—"

"Yes?" Dr. Van Helsing waited, his blue eyes flashing.

My voice dropped to a whisper; I had to force myself to go on, barely able to believe the words even as I spoke them: "They were made by a being who—who sucked her blood! A vampire!"

Dr. Van Helsing nodded grimly. "I think so, Madam. Yes: I think so."

Jonathan's face went chalky white. "A vampire? You are saying that vampires are real, not some folk-tale or superstition? That—that the dead can truly come back to life?"

"There are mysteries, my friend, which men can only guess at, which age by age they may solve only in part. I believe we are on the verge of one: the proof that the *nosferatu*—the Un-Dead—exist."

"Oh!" I cried with a shudder.

"Those women at the castle," Jonathan added with animation, "when I felt the sharp points of one's teeth at my neck, I wondered, *could she be*—but I told myself no, it was impossible, it was madness—"

"Just as bats come in the night and suck dry the veins of their victims," Dr. Van Helsing said, "those women I believe would have done the same to you, Mr. Harker, had they the chance."

"My God!" Jonathan cried, horrified.

"And Count Dracula?" I said. "Is he a vampire, too?"

"The Count neither eats nor drinks; he has inhuman strength; he sleeps by day in a deep trance, on the earth of his homeland—which, it is said, is the only way to restore his strength and powers; and he has been seen to grow young, which we are told the *nosferatu* can do, perhaps when fully fed with blood. I think we can safely assume that Count Dracula is a vampire, yes."

"What other fearsome powers does that monster have?" Jonathan cried. "Can he vanish into thin air, as those awful women did?"

"That, I can only guess at present," Dr. Van Helsing replied, "but after reading your accounts, one thing now seems clear: the Count has attained his designs and has gotten to London. How did he get there? By ship, I believe. And where did he first enter the country? I tell you where: I think he docked at Whitby."

"Whitby?" I said, surprised. Then, all at once, the last piece of the puzzle fell into place, and I saw the facts as Dr. Van Helsing saw them. "The fifty boxes of earth!"

Dr. Van Helsing raised his bushy eyebrows at me with approbation. "You have a good and clever wife, Mr. Harker. She sees; she understands! But Madam Mina: if your husband has not yet read your journal, I think you must explain."

I told Jonathan about the ship *Demeter,* its vanished crew, its dead captain, and its strange cargo. "In your diary, Jonathan, you said you found Count Dracula lying in a box of earth in his chapel, and a total of fifty other such boxes which the gipsies were loading onto wagons. Could it be that Count Dracula was aboard the *Demeter,* inside one of those boxes? And en route—" With a grimace, I finished: "he killed every one of those poor sailors to satiate his appetite?"

"I saw a map of England in the Count's library," Jonathan said excitedly, "with various locations circled. One was near London, where his new estate is situated; another was Exeter; and he had circled port cities from Dover to Newcastle, including Whitby! The Count asked endless questions about the means of making consignments at an English port and the forms to be gone through."

"He planned with great care for his arrival," noted Dr. Van Helsing.

"But if his destination was London," I put in, "would it not have been easier to go straight there, or to some other, larger port to the south? Why go to Whitby?"

"Why, indeed?" Dr. Van Helsing said, his forehead furrowed. "It makes no sense to me that the Count went to Whitby—but to Whitby he *did* go, and to the great misfortune of poor Miss Lucy. For it is there, I think, that he first found her, sleep-walking on the cliffs one night. After she went back to London, whether by coincidence or design, he seems to have again found her there."

My mind revolted with sudden, deep hatred for the man who had so grievously assaulted my dearest friend and who had cruelly tormented my husband. Still, I wondered: "Do we know for certain that it was Count Dracula who attacked Lucy in London? It is a huge city. Could there be other creatures like him?"

"Anything is possible, Madam Mina. But in my years of study, I find these beings are few in number, and keep mostly to their own lands. I hear of no such others in England in recent history. Remember, it is not so easy for the vampire to travel. The Count, he must bring so many boxes of earth by ship from Transylvania; and why? To assure his existence here; for without that earth to rest on every day, he will lose his powers and in time perish."

"That would be one way to defeat him, then, would it not?" I asked. "To deny him access to his boxes of earth?"

"Yes! Or to sterilise that earth with holy objects, and thereby render the boxes useless to him."

"Where did all those boxes go, I wonder, after they arrived in Whitby?" Jonathan mused. "Are they still there? Were they shipped to the Count's place in London? Or did he send them all over the map?"

"I would give much to know this also," Dr. Van Helsing replied. "The key now is to find all fifty boxes. If we have them, we have the Count."

We had finished breakfast by then. Dr. Van Helsing wiped his face with his napkin and regarded us with a beaming smile. "Oh! How can I tell you good people what I owe you? I arrive so much in the dark, seeking answers to Miss Lucy's perplexing illness. Thanks to you and your so wonderful diaries, I have learned much: the very name of our foreign enemy, how he reached this country, and even the place where he maybe hide!"

"Carfax," Jonathan replied with a nod.

"I must say, when I read your diary, Mr. Harker, I am astounded to learn that of all places, our foe has purchased an estate in the village of Purfleet, where Dr. Seward himself resides! Where is this old house called Carfax? Is it close to Dr. Seward's property?"

"Very close, in fact. They are both large estates, but they are adjacent to each other."

"Adjacent! This seems to me a very great coincidence."

"Not really, Doctor. I was the agent who arranged the purchase—and it was Dr. Seward who suggested the place."

"Dr. Seward?"

"Yes. Being unfamiliar with properties in London, I applied to every acquaintance I could think of in town for help. Lucy put me in touch with Seward. I know him only through correspondence—he was away when I scouted the area in February—but he said there was an old house with a chapel on the byroad next to his asylum, which might meet all of my client's requirements. I thought it strange at the time that Count Dracula had sought the services of an agent so far off from London to find him a house, instead of someone resident there. He claimed it was to avoid serving a local firm, who might have their own interests at heart. But now I see the truth behind it: he wanted no one to interfere with his privacy and anonymity when he arrived."

"Just so," Dr. Van Helsing replied, sitting back in his chair pensively.

"To think," Jonathan went on angrily, "that the Count is loose on the streets of London at this very moment, to kill and wreak havoc wherever he may—and that I had a hand in making it happen! Oh! It makes my blood boil! If only I had known—"

"Do not berate yourself, Mr. Harker. Had I but better understood—had I known at the first what I know now—the young and beautiful Miss Lucy Westenra would not be in her tomb in a lonely churchyard at Kingstead, on Hampstead Heath. But we must not look back, only forward, so that other souls will not perish."

"Poor, dear Lucy," I said softly. "At least she is at peace; her suffering has ended."

"Not so. Alas!—not so," cried Dr. Van Helsing, shaking his head. "It is not the end for Miss Lucy, but only the beginning."

I stared at him. "The beginning? What do you mean, Doctor?"

The doctor looked up sharply, as if regretting the words he had just spoken; then he frowned and said only: "There are, I fear, still more great and terrible events yet to come. We must wait and see." Glancing at his pocket-watch, he stood and added quickly: "Forgive me, I am out of time. I must catch the next train back to London."

"I will see you to the station," Jonathan said; and we all headed out to the vestibule.

"May I keep, for now, the copies of the journals you so kindly make?" Dr. Van Helsing asked, as he donned his hat and coat. I said that he could, for we had the originals, should we wish to refer to them. He thanked us for breakfast, then put out his hand to me. "Madam Mina, again I express my deepest gratitude for all you have done. You are one of God's women, fashioned by His own hand: so true, so sweet, so noble. I am greatly in your debt."

"I am glad if I have been of some assistance, Doctor."

"Mr. Harker, may I now ask you a favour? Can you share with me any papers you have, about what went before your going to Transylvania? Letters from Count Dracula and such—and the information about this property at Purfleet?"

"I will give you everything I can find, Doctor. The legal documents I will have to copy out and send to you. What else I can do? What about those fifty boxes of earth? Let me trace them! I remember seeing a letter on the Count's desk, addressed to someone in Whitby—perhaps a consignment company. The name will be in my journal. I can make some enquiries and let you know what I discover."

"You are too good, sir," Dr. Van Helsing said with a bow. "There is so much more I could tell you. I have a great task ahead of me, but I fear that Dr. Seward and I cannot do it alone. Perhaps we can all meet again in London in a few days and share what we learn. Will you help us? Will you come?"

Jonathan glanced at me and saw the answer in my eyes. He reached out and took my hand; it was reassuring to feel its touch—once again so strong, so self-reliant, so resolute. "We shall both come, Doctor."

Dr. Van Helsing bowed again. "Thank you. One last request: Madam Mina, will you bring with you your so valuable typewriter?"

"I will. If there is anything we can do to help you hunt down and destroy this terrible Count Dracula, we are with you heart and soul."

JONATHAN RETURNED FROM THE TRAIN STATION FILLED WITH energy and excitement, clutching several newspapers. "I feel like a new man, Mina! I will help find and stop that monster, if it is the last thing I do."

"Thank God Dr. Seward sent for Dr. Van Helsing, or I do not know where we would be."

"Yes. Although something seemed to alarm him just now when I saw him off."

"What do you mean?" I followed Jonathan into the drawing-room, where we both sat down.

"We had just picked up the morning papers and the London papers from last night. While we were talking at the carriage window, waiting for the train to start, he was looking over the *Westminster Gazette*—I knew it by the green paper it was printed on—and his eyes fixed on some article or other. He read intently, his face growing white as he groaned aloud and cried, 'Mijn God! So soon! So soon!' I asked what was wrong; but just then the whistle blew, and he waved good-bye."

"What article was it that alarmed him so?" I asked, for I saw that Jonathan had another copy of the *Westminster Gazette.*

"I cannot be sure, but I have a feeling it is this one." He handed me the paper, indicating a story on the front page:

A HAMPSTEAD MYSTERY

The neighbourhood of Hampstead is just at present exercised with a series of events which seem to run on

> lines parallel to those of what was known to the writers of headlines as "The Kensington Horror," or "The Stabbing Woman," or "The Woman in Black." During the past two or three days several cases have occurred of young children straying from home or neglecting to return from their playing on the Heath. In all these cases the children were too young to give any properly intelligible account of themselves, but the consensus of their excuses is that they had been with a "bloofer lady." It has always been late in the evening when they have been missed, and on two occasions the children have not been found until early morning . . .

The article continued at some length, adding a very serious side to the mystery: all of the children, when found, had been slightly wounded in the throat, with marks that might have been made by a rat or small dog.

"Oh!" I cried, upset. "The marks at the throat! Is it the work of Count Dracula?"

"It would seem so; and yet, the children all claim to have been with a lady—a 'bloofer lady,' the first child called her, whatever that means."

"It was a very little child. Perhaps he meant 'beautiful.'"

Jonathan nodded; then an odd look crossed his face. "Hampstead Heath: isn't that near Hillingham, where Lucy and her mother lived? Didn't Dr. Van Helsing say that Lucy was buried at a churchyard at Hampstead Heath?"

A great horror came over me, for I saw at once where Jonathan was heading. Lucy had been bitten by a vampire—many times, apparently—before she died. I knew next to nothing about such creatures; until recently, I had not even believed they truly existed. Could it be that my dear friend Lucy was now a vampire herself?

Had she risen from the grave?

WE HEARD NOTHING FROM DR. VAN HELSING FOR THE NEXT THREE days. Reports continued in the *Westminster Gazette.* A child was found, terribly weak, who insisted that he wanted to go back to the Heath and play with the beautiful lady. I tossed and turned at night, thinking about poor Lucy, too filled with horror to sleep.

Anxious for more news, I decided to go up to London to see Dr. Van Helsing. At the same time, Jonathan went to Whitby. He had received a courteous reply to his letter to Mr. Billington, the consignment agent who had received the fifty boxes of earth from the *Demeter,* and felt it best to go down and make his enquiries on the spot.

"I am going to trace that horrid cargo of the Count's if it is the last thing I do," he said, as he kissed me good-bye early that morning before leaving for the station.

"I still do not see why you must go to Whitby," I responded. "If we know the Count has a house at Purfleet, why not go straight there and apprehend him?"

"We cannot be certain that he *is* at Purfleet. He may have other properties by now. We need to know what happened to every one of those boxes if we are to trap the Devil in his lair. Send me word of where you are staying in town, Mina, and I will join you in a day or two."

I sent a telegram to Dr. Van Helsing at the Berkeley Hotel, informing him that I would be coming up by train that day. Just as I finished packing my bags and closing up my typewriter in its carrying case, a letter arrived for me. I thought it would be from Dr. Van Helsing; but to my complete surprise, it was from the director of the orphanage in London where I had grown up. He had written a brief note, explaining that he had found the missing envelope to which I had referred, and that it was duly enclosed.

This news, so utterly unexpected, took me back entirely. My

mind had been so filled with other, terrifying thoughts of late that I had entirely forgotten our visit to the London orphanage the week before. Stunned, I stared at the old, faded envelope enclosed. It was of a cheap sort of paper, and had turned slightly brown at the edges with age. It was addressed in pencil in an uneven hand to: "Miss Wilhelmina Murray: Not to be opened until she reaches 18 years of age."

Was it from my mother? I wondered, my heart pounding.

I went to my husband's desk and retrieved a letter-opener. With trembling fingers, I carefully slid the instrument beneath the envelope's fragile flap, trying to do as little damage as possible as I opened it. I slipped out the two folded sheets of writing paper within, which were likewise inscribed in pencil; there was also a tiny, crumpled, faded, pink ribbon. My pulse pounded in my ears as I stared at these items, which seemed to me as precious as the Holy Grail. I sank down onto the chair and read:

5 May, 1875

My dearest daughter:

I must of walked by the orphanage a hundred times since the day I gived you up, hoping I might get a glimpse of you, but they never took the babies out, and I never dared step inside. Once, a few months past, I thought I might of seed you as you walked to school with the other children, but I couldn't be sure it was you, for your a growed girl of seven now, and so changed from when last I held you in my arms. Maybe you were placed in a good family somewhere ages ago. I hope that is true, for that was my wish and dream.

Wilhelmina, my darling girl, I think of you every day. I wonder how you are and what you look like, if your happy, and if you ever think of me. At night I dream of what I might say if we were to meet, but I know that can never be. I've come on hard times, and

I couldn't bear to see the shame in your eyes, to see me now and know that I'm your mother.

I am writing now because I'm ill. The doctor says I'm not long for this world. I didn't want to leave it without telling you how much I loved you, and how hard I tried to keep you. I loved your father. His name was Cuthbert. I believe he truly loved me for a time. I met him while serving as a chambermaid in Marlborough Gardens, Belgravia. The two years I spent at that house were the happiest of my life. I understood when I had to leave. I did my best by you for as long as I could, but work was hard to come by. You needed food, medicine, and clothes, and all I had to give was love.

I have kept this ribbon from your baby bonnet all this time, but I thought you might some day like to have it. I hope they give this letter to you when you are grown, and old enough to understand. Please do not think too poorly of me, Wilhelmina. I will always love you with all my heart.

Your own Mother,
Anna

As I read this missive, I was overcome with emotion. The salutation alone—*My dearest daughter*—caused my eyes to so fill with blinding tears that I could barely continue, and they kept on rolling down my cheeks long after I had finished reading the last line.

Your own Mother, Anna. So that was my mother's name: Anna! Oh! Such a beautiful name; and such a precious piece of information! What a tumult of thoughts and feelings coursed through me! First: deep sadness that she was gone. And then questions: what was her surname? Was it Murray? How old was she? Where did she come from? And what about my father—who was he? Was he another servant in the house? Or did they meet elsewhere?

All my life, I had felt ashamed to think that my mother had given birth to me out of wedlock. The shame was somewhat mitigated now by the knowledge that I had at least come not from a hurried, sullied, forgotten moment—but from love—true love. For a long while I sat and wept for the mother who had loved me, the mother whom I would never know, filled with a longing so great that I thought my aching heart would burst.

I must have re-read the letter a dozen times on the train to London, fingering the tiny, fragile scrap of pink ribbon while dashing away tears. At length, I felt strong enough to put away the envelope and turn my mind to other things. To my surprise, a wire was delivered to me *en route*:

PURFLEET 29 SEPTEMBER 1890

MRS. MINA HARKER

VAN HELSING CALLED BACK TO AMSTERDAM. I WILL MEET YOU AT STATION.

JOHN SEWARD, M.D.

When I arrived at Paddington Station, I searched through the bustling crowd on the platform for a sign of Dr. Seward, hoping I would be able to pick him out, even though we had never met. As the crowd thinned, I spotted a tall, handsome, strong-jawed gentleman wearing a dark brown suit, who looked to be about thirty years old, and was glancing about uneasily.

I stepped up to him with a hesitant smile. "Dr. Seward, is it not?"

"And you are Mrs. Harker!" He took the hand I offered with a shy, nervous grin. "The professor sends his apologies."

"The professor?"

"I mean Dr. Van Helsing. To me, he will always be the professor, as he was my most valued teacher. He had to dash off very suddenly—he had something to do back home, and will return to-morrow night. I take it you got my wire?" Although he was making every effort to be charming, I sensed that he was very upset about something, a fact which he was struggling to hide.

"Yes. Thank you. I knew you from the description of poor dear Lucy, and—" I stopped, a blush rising to my cheeks; for even though I knew Dr. Seward had proposed to Lucy, it was unlikely *he* knew I was in possession of his secret.

At the mention of Lucy's name his smile fled, and he appeared even more anxious than before. What prompted this reaction? I wondered. Was it grief over Lucy's passing? Had he guessed what I was thinking? Or was it something else of which I was unaware? Just then his eyes met mine, and we shared a brave little smile, which seemed to set us both more at ease.

"Allow me to get your luggage," he said. This accomplished, he went on in a kind and noble but rather distracted manner: "Forgive me, Mrs. Harker, but the professor and I have been much preoccupied the past few days with—with some difficult matters. We did not have a chance to discuss your coming, or how he intends for us to proceed with—" He broke off.

"I understand. I appreciate your meeting me, Dr. Seward. If you would be so kind as to take me to the Berkeley Hotel—I believe that is where Dr. Van Helsing has been staying?—I will simply wait there until he returns."

"No—I did not mean that, Mrs. Harker. You need not go to the expense of a hotel. In fact, it was the professor's express wish that you and your husband should stay with me. I would be happy to provide you with a suite of rooms at my house in Purfleet. Unless—"

"Unless?"

"Did Dr. Van Helsing mention the kind of work that I do?"

"Yes." Although I tried to sound matter-of-fact, a little shiver danced through me. "He said that—that you are the proprietor of a private insane asylum."

"That is so. But be advised that it is a very large country house.

The patients all come from well-to-do families, live on a completely separate floor, and are well looked after. You would not be obliged to see any of them. Given the nature of the work ahead of us, it would be convenient, I think, if you were near at hand. Would you feel comfortable with such an arrangement, Mrs. Harker? If not, you have only to say the word, and I will find you a hotel."

I hesitated. I had never been to an insane asylum, and had had little contact with the mentally ill. It was certainly not the kind of place where I preferred to stay. However, it did make more sense for Jonathan and I to stay with Dr. Seward in Purfleet, rather than in London proper. Another reason came to mind, too, which made the idea particularly appealing: it would afford me an opportunity to see Carfax, the adjacent property belonging to the mysterious Count Dracula. I managed a small smile and said: "Thank you. I will accept your kind offer, Dr. Seward."

He immediately sent a wire to his housekeeper to have a room prepared for me. I sent a wire to Jonathan, informing him of where I was staying. We then took the Underground to Fenchurch Street, a large and bustling station, where we boarded a train to Purfleet, Essex, a journey of some sixteen miles. Since we shared a compartment with several others, I kept my voice low as I informed Dr. Seward about Jonathan's hurried excursion to Whitby. He nodded but made little comment; he still seemed very distracted, and the anxiety I had noticed upon my arrival had not gone away. I wondered what was on his mind and how best to gain his confidence.

"I understand that it was you, Dr. Seward, who first summoned Dr. Van Helsing to London to attend Lucy?"

"Yes."

"For this I must extend my gratitude, for he seems to be a man of fine intellect. If any one can find and bring down this horrible Count Dracula, I think it is he."

"I hope so."

"Have you seen the property that Jonathan purchased for the Count?"

"We have only made a cursory inspection. It does not appear as though any one is living there yet."

"I did not see yesterday's copy of the *Westminster Gazette.* Have there been any more sightings of the mysterious lady on Hampstead Heath?"

Dr. Seward's face went ashen at this. Glancing at the other occupants of the train compartment, he lowered his voice and said, alarmed: "I think it best that we reserve this discussion for a later time, Mrs. Harker."

I fell silent and looked out the window, greatly worried. Were my fears and intuitions about Lucy correct? Had Lucy risen from the grave? Had something else of dire consequence occurred since I last spoke with Dr. Van Helsing? If so, what?

IN SHORT ORDER WE ARRIVED AT DR. SEWARD'S HOUSE, WHICH was situated on lovely, spacious, wooded grounds. It was immense—three storeys high—and built of dark red brick, with a large new wing of clean brick. If not for the discreet sign by the front entrance, which read PURFLEET ASYLUM, I would never have guessed that it was anything other than a respectable gentleman's country seat.

As we crossed the threshold, however, and entered the marbled hall, I heard a strange, low moan emanate from somewhere down the corridor, followed by an eerie laugh. Is this what I could expect to be hearing every day, I thought with a shudder, while staying under this roof?

If Dr. Seward noticed my discomfort, he did not mention it, only saying: "Are you hungry, Mrs. Harker? May I order you something to eat?"

"No thank you. I ate on the train. I am most anxious to speak with you about the matter at hand and to get to work if there is any way that I can be of help."

"In that case, I will have my housekeeper show you promptly to your room. Feel free to meet me in my study as soon as you are settled."

I was directed to a very nice bedroom up on the first floor, where my luggage was deposited. I took only a moment or two to tidy myself, and then went back down-stairs to Dr. Seward's study, which had been pointed out to me. As I approached in the passage, I heard him talking with someone within. I paused a moment outside the door; but at length, since he was expecting me, I knocked. His conversation ceased, and I heard him say: "Come in."

I entered. It was a very large room, lined with bookcases on three sides and furnished so as to serve as a comfortable parlour and study as well as a meeting-room. There was a sofa and an arrangement of tables and armchairs on one side, a long table surrounded by chairs in the centre, and a good-sized desk on the other, where Dr. Seward was sitting. To my surprise, however, there was no one else with him.

Suddenly, I understood to whom—or should I say, to what—he had been speaking. On a table opposite to him was a brand-new machine, a sizeable wooden box with an assortment of metal fittings across the top. One of these fittings was a horizontal, spindle-shaped device holding a wax cylinder, which I knew was designed—incredibly—to record and play back the spoken word.

"Is that a phonograph?" I said excitedly.

"It is indeed."

"I have read about such things! Mr. Edison is a great genius. What do you use it for?"

"I keep my diary in it."

"Your diary? On a phonograph? Why, this outdoes even shorthand! May I hear it say something?"

"Certainly." He stood up to put it in train for speaking; but then he paused, troubled. "On second thought, perhaps not. Everything on these cylinders is about my cases, Mrs. Harker, so it would be awkward—" He stopped.

"Oh! I understand," I replied, trying to help him out of his embarrassment. "A diary is very personal, and your thoughts on your cases, I presume, are not meant to be shared."

"Yes. Thank you."

"Perhaps you could play just one part of it for me."

"Which part is that?"

"You helped attend my dear friend Lucy at the end, did you not?"

"I did."

"Let me hear how she died."

A look of sudden horror crossed his face, and he answered: "No! No! For all the world, I wouldn't let you know that terrible story!"

A grave, terrible feeling came over me. Clearly there *was* more to the story of Lucy's death than had yet been revealed. "If I am to be of any help to you, Doctor, in our effort to find this vile Count, then I should know everything you can tell me—don't you agree? Dr. Van Helsing has already shared the events leading up to Lucy's death. I know that she was deprived of blood time and again by that foul being, and that despite all your efforts, she perished. I am only asking to hear the details as you experienced them; for Lucy was very, very dear to me."

His face was by then a positively deathly pallor, and he stammered: "What happened at the end—the very end—it is too horrifying to tell, Mrs. Harker. I would not wish you to hear my account of it. No! I will leave that to Dr. Van Helsing, when he returns." I noticed that his hand had begun to shake.

My glance now fell on a great batch of typewriting on the table, which was very familiar to me. "I see that you have the transcripts I made of my and my husband's diaries, which I gave to Dr. Van Helsing."

"Yes. I am most anxious to look at them, but I have not had the opportunity. The professor only gave them to me before he left."

"Did he tell you anything of our experiences, or of the discussion we had three days ago?"

"No, nothing." With a tentative little smile, he added: "Other than the fact that you both have a great personal interest in this matter and that you are a 'pearl among women.' "

"There is little basis for his high opinion of me, I fear; it seems to be based solely on the fact that I am a very neat typist." With a sigh, I added: "I see you do not know me, Doctor. When you have read those papers, you will know me better." I glanced out the window; it was late afternoon but still light out. "I have been sitting most of the day. If you will permit me, I think I will take a long walk, and then a nap. That should give you sufficient time to read through those documents; and then, perhaps, you will trust me enough to take me into your confidence."

He bowed his head in assent. "I have called for dinner at eight, Mrs. Harker, but it can be delayed if necessary. Come down whenever you wake from your nap."

I thanked him again, then retrieved my hat and shawl from my room. I left the house in a disquieted state of mind, with one object only—to get some fresh air and exercise—having no inkling of the person I was about to encounter, or the adventure which lay before me.

TEN

As I ventured down the long, gravel drive that led from the asylum's front entrance to the lane, I breathed in deeply of the scents of pine, oak, and elm from the wooded grounds around me. The deciduous trees were on the crest of their colour change, beginning their annual shift from green to dramatic reds and golds. The afternoon sun was low in a hazy sky, and the air was a pleasant temperature, alive with the sounds of birds and distantly bleating sheep. For a few minutes, I allowed myself to forget the reason I had come here and to simply enjoy the pleasure of being in the country-side again.

In reaching the lane, I remembered that Dr. Seward's property was immediately adjacent to the estate which now belonged to Count Dracula. Dr. Seward had pointed the place out to me from the carriage when we passed by earlier upon my arrival.

My pulse began to race excitedly. Did I dare investigate? The doctor had said that no one had moved in next door; but what if he was wrong? So filled with curiosity was I to see the place that I pushed back my fears and hastened down the lane to study the great stone wall which appeared to entirely enclose the neighbouring property. The wall, at least ten feet high, was fronted by a set of very old and rusted iron gates, which were securely chained and locked. Disappointed, I saw that any further exploration would be impossible.

I peered through the iron bars of the gates. The place was just as Jonathan had described it. A long driveway choked with weeds led through spacious grounds, which were dense with trees. Through the foliage, I could make out a dark pond to one side and the great house beyond. It was four storeys high, very large and old, and seemed to have been added on to in different architectural styles at various periods of its history. One part, dating perhaps to late medieval times, was of immensely thick stone with heavily barred windows.

The entire place looked neglected and deserted. The surrounding woods were eerily silent. If indeed the Count had taken up residence, there was no sign of it.

Despite this, as I stood looking in through the front gates, I had the strangest feeling of being watched—a feeling I had not had since that morning nearly two months past, after the great storm at Whitby. My heart lurched as my gaze was drawn to a window in the upper floor of the ancient building. Was that a shadow, or was someone standing within? A quiver ran through my body; then I could not help but laugh at my own folly. Surely it was nothing but the late-afternoon sun glinting weakly against the grimy glass.

Leaving the old residence, I walked down the wooded byroad, which took me to the main road. Another fifteen minutes' walk took me back into the heart of Purfleet. As Dr. Seward and I had gone straight to his house from the train station, I had gotten no more than a glimpse of the pretty little village on the Thames, with the chalk hills in the distance. I saw now that it was a very picturesque place, with a few scattered rows of houses, several small shops, and a Royal Hotel, which advertised its "World Famous Fish Dinners." There was, however, nothing of great interest there to occupy me for any length of time.

As I approached the train station, I passed a young woman walking hand in hand with a little girl. It was clear from their conversation that they were mother and daughter, and were very close. They presented such a charming and affectionate picture that I felt a pang of envy. My mind drifted to the letter I had received that morning from my own mother—Anna—a letter I had already read so many times, I knew much of it by heart: "I loved your father. His name was Cuthbert. I believe he truly loved me for a time. I met him while serving as a chambermaid in Marlborough Gardens, Belgravia. The two years I spent at that house were the happiest of my life . . ."

A sharp whistle sounded from an approaching train. I saw that it was heading in the direction of London. It was not a long journey. It was several hours yet until dinner. I could, I realised, get to town and back before any one would miss me. I could try to find Marlborough Gardens, Belgravia—the street where my mother had lived and worked when she had fallen in love with my father and had created me.

Without further thought, I hurried to the ticket window, purchased my ticket, and breathlessly jumped on board the train. I found an empty compartment and took a seat by the window. A few minutes later, I heard the hissing steam escaping from below me as the train bumped and lurched into motion. A uniformed man took my ticket and withdrew. I was sitting lost in thought, gazing out at the passing country-side, when I heard the compartment door slide open again.

I glanced at the new arrival, who was standing in the doorway—and my heart nearly stopped beating.

It was Mr. Wagner.

❧

I FELT FOR A MOMENT AS IF I COULD NOT BREATHE.

Mr. Wagner took two steps into the compartment and paused, staring at me as if in disbelief. I had thought of him so often since last we met, recalling in infinite detail his handsome face and figure, each time wondering if I was remembering him to be more perfect than he was. Now, I saw that my memory had not done him justice. Oh! How wonderful it was to see that dear face again! He was dressed as always in a black frock coat, with the addition of a magnificent, long, black cloak draped lazily over his broad shoulders.

"From my window, I thought I saw you board the train." His dark blue eyes glowed with astonished happiness as he looked at me. "I could not believe it."

"Mr. Wagner," was all that I could manage. My heart was pounding in such a frenzy, I could scarcely think.

"It has been a long time."

"Six weeks."

"You have been counting."

A blush spread across my cheeks. He smiled and said:

"May I join you?"

"Please." I gestured towards the empty seat across from me, feeling as if I were wrapped in some kind of dream.

He sat, his eyes fixed upon me intensely. For some moments, the only sounds in the compartment were the clicking of the wheels below us and the rhythmic puffing of the engine. "Are you well?"

"I am. And you, sir?"

"Quite well."

I had held so many imaginary conversations with him in my mind; yet now, in his presence, I struggled for words. "I thought you might have long since returned to Austria."

"No. I have often thought of you since that last morning in Whitby. Did you make it to Buda-Pesth?"

"Yes."

"How did you find your man?"

"Very ill. He had been in hospital for quite some time, suffering from a terrible shock."

"A shock?"

"Yes. I helped to nurse him, and—and we were married—and returned home to Exeter."

If he was surprised or disappointed to find me married, he hid it well. "Then it is Miss Murray no longer?"

"It is Mrs. Harker." I blushed despite myself, as I lowered my gaze.

"Congratulations. I hope you are happy?"

"Yes, very."

"I am pleased to hear it. Pray, tell me: to what do I owe this extraordinary coincidence? How is it that you happen to be here to-day, Mrs. Harker, on this very train?"

I hesitated. "My husband had business in town, and I thought to join him. We are staying with a friend in Purfleet. Jonathan is away at Whitby until to-morrow, on—on an errand."

"At Whitby?"

"Yes. It *is* ironic, I suppose," I added with a smile. "The last time I saw you, *I* was at Whitby and Jonathan was away; and now it is the reverse."

He returned my smile. "Indeed. And it is wonderful that we should find each other again so unexpectedly. I am most grateful for it."

"How is it that you come to be here, sir?"

"I have been to see some property in West Essex. I am on my way back to London now. Are you also bound for town?"

"Yes."

"Not for business or shopping, though, I think? It is a bit late in the day for that. You are visiting a friend, perhaps?"

"No." I paused. He continued to look at me so questioningly, that I felt compelled to explain. "If I tell you why I am going, you will think me foolish."

"I doubt that."

With a sigh, I said: "I had a sudden impulse to see the house where my mother lived and worked."

"Your mother?" he replied, surprised. "Have you heard from her, then?"

"She left me a letter many years ago, before she died. I only just received it to-day. I now know her name was Anna, and that my father's surname was Cuthbert. She said she worked for several years at a house in Belgravia."

"Was she indeed a chambermaid? The story you overhead as a child, was it true?"

"It seems that it was." I was flattered that he recalled the details of my little personal history, of which I had spoken so anxiously the day we went boating. From my bag, I took the envelope containing my mother's precious letter and showed it to him. "She said she loved me, sir, and wanted to keep me. It meant a great deal to hear that."

"I imagine it would," he said kindly. "And now, you are on your way to Belgravia to—what?"

"I do not know exactly. To try to find the street where she lived, I suppose. Just to see what it looks like."

"An honourable quest, and not foolish at all. I understand and commend it. Do you have the address?"

"She just said Marlborough Gardens."

"That should not be difficult to find. May I have the honour of accompanying you on this mission, Mrs. Harker? It is not the best idea for a woman to traverse the streets of London on her own at this hour, even in Belgravia. My evening is quite free, and perhaps I can be of some assistance."

"Thank you, Mr. Wagner," I replied instantly and with a smile, grateful for an excuse to spend more time with him. "I would be glad of your company."

We chatted all the way into town. At first, we reminisced about the times we had shared in Whitby. He asked if I had done any more dancing since then. I replied with regret that I had not. Mr. Wagner explained that he had travelled a great deal since we last met and was very fond of trains.

"Your English trains are wonderful, so efficient, and they run so frequently. You can go anyplace you like on a whim—halfway across the country if you wish—spend a few delightful hours, and return just as swiftly." He was equally praiseworthy about the underground railway system. "There is nothing like it anywhere in the world. Such an enormous and progressive undertaking! Such a feat of engineering! I have followed its development in the newspapers with great interest ever since they first began building it."

"Perhaps not since they *first* began," I said with a laugh. "The first section, I believe, opened seven-and-twenty years ago. You would have been a very little boy."

"I took an interest at a very early age."

When we reached town, he hailed a hansom cab to take us to Belgravia. As he sat down beside me within the confines of the cab, his nearness caused a heat to course through me, and my heart continued to pound in the same erratic rhythm that had begun the moment I first saw him. "Have you been in London long?" I asked.

"Some weeks now. I have visited all the great sights you mentioned when last we met, and many more. I find it a far more modern and cosmopolitan city than any capital I have seen in Europe."

"You do not prefer Paris?"

"Not at all." In a deep, thrilling tone, he added: "Paris is old-world. London is everything new: the great, teeming hub of the world."

It was early evening when our hansom cab arrived at Marlborough Gardens, and it had grown quite dark. I suddenly felt very foolish for having dashed off to London on my own on the cusp of night, and was grateful to have Mr. Wagner as my escort.

"How lovely," I murmured, as we began walking down the narrow, tree-lined street, with long rows of tall, white, aristocratic-looking town-houses on either side. All the houses looked exactly alike: five storeys high, with many balconied windows framed by intricately carved cornice work and noble-looking columns.

"Just think," I said in wonder, "my own mother walked up this street hundreds, perhaps thousands of times. She lived inside one of these beautiful houses. She might have swept that very doorstep every day for years. Oh! How I wish I had known her."

"Perhaps you can learn something of her."

"How?"

"You know her name, and your father's surname. We could make a few enquiries and find out if any one remembers them."

"Oh, no! I would not think of disturbing any one. It would be most unlikely that any one could help me. My father could have been any one, from a groom to the postman, and my mother was only a maid. She lived here but a few short years, and it was more than two-and-twenty years ago."

"Yes, but considering the circumstances under which she left—"

My cheeks grew warm. "The scandal, you mean?"

"I do not consider it as such, Mrs. Harker; however, I think people in general do tend to remember such things and enjoy talking about them."

"What would I say?" I replied with a mortified laugh. "That I am looking for a maid called Anna—possibly Anna Murray—who left her employment because she was with child?"

"Precisely."

"I should die of shame!" I turned and began walking rapidly back in the direction from which we had come. "Thank you for helping me find the street, sir. I am happy to have seen it. I am very satisfied. Now let us depart."

"Wait! All your life, you have wondered about your mother," Mr. Wagner said as he kept pace with me, his handsome face bathed in the moonlight. "You have come all this way. Here is your chance to satisfy that curiosity. It would be a shame to leave without at least making an attempt."

I slowed my steps, still filled with embarrassment; but some inner voice told me that he was right.

"What are you afraid of?" he persisted.

"I am afraid," I blurted quietly, "that if any one *should* remember my mother, he will look down on me for being her daughter."

Mr. Wagner touched my arm and stopped me—a contact which sent a tingle up my spine. "If any one does, that is his own problem, not yours. Your mother loved you and did what she thought best for you. You should be proud of that. In any case, you need not say that you are her daughter, if you prefer; only that you are seeking information about her."

I suddenly felt ashamed of my weakness and discomfiture. "You once told me not to care so much about what other people think. You said, 'throw caution to the wind.' But that is more easily said than done."

"Nothing truly worth doing is ever easily done."

I smiled at that, and then took a deep breath, gathering my courage. "Where should we start?"

It was like a little game at first. We stopped at the house directly in front of us and knocked at the door. The maid who answered was even younger than myself, and knew nothing about any servants who had been employed in the vicinity more than two decades before. It was the same at the other houses; even the middle-aged servants and housekeepers, who were old enough to recall the comings and goings in the neighbourhood, had no memory of a maid called Anna or a man called Mr. Cuthbert. We were treated to several other tales, however, about girls who had "got themselves in the family way while in service" over the years, and who had gone off and were never heard from again.

I was ready to give up when Mr. Wagner insisted we try once more place. Once again, the cheerful maid who answered was too young to be of any assistance.

"Sorry, miss," she said. "I've been at this house ten years now, but I wouldn't know nought about what went on before my time."

"Is there a family called Cuthbert in the neighbourhood, or a servant or coachman with that name who is perhaps forty years of age or older?" I asked, a question I had posed at every house along the way.

"No, miss. Not that I know of."

She was about to close the door, when Mr. Wagner asked: "By any chance, is there a man in the area whose Christian name is Cuthbert?"

"Well, there's Sir Cuthbert Sterling who lives at Number 24 down the street. We don't see too much of him, though, for he has a seat in the Parliament. When he's not working, he's out with Lady Sterling."

My pulse quickened. "Has he lived there long?"

"Oh, the Sterlings have lived on this street for ever, or so I'm told—nigh on to fifty years."

We thanked her and walked away. "Well!" Mr. Wagner said, raising his eyebrows. "This is an interesting development."

"The man is in Parliament," I returned sceptically. "He has lived here fifty years. He is probably eighty years old!" The challenge in Mr. Wagner's eyes, however, was impossible to ignore. "All right," I said, laughing. "We will go and ask. But this is positively the *last* enquiry. I must get back before Dr. Seward becomes concerned about me."

I had difficulty making out the house numbers in the dim glow of the street-lamps, but Mr. Wagner could read them with ease. He found Number 24 and knocked. The door was answered by a stout, sensible-looking, middle-aged woman in a starched maid's uniform, whose auburn hair was laced with grey. As she lifted her eyes to mine, her placid expression instantly dissolved, replaced by stunned amazement.

"Good gracious!" she cried, her hand flying to her mouth. "Anna Murray? How can it be? But no, no, forgive me—that's quite impossible."

The woman's outburst—and the name she'd spoken, *Anna Murray*—took me by such surprise that I nearly forgot what I had intended to say. "Is . . . Sir Cuthbert Sterling at home?" I managed, my heart pounding.

"I'm sorry." She glanced at Mr. Wagner, but his charming smile only seemed to add to her discomposure. "He and Lady Sterling are out at present. May I tell them who called?"

"My name is Mrs. Harker. Forgive me—but you called me a name just now: Anna Murray. My maiden name was Murray. I came to enquire about a young woman who worked in this neighbourhood some two-and-twenty years ago. Her name was Anna. I think she was my mother."

A soft look now came into the woman's eyes as she studied me, and her lips began to quiver. "I thought I was seeing a ghost," she said, shaking her head wonderingly. "Yes. Yes. You're the spitting image of her, you are, except for the eyes. Anna had dark brown eyes."

"You knew her, then?" My heart leapt. "Did she work in this house?"

"She did. It was a long time ago, when I first started in service here. We were chambermaids together. She was eighteen years old when she—when she was obliged to leave. I always wondered what became of her."

"It seems she passed away when I was a little girl. I would love to know more about her if you would be willing to share what you remember."

She opened her mouth to reply, then shut it again. The gleam went out of her eyes with the suddenness of a candle blowing out. "I'm afraid that won't be possible."

"I could come back if this is not a convenient time."

The maid shook her head, looking very worried now. "That wouldn't be a good idea. I'm sorry, but I'm going to have to ask you to leave."

"Think how much it would mean to the young lady," Mr. Wagner interjected quickly and gently, gazing directly into the woman's eyes, "to have a tour of the home where her mother once lived and worked. Surely you could spare her a few minutes."

The woman froze, staring at him; then she turned to me and said in a somewhat dazed voice, "You had best come in, ma'am."

I had witnessed a similar reaction once before, I realised: outside the post office at Whitby, when Mr. Wagner had somehow redirected the attentions of my inquisitive landlady. As I darted him a grateful but puzzled look, he only stepped back and said with a smile, "I will wait for you out here."

It was a brief but memorable tour. The maid said her name was Miss Hornsby. She showed me the grand, high-ceilinged drawing-room, a beautiful library, and a sitting-room on the ground floor. As we ascended the staircase to the servants' quarters, I could hear the sounds of children laughing and romping about on the first floor, and the stern voice of someone in command. Knowing that I was climbing the very same steps that my mother had used—and then, seeing the very chamber where my mother used to sleep—filled me with such emotion that I was moved to tears.

"I was one of four chambermaids in the old days," Miss Hornsby said as we made our way back down-stairs, "when the house belonged to Sir Cuthbert's father, God rest his soul. It was a never-ending job keeping this house clean, I can tell you, barely a minute to ourselves, and only one day a month off to go home. Not that Anna had a home to go to."

"She had no parents?"

"No. She never talked much about herself, but she did say she lost both her parents to illness and went into service at a young age. She was a cheerful sort, and very pretty. She didn't have much schooling, but she taught herself to read, and was very fond of books. She was always trying to better herself. And she had a way of knowing things that were going to happen before they did, if you know what I mean."

"No; what do you mean, Miss Hornsby?"

"Well, I remember one time when a gentleman friend was supposed to meet me on a Sunday to walk me to church, and he didn't come. Anna said, 'He's had an accident, hurt his left foot in the stable-yard,' and so it proved. She was like that. She always knew to the minute when young Master Cuthbert was coming home from University for one of his surprise visits, even when his own mother didn't have a clue. I used to tell Anna that she must be descended from gipsy stock, and could have earned her living as a fortune-teller if she chose."

This information so filled me with wonder that I could barely speak—a feeling intensified by the fact that I now had no further doubts as to who my father was. We were approaching the foyer when I finally found my voice again. "Miss Hornsby: you said you were my mother's friend. Is it too much to hope for—when she left, did she by any chance leave any of her belongings behind?"

Miss Hornsby pursed her lips, thinking. "Now that you mention it, I think she did give me something, which I might have kept. I will look for it. You must tell me where to send it."

While she went in search of a piece of paper and a fountain-pen, I heard a carriage draw up outside. Miss Hornsby returned; and while I was writing down my home address, the front door flew open and a well-dressed lady and gentleman entered. They both looked to be about forty years of age. From their manner, and from Miss Hornsby's mortified, averted gaze and deferential curtsey, it was clear that they were the master and mistress of the house.

"Good evening, Hornsby," replied the gentleman heartily, handing her his hat and coat. "And who might this be?" As his eyes caught mine (green eyes that mirrored my own), his mouth dropped open, and he froze, with an expression so stunned that I thought he might drop dead on the marbled floor before me.

"Is this a friend of yours, Hornsby?" asked Lady Sterling in some confusion.

"Yes, and she was just leaving, madam," Miss Hornsby replied quickly.

Sir Cuthbert took two steps back, still staring at me in consternation. Recovering my wits, I gave Miss Hornsby the fountain-pen and paper, saying, "It was so nice to see you. Good-night."

No sooner had I gained the front step than the door slammed shut behind me. Mr. Wagner, who was waiting beneath a near-by tree, hurried to join me. "I saw them draw up. Was he—"

"Yes. I fear I gave him quite a shock."

"Forgive me. I placed you in a very awkward situation."

"Please, do not apologise. I am glad I did it." I smiled; and then a little laugh bubbled up from inside me. "If not for you, I would never have knocked on a single door on this street, and I would still know nothing about my parents. Now I think I can say with assurance that I am the daughter of a member of Parliament and a gipsy!"

ELEVEN

In the cab back to the train station, I told Mr. Wagner everything that had passed during my brief visit to the Sterlings' mansion.

"How remarkable to think that you look so much like your mother."

"I did not know whether to laugh or cry when Sir Cuthbert caught sight of me. Did he think I was my mother's ghost come back to haunt him? Or did he realise that I was his daughter?"

"For all we know, he may never have been aware of your existence."

"True."

"Do you intend to contact him again?"

"No."

"Why not?"

"I want nothing from him. He has a wife and family. I think I can safely assume that they know nothing about me. My mother was eighteen years old when she left that house; he could not have been much older. I am a mistake from his past. I am happy—very happy—to have seen his face this once, to have the mystery of my birth solved, and to know that my mother loved him; but I would not wish to cause him any pain."

"An admirable view," he said quietly, with a smile.

When we reached the train station, I expected to say good-bye to Mr. Wagner, a circumstance I anticipated with great melancholy. To my surprise, he bought tickets for both of us back to Purfleet.

"But you are staying in London," I said. "Please do not go so far out of town on my account."

"I would not think of allowing you to return unaccompanied at this hour," he insisted.

We were obliged to share a train compartment with three other people and remained silent for most of the journey, my mind full of all that had just happened.

When we exited the train at Purfleet, Mr. Wagner said, "It is late. I will not be satisfied until I have delivered you to your door. Where you are staying?"

I hesitated before answering. I knew I would have to devise some explanation were I to be seen arriving at the house in Mr. Wagner's company; but I was also relieved by his offer, for I had not looked forward to walking down the dark country lanes alone. It was with some embarrassment that I admitted: "I am staying at Purfleet Asylum, about a mile down the road."

"An asylum? Indeed?"

It had grown chilly, and I wrapped my shawl more tightly around me. "I know it sounds strange, but a friend of mine is the proprietor of the establishment. The house is large and very comfortable."

"It is too cold to walk. Wait here, while I find a cab."

There were no cabs to be found, but Mr. Wagner persuaded a local man to let him hire his gig for an hour, apparently paying very well for the privilege. As its owner happily walked off towards the inn with coin in hand, Mr. Wagner assisted me to board the vehicle and moved around to the driver's side.

Just then, the wind picked up, gusting through the area with such force that it stirred up a quantity of rubbish near-by and sent a pile of empty crates clattering to the ground. The horse reared up and whinnied in alarm. Mr. Wagner darted up to the horse and placed his hands upon its face, petting it and speaking to it in a low, soothing tone; he then whispered something in its ears. Under his caresses, the horse immediately quieted down.

When Mr. Wagner leapt on board, I said admiringly: "You have quite a way with horses."

"'The wind of heaven is that which blows between a horse's ears.'"

I recognised the Arabian proverb, and smiled. We got under way. I soon found myself trembling, a reaction which I suspect had more to do with the touch of Mr. Wagner's thigh against mine than the temperature of the night air.

"Take my cloak," he said, as he removed said garment and draped it about my shoulders.

"Then you will be cold, sir."

"I promise you, I will not."

We rode in silence for a while. Sadness welled up within me, aware as I was that every movement of the chaise only brought me closer to the moment when Mr. Wagner and I would be obliged to part. "I am grateful to you, sir," I murmured. "You gave me courage to-night when I needed it most; the courage to fulfill a dream."

"I am glad."

"How can I ever thank you?"

As he drove, Mr. Wagner took my gloved hand in his and brought it to his lips, saying softly: "By allowing me to see you again."

My heart began to pound. "You are always welcome to visit me and my husband, sir, while we are in town."

"Your husband?" He dropped my hand and let out a low, ironic laugh. "I have no interest in seeing your husband, madam."

I had no answer to that and fell silent, my cheeks growing hot.

He looked at me. "All these weeks, since last we saw each other—have you ever thought of me?"

"Of course I have," I responded in a voice I barely recognised.

He commanded the horses to stop and turned to me, his handsome face glowing in the moonlight as his eyes met mine. He rested his cool hand upon my burning cheek, a touch so intimate that it caused me to gasp aloud. In a soft, deep voice, he said: "I have thought of little else but you."

"Every day, I wondered where you were and how you were," I whispered.

"I have done the same. I thought you were lost to me for ever; yet I could not forget you. I can never forget you, Mina."

It was the first time he had called me Mina, a familiarity reserved for only the closest of relations. He leaned nearer now, until his face was just inches from mine. Desire coursed through me. I was possessed by a desperate need to feel his lips pressed against my own. Hot tears threatened, and it seemed as if my very throat might close.

"Perhaps," I said brokenly, "if I had not been engaged when we first met, things would be different. But I *was* engaged. And now I am married!" I broke away from him and threw off his cloak. "This is wrong. Wrong! I am sorry. I cannot see you again!"

I flung open the door, leapt down from the chaise, and ran off in anguish down the wooded lane.

AT THE ASYLUM'S FRONT DOOR, A MAID ANSWERED MY QUIET knock. I hurried up to my room, where I sank down upon the bed and burst into tears.

Oh! The folly of the human heart! There was no longer any point denying it: I was in love with Mr. Wagner! Madly, deeply, desperately in love! How was it possible, I wondered miserably, to love two men at the same time? For I did love my husband, very dearly. My feelings for Jonathan were different, however, than those I had for Mr. Wagner. They were softer and quieter, founded in a life-long friendship and respect.

The very thought of Mr. Wagner, on the other hand, caused my pulse to race; and being in his company—hearing his voice—feeling his touch—filled me with an electric excitement such as I had never before experienced. In saying good-bye to him, I felt as though my body had been cut in two. But what other choice had I? None. None! I was a married woman; and to be in his presence was, and always had been, a temptation nearly impossible to resist. I had already gone far beyond the bounds of propriety just in spending so much time alone with him; and the thoughts now coursing through my mind and heart went against any semblance of decency and morality.

For some minutes I lay on the bed, crying bitterly; but this, I knew, would never do. Gathering my strength of mind, I dried my eyes and repeated aloud the lines from my favourite Shakespeare sonnet:

. . . Love is not love
Which alters when it alteration finds,
Or bends with the remover to remove:
O no! it is an ever-fixed mark
That looks on tempests and is never shaken . . .

My love for Jonathan, I reminded myself, was an ever-fixed mark. It was constant and true. It could not be shaken by adversity or changed by time. I had felt temptation, and I had not wavered. My love would bear out, as Shakespeare had written, even until the edge of doom.

I glanced up at the clock on the mantel: it was nearly half-past eight. Dr. Seward must wonder what had become of me. I went to the basin, splashed water on my face, and straightened my hair, determined to put an end to this paroxysm of emotion and to keep my evening's outing to myself.

I VENTURED DOWN-STAIRS TO DR. SEWARD'S STUDY, WHERE I found him at his desk, absorbed in reading my typewritten pages. Upon seeing me, he leapt to his feet. "Mrs. Harker. I told the cook to hold supper, as I did not wish to disturb you."

"Thank you," I replied, relieved to learn that he had not missed me.

He eyed me with concern. "Are you quite well?"

I lied: "I am; although—I have been thinking about poor Lucy, and about all that Jonathan has suffered."

"Ah. I understand your distress. I have read your diary, and I am more than halfway through with your husband's. You were right, Mrs. Harker. You have both been through a great deal. I should have trusted you earlier, for Lucy spoke so highly of you." He moved around the desk to stand beside me. "You said you wanted to know how Lucy died."

"Yes."

"I warn you: it is a terrible tale, but if you still wish to hear it—"

"I do, Doctor."

"Then you can begin listening to my phonograph recordings any time you like."

❧

After supper we returned to Dr. Seward's study, where he placed me in a comfortable chair beside the phonograph. He opened a large drawer, in which were arranged in order a number of hollow cylinders of metal covered with dark wax; but instead of selecting one, he paused as a sudden thought struck him.

"You know, I have been keeping this diary for months, but it never occurred to me until now: I have no idea how to pick out any particular part of it. To find the passages about Lucy, I am afraid you will have to listen to it all from the beginning."

"That is quite all right, Doctor. I have the whole night before me, and I am not at all sleepy." And I was desperate, I mused silently, for anything which might help divert my mind from thoughts of Mr. Wagner.

Dr. Seward put the first cylinder into the instrument and adjusted it for me, showing me how to start and stop it in case I should wish to pause. "The first half-dozen of these cylinders will not horrify you, and should tell you something of which you want to know. After that . . ." He did not finish the thought; instead, he handed me a folder that contained a collection of pages. "No doubt there will be gaps in the story. You may find this correspondence of interest, which is related to the case. Arthur Holmwood—Lord Godalming, now—returned my letters, so that we could keep a record of all that had happened. We also have Lucy's few diary pages, including the entry she wrote several nights before she died, describing the wolf who broke through her bedroom window."

"Lucy's diary pages?" I opened the folder and glanced through it, a jolt of emotion coursing through me when I beheld a page with my friend's familiar handwriting.

"I suggest you go through it in chronological order, or I fear it will make little sense to you." With a grim look, Dr. Seward crossed the room and—as if trying to afford me some privacy—sat down with his back to me and returned to his reading.

Although I longed to read Lucy's words, I set aside the folder for the moment. Starting up the phonograph, I put the forked metal to my ears and began to listen. Although the first part of Dr. Seward's diary was a long and disturbing observation of one of his patients—a mentally unbalanced man called Renfield, who had a predilection for catching and eating flies, spiders, and small birds—it was the first time I had ever heard a machine talk, and I found myself riveted by his every word.

For the next few hours, I never moved from my chair except to change a cylinder. This madman Renfield (with whom I was shortly to become acquainted) seemed to be of great interest to Dr. Seward. Mr. Renfield alternated between bouts of gentleness and violence. One night he escaped from the asylum and ran off into the woods, where he scaled the high wall into the grounds of Carfax, the deserted house next door. They found him pressed against the door to the old chapel behind the house, crying:

"I am here to do Your bidding, Master! I am Your slave, and You will reward me, for I shall be faithful. I have worshipped You long and afar off. Now that You are near, I await Your commands!"

Another, similar incident followed, equally strange. When they captured him, Mr. Renfield grew calm upon seeing a large bat flapping its silent way to the west across the moonlit sky. Dr. Seward was puzzled by these occurrences at the time. Now that we knew the house in question belonged to Count Dracula, I wondered: was Dracula himself inside the chapel at the time? Did this lunatic Renfield's mania in some way connect him to the Count?

The story then progressed to focus on dear Lucy, the part of greatest interest to me. It alternated between Dr. Seward's phonograph diary entries and his correspondence with Arthur Holmwood and others. Tears streamed down my face as I listened to Dr. Seward's anguished voice, telling the details of Lucy's suffering in those last, agonising weeks of her life.

Oh! If only I could have been there to help her! If only the four good men attending her had known what we knew now, about the nature of Lucy's ailment and the identity of her foe! But they had all been in the dark—all save Dr. Van Helsing, of course—but his efforts were in vain, and he dared not voice his terrible suspicions until he had proof.

Dr. Van Helsing performed four separate blood transfusions on Lucy, taking blood first from Lord Godalming, then from Dr. Seward, then from himself, and then—when it seemed that there was no one else to ask—from Mr. Quincey Morris, the wealthy, young American from Texas who had also loved Lucy to distraction and had come in response to a telegram from his old friend, Lord Godalming. Four transfusions in only ten days! It was incredible! Each one seemed to briefly breathe life back into her, but by morning Lucy appeared to be sick and bloodless again. Her appetite disappeared. She grew weaker and thinner. At last it was clear that she was dying.

As the men gathered around Lucy's death-bed in misery, she sank to sleep; but then there came a strange change. Lucy's eyes flew open; they were dull and hard, and when she opened her mouth, her canine teeth were visibly sharper than all the rest. In a soft, voluptuous voice which the men had never heard before, Lucy said:

"Arthur! Oh, my love, I am so glad you have come! Kiss me!"

Although startled by this transformation, Arthur bent eagerly to kiss her; but Van Helsing caught him by the neck and hurled him almost across the room, crying, "Not for your life! Not for your living soul and hers!"

As Dr. Van Helsing stood between them like a lion at bay,

a spasm of rage flitted like a shadow over Lucy's face; then she blinked, and her eyes and face returned to their sweet, innocent loveliness. Putting out her poor, pale, thin hand, she took Dr. Van Helsing's hand and drew it to her. "My true friend," she said in a faint voice. "My true friend, and his. Oh, guard him, and give me peace!"

Moments later, Lucy died. The men who loved her and had been devotedly caring for her were broken down with grief.

"Poor girl, there is peace for her at last," Dr. Seward said quietly, dashing tears from his eyes. "It is the end."

"Not so; alas!" Dr. Van Helsing replied grimly and enigmatically. "Not so. I fear it is only the beginning!"

At the funeral-house where Lucy's body lay in state, Dr. Seward and Lord Godalming were astonished to discover that all of Lucy's colour and loveliness had come back to her in death. Indeed, she looked so beautiful, they found it hard to believe that they were looking at a corpse. It was only a day or two after Lucy and her mother were laid to rest in their family tomb near Hampstead Heath that the mysterious woman in white began making appearances in late evening, leaving little children paler than she found them, with tiny wounds in their throats.

By then, Dr. Van Helsing had returned from his trip to Exeter to see me. Armed with the new information from the journals I had given him, he at last openly declared his suspicions about the vile creature who had bitten Lucy and the fact that the strange woman on the Heath was Lucy Westenra herself, now a vampire and risen from the dead!

Dr. Seward thought his friend had gone mad. Dr. Van Helsing set out to prove his theory. That night, he and Dr. Seward went to the eerie graveyard and entered the Westenra tomb, where the professor sawed open Lucy's coffin—and proved that it was empty. Dr. Seward at first blamed grave robbers; and even when, after leaving the tomb, they rescued a missing child and observed a white figure flitting back towards Lucy's grave, Dr. Seward refused to believe that it could be Lucy.

The next day, however, when they opened Lucy's coffin again, they found her lying within as if asleep. Although nearly a week had passed since she was buried, she appeared more radiantly beautiful than ever.

"Are you convinced now?" said the professor, as he pulled back Lucy's lips to reveal her sharp fangs. "She is Un-Dead! Here she rests by day, and she walks by night. With these teeth, the little children can be bitten. Lucy is young vampire. She start with small things, and have yet no life taken; but in time she will move on to larger ones and prove of great danger to all." With a woeful sigh he added: "It is hard to think that one so beautiful I must kill in her sleep."

Dr. Seward was horrified, even more so when Van Helsing revealed the known method to kill the Un-Dead: they must drive a stake through her body, fill her mouth with garlic, and cut off her head. It made Dr. Seward shudder to think of so mutilating the body of the woman he had loved; and yet, was it really so terrifying if Lucy was already dead?

Dr. Van Helsing decided not to perform the final deed on the spot. He feared that Arthur, who was still in a quandary over how lifelike Lucy had appeared after she died, might be haunted for ever by fears that they had made a terrible mistake and buried his love alive.

And so it was that in the wee hours of the 29th of September, Dr. Van Helsing and Dr. Seward revealed to Arthur and Quincey all that they had learned, and what they meant to do. It was only with the greatest insistence that Van Helsing was able to persuade them to put their doubts aside and their faith in him, for they had a great and terrible task to perform—but he would not do it without their blessing.

As I listened to Dr. Seward's account of the ensuing events, the horrifying images he created were so vivid in my mind, I felt as if the proceedings were unfolding before my very eyes.

Late that night at the churchyard, Dr. Van Helsing proved to the startled men that Lucy's coffin was again empty. He re-locked the Westenra tomb, then pressed into the crevices around the door a putty made of crumbled Host (sacred holy wafers, consecrated in the celebration of the Eucharist) which he had brought with him from Amsterdam, and which he said would make it difficult for the Un-Dead to enter. After this, the foursome waited in ominous silence amid the gravestones. In time, the group spied a woman advancing towards the moonlit tomb, dressed in the white cerements of the grave and carrying a little child.

"I could hear the gasp of Arthur," Dr. Seward explained, "as we recognised the features of Lucy Westenra. Lucy Westenra, but yet how changed! The sweetness was turned to adamantine, heartless cruelty, and the purity to voluptuous wantonness."

Van Helsing raised his lantern; the men shuddered with horror, for Lucy's lips were crimson with fresh blood which trickled over her chin and stained her white death-robe. When Lucy—or the thing that once was Lucy—saw them, she drew back with an angry snarl, carelessly flinging to the ground the child she had been holding. As the child lay there moaning, Lucy's lips curved in a wanton smile, and she advanced languorously towards Arthur with outstretched arms.

"Come to me, Arthur," she said, in a tone that was diabolically sweet. "Leave these others and come to me. My arms are hungry for you. Come, and we can rest together. Come, my husband, come!"

Arthur, although horror-struck, opened his arms to receive her as if under a spell. Van Helsing sprang between them and held up a golden crucifix, from which the vampire Lucy recoiled. She dashed for the tomb, but was stopped outside the door as if by some irresistible force: the Host! Lucy turned to them, her eyes throwing out sparks of hell-fire, and her features contorted with rage and baffled malice, such as Dr. Seward had never before seen on any living face.

"Answer me, oh my friend!" Van Helsing called to Arthur. "Am I to proceed in my work?"

Hiding his face in his hands, Arthur groaned and answered: "Do as you will. There can be no horror like this ever any more."

From the chinks around the tomb's door, Van Helsing removed some of the sacred substance which he had placed there. The men looked on in horrified amazement as Lucy, who had at that moment a corporeal body as real as their own, dashed up to this interstice, which was no wider than a knife blade, and somehow vanished entirely through it.

They could do no more that night; so they took the little child to safety and returned in the light of afternoon with the tools required to finish the deed. The churchyard was deserted. Once more they entered the tomb, where they found Lucy lying in her coffin in all her death-beauty. Dr. Van Helsing explained:

"The lore and experience of the ancients, and of all those who have studied the powers of the Un-Dead, tell us that they are cursed with immortality. They go on age after age, preying on new victims, who become themselves Un-Dead; and so the circle goes on ever widening. Friend Arthur, if you had met that kiss before Miss Lucy die, and again last night when she called to you, you might have become *nosferatu* yourself when you die. The children whose blood she sucked are not yet so much the worse; but the more she draw their blood, the more power she will have over them, and the more they will come to her. But if she die in truth, then all cease; the tiny wounds of their throats disappear, and they go back to what they were before and live in peace."

The men nodded in silent understanding. This gave way to horror when Dr. Van Helsing removed from his tool bag a heavy hammer and a wooden stake, some three feet long, one end of which was sharpened to a fine point.

"What we do here is a blessing, my friends," the professor went on stoically. "When by our hand, this now Un-Dead be made to rest as true dead, then the soul of the poor dear lady whom we all love shall again be free. Instead of working wickedness by night, she will take her rightful place among the angels. Who shall strike the blow that sets her free?"

Dr. Van Helsing was willing to do the deed; but he felt, for Lucy's sake, it should be done by the hand of he who loved her best. Arthur, trembling, agreed to do it. Taking the instruments from Dr. Van Helsing's hands, Arthur placed the point of the stake over Lucy's heart and struck with all his might. The creature in the coffin writhed and contorted and screamed, while blood from its pierced heart welled and spurted up around it; but at last the body fell still, and a calm fell over it. Suddenly, the men found themselves looking once again upon Lucy as they had seen her in life, in all her purity and sweetness.

"And now, Arthur my friend, am I forgiven?" Dr. Van Helsing asked, laying his hand on Lord Godalming's shoulder.

"Forgiven?" Arthur said. "God bless you that you have given my dear one her soul again, and me peace." He shed tears as he pressed his lips to Lucy's for a final kiss.

They then completed the last, terrible act—cutting off Lucy's head, and filling the mouth with garlic—to ensure that vampire Lucy could never return and that her soul would be for ever at rest.

"One step of our work is now done," Dr. Van Helsing said with a sigh, as the group emerged into the early-afternoon sun and air, which seemed doubly sweet after the horrors of the confining tomb. "But there remains a greater task: to find out the author of all this sorrow and to stamp him out. Shall you all help me?"

The men vowed that they would. They all agreed to meet at

Dr. Seward's house in two days' time, to form a plan to find and destroy Count Dracula.

I TURNED OFF THE PHONOGRAPH AND LAY BACK IN MY CHAIR, powerless. My cheeks were streaked with tears, and a small, sad sob escaped my lips. Dr. Seward must have heard it, for he jumped up with a worried exclamation, took a case-bottle from a cupboard, and poured me a glass of brandy.

I sipped the spirits gratefully, drying my eyes with the handkerchief the kind doctor offered. "My God," I finally said, my voice low and broken. "Had I not already known of Jonathan's experience in Transylvania, I could never believe the multitude of horrors which I have just heard."

"I was there, and I can scarcely believe it myself," he replied grimly.

"Through it all, there is only one ray of light: that our dear Lucy is at last at peace."

"Yes."

A sudden thought occurred to me. "If I am not mistaken, Doctor, this last dreadful episode, when you—when you killed the vampire Lucy at the graveyard—it only just occurred. In fact, it happened early this very afternoon, shortly before I arrived, did it not?"

"It did, Mrs. Harker. I had just taken Dr. Van Helsing to his hotel afterwards to pack for his trip to Amsterdam, when he received your telegram informing us of your arrival. I finished dictating the last section this afternoon, while you were out."

"Oh! You poor man. No wonder you seemed so upset to-day at the train station! To think, after all you had just been through, you had to run and meet me—I am so sorry."

"Do not be. I am glad you are here, ma'am. While you have

been listening to my story, I have been reading your husband's wonderful journal. I have read parts of it twice now, in fact, and it sheds light on many things. Mr. Harker is uncommonly clever, and a man of great nerve."

"Yes, he is."

"Scaling that castle wall, and going down to the vault a second time—that was a remarkable piece of daring. I see now why the professor was so keen to have you both join us in our quest."

"There is one way in which I think I could be of immediate help, Doctor."

"What is that?"

"You said you would not know how to pick out any particular part of your phonographic diary, should you have a case you wished to look up. Your detailed observations will, I think, prove invaluable in the task before us. Will you let me copy it all out for you now on my typewriter, as I did with my journal and my husband's? Then we will be ready for Dr. Van Helsing when he returns to-morrow."

"A fine idea, Mrs. Harker; but it is well past midnight. You must be tired. Let us return to this in the morning."

"After all I have just heard, I could never sleep a wink. Please, Doctor: I would be grateful for something to do."

Dr. Seward capitulated. I brought down my typewriter and set it up on the small table beside the phonograph. He set the instrument at a slow pace, and I began to typewrite from the beginning, using manifold-paper to make three copies. Dr. Seward made a round of his patients while I worked; he then returned and sat near me, reading, to keep me company. At length, he fell asleep in his chair. I typed long into the night, not finishing until after the sun came up. Leaving the typed pages neatly on Dr. Seward's desk, I slipped quietly upstairs and fell into bed for some much-needed rest.

I had three dreams.

In the first dream, I saw Lucy as a vampire, dressed in her death-robe as she wandered aimlessly across the Heath. She came upon a little child and snatched it up, her eyes blazing like red flames as she bared her fangs and clenched them on the child's throat. That vision was so real and so frightening that it took me a while to fall back to sleep.

My second dream was a vast improvement—wonderful, in fact. I was sitting in a rocking chair in my house at Exeter, holding an infant to my breast. As I cradled the tiny, chubby form in my arms, I kissed his soft, warm head, inhaling his lovely baby scent as I stroked his tufts of dark hair. He was *my* baby: my very own child, the first true blood relative I had ever known, a being who was a part of me and Jonathan together. I felt my heart spilling over with love, so much love, more love than I had ever imagined I had inside of me. I knew that I would do anything to protect this child, anything. I awoke glowing with happiness. *Some day,* I thought: some day when all this madness was over, when the evil Dracula was dead and we could all return to our normal lives, I would have that baby. I would have many babies: to hold, cuddle, sing to, read to, play with, and raise into happy, healthy children. I drifted off again in a blissful haze.

The third dream was about Mr. Wagner. I was back at the Whitby pavilion, and we were whirling about the dance floor. I was floating, floating, transported by the music and the thrill of being in his arms. The music rose to a crescendo as we waltzed out to the terrace, where he drew me more closely to him, gazing into my eyes with deepest love; and then he kissed me. A long, heartfelt, magical kiss—

I awoke flushed and perspiring, my heart pounding so loudly I thought it might leap from my chest. Oh! Why must I dream of *him*? What a treacherous thing the subconscious mind was! Such dreams and imaginings, I believed, were as much a betrayal of my marriage vows as any physical act. And yet, I found myself lying in the dark for several shameful minutes, savoring the imagined memory of his embrace and the feel of his kiss. Then I gave myself a mental shake and reproached myself sternly: *Mina Harker: you must think of him no more.*

I sat up and threw off the bed-clothes. The curtains were open. Sunlight streamed into the room, and the clock announced that it was a quarter past noon. I saw with a start that Jonathan's luggage was standing just inside the door. He was here—returned from Whitby!

I quickly washed and dressed, relieved that there was work to be done; for our quest to find and destroy the vile Count Dracula would surely take my mind off my longing for Mr. Wagner, a man I loved but could never have.

TWELVE

I found Jonathan down-stairs in the dining-room, deep in conversation with Dr. Seward, just as luncheon was being served. The sight of my husband's dear face filled me with quiet joy. He looked and sounded resolute and full of volcanic energy, as if his trip had done him good. Indeed, any one seeing him to-day would find it difficult to believe that this strong and determined man was the same beaten-down individual I had discovered in hospital only six weeks before in Buda-Pesth.

"Darling! There you are," Jonathan said, leaping up from his chair with a welcoming smile as I entered. "Dr. Seward said you were up all night, so I let you sleep."

"Thank you." I crossed to him and we exchanged an affectionate kiss. "I see that you two have become acquainted."

"Yes," Dr. Seward said, rising and gesturing towards a place at the table, which had been set for me. "Your husband is an excellent fellow."

"May I say the same about you, sir," Jonathan responded with a sincere and gracious nod. As we all took our seats, he covered my hand with his and added gravely: "We have been discussing the case all morning, dearest, ever since I arrived. Dr. Seward has told me all about what happened to Lucy. It is so hard to believe; and yet, it must be true."

"At least Lucy's soul is at peace now," I said sadly.

"Little consolation for the loss of one so young and beautiful and so dear," remarked Dr. Seward bitterly.

"We will hunt that Thing down and rid the world of him!" Jonathan insisted with fierce determination. "We have all the facts now, and to-night we can proceed."

"Did you find what you needed to know in Whitby, then?" I asked.

"Everything and more," Jonathan replied with satisfaction. As we all began to eat, he continued: "Everyone from the coast-guardsmen to the harbour-master had something to say about the strange entry of the ship *Demeter,* which is already taking its place in local tradition. Then I saw Mr. Billington—stayed at his house, in fact—that's true Yorkshire hospitality for you. Billington showed me all the letters and invoices concerning the consignment of the boxes. 'Fifty cases of common earth, to be used for experimental purposes,' they said. It gave me quite a turn to see again one of the letters which I had seen on the Count's table at the castle, before I knew of his diabolical plan. He had thought everything out very carefully and executed it with systematic precision, preparing in advance for every obstacle which might come in his way."

"And the boxes?" I said. "What happened to them?"

"At first, they were put into storage in a Whitby warehouse."

"No doubt the Count sneaked in and took shelter inside one of them during the day," Dr. Seward said.

"Yes," I murmured, "for it was only a couple of days after the ship arrived that Lucy was first attacked up on the cliff."

"On the 19th of August, they got a sudden notice to ship them all to London. When I arrived at King's Cross Station this morning, the officials kindly showed me their records, confirming that all fifty boxes had arrived late on the evening of the 19th. I followed another lead, and found the carrier's men who delivered the boxes to the chapel at Carfax, the very next day."

"Then Count Dracula has indeed taken possession of the house next door?" I asked. An ominous feeling came over me as I recalled standing outside the rusting gates the day before, and the strange sensation that I was being watched.

"I cannot say if Dracula is there or not, but all fifty boxes should be, unless any have since been removed."

"I fear that may be the case," Dr. Seward said, frowning. "A little more than a week ago, while I was at Hillingham looking after Lucy, the doctor I left in charge reported seeing a carrier's cart leaving that house, loaded with some great wooden boxes. The only reason he reported it was because one of our patients escaped and attacked the carriers, accusing them of robbery and shouting that he would 'fight for his Lord and Master.' "

"His Lord and Master?" Jonathan repeated, intrigued.

"What patient was that? Was it Renfield?" I asked.

"Yes."

"Who is Renfield?" Jonathan asked.

Dr. Seward gave him a brief summary of the lunatic who was under his care, to which Jonathan replied: "Do you think he knows something of this business with the Count?"

"I do," I interjected. "While listening to Dr. Seward's phonographic diary last night, I sensed that somehow, in his madness, this Mr. Renfield has a mental connection with Count Dracula. I have a feeling that if we look at the dates carefully, we may find they are a sort of index to the comings and goings of the Count. The first time Renfield escaped from the asylum, for example, and ran next door—I believe it may correspond with the date the Count arrived at Carfax."

"Interesting," Dr. Seward mused. "What a good thing you put my cylinders into type, Mrs. Harker! We could never find the dates otherwise."

"In this matter, I think dates are everything," I replied. "If we get all our material together, and put every scrap of evidence into chronological order, we should be able to make real sense of it—and make a good start on this case to-night, when the others arrive."

AFTER LUNCHEON, JONATHAN AND I WENT UP TO OUR ROOM. While he read my typescript of Dr. Seward's diary, I typed up in triplicate all the rest of the related correspondence, as well as Jonathan's newest journal entries and the information he had brought back from Whitby. We then put all the papers into order in folders for the members of the party who had not read them.

At three o'clock, Dr. Seward was obliged to leave on some other business, and Jonathan went out to visit the carrier's men who had been seen hauling away some of the boxes from Carfax. I was about to take a nap when the maid knocked on my door and announced that Lord Godalming and Mr. Morris had arrived some hours ahead of schedule. As Dr. Seward was not at home, would I be willing to receive them?

I issued down-stairs and greeted the gentlemen in the foyer with a brave smile and a heavy heart, for we all shared a common bond and purpose, rooted in the sorrow of Lucy's death. I had only met Arthur Holmwood once before, the previous spring, when he had called on Lucy during one of my visits—and although still very handsome, his face was so lined with suffering, it seemed as if he had aged a decade since then.

"Lord Godalming," I said, as I gave him my hand, "I am so sorry for your loss, both for dear Lucy and for your father."

"Thank you, Mrs. Harker," he replied gravely, "but I know you and Lucy were like sisters. Her loss has been deeply felt by all of us, I fear."

"You are right, sir." I then turned to Mr. Morris. He was tall like his friend, and very young—perhaps a few years older than myself—with a thick moustache, wavy auburn hair, piercing hazel eyes, and a firm grip. From the phonographic journal and letters I had typed the previous night, I deduced that Mr. Morris, Dr. Seward, and Lord Godalming had all shared in many past adventures in their youth, in remote places from the Marquesas Islands to the shores of Lake Titicaca in Peru. "How do you do, sir?" I said, holding out my hand.

"As well as can be expected, ma'am, under the circumstances," Mr. Morris replied in an accent which I took to be the American Texas twang I had read about in books. As I led the men down the corridor, Mr. Morris continued: "We've heard tell a lot about you, Mrs. Harker. Dr. Van Helsing has been blowing your trumpet. He says you have a man's brain—a brain that a man should have, that is, if he were gifted—and a woman's heart."

"Where Dr. Van Helsing gets that idea, I could not say. Indeed, I have spent very little time in his company."

We entered Dr. Seward's study. Both men stood awkwardly in the centre of the room, as if unsure of what to say or do.

"Please forgive us for coming so early," Lord Godalming remarked uncertainly, "but I have been pacing the halls since yesterday, and I thought if I could just come over here and be given something useful to do—" He then lapsed into silence.

"Gentlemen," I said, wishing to put them at ease, "let us speak openly. Last night, I listened to Dr. Seward's detailed phonographic account of everything that has happened thus far. I know that our foe is a vampire, and I know all about Lucy's death—her *real* death—yesterday, at the graveyard."

The men's eyes widened. "You don't say!" exclaimed Mr. Morris. "You know all about it?"

"I not only know about it, sir, I have typed it all up, along with all the papers and diaries everyone has kept."

I gave them each a copy of the rather sizeable manuscript. "Did you really typewrite all this, Mrs. Harker?" Lord Godalming asked.

I nodded. Mr. Morris eyed me in wonder and said: "May I read this now?"

"You may, sir."

As Lord Godalming stared at the papers, I saw that his eyes were laced with sudden tears. Mr. Morris laid a hand on Lord Godalming's shoulder for a moment; then, with quiet delicacy, he took the manuscript I had given him and walked out of the room.

Finding himself alone with me, Lord Godalming sank down onto the sofa and began to cry. I sat beside him in heartfelt sympathy, saying whatever I could think of to ease his sorrow. When our grief subsided and we had dried our tears, he thanked me for my words of comfort; and then a thought seemed to occur to him. From his coat-pocket, he withdrew a small box and offered it to me. "I almost forgot. I have something for you, Mrs. Harker. Before Lucy died, she asked me to give you this."

I opened the box. I recognised the contents at once: it was the black velvet neckband with the exquisite diamond buckle that Lucy had so loved. "Oh! I cannot accept this, Lord Godalming. It is far too valuable, and your family heirloom. Did it not once belong to your mother?"

"Yes, but Lucy wanted you to have it. She made me issue my most solemn promise that I would see it safely into your hands. I would be happy to have you wear it in Lucy's memory."

"Then I must not refuse. Thank you, sir. Every time I wear it, I will think of her."

❧

WHEN DR. SEWARD RETURNED, I HAD TEA SERVED, WHICH SEEMED to revitalize everyone.

"May I ask a favour, Doctor?" I said, as I replaced my empty tea-cup in my saucer. "I would like to see your patient, Mr. Renfield."

"Renfield?" Dr. Seward looked at me in alarm. "Why do you wish to see him?"

"What you have said of him in your diary interests me very much."

"It is not a good idea, Mrs. Harker. Renfield is the most pronounced lunatic I have ever met with, and he can be very dangerous. Two weeks ago, he escaped and stabbed me in the wrist with a stolen dinner-knife, and then tried to lap up my blood."

"I know." I also knew that Mr. Renfield was fifty-nine years old, and a man of great physical strength, who alternated between periods of morbid excitability and deep gloom. "But he has no reason to wish me harm, Doctor—and I will be safe if you are with me. I would like to talk to him, to see if I can get him to admit anything about his mental connection to Count Dracula—if indeed there is one."

He sighed. "Well, I suppose you could have a shot at it. I haven't been able to get a useful word out of him of late. But under no circumstances will I leave you alone with him."

Dr. Seward led me down the corridor to the patient's room, which was situated one floor below mine, on the same side of the building. "Wait here," he said, as he unlocked the door and slipped inside the chamber. I could hear the murmur of a brief conversation within; shortly thereafter, Dr. Seward reappeared and shut the door with a disgusted look on his face.

"What is wrong?" I enquired.

"Mr. Renfield's method of preparing to greet guests is very singular. He just swallowed up a great quantity of flies and spiders that he has been collecting—no doubt to prevent us from stealing them."

This pronouncement was disturbing, but not wholly unexpected. "I am well-acquainted with Mr. Renfield's zoöphagous habits, having heard about them in some detail in your diary."

Dr. Seward paused uncertainly, as if silently debating whether or not to allow the interview. With a reluctant sigh, he finally said: "All right. But do not be fooled by his quiet mood. He cannot be trusted."

Dr. Seward preceded me into the room, which was small and starkly furnished. Mr. Renfield was a man of average height with wide shoulders and a very pale face. He was sitting on the edge of the bed in an eerie position: his head was down, but his eyelids were raised, and his eyes were fixed warily on me, with a look so dark and intense, it sent a chill up my spine.

Dr. Seward stood in close proximity to him, as if prepared to seize the madman at once, in case he attempted to make a spring at me. I swallowed my fear, held out my hand, and approached the patient with what I hoped would appear to be ease and gracefulness. "Good evening, Mr. Renfield. Dr. Seward has told me a great deal about you."

Mr. Renfield made no immediate reply but studied me intently. At length, his eyebrows raised as a curious look crossed his face. "You're not the girl the doctor wanted to marry, are you? No—you can't be, for she's dead."

Dr. Seward looked taken aback by this statement.

"Oh no!" I replied, smiling. "I have a husband of my own, to whom I was married before I ever saw Dr. Seward, or he me. I am Mrs. Harker. I am here visiting Dr. Seward."

Dr. Seward said quickly: "What makes you think I wanted to marry any one?"

Mr. Renfield snorted contemptuously, "What an asinine question!" Turning back to me, his manner suddenly changed, as quickly as the shifting of a wind, to a tone of courtesy and respect. "When a man is so loved and honoured as our host is, Mrs. Harker, everything regarding him is of interest in our little community." He added that Dr. Seward was loved not only by his household and friends, but also by his patients, despite—or perhaps because of—their precarious mental equilibrium. He then went on to make some lengthy, erudite, and philosophical observations about the inmates at the asylum, and about the state of the world we lived in.

Whatever I had expected from Mr. Renfield, it was not this. His speech and manners were so much those of a polished gentleman that he appeared for all the world to be perfectly sane. It seemed impossible to believe that he had been eating up spiders and flies not five minutes before I entered the room. Dr. Seward seemed equally astonished; he stood in silence, looking at me as if I had some rare gift or power.

"If Dr. Seward's patients love him," I said, "it is with good reason, for he is a very kind and thoughtful individual, and has their best interests at heart."

"That may be true for the others," Mr. Renfield said emphatically, "but not for me. The doctor does not like me, and he has gotten in my way."

"How so?" I asked.

"He thinks that I have a strange belief—and perhaps I did. I used to think that by consuming a multitude of live things, no matter how low in the scale of creation, one might indefinitely prolong life. At times, I have held the belief so strongly that I tried to take human life, for the purpose of strengthening my vital powers by the assimilation of that person's blood—relying, of course, upon the Scriptural phrase, 'For the blood is the life.' Though the vendor of a certain nostrum—Clarke's 'World Famous Blood Purifier,' to be precise—has now turned that truism into a marketing slogan, which has vulgarised it to the very point of contempt. Don't you agree?"

I nodded, familiar with the product to which he referred, and still taken aback by his genteel and lucid manner. The content of his discourse, however, depicted his psychosis, and I hoped to take full advantage of this. "Mr. Renfield. You said Dr. Seward has gotten in your way. Were you referring to the times when you tried to escape from this institution, and he brought you back?"

"Yes, and the fact that he won't give me a cat."

Knowing the patient's predilection for consuming live creatures, I ignored this disturbing comment, and went on: "I understand that you ran to the property next door. Can you tell me why that is?"

He hesitated. "I was looking for the Master."

"Who is the Master?"

Fear crept into his voice. "I do not know his name. I have never seen him. I only feel his presence. He comes and goes."

"How do you feel his presence? How do you know when he comes and goes?"

"I don't want to talk about this." Mr. Renfield was suddenly anxious and upset. "Stop talking about it. I think now it was a mistake to let the Master know I am here. I don't know. I don't know!"

"Why do you call him the Master?"

Mr. Renfield stared up at me in agitation. "Why are you asking me all these questions? You of all people! You know the Master better than I do!"

"Me?" I replied in surprise. "I do not know him at all."

"But you do! You know him, Mrs. Harker. You do! You do!"

"All right, that's enough! This interview is over," Dr. Seward interjected, taking me by the arm and leading me to the door.

"Good-bye, Mr. Renfield," I said.

"Good-bye." As the door shut behind me, I heard him cry inexplicably: "I pray God I may never see your face again! May He bless and keep you."

My meeting with Mr. Renfield left me both confused and disturbed. It seemed that the patient did indeed have some kind of strange connection with this being he called "the Master," even if he did not understand that connection—and "the Master" could be none other than Count Dracula. I was very puzzled, however, by his assertion that I knew "the Master." Did he mean that I knew Count Dracula because I had learned so much about him over the past few days? Or was he referring to the single time that I had observed the Count on the street in Piccadilly? When I shared my thoughts with Dr. Seward, he assured me that the statement meant nothing other than the fact that Mr. Renfield was a certified lunatic.

Jonathan soon returned from his scouting mission, which had so far proven unsuccessful. Dr. Seward picked up Dr. Van Helsing at the train station. The professor was delighted to learn about the work Jonathan and I had done. He asked me please to continue gathering and typing up information as it came in, so as to keep all our information in exact order and up to the moment.

After a quick, early dinner, he skimmed through what I had written the night before.

At eight o'clock, the six of us gathered in Dr. Seward's study, all seated around his table like a sort of committee. Dr. Van Helsing took the head of the table and asked me to act as secretary. Holding up a copy of the manuscript, he asked if we were all acquainted with the facts that were in the papers. When we all expressed assent, Dr. Van Helsing said grimly:

"My friends, we are face to face with a momentous duty, and there is great danger in it. We all know now that there are such beings as vampires. We must destroy this mighty foe before us. In this battle, some may lose their lives. But to fail here is not mere life or death—no! Others of us—God forbid!—may fall further victim and become as him, as foul things of the night, without heart or conscience, preying on the bodies and the souls of others, to go on abhorred for all time. This risk we must accept, for it is real."

I felt my heart grow icy cold, and shuddered. What a dreadful fate it would be, to become a member of the Un-Dead!

"I am old; but you are all young and have fair days yet in store," Dr. Van Helsing went on. "If any wish to leave, speak up now, and we will think not the less of you." The room fell silent. "What say you? Who shall join me to the bitter end?"

Jonathan stretched out his hand towards mine beneath the table. At first, I feared that the appalling nature of our danger was overcoming him, and he was appealing to me for silent strength; but the reverse proved true. As his fingers closed around mine—so firm, so self-reliant, so comforting—I knew that he was reaching out to offer me *his* strength. He looked in my eyes, and I in his; without a word, I knew he read my assent.

"I can answer for Mina and myself," Jonathan said calmly.

"Count me in, Professor," put in Mr. Morris.

"I am with you," said Lord Godalming, "for Lucy's sake, if for no other reason."

Dr. Seward simply nodded. We then all joined hands around the table, and our solemn pact was made.

The professor took a deep breath. "Well then, I think it good to tell you more about the kind of enemy with which we have to deal. The *nosferatu* or *wampyr* is found in teachings and legends everywhere that men have been from times of old, from ancient Greece, Rome, and China to India and Iceland, to name a few. And yet this creature is new to us, and so is still a mystery, an unknown. All we have to rely upon are traditions and superstitions of the past, and that which we have seen with our own eyes. It is said that the *nosferatu* is immortal; he cannot die unless by extraordinary means. He eats not as others but survives by consuming the blood of the living. With this steady diet of blood, it seems he can even grow younger! As Jonathan also observe, it seems he make in the mirror no reflection. We are told he has the strength of twenty men; and he can, within limitations, appear at will in any of the forms that are available to him."

"What do you mean, Professor?" interjected Lord Godalming. "What kind of forms can he take?"

"Of two, we can be fairly certain: he can transform himself into a large dog or perhaps a wolf, for such is the only creature seen to depart the ship at Whitby. And he can be as bat, as Madam Mina saw on the window at Whitby, and friend Quincey saw at the window of Miss Lucy in London, and friend Jack saw fly from the house next door."

"That was Count Dracula I saw flapping away into the night?" Dr. Seward said, in wonder.

"It was, my friend; I am sure of it. As to his other powers: on my last trip to Amsterdam, I met with my friend Arminius from Buda-Pesth University, who specialize in this study. He said there is rumoured to be one old and very great vampire who live in Transylvania, who is mightier than all the rest. We believe this is the same Count Dracula whom we seek. This mighty vampire, he can, within his range, direct the elements—the storm, the wind, the fog, the thunder—a gift which maybe help him control the arrival of the ship that carried him to this country. He can, we think, command all the meaner creatures: the rat, the owl, the bat, the moth, the fox, and the wolf—as you, friend Jonathan, saw him do."

"Yes," Jonathan replied. "He seemed to have power over all the wolves in Transylvania—and I saw him talk to horses, as well."

"There is more," the professor said. "He is clever and cunning and has a mighty brain, which he has educated for centuries. He can see in the dark; no small power, in a world which is one-half shut from the light. He can—like the young vampire—vanish at will and become invisible, or slip through a hairbreadth space, as we saw Lucy do at the tomb door. He can come in mist which he creates, or on moonlight rays as elemental dust—as was recorded in the writings of Miss Lucy, and as Jonathan saw those weird sisters do in the castle of Dracula."

"If this monster can do all that," Mr. Morris said, shaking his head, "how on God's green earth do you expect us to catch him and kill him?"

"Ah, but hear me out. He can do all these things, yes; but he is not free. Nay; the vampire is even more prisoner than the slave of the galley, or the madman in his cell. As we know, he must carry the earth of his homeland with him to rest upon if he is to retain his powers. According to legend and superstition, he cannot go anywhere he wishes at any time. To the point, he may not enter a house at the first, unless there be someone of the household who bid him to come."

"Are you saying someone has to invite him in?" I asked.

"The first time, yes. After, he can come as he please."

"How strange," Lord Godalming said.

"All this is strange, is it not? And yet it is so. As to his powers: it is said that they cease at the coming of the sunrise. He can walk by day, although he avoids the sun's brightest rays; but during this interval he is as powerless as any human, and must keep until sunset the form he had chosen before the sun came up."

Dr. Van Helsing shared other theories, such as a claim that the vampire must be carried over running water, and that garlic and the wild rose could secure him in his coffin. He then laid a lovely golden crucifix on the table. "All things sacred, such as this symbol, Host, and holy water, we believe he greatly dreads, and can only view from far off and with respect. We proved this with the holy wafer, which had so great effect when we applied it around the door to Miss Lucy's tomb."

"But all these things just scare him off," Jonathan observed with an impatient wave of his hand. "What's important is that we know how to kill him! A stake through the heart, and we cut off his head!"

"Yes, my friend. But to kill him we must first be able to find him, with full knowledge of every single one of his abilities, for he has much power to outwit us—and to harm us."

We all fell silent for a moment, and I believe we were all thinking of poor Lucy; for every face at the table mirrored the sadness I felt for my friend as well as contempt for her murderer.

"Who is Count Dracula?" I asked. "I understand that he is from Transylvania, but how old is he? Who was he before he became a vampire?"

"Of this monster's background, we know but little," Dr. Van Helsing admitted. "My friend Arminius claim the Draculas were once a great and noble race. From dates on the gold coins friend Jonathan find at Dracula's castle, I conjecture that he is at least three hundred years old, and probably more." To Jonathan, he added: "You say in your journal that he spoke about his country's history, and his ancestors' fight in the wars against the Turks. Did he tell anything about himself, his own personal story?"

"Not a word," Jonathan replied.

"He maintains that he is a count," Dr. Van Helsing said, "but of course he must invent a new identity for each new generation."

"Who were those three horrid women at the castle?" Jonathan asked. "His vampire brides?"

"I suspect so," the professor replied.

"You said Count Dracula is more powerful than other vampires," Lord Godalming said. "How did he get that way?"

"We do not know. Perhaps the longer a vampire exists, the greater his powers become."

During this last conversation, I observed that Mr. Morris was looking out the window. He suddenly got up and, without a word, hastened out of the room. The professor glanced after him curiously, and went on: "I have said enough for now. You know what we have to contend against. Our foe is formidable; but we, too, are not without strength. We are six minds to his one. We have sources of science at our disposal. Most important perhaps, we have self-devotion in a good cause, an end to achieve which is not an evil and selfish one. For this alone, I believe we can succeed, for we have God on our side. Now we must lay out our campaign to find and destroy this monster. I propose we begin with the Count's boxes of earth. Once we ascertain how many boxes still remain in that house beyond the wall—"

There came the sudden, startling sound of a pistol-shot from outside, and the shattering of glass, as one of the study windows burst into fragments. I shrieked. The men jumped to their feet. Lord Godalming raced to the broken window and threw up the sash.

"Sorry!" came Mr. Morris's voice from outside. "Is everyone all right?" When Lord Godalming assured him that we were, Mr.

Morris called out: "I'll come in and explain." A minute later, he returned and said: "I fear I must have greatly alarmed you—but I saw a bat land on the window-sill while you were talking, Professor."

"A bat!" cried Dr. Van Helsing.

"A great big one. I hate the damned things, and thought it might be Dracula himself, so I went out to have a shot."

"It must have been the Count!" Dr. Van Helsing replied. "No doubt he was spying on us. Did you hit it?"

"I don't know. I fancy not, for it flew away into the wood."

"Here is the bullet, embedded in the wall," observed Jonathan.

"I ask your pardon," Mr. Morris said, shamefaced. "It was an idiotic thing to do. I could have killed somebody."

"But you would have not killed the bat," explained the professor solemnly. "A bullet might make that creature bleed, but it would not die; for the being that animates it is already Un-Dead."

When we had all calmed down from this incident and resumed our seats, Dr. Van Helsing returned to the subject at hand. He suggested that our best course of action would be to try to capture or kill Count Dracula during the day when he was in the form of a man, and at his weakest. "If we are lucky, we will find him to-morrow in his own lair next door."

"I vote we have a look at his house right now," Mr. Morris said.

"No," insisted the professor. "It is too dangerous. His powers are too great at night. And if that bat was truly him, he knows we plot against him."

"But time is everything with him," Dr. Seward interjected. "Swift action on our part may save another victim."

"Professor," Jonathan added, "you said if we sterilise that earth of his—with some kind of sacred object, I assume—it will be useless to him. Isn't that right?"

"That is correct, friend Jonathan."

"Then I say we go over there this very night and sterilise all the boxes we can find. If we run into the monster, so be it; we will take him on."

"Hear, hear," responded all the men, save for the professor.

After a pause, Dr. Van Helsing said with a frown, "I must yield to the majority, but on one condition: that we leave Madam Mina behind. She is too precious to put at risk, and this is a grave danger that we face."

I protested this chivalrous stance, insisting that I should go, as there was strength in numbers; but the professor's mind was made up, and all the men agreed and seemed relieved.

"You must stay home to-night, Mina," Jonathan insisted, squeezing my hand. "We shall act all the more freely, knowing that you are safe."

The group spent several hours discussing the method of their attack and gathering the required objects for their foray, which included tools, weapons, skeleton keys, crucifixes, small vials of holy water, and sacred wafers. The process greatly unnerved me, but I did not want to appear as a hindrance to their work, for fear that they might leave me out of their future counsels altogether; so I maintained an appearance of calm and made as many helpful suggestions as I could.

At three o'clock in the morning, just as the men were about to leave the house, an urgent message was brought to Dr. Seward from Mr. Renfield, who wanted to be seen at once.

"Tell Mr. Renfield I will see him in the morning," Dr. Seward told the attendant.

The attendant insisted that he had never seen Mr. Renfield so eager. "I don't know but what, if you don't talk to him soon, sir, he will have one of his violent fits."

Dr. Seward reluctantly agreed to go; all the men, intrigued, accompanied him, but I was told to stay behind.

I waited in Dr. Seward's study, too anxious to do anything but pace and worry. From down the hall, I heard the sounds of their conversation, and what appeared to be a long, impassioned speech from Mr. Renfield. Then I heard him shriek, followed by a torrent of emotion. The doctor must have opened the patient's door then, for I heard Mr. Renfield cry:

"Oh, hear me! Hear me! Let me go! Let me go! Let me go!"

A few minutes later, the party reappeared. "What is the matter with him?" I asked.

"He wants us to set him free," Dr. Seward replied with a bemused shake of his head. "To let him walk away, here and now."

"At three o'clock in the morning?" I said, startled. "But why?"

"He would not say," Lord Godalming replied. "He just kept insisting that he must leave or perish. He seemed to be terrified of something."

"Except for that last hysterical outburst, he is about the sanest lunatic I ever saw," said Mr. Morris. "I'm not sure, but I believe that he had some serious purpose."

"I could almost agree with you," Dr. Seward said, "if I did not recall how he prayed with equal fervour for a cat, which he no doubt would have eaten on the spot. This change in intellectual method is but another form or phase of his madness; I could not in good conscience set him loose in the country-side at this or any other hour."

"Besides, he called the Count 'Lord and Master,'" Jonathan pointed out. "He may want to get out to help him in some diabolical way."

"If that horrid thing has the wolves and rats to help him, I suppose he isn't above trying to use a near-by lunatic," Dr. Seward agreed with a deep sigh. "Let us go now. We have work to do."

After the men left, I put on my nightdress, brushed my long blonde hair, and went to bed, leaving the gas-light lit but turned down low for Jonathan's return.

I could not sleep. What woman *could* rest, knowing that her husband and so many brave souls were going into danger? I lay in bed, thinking over all that had happened thus far, and poor Lucy's fate. Oh! If only I had not gone to Whitby and taken to visiting in that churchyard, perhaps Lucy would never have taken to sleep-walking, and that monster could not have destroyed her. I shed tears for my dear, departed friend, and then rebuked myself for crying. If Jonathan should know I had been weeping, he would fret his heart out.

Suddenly, I heard the barking of dogs, followed by a lot of queer sounds—like praying on a very tumultuous scale—coming from the floor below mine, in the direction of Mr. Renfield's room. An eerie silence followed. I got up and went to the tall casement windows, looking out beyond the narrow balcony to the grounds below. All was dark without. Not a thing seemed to be stirring.

Then, in the black shadows thrown by the moonlight, I became aware of a thin streak of white mist creeping with almost imperceptible slowness across the grass towards the house. The mist seemed to have a sentience and a vitality of its own. It kept spreading and moving forward, until it lay thick and white against the wall of the house, and settled against the window which I believed led to Mr. Renfield's room. The mist then slowly evaporated, dissipating into the night air.

The patient's muted cries became louder than ever. Although I could not distinguish a word he said, I recognised in his tone some kind of passionate entreaty on his part. There came the sound of a struggle. I was suddenly frightened, although from what cause I could not say. I assumed the attendants were dealing with Mr. Renfield, and surely he did not present any particular danger to me.

Taking care that the window was shut and the door securely locked, I crept back into bed and pulled the clothes over my head. For some long minutes I lay trembling in the dark, uncertain why I felt so overwhelmed by fear and wishing that the men had not all quit the premises together, leaving me so entirely alone. Despite the bed-clothes that covered me, I soon began to sense that the air in the room had somehow grown heavier, and seemed dank and cold.

I threw off the covers and sat up. To my astonishment, the room was filling with white mist, which I saw pouring in through the joinings of the door. My heart began to pound in terror and confusion as I watched the mist become thicker and thicker, until it seemed to concentrate into a sort of pillar of cloud in the centre of the room. What was this? What was happening? Suddenly the horror burst upon me that it was in this same manner that Jonathan had seen those awful vampire women at Castle Dracula growing into reality through the whirling mist in the moonlight.

Then, before my terrified eyes, the ghostly column took the form and shape of a dazzling, handsome young man:

Mr. Wagner.

I wanted to scream but was powerless to do so. My limbs felt so leaden, I could not move. Had I lost my senses? Was I dreaming? How could Mr. Wagner suddenly appear out of a mist before me?

"Please. Don't be afraid," he said quietly.

I was so stunned, I could scarcely think. It was one thing to be told a story about a living creature appearing out of mist or thin air; but to see the actual phenomenon take place right before one's eyes—it was petrifying, and enough to make one doubt one's very sanity!

All at once, a chaotic jumble of memories and images descended on my brain: how I had met Mr. Wagner on the very day that the *Demeter* had arrived at Whitby; the speed with which he had rescued my errant hat; how he never ate or drank while in my presence; how it had seemed that he cast no reflection in the river-water; the magnetic powers of persuasion he had exhibited over strangers; how cool his fingers had always felt against my skin; the smoldering look in his eyes as he had stared at my throat, before shoving me away; his ability to read the street numbers so well in the dark; the odd sensation that I was being watched from the house next door, and his sudden appearance shortly thereafter on the train.

"No!" I gasped, staring at him. "It cannot be true! You cannot be he!"

"I am sorry, Mina, that you had to find out this way. I had planned to tell you very differently. However—" He let out a rueful laugh and went on bitterly: "I just discovered that you and those men of yours—based on some misguided notion that I mean you harm—are plotting to kill me."

THIRTEEN

I LEAPT FROM MY BED AND SHRANK BACK AGAINST THE FAR wall in terror and confusion. Was it possible? Could the man I loved be the very monster that I despised . . . and the same beast that we were all committed to destroy? All that had come before this, everything "Mr. Wagner" and I had shared—was it just part of some devious, incomprehensible plot? Was he here to murder me?

If so, I was entirely at his mercy. I was clad in nothing but a thin white nightdress, and left alone in a house with no one but incarcerated madmen and a few servants and attendants who resided in a separate wing. I was heartbroken, bewildered, terrified, and aghast, all at the same time.

"How?" I whispered. "How can it be? Jonathan said that Count Dracula was an old man, but you are—"

"When I met your Mr. Harker in Transylvania, I took the form that I present to the locals. I had not fed in a long while. The peasants, with their superstitious fears, take care to guard both themselves and their livestock against me."

"So it is true, then?" I cried in horror. "The reason you have come to England is to gorge yourself on our defenseless citizens—to murder them and create more of your own kind?"

He let out a groan of frustration and disgust, eyeing me with such fury that I feared he might leap across the room and kill me on the spot. "So this is what your precious Professor Van Helsing has told you of me? I guessed as much when I heard your plans earlier this evening. What fallacies mankind creates, in its ignorance! Mina: do you really imagine that I have been murdering the innocent residents of London? Have there been any such reports in the newspapers? With the Ripper killings still so fresh in everyone's minds, if people were turning up dead in alleys at night with bite marks on their throats, do not you think someone would have noticed?"

Faintly, I managed: "I—suppose so. But—"

"I know of your professor by reputation." Dracula seemed to be straining every nerve he possessed to hold his anger in check as he paced the room. "He fancies himself something of a vampire expert—although to my knowledge he had never seen one, let alone killed one, until yesterday at Hampstead cemetery. What other lies has this 'expert' told you about me? I have little interest in making more of my own kind, Mina. The other vampires I have met or known are mostly foul creatures with whom I have nothing in common besides a thirst for blood. The last thing I would wish is to populate the earth with more of them."

"Then why are you here?"

"I left Transylvania because after centuries of stagnation in the darkness, surrounded by people who hate and fear me, I wished to live in the light and the world again. I wished to be amongst interesting, energetic, educated people who were *doing* things: to enjoy and experience the delights of culture and the wonders of science and technology, which I could only read about from afar. That this great city offers me more opportunities to feed, I cannot ignore. I survive as I must—as any one would do. It is a law of nature. In truth, my eating habits are not all that different from yours, Mina: blood for me; a cooked bird or animal for you."

"They are entirely different! It is the difference between good and evil!"

"Is it? If so, then I believe your cooked bird is the act of evil—because I rarely feed to kill. I have no need to do so. I prefer human blood, but I will resort to animal blood if required. As a rule, I take but little, which the body easily replenishes. The wounds heal in time, the creature goes off unharmed, and, under my power of suggestion, rarely recalls a thing about it."

Intense loathing welled up within me. "Lucy did not go off unharmed! It was you who attacked her in Whitby and London, was it not?"

"I would hardly use the term *attacked;* but yes, I did feed from her."

"And then you killed her!"

"I did not kill Lucy. *That* was the work of Dr. Van Helsing."

"What? How dare you say so! The professor only killed the false, *vampire* Lucy to save her soul. But *you* murdered my sweet friend! You made Lucy into a vampire! Do you deny it?"

"I have no wish to deny it. I made Lucy a vampire at her request, to save her life in the only way I could, because she was dying—dying because the professor was killing her with his blood transfusions."

I stared at him, taken aback entirely. "What do you mean? What are you saying? Those transfusions were to try and save her."

"And yet they killed her."

"I don't understand."

"Mina," he explained patiently, "Lucy told me that Van Helsing gave her four separate blood transfusions in ten days, from *four different men.* I am an expert of sorts when it comes to the blood. And I can tell you—even though modern science is as yet oblivious of the fact—there are, without question, different types and kinds of blood, and I am certain they do not mix. Why do you think so many—I should say *most*—of the patients who have been transfused in the past decades have died? It was the professor's misguided medicine that killed Lucy. She may have seemed to benefit from the first donation of blood, but it soon sickened her; and each subsequent transfusion only made her increasingly ill, until she died."

I shook my head in disbelief. "You are lying. Lucy was bloodless, they said, and ghostly pale—you took her blood time and again, and left her on the verge of death!"

"That is not true. In Whitby, I never took enough to sicken her or to change her. Perhaps she suffered from some other malady, like her mother. And I only came to her in London because she called to me."

"She called to you?" I repeated incredulously. "Oh! Do you really expect me to believe that, Mr.—" I stopped myself, reminding myself that this was not Mr. Wagner; there had never been a Mr. Wagner. With increasing despair and disgust, I went on: "I believed you to be a man of character, yet you are no man at all. You are a . . . a Thing. An Un-Dead Thing. Unholy. Unreal. I know I have been blind and gullible up until now, but please do not further insult my intelligence by saying she 'called to you.' And take care not to sully my best friend's memory! I loved Lucy truly, even as I thought I—" Tears sprang into my eyes, and I could not finish the sentence.

"I see I have much to explain if you are ever to understand the true facts of the case," he said quietly.

"I do not wish to hear your explanations. You are a murderer and a monster! Get out of my sight! Go!"

"I will not leave, Mina; not until you hear what I have to say.

I may never have this opportunity again. I overheard your little committee's plans to-night. Your men are searching my house as we speak, hoping to defile the precious cargo I took such care to bring here. I could have stopped them; I could have killed every one of them; but I did not. I would not harm them, for your sake. I sent a small deterrent instead."

"What deterrent?"

"A few thousand rats."

"Oh!" I cried in repugnance.

"It will disrupt their activities to-night; however, I fear it will only put off the inevitable." He whirled on me abruptly, his blue eyes smoldering at their centres now like red flames, a sight which made my blood run cold. "Do you think this is a little pleasure trip I have taken to your country, Mina? Do you imagine it was easy for me to get here? No. It is the culmination of five decades of planning! I learned your language. I studied your culture, your laws, your politics, your social life. It required an immense financial investment. It is the fulfillment of a dream. Now you and your men seek to destroy everything I have worked so hard to build. Somehow, I must make you understand the truth!"

He moved to the mantel, where he stood with his back to me for some moments, as if struggling to regain control over his temper and emotions. When he turned back to stare intently at me, his eyes had returned to their natural deep blue. "Allow me to tell you why I came to Whitby in the first place. It began with a photograph."

"A photograph? Of whom?"

"Of you. Mr. Harker had brought it with him to Transylvania."

I knew the photograph he spoke of. Jonathan had taken it with his Kodak camera shortly after we became engaged, and he used to carry it with him everywhere in his pocketbook.

"He showed the photograph to me one evening, and talked about you at length. I could see that you were not only a beautiful but a remarkable woman, and that he was deeply in love with you. I admit: I was . . . envious. It had been centuries since I had felt that kind of passion for a woman, or since any one had held such deep feelings for me. And then . . . your letters arrived."

"The letters I wrote to Jonathan, which he never received!"

"Yes." He glanced away, suddenly unable to look me in the eye.

"Why did you keep them from him? How could you?"

"Forgive me. I should not have opened those letters, Mina; but from the moment the first envelope touched my hand, I felt something that I cannot explain. I read your precious words. It was as if your spirit were emanating off the page. I could not bear to part with them."

His voice was filled with such emotion and apparent sincerity that—despite myself—it made a tiny chink in my wall of fear and hatred.

"I was overcome with the need to meet you; to know you," he went on. "From your correspondence, I knew where and when you would be staying in Whitby. And so, out of all the ports I had been considering as my entry point into England, I chose Whitby. Perhaps it was foolish of me; I could have employed the ship to sail directly up the Thames to London harbour with far more expediency, and in the long run at far less expense. But I was determined to find you at any cost."

I stared at him, bewildered. "You came to Whitby . . . because of me?"

"For no other reason."

"But those sailors on the ship! You murdered them all!"

"I did not. I admit, I was obliged to kill one man under duress—but I never laid a hand on the others."

"You did!"

"Mina: what possible reason could I have had for killing the crew of the *Demeter*? I needed them all alive and well to sail the ship, if I was to make safe harbour with my cargo. If that ship had sunk, my boxes of Transylvanian earth would have all been lost, and I would have been a thousand miles from home, with little hope of survival. Not to mention that a ship arriving with a missing crew would surely call attention to itself, something I greatly wished to avoid."

I listened in growing wonder. How was it that none of this had occurred to Dr. Van Helsing or the rest of us when we had blamed the Count for the crew's demise? "If you did not kill all those men, then what happened to them?" I demanded.

"I can only tell you what I know, for I spent the greater part of the voyage in the hold below. I had taken care to feed fully before I left Varna. I require very little blood any more, unless I am trying to maintain the healthy pink skin tone that is so pleasing to mortals. What little I needed to survive during the month-long voyage, I took from the rats on board. We were eleven days at sea, when, late one night, I went up on deck for some fresh air. This turned out to be a great blunder, as I was soon to discover. The next day, the entire crew came down to search the hold. I was safe in one of my boxes, which fortunately they did not think to open. From their conversation, I learned that one of the crew, Petrofsky—a man who they said was very fond of the drink—had mysteriously gone missing two nights earlier, and that a strange, tall man had been briefly spotted on deck by the man on watch the night before.

"I can only deduce that Petrofsky accidentally fell overboard in a drunken stupor. His disappearance, however, combined with the unfortunate sighting of me, gave rise to a panic of superstitious fear amongst the crew, who now feared that something or someone strange was aboard. Not wishing to cause any further trouble, I stayed in my box for the next six days straight, but such captivity and immobility is not easy to endure. At last I could stand it no longer. I went up on deck again, unaware that the watchman was in hiding, looking for me. He pounced on me with his blade. I had no choice but to kill him and throw him overboard."

"Did you feed on him before you—"

"Would it matter if I did? The point is: my very survival was at stake. He would have told the others what he had seen, and they might have discovered my hiding place. I kept to the hold after that, but it appears that chaos soon ensued. The first mate, a superstitious Romanian, seems to have taken this second man's disappearance as a sign, and—as the captain recorded in his log—the mate went virtually insane. As far as I can ascertain, he made it his mission to stab every member of the crew he encountered alone on deck at night and throw him to the sharks, perhaps hoping to protect them from becoming vampires, or fearing that they had already been turned. All this I only discovered when we had nearly reached our destination."

"You are saying that you had nothing to do with their deaths? That it was the first mate who killed the rest of the crew?"

"Yes."

"Why did the first mate say that when he later encountered the stranger on board, he knifed him—and his blade went through empty air?"

"Could I allow a repetition of earlier events? When he came upon me, should I have let him stab me? No; this time, I vanished to the hold. The mate himself described me as 'ghastly pale'—which I assure you, Mina, would never have been the case, had I just fed on seven crew members in rapid succession. When he came down and spotted me again, I saw the terror in his eyes. He jumped off the ship of his own volition, to 'save his soul'; you will find that, too, in the published log. As for the captain, when I realised that we were the only two left on board, I appeared before him and offered my help to sail his ship. I speak perfectly fluent Russian; however, the poor soul was too overcome with fear to listen. He went mad, and later lashed himself to the helm. I was obliged to steer the ship all on my own, by controlling the fog and wind and storm; no easy feat, I can tell you, for I have next to nothing in the way of experience as a sailor."

I stared at him confounded, trying to make sense of all he was telling me. "And the dog—or wolf—they saw leaping off the ship?"

"People were watching, in the glare of the coastguard's searchlight. It seemed the best method of locomotion at the time. A trail of mist or a blur of motion would have been far more strange and conspicuous."

"Who . . . killed old Mr. Swales?"

"You mean the old man on the East Cliff? I regret to say that I appeared one night immediately before him. I believe it frightened him to death."

I leaned back against the wall, my mind a whirl of confusion. Should I believe him? What if he was just inventing these explanations to win me to his side? I had no way to verify any of it, and surely he knew that. But . . . what if it was true? Could it be that this man was not the terrible monster that we all imagined?

"The day I met you on the cliff . . ." I said slowly, recalling the way my hat had blown off, and how he had rescued it for me. "Was that—"

"I had been following you since early morning from your lodging-house. I waited for an opportunity. And then, a little puff of wind—" He shrugged. "Not all my powers completely vanish with the daylight, despite what your 'learned' professor may tell you." With catlike grace, he skirted around the bed until he stood directly in front of me, and said softly:

"Mina: for centuries, I have been alone. I have nearly perished from loneliness, and yet I could not die. I have longed to meet a woman I could truly love: a kindred spirit who shared my dreams, my interests, my passions. When I saw your photograph and read your letters, I had an uncanny premonition that you were destined for me; and once we met, I knew it with a certainty."

His eyes and voice blazed with such passion that all the fear and rancor that had built up within me began to fade away, evaporating like the very mist which had brought him here. He went on:

"From the moment I set eyes on you on that first day at Whitby, I have wanted you—needed you—loved you. But I did not just want you for your blood: I wanted all of you: your mind, your heart, your body, your soul. *I wanted you to want me*; to become mine of your own free will. The time we shared in Whitby was the sweetest of my existence. When you left so abruptly, I nearly went mad. I thought I would never see you again. I left for London that same day, but it proved meaningless to me. I could think of nothing but you. Were you well and safe? Had you returned from Buda-Pesth? At last, when I could stand it no longer, I went down to Exeter to try and find you. I saw you—and your husband—on your balcony."

"That was you?" I said breathlessly, recalling the bat we had seen fly away.

"Yes. You looked so happy, so serene. I could not bear to disturb you. Leaving you that night, in the arms of another man—a man I had come to despise, a man who had once tried to kill me—was the hardest thing I have ever done. But I was determined to leave you be, to let you live the life you had chosen for yourself."

He placed his cool hand against my cheek, a touch which sent a shock like pure electricity running through me. My heart twisted, even as I felt my body tingle with sudden desire.

"Yesterday, by what seemed to be the most astonishing twist of fate, I thought I saw you standing on the road outside my very gates! I had to know if it was really you. I dashed after you. I leapt upon the train. Finding you again, it was like . . . a miracle."

His eyes as they gazed into mine were so filled with affection that my mind reeled, and my pulse drummed in my ears. *No. No,* I told myself. *You are a married woman. This is wrong.* But I could not listen. At that moment, I yearned for nothing more in all the world but for him to pull me into his arms and to kiss me.

"I love you, Mina. I love you. If you do not want me, if you must break my heart, please say so now: tell me to go, and I will leave you for ever and not return. But I must hear it from your own lips. What shall it be? Do you want me? Do you love me? Will you let me love you?"

"Yes," I whispered. "I love you! I want you!"

With an impassioned moan, he pulled me to him. His lips found mine. I gave myself up to the joy of his embrace, returning his kiss with a fervour equal to his own. My eyes closed. My arms wrapped around his neck. My hands tangled in his hair. I felt the pressure of his hands roving up and down my back, pressing me more tightly against him. After the first few minutes of heated, heartfelt contact, the nature of his kiss changed to something slower, deeper, and softer.

Oh! What a kiss! It was a kiss unlike anything that I had ever before experienced. As his tongue went on a gentle quest, exploring the delicate interior of my mouth, a myriad of new sensations were awakened within me. I began to tremble. A tingling began in the tips of my breasts that seemed to move and settle in the very centre of my womanhood. I was carried away, on fire. The kiss seemed to go on for ever; I *wanted* it to go on for ever; yet all too soon, it was over. Bereft, I opened my eyes—and I gasped, my heart pounding in sudden terror. For I saw that his eyes were now no longer blue, but blazing like hot red flames, and his canine teeth had grown longer and sharper.

I was too stunned to think or move. I knew he desired my blood. And yet I did not want to hinder him. With a flick of his fingers, he untied the ribbon at my collar and pulled open my nightdress at my neck, exposing my collar-bone and upper chest. His mouth instantly found the supersensitive skin at the side of my throat, and at his first, butterfly touch, I quivered and moaned in ecstasy. Suddenly, I felt two sharp pricks against my flesh, and I gasped again. The pain was trivial, quickly replaced by a feeling of languid pleasure such as I had never before imagined. It was as if I could feel my blood seeping out of me, and at the same time, something new, magical, and effervescent seemed to be mingling with my own life essence. Soon, it felt as if the tingling, liquid glow that had been throbbing in my very centre was pulsating throughout all the veins in my body, as if every one of my senses was alive and heightened to a fever-pitch—and with it came a sense of impending danger. Deep down inside of me, I knew that this was bad for me—*very bad*—that if he took too much blood it would kill me—that I must put a stop to it before it was too late. But I had no will to stop it. I heard a strange vibration, like singing through deep water. My head fell back; I heard myself sigh with intense pleasure; my knees began to buckle beneath me. If nirvana existed, I thought, in the remote corner of my mind which could still think, this must be it. I never wanted it to end.

Abruptly, his mouth left my throat. "Enough," he said softly.

I moaned in disappointment. He held me tightly. I felt dizzy and light-headed; had he let me go, I believe I would have fainted. Suddenly, I was very, very cold; but *his* touch was strangely warm.

All at once, he whispered: "They are here."

I had no idea what he meant; I could hear nothing except the thundering beat of my own heart in my ears.

"I will be back to-morrow night," he whispered, pressing his lips to mine one last time. Then he took a step back and vanished into a cloud of mist, which, through dazed eyes, I watched trail out around the edges of the window.

I SANK TO THE FLOOR, DRAINED AND SPENT, MY HEART STILL pounding, but too weak to move. I felt as if every cell in my body had dissolved into a hot, liquid, molten pool. I became hazily aware of the voices of the men below, returning from their search party. My arms felt like leaden weights. With difficulty, I raised my hand to touch my throat, and felt the fresh teeth-marks embedded there.

Sudden guilt overcame me in a rush. Oh! What had I done? How could I have allowed Mr. Wagner—*no, no, Count Dracula*—to kiss me, and to drink my blood? It was bad enough that I had thought of him, dreamt of him, *longed for him,* when I thought he was Mr. Wagner, a flesh and blood man—but to give myself to one who was Un-Dead—a vampire, a Thing I had come to hate—it was unthinkable!

And yet . . . and yet . . .

In my arms, Dracula had felt as real and alive as any human man. In his embrace, I had undergone the most wondrous physical sensations I had ever experienced. And in spite of who or what he was . . . in spite of every terrible thing I knew about him . . . *I loved him.*

Was it possible to be both violently attracted to and repelled by a man at the same time? Is this what Jonathan had felt, I wondered, for those awful vampire women at Dracula's castle? And what about my mother? Is this attraction what she had felt, when she gave herself so willingly to the young master of the Sterling household?

I heard footsteps on the stairs. I forced myself to rise. Dizzily, I slipped into bed, retying the collar of my nightdress and pulling up the bed-clothes just as I heard the door to my chamber unlock and open. I feigned sleep, willing my pulse and breathing to slow to a soft and natural state as I listened to Jonathan quietly undress and slip into bed, terrified lest he should gain the slightest inkling of what had just occurred.

Oh! What on earth was I to do?

Dr. Van Helsing and Jonathan had both insisted that Count Dracula was an evil being, without conscience, intent on doing harm to every human he met. Was that so? How was I to reconcile the monster they described with the man I had come to know and love at Whitby, and the man who had just expressed his love to me so ardently and passionately?

I longed to share with the others all that Dracula had told me in his defence. But how could I? To do so, I would have to admit to everything, all the way back to the times we had shared at Whitby. I would be obliged to reveal that we had spoken to-night in this very bedchamber. Jonathan would surely discover that I had been bitten. No doubt, the group would immediately leap to the conclusion that I had been poisoned, both mentally and physically, into collaborating with the enemy—as perhaps I had been. If I pretended that I had been unwillingly attacked, I feared it would only whip them into a frenzy of deeper hatred. And most certainly, I could never tell Jonathan or any of the others about my true feelings for Dracula—*never*! Never! To do so I would be labeled as a debased, wanton woman. My husband would never touch me again. No, I thought, as I pulled up the collar of my nightdress to cover the fresh wounds at my throat; this must remain my secret, for ever.

And it must never happen again.

But how on earth, I wondered, was I to accomplish that? The Count had said he would return to-morrow night! A little voice told me that I should simply refuse to see him or talk to him; but was he the kind of being that one *could* refuse? Moreover, his powers of persuasion were so great, and my feelings for him were so intense, that I was not certain I could withstand any further advances on his part. Still, I would have to try.

My thoughts began to scatter. As I drifted off to sleep, I made a resolution. If Dracula came to me again, I would be strong. I would not allow him to kiss me or touch me in any way. I had so many questions. I would use the opportunity to learn all that I could about him.

To-morrow, I vowed, I would prepare myself for my next audience with the vampire.

I DID NOT WAKE UNTIL WELL PAST NOON, WHEN I OPENED MY EYES to find Jonathan shaking me gently and anxiously as he stood over the bed.

"Mina! Are you all right?"

"I am fine," I responded groggily, as I struggled to emerge from a deep, lethargic slumber.

"You look pale. I had to call your name three times before you came round."

The memory of all that had happened the night before came back in a rush. I felt myself blush and buried my face in the pillow to hide a smile I could not prevent. "I am just tired. I did not sleep well."

"I am sorry I woke you, then," he said sweetly, as he kissed the back of my head. "Go back to sleep. I have things to do. I will see you this evening."

I heard the door close, and I drifted off again.

The afternoon sun was low in the sky when I finally got up. The dizziness and weakness had passed. I glanced in the looking-glass. I was a bit pale, but not alarmingly so. I pulled back my long hair, wincing when I saw the small puncture wounds on my throat. They only smarted slightly, but they were ugly. How fortunate I was that Jonathan had not noticed them when he awakened me earlier. For once, I was grateful to the dictates of fashion, since the high collar of my blouse neatly hid the two marks.

I went down-stairs and found the house very quiet. Dr. Seward's study was empty. I stole inside, where I searched and soon found what I was seeking: a medical book regarding the study of blood. I leafed through it to an article about the history of blood transfusions. The text, which was boldly illustrated with pictures of needles, syringes, tubes, and drawings of patients undergoing some rather frightening-looking procedures, depicted an appalling record. Indeed: far more patients had died over the years from this little-understood technique than had lived.

I was deep in contemplation as to the implications of this knowledge when Dr. Van Helsing startled me by entering the room.

"You read medical books for pleasure, Madam Mina?" he said with a smile.

"Anything that can be of help in our quest is of interest to me." I quickly replaced the volume on the shelf and turned to him. "Doctor: I have been thinking about Lucy. I know that you gave her four blood transfusions. I suppose you must have a great deal of experience with that kind of operation?"

"Oh yes, I have transfused many patients in the past."

"Were your other transfusions successful?"

Dr. Van Helsing hesitated. He seemed unsure how to reply; but honest man that he was, he finally said: "I succeeded with one patient, yes."

"So all the other patients—they died?"

"It is a new and inexact science. I did my best for Miss Lucy," he said defensively.

"I am certain you did." Changing the subject, I asked where the others were, and he replied enigmatically:

"Your husband, Mr. Morris, and Lord Godalming have gone out. Dr. Seward is with his patients, I believe."

"And how did your foray go last night?"

"It went well; but I say no more. We think it best that we not draw you further into this awful work, Madam Mina. These are strange and dangerous times, and it is no place for a woman. Until we have rid the earth of this monster of the nether world, we will keep silent about our doings. You understand, I hope."

"I understand," I replied.

Oh! How ironic it was, I thought; if only he knew that while his brave posse had been inside the Count's house the night before, the very man they were trying to protect me from had made a most personal and intimate visit to my own chamber! I was resolute: none of them could ever know the truth. When I later wrote in my journal, I recorded only a partial, altered version of the previous night's events, pretending that I had only had a very strange dream.

All afternoon, I could think of nothing but the night to come. Would Dracula visit me again, as he had promised? The thought both thrilled and terrified me. When and how would he come? Would I be in any danger? I knew he was a powerful being. I had seen evidence of his temper, and I knew he could kill me on a whim. He had said he loved me, and that he had gone to Whitby expressly to meet me. After all the time we had spent in each other's company, all the feelings we had shared, and the very passionate manner in which he had kissed me—and drunk from me—I could not help but believe him.

And yet, just because Dracula loved me—and I returned those feelings—it did not mean that he held my best interests at heart, or that he posed no threat to the population at large. He was well aware that I was party to a group of men plotting his destruction. I had no real proof that the Count could be trusted or that he would not harm me.

This time, I intended to be ready for him. His explanation for Lucy's death now seemed plausible to me, as did everything else he had stated in his own defence—as far as it went. Perhaps it was true that he had come to England only to build a new life for himself, and that he never killed the people and animals whose blood he took. But he still had a great deal to answer for. Although I knew the contents of Jonathan's journal and our other transcripts nearly by heart, I went over them again, making a mental list of questions to ask him. If I deemed Dracula to be a trickster or a liar, I decided, or if I believed that he might prove a danger to others, I could always pretend to play along; and perhaps I could learn something which might prove useful in stopping him.

I determined, as well, to have some kind of protection with me this time. Stealing back down to Dr. Seward's study, I found the bag of tools and charms against the vampire which the professor had given him, and I stole a tiny vial of holy water.

❧

At dinner, the conversation was awkward and stilted. I was preoccupied by my own thoughts; and the men, determined not to discuss anything about the case in front me, strained to keep to neutral subjects.

I had been wearing mourning for over a week, in memory of Mr. Hawkins, Lucy, and Mrs. Westenra. In those two short weeks in Exeter, after Jonathan and I had returned from Buda-Pesth, I had only had time to have two new dresses made, and to-night I wore one of them: a beaded evening gown of black silk. I had taken special care with my hair, pinning it up into a style I thought most becoming. As I fingered the soft velvet of the black neckband, which hid the puncture marks on my throat, I thought: how sweet of Lucy, to leave me such a precious treasure! At the same time, I wondered if she had, somehow, sensed that I might one day have the same need of it as she had. And yet, if so, then why did she not warn me about him? Did she not recognise her own attacker as Mr. Wagner?

After dinner, Jonathan kissed me good-night and closed himself up with the others in Dr. Seward's study, with the shades drawn—to "smoke together," as they said—but I knew they wanted to talk about what had occurred to each during the day, and discuss their future plans. After being in Jonathan's full confidence for so many years, it was strange suddenly to be kept in the dark; and yet, was I not doing the very same thing to him?

It was not yet nine o'clock. Having slept most of the day, I was not at all tired and had no intention of going to bed yet. I went up to my room and waited. Would Dracula dare to come now, I wondered, while the men were occupied down-stairs? More likely, he would wait until everyone was asleep. I hid the vial of holy water between my breasts, deep inside my corset. I took up a book, then threw it down again, too agitated to read. I drew open the blinds, opened the tall casement windows, and stepped out onto the small, railed balcony beyond. All was silent without. The night sky was inky black, the stars obscured by thick clouds.

I had been standing on the balcony for some minutes, when a ray of moonlight broke through the thick clouds above, shining its bright beams on the grass and trees which studded the wide grounds below. I began to notice some tiny, grey specks floating in the moonlight's distant rays. They were like infinitesimal grains of sand or dust, and they wheeled and circled in the air, gathering in clusters and then dispersing again, as they moved ever closer to where I stood.

My pulse began to race in fear and anticipation. Was it possible? Could it be he? I backed away into the room. The motes of dust continued to dance in the moonbeams as they approached, whirling faster and faster until they blew in through the open window, finally assembling into a phantom shape a few feet from where I stood. In the blink of an eye, the shape transformed into the man himself! I gasped and clutched at a piece of furniture to steady myself, still finding it difficult to accept the reality of such an unearthly spectacle.

"You look beautiful," he said softly; then with concern, he added: "You are well, I hope?"

"Yes." I fought to master my pounding heart, determined not to betray the apprehension that coursed through me. "I am just unaccustomed to these sudden and rather dramatic appearances. Last night it was mist. To-night it is—dust?"

"I have a variety of modes of transport at my disposal." He moved in close and touched the velvet band at my throat. "A gift from Lucy?"

This reference to my dear departed friend put me instantly on the defensive. Bitterly, I replied: "Yes."

"It suits you."

Abruptly, I said: "How did you get in here last night? I thought a vampire required an invitation to enter a place the first time."

"True. Mr. Renfield provided that service—a bit reluctantly, I think. God knows how that madman became attuned to my presence, but he seems to have been expecting me before I even took residence at Carfax. At first, he sought me desperately and was quite an annoyance. Now he seems to fear me. The man is truly insane."

"For that, I pity him."

"You should *beware* of him, Mina. He has designs on you. Do not trust a thing he says."

As he moved towards me, he passed in front of the looking-glass. I saw that he cast no reflection, and despite myself, I gave a sudden, startled gasp. Seeing my reaction, he quickly moved out of the mirror's line of sight.

"I despise mirrors," he said testily. "They are a sign of man's vanity, and a reminder that I—" He broke off, his dark brows furrowing. "Does it bother you?"

I swallowed hard. "What? That you have no reflection? It—is very disconcerting. I do not understand it."

"It is one of those mysteries that cannot be explained. It just is. Which is particularly unsettling, I know, in this great scientific age, which demands explanations for everything." As Dracula spoke, he picked up my black shawl and wrapped it about my shoulders. He now gazed down at me and insisted urgently: "Come with me."

"Come where?" I asked.

"To my house next door."

Alarm spread through me. I had not anticipated this. "I cannot leave!" I insisted. "The men are all down-stairs."

"They will be locked up in that study for hours. They think you are asleep. Come. I have something to show you. I promise to have you back before they miss you."

"Surely you must understand that I dare not go anywhere with you."

He moved closer, cupping my chin with his fingers (once more as cool as summer rain) and raising it until my eyes met his. I had promised myself that I would not let him touch me, that I would not allow myself to fall under his spell; but with his eyes on mine, and his touch against my flesh, I was powerless to resist, as putty in his hands. "What are you afraid of?" he said tenderly. "That I will take advantage of your virtue? Or that I will bite you and feed a bit too long and avidly?"

Both, I thought. Aloud, I said breathlessly: "Should I fear these things?"

"Perhaps you should. I cannot deny it: I have long desired both your body and your blood. But had I wished to take you by force, Mina, I could have—and would have—long ago. I am willing to wait as long as it takes to possess those parts of you which mean the most to me: your mind and heart."

The heart he spoke of continued to hammer in my chest, in close proximity to the vial of holy water which I had hidden between my breasts. "If you hoped to endear me to you with such a speech, you have failed," I said, my breathing shallow and laboured. "You have only increased my fear." But was it really due to fear? Or was it due to something else?

He winced at that. As if annoyed with himself, he lowered his hand and stepped back, his gaze still holding mine. "Forgive me. You were never afraid when I was Mr. Wagner. Do not fear me now. I am the same man, Mina. Nothing has changed, except your perception of me. Trust me when I tell you: I love you, and I would never harm you."

The affection in his eyes and the sincerity in his voice were nearly impossible to resist. It took every ounce of will-power I possessed not to say yes to him at that very instant. Sensing my hesitation, he said:

"Come or not; the choice is entirely up to you. But I truly hope you will."

I guessed what lay unspoken: that he could employ his hypnotic powers of persuasion if he wished, but he had chosen not to. For better or worse, I made my decision. I fought back my fear and took the hand he offered. I expected him to lead me to the door. Instead, to my surprise, he effortlessly swept me up into his arms and carried me outside onto the balcony. "Hold on tight."

"What are you doing?" I asked, startled.

"I am taking you home."

FOURTEEN

I FELT A SUDDEN BLAST OF ICY WIND, ACCOMPANIED BY THE sensation of rapid movement, a flash of colourful images, and a great, whirring vibration in my ears. All at once, we were standing in the moonlight on what appeared to be the back porch of an immense, old, stone mansion: the house next door.

"How did you do that?" I said, dumbfounded, as he set me on my feet.

"A simple matter of physics." With affection, he brushed back a lock of my hair that had blown loose, adding: "'There are more things in heaven and earth, Horatio, than are dreamt of in your philosophy.'"

Although wobbly and still struggling to regain my wits, I recognised the quote from *Hamlet.* I shook my head in disbelief. "But—we were up on a first-floor balcony—and there is a high wall separating our properties. Can you fly?"

He laughed. "Not as a man. But I can leap, and move faster than the human eye can follow. I cannot do so for great distances, however, as it saps much of my strength."

I struggled to rise above my amazement as he unlocked the door and motioned for me to enter. It was pitch-dark and very cold inside. As I shivered in the dank air, he lit a candle. In its flickering light, I saw that we were in a large, old, empty vestibule. The floor was blanketed with a thick layer of dust, and the high walls were laced with cobwebs that hung down like flags, thick with dust.

"Please excuse the deplorable lack of housekeeping. This house is vast and has been empty for quite some time." It was all I could do to keep up with him as he bounded up several long flights of stairs. "I have put all my energy into making one particular chamber habitable. Thankfully, it appears to have been undiscovered by your men's search party last night."

We reached the top floor of the building. Midway down the long, dark corridor, he waved his hand and part of the panelled wall slid back.

"Welcome to my parlour," he said.

We entered. I stopped and stared in abject wonder. Whatever I had expected to find upstairs in this ancient, part-medieval mansion, it was not this. The room was warm, inviting, and elegantly panelled in oak, with long, dark red velvet draperies shrouding the tall windows. Candles glowed in several tall candelabras, accompanied by two gas-lamps, which combined to fill the room with a soft golden light. The furnishings and thick Turkey carpets looked expensive and luxurious. I was most surprised, however, by the oak bookcases lining two long walls from floor to ceiling, which were half-filled with books of all sizes and descriptions. A sea of boxes lying open and scattered on the floor contained more books, as if they were still in the process of being unpacked. The volumes seemed to number into the tens of thousands.

"It is more like a library than a parlour," I said, thunder-struck, glancing at the titles of some of the books on the shelves, many of which appeared to be very old. They encompassed a wide variety of topics, including history, biography, philosophy, science, medicine, poetry, and fiction—from the ancient classics to the modern—both the popular and the obscure. There was also, I noticed, a collection of volumes on witchcraft, alchemy, and superstition. Many of the titles I had never heard of, and I found myself longing to take them up and read them.

"Where did you get all these books?" I asked.

"They are from my castle in Transylvania. This is but a tiny portion of my library there. Did you really think it was only earth in all of those crates I brought with me?"

I nodded, speechless—yet wondering why I should be so surprised. Mr. Wagner and I had, after all, discussed literature often and at great length. The two halves of the man I knew were coming together for me now to make up a fascinating whole—and there were more surprises to come. On a table near-by I spied a typewriter, along with Gregg's book on shorthand, and a flurry of sheets which revealed attempts at practicing both techniques.

I glanced at him with a confused smile, and he shrugged: "I thought I might teach myself these arts, which were of such interest to you."

His expression caused a heat to rise to my face; a heat which made me realise, all of a sudden, that I was no longer cold at all. As I removed my shawl, my attention was drawn to a substantial fire burning brightly in the hearth, which gave off a comforting heat. "Oh!" I cried in alarm. "Are you not worried that someone will see the smoke?"

"It is a smokeless fire."

Indeed, as I studied it again, I saw that the flames blazed more red than yellow, and that although they appeared to be consuming real logs, they emitted not a single puff of smoke. "Just another simple matter of physics, I suppose?"

"Something like that."

I stared at him in wonder. Was all this just another one of my strange dreams? But no; something deep in my bones told me that I was fully sentient. Upon first entering the room, I had been aware of a unique, pungent smell which was at once rich, deep, and oddly familiar. I now caught sight of the source: an easel was set up in one corner, with a canvas upon it that faced the opposite way. Beside the easel, a table held jars of oil paints, pencils, brushes, mineral spirits, sketch-books, and a palette dotted with multiple colours. This discovery was so entirely unexpected that I blurted rather unnecessarily:

"Do you paint?"

"I dabble."

I crossed to the easel and turned to stop in full view of the canvas. It was a portrait in oils—still fresh and new, and so perfectly and exquisitely rendered, that it might have been a work by Rembrandt or Leonardo Da Vinci. I stared at it, stunned.

It was a portrait of me.

In the painting, I was dressed in a beautiful, emerald green evening gown, with a low-cut bodice adorned with elaborate beading. My blonde hair was swept up high upon my head, exposing my pale throat. I was smiling demurely at the viewer, as if in happy possession of a secret. There was no doubting the artist's affection for his subject; for although I clearly recognised myself, he had somehow made me appear far more beautiful than I believed myself to be. It was then that I noticed, on the table beside the easel, the tiny photograph of me which Jonathan had taken a year before. The faded, sepia-toned print seemed pale and lifeless in comparison with the glowing woman in the portrait.

I heard him move up close behind me.

"Do you like it?" he asked quietly.

My pulse quickened at his nearness. "Yes. When did you paint it?"

"I began many weeks ago, when I first arrived here. It was my solace."

I hardly knew what to say. "You are a wonderful artist."

"One can become proficient at most anything, I find, with a modicum of aptitude and an eternity to indulge it." He closed the gap between us now, his body resting against the back of mine, his hands settling on my shoulders. This was my moment to move away, I knew. I must insist on maintaining a safe distance between us. I must steel myself against him. But his touch made me feel weak with sudden longing, and I could not bring myself to do it.

I felt his lips press against my hair, then move lower to tenderly kiss my neck. "Mina: for weeks, I have dreamt of bringing you here. I never imagined it could ever be so; yet here you are."

My heart began to pound in earnest now. Did he mean to bite me again? I feared it; yet to my mortification, I wanted him to. I desperately craved the feel of his teeth piercing my flesh, and the intense, erotic rush of pleasure that I knew would follow. I closed my eyes, unable to prevent the anxious gasp that escaped my lips.

I felt him tense. "You are still afraid," he said with deep regret. He let me go abruptly, and stepped back with a small, self-derisive laugh. "Forgive me. I told myself I could be with you and not be tempted. I was wrong. I will do my best to control my appetite hereafter."

I stood in disappointed silence, attempting to regulate my breathing and slow the rapid cadence of my heart as I watched him cross the room. He opened a large wooden chest, from which he withdrew a stunning, beaded evening gown of emerald green silk—the same gown that I was wearing in the portrait.

"I had this made for you by a dressmaker in Whitby," he said, bringing me the garment. "I thought the colour would match your eyes. I hoped to give it to you there, but—you left very suddenly."

"Oh! It is exquisite." I had never dreamt of owning anything like it. But it was too much; I felt as if all my senses were being assaulted by too many new and stunning wonders in too small a space of time. "But—you must know I cannot accept it. How could I ever explain it?"

"Perhaps you could indulge me, then, and wear it while you are here?"

"I had best not. But I thank you all the same."

Disappointed, he laid the garment aside and led me to a small table in the centre of the room, which was elegantly set with gilded china, fine crystal, and heavily scrolled silver. He pulled out a chair for me.

"May I offer you some refreshment, then? I was not sure what kind of foods would be your favourites, so I have provided a variety."

He lifted a silver cover from the plate before me to reveal a delicious-looking assortment of cold meats, cheeses, breads, and fruits, whose appetizing aromas made my mouth water. I was flattered that he had gone to much effort on my behalf, and suddenly realised that despite my nerves, I was famished, having been too tense to eat much at dinner earlier. I took the chair he offered. "Thank you."

"Would you like a glass of wine?"

"That would be lovely." As I watched him uncork a bottle of Bordeaux—(Red, I thought: how appropriate)—my mind and emotions continued to spin in confusion. The refined gentleman before me was so interesting, so passionate, learned, accomplished. How could he be the same monster that we were all hunting: an other-worldly being who yearned to drink my blood?

"What are you thinking?" he asked, as he poured the burgundy-coloured vintage into a delicate crystal goblet.

"I was thinking how strange it feels to be sitting here as your honoured guest," I lied, "and that . . . I do not know what to call you now. I still think of you as Mr. Wagner. Where did that name come from?"

He shrugged. "I admire his music."

"Somehow, 'Count Dracula' seems too formal . . ."

"Call me Nicolae."

"Nicolae." I recalled seeing that name when I had studied the title deed to this property. Despite myself, my hand trembled a little as I took the glass he offered—a reaction he did not fail to notice.

With a frown, he sat down across from me. I cut a slice of cheese, placed it atop a piece of bread, and took a bite. It was delectable. He did not remove the silver cover from his own plate but sat watching me as I ate.

"Is it true that you cannot eat food?" I asked.

"Regrettably, that pleasure is denied to me."

"Why? If you can swallow blood, why cannot you eat or drink?"

"Think: carnivore versus herbivore. My organs function in a similar manner to yours, but my body chemistry has been permanently altered. I can now digest only blood."

I nodded. "What have you been . . . living on . . . since you came to England?"

"For the most part, I have taken what little I require as a bat or a wolf, by feeding on wild animals. Although I admit: both for pleasure and sustenance, I took the blood of several people whom I encountered alone on the street late at night. They were frightened at first, as always, but then they seemed to rather enjoy the experience; and I made certain they had no memory of it afterwards."

I did not wonder that these strangers enjoyed the bloodletting, if they experienced anything even halfway similar to what I had felt. "But I remember *everything* that happened," I said.

He looked at me with a silent raising of his eyebrows, making it clear that that had been his intention. I felt myself blush.

"So then: you never kill the people you feed from?"

"Only if I lose control and drink too much, or feed too often—

but that very rarely happens." He smiled and said calmly: "Do not look so worried: I promise never to overindulge or lose control with you."

Apprehension speared through me. He made the promise so matter-of-factly; yet he was talking about *my life*! My life, which he could end in an instant, whether inadvertently or by intention. I tried not to think about that possibility as I went on:

"Do you breathe?"

"Sometimes. Out of habit, not necessity."

"If I prick you, do you bleed?"

"Yes. But I heal so quickly, it is almost as if I was never wounded at all."

It was all so incredibly uncanny. My stomach was in knots again. I put down the grapes in my hand, no longer able to eat.

"What can I do to set you at ease?" he asked gently.

"Talk to me."

"With pleasure. Since the day we met, talking with you has been one of my greatest delights. It is why I brought you here. I imagine you must have many questions for me."

"I do."

"Ask away. I will tell you anything you wish to know."

I hardly knew where to begin. I sipped my wine. After some hesitation, I said: "You insist that I should not fear you. But I know who and what you are. I see how difficult it is for you to—as you say—control your appetite. You admit that you took Lucy's blood, yet you say you did not kill her. How can I believe you?"

"I told you last night: Lucy's death was tragic, but it was not my fault."

"It was! I saw you with her that first night, on the cliff at Whitby. You attacked her—an innocent, defenseless girl, who was walking in her sleep!"

"Is that what she told you? I suppose I should not be surprised. I am afraid, my dear Mina, it did not quite happen that way."

"What did happen, then?"

"I was strolling through the Whitby graveyard: a place which had become very dear to me, for it was there that I had first met you. Lucy had a very sensitive mind. I think it was because of that—or perhaps because you two slept in such proximity in the same room—that she received thoughts that were meant for you."

"Thoughts meant for me?"

"I was thinking—rather vividly as I recall—of a future day when you would be mine."

Suddenly I remembered the dream I had had, that very night—about a tall, dark figure with red eyes who had intoned, *"You will be mine!"*—and my earlier dream, the night of the storm, when I had encountered the same faceless creature in an eerie corridor.

"Before long, I saw a young woman appear in the graveyard, barefoot and clad in a white nightdress. I recognised her, for I had seen Lucy previously with you. Not wishing to frighten her, I hid in the shadows, not far from the bench which you two so often frequented. She caught sight of me and crossed to where I stood, staring at me with her lovely blue eyes. She said: 'Sir: will you dance with me?' "

"She asked you to dance with her?" I replied, incredulous.

"I quickly deduced that she was walking in her sleep. I asked if she truly wished to dance there and then, in a graveyard, with no music playing? With a slow smile, she moved closer and said: 'Sir, ever since I came to Whitby, I have been longing to dance at the pavilion. I will be married soon. I will never dance with a stranger again. Please: dance with me! I will waltz to the music inside my head.' I could see no harm in yielding to her sweet request. And so I took your friend in my arms."

"Oh!" I said softly. I knew Lucy only too well—and was too familiar with her sleep-walking tendencies, and her appetites where men and dancing were concerned—to doubt his story.

"She began to hum *The Blue Danube,*" he continued, "and

there on the grass atop the cliff, we waltzed for a minute or two. She was a decent dancer, even in her sleep, although in no way as accomplished as yourself. As I held her in my arms, I could not help but feel a growing hunger, for she was very beautiful; but I restrained myself, knowing her to be your friend.

"Lucy's eyes soon closed, and I felt her go limp in my arms. I took her to the bench and laid her down. I would have left her there; but her eyes suddenly blinked open again. She came fully awake. She looked confused for an instant, and she blushed. Then she grabbed hold of me, drew my face down to hers, and kissed me. It was a lovely kiss; and it was then that I lost control. She was young; she was lovely; and I could not resist what she offered. I took her blood. I heard the clock in the church tower strike one, and soon after a faint voice calling 'Lucy! Lucy!' I looked up and saw someone, far away on the opposite cliff. I did not realise until later that it was you. I turned to leave, but Lucy grabbed me again and pulled me down to her, forcing my mouth back to her throat. I drank again. When I left her, she had fallen asleep once more. I watched as you woke her, then I followed you both home to ensure that you arrived in safety."

I listened to this story in silent astonishment. It was so different from the picture I had painted in my head—the picture of a villainous monster who had preyed without conscience on my unknowing, innocent friend. I remembered, too, certain odd behaviour on Lucy's part, which implied that she came to remember full well what had happened that night, and on subsequent nights—that she was hiding something.

"I introduced her to you the very next night at the pavilion," I said slowly, as I set down my wine-glass. "Why didn't she recognise you?"

"I believe she did, in some corner of her mind; but I did not appear to her on the cliff as I do to you."

I looked at him, wondering if, that night, he had looked anything like the version of himself that Jonathan and I had spotted in Piccadilly. I said: "I locked Lucy in our room to protect her, yet you came back for her—as a bat."

"She asked me to come."

"Asked you? How?"

"As I said, Lucy had a strong will and a sensitive mind. I cannot usually hear the thoughts of others, but at times, I could hear hers. I suspect this is why she recalled the times I fed from her, despite my attempts to wipe them from her memory. She must have enjoyed that first blood exchange and craved more. I needed blood; why not take what was so freely offered? Believe me, though—the amount of blood I took from Lucy as a bat could not have harmed an infant, much less a young woman of her age and size. Why Lucy declined in Whitby is beyond me; perhaps she did not have a hardy constitution, or had a heart condition like her mother. Why she grew ill in London is another story—which I have already explained. I only visited her there because I heard her call, and I thought it might be a way I could learn something about you."

"About me?"

"I was tormented, desperate to know if you had reached Buda-Pesth, if you were safe, if you were married or not . . . Lucy met me in the garden at Hillingham. To my frustration, she had not yet heard from you. She had no information to share. I walked away, but—she was not shy, your Lucy. I think she fancied herself a little bit in love with me. She ran up and pulled me into her arms, insisting that I bite her again, there and then; that she missed it and craved it. And the mental state I was in—let us say, I was in no mood to refuse. For the next ten days, I was busy here and elsewhere—unaware that your Dr. Van Helsing was killing her with his spectacularly unsound medical experiments."

Again, I found myself at a loss for words. It was possible that he was lying—weaving this story only to overcome my prejudice—

and yet everything he'd said about Lucy's nature rang completely true. And who but I could better understand her cravings—I, who had experienced Dracula's vampire bite only once! Tears sprang into my eyes; in fury and anguish, I thought: Oh, Lucy, Lucy! We both fell in love with the same man; and you lost your life because of it!

"I am sorry," he said softly. "I have made you sad. I know you loved your friend, and you must miss her."

"I am sad, but I am angry, too! Even if events did transpire exactly as you say, the fact is: Lucy would never have looked so pale as to require a blood transfusion in the first place if not for you!"

There was a flash of something immensely threatening in his eyes, and he looked away, his lips pressed together in a tight, thin line. He said angrily: "She did not *require* a transfusion. I may have left Lucy more bloodless that night than I ought to—*that* was a mistake—but left alone, in time, her blood would have replaced itself. She would have recovered on her own. Part of me curses the fact that I ever went to her in London, for it was that visit which alerted your *friends* to my existence! Another part of me is glad for it—" (His eyes darted back to mine now, once more calm and darkly compelling) "—for it brought you to me."

It was frightening, the way he blew so hot and cold. Yet it was difficult to think when he looked at me that way. "You do not seem to regret that she died, only that it made things difficult for you."

"I regret that she died young, and that her death caused you pain. I regret that, due to Van Helsing's incompetency, I was obliged to turn her into a vampire. But everyone dies. I made Lucy immortal."

"You said yesterday that you made her a vampire at her request. How can that be?"

"The next time I saw Lucy, she was dying; too weak to rise from her bed even to issue the invitation I required to enter the house. A wolf whom I had befriended at the zoo came to my call, and broke through the window for me. Lucy then asked me in—but it was too late to save her. She knew what I was. She insisted that I make her a vampire. I tried to convince her otherwise; but she saw it as a better alternative than death."

"That is not how she explained it in her diary. Lucy said that she saw specks of dust fly into the room through the broken window, and felt as if a spell had been placed upon her. Then she lost consciousness."

"I am not responsible for any tale she may have fabricated to cover up the truth."

The colour rose in my cheeks as his words hit home. I had fabricated a tale in my own journal the night before, to prevent any one from learning the truth about Dracula's visit; and I had deliberately left out any mention of Mr. Wagner ever since I began my diary at Whitby. "Even if all that is true," I said, "how could you agree to her request, knowing that you were dooming her to life as a monster—a vile seductress and a hunter of children!"

"I could have cured her of that! In all my years as a member of the Un-Dead, I have made very few of my kind, Mina. The last thing I wanted was to let loose an untrained, fledgling vampire on London, a being who was rampant with uncontrolled desire and lust; I feared it would call attention to me and might threaten my own safety—as indeed it has. But after what happened, I felt a . . . responsibility to Lucy. I warned her of what to expect. I tried to coach and guide her in those first, crucial days after she was changed—but Lucy was stubborn, and ignored my warnings. If I had had more time to work with her, I believe she would have been fine. She would have learned to restrain herself. She would have enjoyed eternal life. But when I came back, I found her mangled remains within her tomb. Van Helsing and his companions had butchered her."

Tears now flowed freely down my cheeks. "They had no choice! They butchered her to save her soul! To save her from becoming—" I could not finish. I rose from the table and walked some distance away, mourning my dear friend's loss. Dracula appeared beside me and silently gave me a linen handkerchief.

As I struggled to regain my composure, I wondered again: should I trust him? How could I be certain that all he had said was true?

I whirled to face him. "All right. Perhaps I am a fool, but you have convinced me. I understand your part where Lucy is concerned. Still, that does not explain everything that happened when Jonathan went to visit you in Transylvania. Why did you torment him so?"

Dracula sighed. "Mina, the man was my guest. I enjoyed his company at first—particularly our conversations about you. I showed him only the utmost courtesy during his visit, even though he became increasingly antagonistic towards me. He tormented himself."

"How so?" I said sceptically.

Dracula began to pace the room, speaking with great animation. "I had not entertained a guest for more than half a century, ever since a pair of erudite, adventuresome Englishmen appeared at my door one night, lost in a storm. We liked each other at once. They stayed for months. It was with their help that I perfected my English, and through them that I began to harbour a great interest and affection for your country and its countrymen. When Mr. Harker came years later, I knew that my servants—the few gipsies who dared to work for me on occasion—were not up to British standards. So I waited on Mr. Harker myself. He seemed to think this very strange. Then one morning when I greeted him while he was shaving, he accidentally cut himself, and went mad with fright for no reason."

"Jonathan said he was startled because he saw no reflection of you in his mirror—and that in a fury, you threw the mirror out the window."

"Is that why he was so afraid? The reflection? I should have guessed. What upset me was the crucifix I saw around his neck, proof that the locals had warned him against me. I threw out the mirror in a fit of temper, thinking it best that he give up shaving if he was prone to cutting himself—for my three sisters might smell his blood and ignore my warnings to leave him alone."

"Your sisters?" I said, astonished. "Those three strange women, they are your sisters?"

"Yes." In that single word, his look and tone conveyed his extreme antipathy for them. "They are one of the banes of my existence. Despite my best efforts to teach them, they have never mastered the art of self-control. I did my best to keep Mr. Harker out of harm's way by locking most of the doors in the castle, and warning him not to sleep anywhere but his own room. Finding locked doors, however, he imagined himself to be a prisoner and fell into a panic."

"But he *was* a prisoner! You forced him to stay against his will for two long months!"

"I did not force him. I *asked* him to stay."

"You made him write letters home in advance!"

Dracula glanced away, saying suavely: "It was a precaution. Our postal system is very unreliable—and I had become concerned. I had gone to great trouble and expense to set up a new life in your country. I wished to arrive unnoticed and remain undisturbed. Mr. Harker had become afraid of me. He knew all about this property, and a great deal about my business affairs. If he returned to England before I reached its shores, I feared he might spread word about me that would make my reception there unwelcome. So I requested that he stay until I was ready to leave."

"Was that really the reason?"

He looked back at me. "What do you mean?"

I eyed him levelly. "You said last night that you were determined to meet me. Be honest. Did that . . . *determination* . . .

influence your decision to keep Jonathan in Transylvania, and ignorant of my whereabouts, so that you could reach Whitby yourself before he did?"

His eyes flashed red with sudden anger. He slammed his fist down on a small table with such force that the top splintered into fragments, as he cried "No!"—actions which caused me to leap to my feet and cry out in alarm and fear, my chair crashing to the floor behind me. For the first time since I arrived, I wondered if I might have need of the secret vial of holy water I had brought with me.

An awful silence ensued. Heart pounding in trepidation, I watched him as he stood frozen in place, struggling to regain control of himself, a far-away look in his now-blue eyes. At length his features softened and his gaze again met mine. A sense of calm pervaded his voice as (a bit abashed, and with undisguised affection) he said: "Forgive me. Perhaps there is an element of truth in what you say, even if I did not acknowledge it to myself at the time."

At least he is man enough to admit it, I thought. I hated what he had done. It distressed me terribly to think that Jonathan had suffered, ultimately, because of me. And yet . . . as Dracula strode over to me, straightened my chair, and held out his hand, his look was so apologetic, so beseeching, that I found myself wanting to forgive him. He led me to a comfortable chair before the hearth, where I sat down. Striving for calm, I said quietly:

"Be honest about this, too: with the same motive, did you try to drive Jonathan mad?"

Dracula shook his head and replied with deep sincerity: "No. Whatever may have been behind my desire to delay Mr. Harker's departure, I did not intentionally threaten his sanity. In fact, I tried to protect him. It was about this time that he deliberately forced his way into a wing of the castle which I had expressly warned him against. My wretched sisters found him and attempted to seduce him. I rescued him—in the nick of time, I think. Of course, he never thanked me. I fear from that point on, his mind became unhinged. He seemed to doubt his own grasp of reality."

"With good reason, considering all that he witnessed! He saw your sisters vanish into thin air before him, and twice he saw you crawl down the castle wall like a lizard!"

Dracula looked at me in puzzlement. "A lizard?"

"He saw you emerge from a window and crawl head down along the sheer castle wall, before disappearing into a hole. The second time you were wearing his own suit of clothes!"

"His clothes?"

"Yes! Why did you do that?"

He fell briefly silent, frowning. "He said I was head down? So he did not actually see my face?"

"I suppose he did not."

He nodded. "It must have been one of my sisters, playing a malicious trick on him. They have been known to steal my own clothes, dress up in them, and alter their appearance when they go out foraging, to deliberately frighten the locals."

This explanation took me aback. "If it *was* one of your sisters, it truly terrified him."

"Yet I knew nothing about it." Dracula shook his head in frustration. "Sensing his fears, I suppose I should have tried harder to assuage them; but in his self-induced panic, and his growing hatred of me, I doubt he would have listened. When he at last announced his wish to leave, I was concerned about his walking that long road alone in the dark, but I had no intention of stopping him."

"You called wolves to the door!"

"I did not call the wolves, but I sensed that they were there. I planned to calm and persuade them into accompanying Mr.

Harker on his journey; but he backed off in terror and fled. The next morning, he found me lying in a trance, testing one of my earth boxes before travel—and he tried to kill me! Not that a blow from a spade could have so final an effect. I could have risen and dispatched him in an instant, but I chose not to."

I stared at him in consternation. He had an answer for everything! "Why, on Jonathan's last night at your castle, did you tell those women, 'Have patience. To-morrow night is yours!' "

"I said that so they would leave him alone. I knew that Mr. Harker was leaving the next morning. I had arranged for the Szgany to convey him on the first leg of his homeward journey. Believe me, Mina, if I had possessed some perverse desire to offer up Mr. Harker to them on a platter, I would have done so much earlier. And had I wished to drink his blood myself, I could have done so at any time—but I never did."

I could not deny the logic in that. "What about that horrible bag?"

"What bag?"

"Jonathan said in his journal that you gave a bag to those three sisters of yours—a bag which contained a squirming, half-smothered child! An innocent child to satisfy their bloodthirsty appetites!"

"A child? He thought it was a child?" Dracula let out a sudden laugh. "No wonder he passed out in shock. There was no child inside that bag, Mina. It was a lamb."

"A lamb?"

"A gift from a farmer, to thank me for removing a rather devastating blight to his field of crops. Sheep's blood is not nearly as satisfying as that of humans, but at times we must make do. One animal sufficed for the four of us, with an added benefit: after we had drained its blood, I cooked it and it made an excellent supper for our human guest."

I stood and walked away, caught between relief, disbelief, and dismay at this revelation. "And the woman who was devoured by wolves?" I said quietly. "What do you have to say about that?"

"What woman?"

"Jonathan saw her beating on the castle gates, sobbing and demanding that you return her missing child. Then a pack of wolves surrounded her and killed her."

"My God. Is that what Harker thought he perceived? More and more, I understand why he began to recoil from me in such horror." Shaking his head, Dracula continued: "Why did he think she died? Did he see a dead body?"

"No. He said she disappeared."

"Does your husband speak my native tongue?"

"No."

"Then how could he know what that woman even said? That polyglot dictionary he brought with him seems to have done more harm than good. The locals know me, Mina. They understand and fear my powers, and generally shun me; but occasionally, in times of desperation—as with the farmer—they come to me for a service. That woman was not accusing me of anything. She came to me for help in *finding* her missing child. I sent those wolves to look for him. They drove the little boy back into the courtyard, right into her arms, and she quickly disappeared home—hopefully to reprimand it for causing so much trouble in the first place. Clearly, Mr. Harker misinterpreted what he saw. I wish he had said something about these fears of his. I would have set him straight; but he was—he is—very English. He never breathed a word."

I caught hold of a chair, staring at him in stunned silence. I did not know what to think. It suddenly occurred to me that—with the exception of his deliberate detention of Jonathan in Transylvania on my account—nearly every incidence of evil connected with Count Dracula had been reported to me second-hand. Everything that had been witnessed, explained, or described by others could have been misinterpreted or based on faulty information—could it not?

Had we all seriously misjudged this man? He was not what one would consider entirely good, but perhaps he was not evil either?

Dracula crossed to me then and stopped, touching my cheek with one hand as he gazed deeply into my eyes. "Mina," he said gently, "I swear to you, upon my honour: the only real wrong I have ever done your husband—and I admit it is an egregious one—is to covet the woman he loves."

My breath caught in my throat. He was so near, so very near. I could read the fervent desire in his blue eyes, and I felt an answering need well up within me. All at once, my anger, fears, and doubts evaporated. I did not care if he was lying or not. I did not care whether he was good or evil. All I cared about was that this man's arms should wrap around me, that his body should press close against me, and that his lips should find mine.

"They are all bent on destroying you," I whispered. "What shall I do? How can I help you?"

"I do not think you *can* help me, my darling. But do not worry. I can take care of myself."

He drew me close then and kissed me. It was a long and passionate kiss. Desire coursed through me. When his lips left my mouth and travelled down to my throat, I quivered in anticipation, knowing what would come next, wanting it. *He promised that I will be safe,* I reminded myself. *He promised not to harm me.* He unbuckled the velvet band around my neck and tossed it aside. His eyes—now red—met mine; I gave him my silent ascent, waiting in breathless ecstasy as my head fell back.

Then I felt it: the prick of his teeth piercing my flesh, and the exquisite joy as my warm blood pulsed from my body into his.

FIFTEEN

I awakened very late the next morning, the sunlight making its presence known despite the cover of the thick yellow window-blinds. I sat up in a daze to find myself alone atop my bed in my own room, fully dressed, my diamond neck-band once more securely fastened around my throat. How, I wondered, had I come to be there? The last thing I remembered was Dracula kissing me—biting me. I must have lost consciousness. He must have carried me back, no doubt at some risk to himself. I had no memory of Jonathan coming to bed, but saw that the pillow and bed-clothes were tousled beside me.

I lay back down, feeling dizzy, weak, and confused—yet at the same time curiously happy, as if a sense of deep satisfaction pervaded my whole being. The two small tooth-marks on my neck, hidden beneath the black velvet ribbon, throbbed slightly. As I recalled everything that had happened the night before, and all that I had seen and learned, I could only shake my head in silent wonder. My cheeks flamed. For so many years, I had led such a clean and blameless life. I had never looked at or thought about another man once I became engaged to Jonathan. Yet ever since the first moment I had laid eyes upon Mr. Wagner—Dracula—at Whitby, I had been carrying on a secret affair of the mind and heart; and for the past two nights, I had behaved in such a base and immoral manner!

I loved my husband. I loved him dearly, and I had betrayed his trust. I had willingly, wantonly, allowed myself to be taken in Dracula's arms and given myself up to his vampire's kiss. Wicked, wicked Mina! Scarlet woman! And yet I knew, were Dracula to appear in my chamber at that very instant, I would again walk willingly into his embrace.

Everything that Dracula had told me in his defence seemed logical and rang true to me. It appeared that he was truly innocent of any real wrong-doing. He was a fascinating, complicated man. I loved him, and I believed that he loved me. Yes, he was Un-Dead. Yes, he possessed uncanny skills and powers that made my head spin. But I understood now that he was not our enemy—not any one's enemy. And yet . . . he was the very being that my husband, Dr. Van Helsing, and the other men were determined to exterminate!

If only I could share with them all that I had learned. If only I could clear Nicolae's name! But that was impossible. If I admitted *how* I knew what I knew, scandal would ensue—and for what purpose? Those men would never believe in his innocence. They all had a fixed idea in their minds of what a vampire was. They had seen the horror of Lucy's death and resurrection, and had been the instruments of her true death; after that, it was unlikely that they would accept anything I said, no matter how cautiously or prettily I presented it.

No; I would have to leave the matter in Dracula's hands and pray that he could find a way to save himself without harming any one I loved. And then . . . and then . . . I could not think beyond "then." The future was an enigma to me. *Please, God,* I prayed, *help me find a way to sort out this confusion of feeling. Show me what it is that I am meant to do.*

My dizziness had finally passed. I rose, washed, and put on my day gown. As I neatly repinned my long hair, the face before me in the glass looked slightly more pale than the day before. I pinched my cheeks, attempting to add more colour to them, to little avail.

The men were all gone again on their mysterious errands. After lunch, an attendant told me that Mr. Renfield had asked if he might see me. The request worried me a little. I could not forget his erratic behaviour on my previous visit, or the warnings that Dr. Seward and Dracula had issued. But I was, in an odd way, grateful to the man—for it was only because of him that Dracula had been able to enter the house to see me—and so I felt I should not refuse. I insisted, however, that the attendant accompany me.

We found Mr. Renfield crouched on the floor in a corner of his room, mumbling to himself and biting his fingernails in an agitated manner. He seemed unaware that we had entered until I spoke:

"Good afternoon, Mr. Renfield. How are you?"

He looked up then, his mouth widening into a slow smile. "Mrs. Harker. How good of you to come. Won't you sit down?"

Something about his tone of voice, and the look in his eyes, sent a little shiver down my spine; and yet he spoke like a perfect gentleman. "I prefer to stand, thank you."

"Then I will stand as well." He rose and moved towards me, suddenly noticing the attendant at my side. "What is he doing here? I requested a private interview. Tell him to go away."

"I would like him to stay. What was it you wanted to see me about?"

"Oh, nothing in particular, Mrs. Harker. I just wanted to look at you and hear your voice. You have a very pleasant voice. And you are the prettiest thing to enter these four walls in a very long time. Looking at you gives me great pleasure. But—" He frowned, staring at me. "Something is wrong. You aren't the same to-day."

"Not the same? What do you mean?"

"Your face. It is like tea after the teapot has been watered. I don't care for pale people; I like people with lots of blood in them. Yours seems to have all run out."

I felt a heat rise to my cheeks at this perceptive observation, a blush strong enough, I hoped, to restore all of the missing colour that seemed to so offend him. "I am a little tired to-day, that is all," I said quickly.

"Well. You look a *little* better now—but something is different about you this afternoon. I wish I could put my finger on what it is." He shook his head, then added solemnly: " 'There's no art to find the mind's construction in the face.' "

"*Macbeth,*" I said.

"It is my favourite play." Staring hard at me with a sly smile, he further quoted: " 'Stars, hide your fires! Let not light see my black and deep desires!' "

I blushed again. Was Mr. Renfield merely quoting a line at random from the play? Was he referring to dark desires of his own? Or . . . was he somehow aware of my guilty secret? "Macbeth was a man of great ambition."

"He was a hero," he replied.

"I disagree. I think him an unredeemable murderer and a villain of the highest order."

"Well, there you are wrong." We discussed Shakespeare for a few minutes more, a conversation in which Mr. Renfield seemed so intelligent, so well-read, and so entirely sane, that it was difficult to believe he was a lunatic being held in a cell.

At length, I told him I must take my leave. "It was good to see you, Mr. Renfield."

He sighed and—very gently—reached out and took my hand,

then brought it to his lips and kissed it. "God bless you, ma'am, for coming. Have a pleasant afternoon and evening. I wish only the best for you."

"Thank you, Mr. Renfield." I turned to go, but he held tightly to my hand and added:

"One more thing, Mrs. Harker. I have been wondering: do you keep your corset on beneath your nightdress when you sleep, or are you quite free and naked underneath it?"

I yanked my hand away, gasping in shock and mortification at this impertinent question. He laughed loudly, a victorious look in his eyes as he cried:

"There! That's what I like! Now I see some real colour in those cheeks!"

"That's enough out of you, Renfield!" cried the attendant as he hurried me to the door.

" 'Look like the innocent flower, but be the serpent under it!' " I heard Mr. Renfield quote with glee, as the attendant slammed and locked the door behind us.

I returned to my rooms, greatly unnerved by the strange meeting; but although Mr. Renfield had made me feel uncomfortable, I could not help feeling sorry for the man. It was not his fault that he had gone mad; and what a terrible fate it would be, I thought, to be locked up in an institution all one's life!

JONATHAN AND THE OTHERS WERE OUT UNTIL DINNER-TIME. THEY all came in very tired. I did what I could to brighten them up, worrying that they might suspect, as Mr. Renfield had, that something was different about me; but they seemed too preoccupied by their own secret business to pay much attention to me. Jonathan did mention that I had fallen asleep on our bed the night before fully dressed, but he did not seem to wonder at it.

Dinner was once again an awkward and rather silent affair, with the men avoiding any discussion of their activities that day. It had occurred to me that if I could learn something of their plans, I could warn Dracula about them. So I said:

"I know that you wish to shield me from all you do in relation to the Count—but I am greatly concerned about you all. It would set my mind at ease if you would at least tell me whether or not you have any plans to go out to-night."

Jonathan shot a glance at Dr. Van Helsing, who nodded his assent. "We are not going out to-night, dear. We have a great deal to discuss after dinner."

"Rest assured, Madam Mina," Dr. Van Helsing added, "that we have learned much these past few days. Very soon we will take our stance against that monster."

"We will trap the Devil and we will kill him!" Dr. Seward added with enthusiasm.

My pulse raced with alarm. "How . . . do you mean to trap him?"

The men exchanged another look. "Mrs. Harker," Lord Godalming said, "we have agreed to say nothing of our plans. It is best that you stay out of it."

"But—will you be in any danger?"

"Don't you fret, little lady," Mr. Morris said. "We'll be just fine."

I nodded silently, trying to hide my anguish.

"Dearest," Jonathan said, "you look so frightfully worried. You needn't be. We are men. We know what we are doing. We will take care of this, and we will take care of you." Giving my hand a squeeze, he turned to Dr. Seward and added, "I say Jack, would you mind mixing up a sleeping draught for Mina, so that she can rest undisturbed to-night?"

"Not a problem," Dr. Seward replied.

I nearly gasped in dismay. I did not want any drugs putting me to sleep! I had no idea if Nicolae planned to visit me that night; but God forgive me, I *hoped* he would, and I wanted to be conscious for the event. "That is not necessary," I said quickly. "I am very tired, and I am certain I will sleep just fine without a draught."

"All the same, I think you should take something," Jonathan insisted as we rose from the table, and Dr. Seward agreed.

The doctor later handed me a tiny medicine box containing an opiate of some kind. "This is very mild and will do you no harm, Mrs. Harker, but it should help you sleep. Simply mix the powder into a glass of water."

I thanked him. Jonathan told me that they might be working very late, but he would look in on me in a little while to make certain I was all right.

"There is no need for that. Enjoy your meeting, dearest. I am sure I will sleep like a baby."

"Good-night, then," Jonathan said, kissing me. "I will see you in the morning."

I bade the men good-night and went upstairs. The moment I reached my room, I opened the box with the sleeping powder draught, removed the little paper envelope within, and took it out onto the balcony, where I let its contents spill out into the night air. Then I came back inside and sat down to wait.

And wait. And wait.

The clock ticked the hours away. Nine o'clock. Ten o'clock. Eleven.

I stood up. I paced. I sat down again. I stared out the window at the night sky, hoping for a glimpse of white mist crossing the grass, or particles of dust whirling in the moonlight. To my disappointment, there was nothing. Nothing at all. All without was still and silent as the grave. A dog's bark made me leap up with sudden hope, but then it ceased.

The clock struck twelve. Clearly, I thought, Nicolae does not mean to come to-night at all. I suddenly felt very foolish. What kind of woman was I, I wondered, waiting with bated breath for a lover to pay a clandestine call? I had a good husband who was very dear to me—and how was I repaying that love and devotion? With dishonesty and betrayal! Flushed with guilt, I closed the windows, put on my nightdress, unpinned and brushed my hair, and went to bed.

Self-recrimination and doubt kept me tossing and turning for a while. When at last I drifted off to sleep, I had a nightmare.

In my dream, I was in an unfamiliar forest landscape, standing on the rocky outcropping of a steep hill-side, surrounded by endless wilderness as far as the eye could see. Beneath me was a long, twisting stretch of dirt road. Patches of snow clung to the ground, and it was bitterly cold. From around a bend, a horse-drawn cart appeared, containing a large, open, wooden box, about the size of a coffin. There was a man's body in the box, but who it was, I could not determine. The cart was accompanied by a large group of robust, dark-skinned, long-haired men wearing big hats, heavy leather belts, and dirty, baggy, white trousers. From their picturesque dress and appearance, I ascertained them to be gipsies—the kind of gipsies Jonathan had described in his foreign journal.

As I watched the approaching procession below, a terrible feeling came over me of impending danger. The wagon came closer now. I could clearly see the face of the dead man in the box. It was Dracula! To my horror he was dead, truly dead!

All at once, from out of the trees came four men on horseback: Jonathan, Dr. Seward, Lord Godalming, and Mr. Morris! The foursome charged at the wagon and its escort, firing at them with rifles. The gipsies shouted in alarm, drawing forth knives and other weapons. The horsemen dismounted, and a fierce battle ensued. I watched the unfolding chaos in helpless horror, flinching at the report of each gunshot and the flash of each knife-blade.

Suddenly, a gipsy viciously stabbed one of the Englishmen, who crumpled to the ground, bleeding. Who was it? I could not see his face! Which one of my men had died? Was it Jonathan?

"No!" I screamed in agony, but my voice was no more than a whisper. "No!"

I awoke in a panic, bathed in perspiration, flung from that terrifying reality into the quiet of the present, my heart pounding. Something touched my arm, and I screamed in earnest, my eyes blinking open.

"Mina! Mina," came Jonathan's gentle voice.

Although the lamp had been extinguished, the moonlight was bright enough that even through the thick yellow blinds, there was light enough to see. I felt Jonathan snuggle up behind me and sleepily wrap an arm around me. "You were having a bad dream, dearest."

"Oh, Jonathan." I turned over in his embrace and buried my face against his neck as I struggled to calm myself. "I am so frightened."

"You are all right now." His voice was heavy with sleep. "It was just a dream."

"It was more than a dream. I have a feeling something terrible is going to happen."

"Nothing terrible will happen to you, dearest."

"It is not me I am worried about. It is one of you. I feel certain that if you proceed with your plans against Dracula, someone—a member of our party—is going to die!"

"Mina: shhh. You are still half-asleep. It is the draught you took."

"I did not take the draught! I am wide awake. I know what I am talking about. It was a premonition, Jonathan!"

He drew back slightly, staring at me now as he stroked my hair affectionately. "Mina, I am well-acquainted with these dreams and premonitions of yours. I have been hearing about them all my life. But they—"

"They often come true! Do you remember the time you decided to climb that big tree in the garden behind the orphanage? You were ten, I think. I said: 'Don't do it, Jonathan.' I'd had a dream that you tried to climb that tree, and a limb broke and you fell and were gravely injured. But you did not listen to me."

"I will never forget it. I did fall, and I broke my arm."

"Years later, I told you that you were going to win the literature prize at school. I had seen a grey-haired man handing you a red leather book, inscribed with your name. And that was exactly how it happened!"

"But your dreams do not always come true, dear. Do you recall the time, some years ago, when you were going on holiday with the Westenras, and you were absolutely terrified that there was going to be a railway accident, and that you and Lucy would both die?"

I sighed impatiently. "Yes, but—"

"This dream is like that one. It is founded only on fear—not intuition. You must stop worrying. We will all be fine."

"You cannot know that! Oh, Jonathan. It might be you! I could not bear it if anything happened to you!" Nor could I bear it, I thought, if anything happened to Nicolae. "Please: let us leave this place."

"What do you mean, leave?"

"I want to go home—now, this instant. Let us pack our things and walk to the village and take the first train out. We could be back in Exeter in time for breakfast."

"Mina, we cannot leave. We have a job to do. We are on the brink of victory. Our day of reckoning is at hand."

"No! This whole thing is a great mistake. You must tell the professor to call it off!"

"I understand that you are anxious. We have all been under a great deal of stress lately, but I promise you, we will defeat this deadly foe—"

"He is not a foe! Listen to me: Count Dracula is innocent. Innocent! There is an explanation for everything he has done. He has been entirely misunderstood!"

"Now you are talking nonsense."

"I am not!"

"Calm down. You had a bad dream, and it has made you hysterical. Everything will be fine, Mina. We are doing a good and brave thing. We are making the world safe for our children."

"It is those very children that I am thinking of." I found his hand beneath the bed-clothes and brought it up to my lips and kissed it. "I want the future that we have planned for ourselves, Jonathan. I want children—lots and lots of them."

"So do I, my dear. And we will have them." He kissed my forehead. "Now go back to sleep. It is late, I am very tired, and we have a big day ahead of us to-morrow."

Jonathan rolled away from me towards the wall and promptly fell asleep. Disappointment surged through me as I sank back against my pillow. I had tried, but I could not make him understand. Heaving a deep sigh, I turned over to face the centre of the room—only to meet a sight which caused me to jerk upright with a violent start:

Dracula was standing at the side of my bed, barely a foot away, looking down at me.

I GASPED IN SURPRISE AND ALARM, CASTING A QUICK, ANXIOUS glance at Jonathan beside me. Dracula only waved a quick, deliberate hand at Jonathan's inert form, saying:

"He will not waken. Are you all right?"

Too stunned to think of a coherent reply, I merely nodded. In the dim light, I perceived that Dracula was clad in black trousers, tall black boots, and a loose white shirt. He looked as handsome as ever—more like a pirate than a vampire—and I thought I detected a hint of fury in his eyes, which he was struggling to hide. He held out a hand to me.

"Come."

I shook my head, glancing meaningfully at Jonathan again, and whispered: "I cannot. Is something wrong?"

He hesitated. "I will tell you presently. Forgive my late arrival. I have been much occupied with preparations for my own defence. Your men intend to destroy all my resting-places to-morrow—or should I say, to-day."

"What will you do?" I asked anxiously.

"I will ensure they do not succeed."

He took both my hands in his, urging me to my feet. I shivered as my bare feet touched the cold wooden floor.

"My love," he said gently, as one hand reached up to caress my face, "you are not still afraid of me?"

"No." My voice seemed to be coming to me from a far-off place. "But we cannot . . . my husband, I—"

"I assure you, he will remain unconscious. He will never know that I was here."

He drew me to him. I found myself melting into his embrace. It was as if my will had left me; I could no more have pushed him away than I could have ceased to breathe. As he kissed me, I felt all my vows of resistance evaporate, replaced by growing desire. Oh! How could any woman refuse the advances of such a man? I wanted him! How I wanted him!

His mouth left mine, and he looked down at me, his eyes like red flames. I knew what he needed. My heart pounded. I knew I should refuse; but I yearned for it. I untied my nightdress at the collar. He pulled it open to expose my throat. As he bent his head and fastened there, I gave out a sigh, drawing pleasure from it. *Yes. Yes. Yes. Liquid, molten ecstasy. Nirvana.*

To my regret, he did not feast long. As if with a superhuman effort, he stopped and stepped back slightly, a trickle of blood dripping from his mouth.

"I do not wish to weaken you further. I took more blood than I ought to last night."

"What do you mean?" I asked, in sudden trepidation. "Am I . . . am I in danger of becoming a—?"

"In danger of becoming a vampire?" At my worried nod, he answered: "Not yet. But if things go on as they are, at some point, you . . ." His voice trailed off.

We stood in silence for a long moment, regarding each other as we fought to regain mastery of ourselves. I suppose it was very remiss of me, but I had not, until that moment, considered the possibility that his vampire bites might change me into a being like him. Lucy had, after all, been bitten many times without permanent injury—until the very end, when he said he had changed her at her bidding.

I loved Dracula desperately, against all sense of propriety and despite all reason. But I believed him to be a unique being. I did not think he was representative of his kind. He had described his sisters as wanton creatures without conscience or self-control; and the same thing had happened to Lucy when she became Un-Dead. I had no wish to be like them. I would not, *could not* become a vampire; and I certainly did not wish to die! Dracula must know this. I believed, with every beating of my heart, that he would never do anything that would be detrimental to my well-being.

"Nicolae: will you promise me something?"

"Anything, my love."

"Whatever happens later to-day; will you promise not to harm my husband, or any of the others?"

It took a moment before he answered, and the reply seemed to cost him dearly. "I give you my word. But Mina: in spite of all I do to protect myself, if your men persist with their intentions, and I do nothing to stop them, there may come a time, and soon, when I am forced to leave England or perish."

"Oh!" I cried, quite miserable at the thought.

"Having found you again, I cannot bear to leave you. And I cannot lose you! If all communication between us should cease, if I cannot discover how you are or where you are, it will drive me mad."

"I will feel the same."

After a pause, he said slowly: "There is something we can do: a way that we can create a bond between us—a telepathic bond—so that I can read your thoughts and you can read mine. We can be together that way and find each other again."

"How would we create such a bond?"

"You must drink my blood."

My pulse quickened. "Drink your blood?"

"Yes. Will you do it?"

I did not hesitate. "Show me how."

I thought he might teach me how to bite his throat, as he had done to mine. Instead, he lifted me and placed me back upon the bed, facing him, on my knees. He then unbuttoned his shirt and pulled it open, revealing his beautiful, sculpted chest. All at once, the nail of his index finger grew long and sharp, and with it he pierced his flesh. Immediately, a thin stream of red blood trickled from his breast.

"Drink," he said.

I pressed my mouth to the wound, first lapping up the blood as it flowed out, and then sucking deeply from it. I had only tasted blood a few times before, when I had sucked on an injured fingertip. The blood I now imbibed was nothing like the mild, slightly salty liquid that ran in my own veins. Dracula's blood was delicious. It tasted like a deep, rich, full-bodied wine, with a dark, delectable tang. It was ambrosia; I felt as if I could not get enough of it. As I drank, I heard him give an ecstatic little moan. His hand cradled the back of my head and held it there, urging me to continue, while his other hand found and clasped both my hands lovingly in his.

As I drank his blood, I felt a fevered glow begin to course through me, even stronger than the glorious, pulsing sensation I had experienced when he drank from me. My ears began to ring with a strange and wonderful hum that steadily increased in pitch and volume. Soon, I was wrapped in a cocoon of sound and sensation that drowned out everything else in the world but him, and me, and this wondrous exchange of his magnificent blood.

Gradually, I became aware of a new and different set of sounds, which hovered at the edges of my consciousness: the sharp murmur of conversation. A mighty crash. The tumble of heavy footsteps. Male voices exclaiming in horror and dismay. So entranced was I in my occupation, however, that I perceived these sounds as no more than an unwelcome annoyance—and apparently Dracula was equally entranced. Suddenly, however, I heard and felt Dracula let out a roar of fury. He shoved me down upon the bed, where I wiped blood from my lips and took in the scene before me in dazed consternation:

Just inside the splintered door-frame stood Dr. Seward, Lord Godalming, and Mr. Morris, as Dr. Van Helsing—who must have fallen in his exertion—rose up from his hands and knees beside them. All were staring in fear, shock, and disgust at me and my companion—who, as he whirled to face them, was no longer the Dracula I knew and loved. To my horror, all the colour had drained from his skin and hair, changing them to pasty white. His face contorted with rage into a wrinkled, waxen mask of Death, and his eyes flamed red with malice, like some fiend from Hell.

Before I could blink, the hideous Dracula sprang at the intruders with another roar, then stopped and faltered back as Dr. Van

Helsing advanced towards him, holding up an envelope containing I knew not what. Now the entire party held up small crucifixes and advanced upon him. Instantly, it grew very dark, as if a great black cloud had obscured the moon. Then the gas-light sprang up under Mr. Morris's match. Dracula had vanished into a wisp of vapour.

I screamed. It was an ear-piercing shriek that embodied all my terror, guilt, mortification, and despair. Terror, because my love had just transformed into a hideous beast before my eyes; guilt, over my own debased behaviour; mortification, to have been discovered by these men in such a compromising position; and in despair over what would follow. Would they perceive that I was drinking Dracula's blood willingly? Would they guess at our former liaisons? Would their hatred of him increase, and put him—and them—in further danger? And what would become of me?

SIXTEEN

I PUT MY HANDS OVER MY FACE, LAY ON THE BED, AND SOBBED as if my heart would break.

"My God," I heard Mr. Morris say. "That beast is the Devil incarnate. Let's see where he's gotten to!"

I heard departing footsteps, then felt the coverlet being drawn over my body as gentle fingers brushed back the hair from my neck, exposing the two bite marks thereupon to view. Dr. Van Helsing gave a little gasp. Then he whispered:

"We can do nothing with poor Madam Mina for a few moments till she recovers herself. Jonathan is in a stupor such as we know the vampire can produce. I must wake him."

A moment later, I heard Jonathan's startled exclamation as he woke and started up. I turned to him instinctively to comfort him; but then I spied the blood which stained the front and sleeves of my white nightdress, and I drew my hands back again, letting out a sob so strong it made the bed beneath us shake.

"In God's name what does this mean?" Jonathan cried. "Dr. Seward, Dr. Van Helsing, what is it? What has happened? What is wrong? Mina, dear, what is it? What does that blood mean?"

"I am so sorry, my friend," Dr. Van Helsing replied in an agonised tone. "Our dreaded foe has come and gone, and taken of our poor Madam Mina what he wanted."

"My God, my God! Has it come to this?" Jonathan cried in horror.

"I fear it is not the first time," Dr. Van Helsing said with anguish. "I fear he has attacked her before, in her sleep."

"How do you know?" Jonathan exclaimed.

"Mr. Renfield told us," answered Dr. Seward. "It was Renfield who invited him in, and who just now warned us that she was in danger. We were imbeciles to leave her unprotected! Mr. Renfield alone noticed your wife's pallor and guessed the terrible truth behind it—and he has paid dearly for it."

With a little, confused shock, I understood now that my secret was safe. The men's collective guilt at leaving me undefended had blinded them from perceiving my own guilt. At the same time, I latched onto the last words Dr. Van Helsing had spoken: *he has paid dearly for it*. Before I could ask what that meant, Jonathan let out a cry of horror, jumped from the bed, and pulled on his clothes. "God help us! Dr. Van Helsing, as you love Mina, do something to save her. It cannot have gone too far yet. Guard her while I look for *him*!"

Frantic lest Jonathan in his fury should find and kill Dracula, or far more likely die in the attempt, I seized hold of him and cried out: "No! No, Jonathan, you must not leave me. I could not bear it if he were to harm you." I pulled him down to sit on the bed beside me and began to sob afresh.

"Calm yourself, Mr. Harker. And do not fear, my dear Madam Mina," Dr. Van Helsing said soothingly, as he crouched before us, holding up his little golden crucifix. "We are here; and whilst this is close to you, no foul thing can approach. You are safe for to-night."

As I tried to regain control of my emotions, Dr. Seward quietly told Jonathan what he had seen upon entering the room. A few minutes later, Mr. Morris and Lord Godalming returned, explaining that they had seen no further sign of the intruder, but they had spied a bat flying westward.

"We looked into Renfield's room," Lord Godalming added. "The poor fellow is dead."

"Dead?" I exclaimed. "Mr. Renfield? But how?"

"The Count brutally attacked him in his room on his way in," Dr. Seward replied angrily.

I leapt to my feet in horror. "How do you know it was Dracula who attacked him?"

"Renfield told us all about it as he lay dying, when he warned us to look after you," Dr. Seward said. "That monster left him, broken and mutilated, in a pool of his own blood. We tried to help him, but he was beyond saving."

"I want to see him," I cried, starting for the door, but Lord Godalming stepped in front of me and replied:

"No, Mrs. Harker. It is not a sight for a lady's eyes."

I shook my head in stunned dismay. How could Dracula have murdered a man in cold blood just moments before taking me in his arms? And yet, I remembered how angry and distracted he had seemed when he first arrived in my chamber. Was it possible . . . ?

"This cruel, inhuman act does not surprise me," Dr. Van Helsing said. "My friend from Buda-Pesth University thinks that this Dracula, in his living life, was none other than Vlad Dracula, or Vlad the Impaler, the sadistic ruler of Wallachia who tortured and murdered tens of thousands of people in the fifteenth century."

A wave of terror and nausea overcame me, even as my mind rejected this notion. Could the Dracula I knew and loved have been a sadistic monster in his former life? No; impossible.

"What will happen to Mina now?" Jonathan asked hoarsely. "Will she—God forbid—will she become a—a—?"

"Not from a few feedings, I think, will she become a vampire," replied Dr. Van Helsing. Jonathan looked relieved at this, until a great sob rose in the professor's throat, and, gulping it down and shaking his head, he went on: "But alas, there is more to fear! Count Dracula forced Madam Mina to drink his blood. It is the vampire's baptism! By this act, he create a spiritual bond between them to control her. She has now been so infected that she will become even as he is whenever she die!"

All the men gasped. Jonathan let out a wail, and then began to weep. I stared at the professor, unable at first to process what he had just relayed. Yes, I had drunk Dracula's blood; but only because he had said it would create a telepathic bond between us. He had said nothing about *a bond to control me,* nor had he explained that there would be this far more dreadful consequence.

"Are you saying," I whispered slowly, "that by drinking Dracula's blood, I am doomed upon my death to become a vampire?"

"Alas, it is true!" Dr. Van Helsing cried in fury, slamming his fist on a table.

I sank down upon the bed, as a scream issued from the very core of my being. Oh! Horror of horrors! What had I done? What had I done? All that had happened over the past three nights—the passionate embraces Dracula and I had shared, all that I had learned, every good feeling he had inspired it me—it all shattered into a thousand pieces in the face of this horrendous new reality.

I had trusted Dracula. I loved him! But what manner of being was it that I loved? Was he nothing but a murderer and a liar, hiding his true aims behind a handsome face? No; no! I could not believe that. And yet . . . he had deliberately, knowingly, without my consent, persuaded me to commit an act which would turn me into an Un-Dead being like himself. How could he do such a thing?

Had I been consorting with the Devil?

In a terrible rush, I suddenly understood, for the first time, what Jonathan must have felt back in Exeter when he said, "You cannot know what it is to doubt everything, even yourself!"

Could it be that everything Dracula had said and done since the first day we met was nothing more than a sadistic kind of courtship, with one selfish, foul aim in mind: to bring me under his control and to make me his minion or companion when I died? Was I the prize in a diabolical revenge upon Jonathan because he had tried to kill Dracula and had escaped from his castle? Did Dracula have some other, fiendish reason for choosing me? Or did he truly believe he loved me, and that I would welcome eternal existence at his side? Either way, I saw it now: I had fallen right into his hands. I had been duped! Befouled! Like the mythological Leda, I had allowed Zeus to seduce me as a swan. And I was now damned to Hell for ever more!

"Oh! I am unclean! Unclean!" I cried.

Jonathan took me in his arms, his voice breaking as he said: "Nonsense, Mina. I will not hear such words from you."

For a while I sobbed against his chest as the other men hovered in sympathy and anguish. When I had regained a measure of control over myself, Dr. Van Helsing knelt beside me and clasped my hand very tenderly. "Madam Mina: have no fear. There is a way that you can escape this terrible fate."

"What way is that, Professor?" I asked tearfully.

"If that other being who has so fouled your sweet life is true dead first, then you will not become as him."

"Is that so?" Jonathan asked, with hope in his eyes.

"It is," Dr. Van Helsing asserted. "And this I vow, Madam Mina: we will slay this foul monster while you still live, and this will set you free."

Jonathan pressed me to him with a cry of relief.

Good, I thought, as I dried my tears. *Let them find and kill Drac-*

ula if they can and free me of this terrible curse! Silently, I prayed: *Dear God: grant me a second chance. I shall be true to my husband. I shall never stray again.*

Dr. Van Helsing went on: "God knows that you have been through enough, Madam Mina, and I do not want you to be further pained; but it is need that we know all. Will you tell us, please, exactly what happened to-night?"

And so I told them.

I dared not reveal what had really happened, of course. No; I could never breathe a word of that! In my rage and horror, I spun a terrible story, painting myself as the most innocent and persecuted of victims, and depicting Count Dracula as the monster they all expected, and which I finally knew him to be.

I described his arrival in my room as it had been on that first night, when he had stepped out of a cloud of mist.

I told them that I had been paralysed with terror; that Dracula had threatened, if I made a sound, to take Jonathan and dash his brains out before my eyes.

I told them that he had sucked my blood and then had spoken to me in an evil tone, deriding the men's efforts to thwart him and threatening to punish me for aiding them. Then, I claimed, he had forced me to drink his blood or suffocate.

The men listened to my tale in wide-eyed silence and growing anger. By the time I had finished, the first red streaks of dawn had stolen over the eastern sky.

"My God!" I cried, desolate and forlorn. "What have I done to deserve such a fate?" But I knew in my heart exactly what I had done: I had, against any semblance of morality, given myself willingly to the enemy.

"I will wipe this brute from the face of creation and send him straight to Hell!" Jonathan said between clenched teeth.

"To-day, the deed shall be done," Dr. Van Helsing promised solemnly.

Jonathan embraced me again, and in an anguished voice he said, "Do not despair, my dearest. We must keep on trusting that God will aid us up until the end."

"What end will that be?" I whispered.

"I do not know. But whatever happens, I am your husband. I am here for you."

No one returned to bed. The men agreed that from that point on, I should be kept in full confidence; that nothing of any sort, no matter how painful, should be kept from me. We gathered in the study, where they explained to me everything that they had discovered in their investigations over the past few days.

"Count Dracula now has three other houses that we know of besides Carfax, in different parts of the city," Dr. Van Helsing announced, to my surprise. "He purchased these places under assumed names, one of which is 'the Count de Ville'—a sly wink at the Devil."

"One house is at Bermondsey, another at Mile End, and one very centrally situated in Piccadilly," Jonathan continued. "He may have others. We only counted twenty-nine boxes out of the original fifty in the old chapel next door, before we were obliged to leave, because of an infestation of rats. We have evidence that the rest of the boxes were moved to his other lairs."

"The boxes you found in the chapel next door—were they all filled with earth?" I asked, remembering that Dracula had used many of them to transport his books and other things.

"Every one of them," Dr. Seward said. "The native soil of Transylvania."

I knew that to be untrue. Dracula must have filled the empty ones with local dirt to deceive them; but it hardly mattered now.

"What do you think he intends to do with these other residences?" I asked.

"They safeguard his life," Dr. Van Helsing replied. "If one resting-place should be discovered and destroyed, he will always have another."

"And they give him quick access to victims in every part of London," Dr. Seward said with a disgusted noise.

"Professor: you said this monster was once Vlad something-or-other, who tortured and murdered people?" Jonathan said.

"Yes."

"What else do you know about him?" Jonathan asked. "Anything you can tell us might be useful when we confront him."

"We think his father was Vlad II, who in the early fifteenth century was ruler of Wallachia, an area of the Balkans in present-day Romania, adjacent to Transylvania. His name, Dracula, it come from the Order of the Dragon, a secret fraternal order of knights to which Vlad II belonged. It was founded to defend Christianity against the Ottoman Turks."

Dr. Van Helsing withdrew an old book from his bag and flipped through it. He showed us a page with a magnificent illustration of an armored knight, whose shield and tabard bore the emblem of a dragon with wings extended, hanging on a cross.

"The word for dragon in Romanian is 'drac' and 'ul' is the article. Thus Vlad II came to be known as 'Vlad Dracul,' or 'Vlad the dragon.' Even his coinage bore the dragon symbol. The ending 'ulea' means 'the son of'—and so his sons came to be known as Dracula, or 'the son of the dragon.' But 'Dracul' also means 'the Devil' in Romanian—a double meaning which take on great significance in the eyes of Dracula's enemies."

"So this Dracula we now face—he was the son of Vlad II?" Lord Godalming asked.

"It would seem so. He had many names: Vlad III, Vlad Tepes,

Vlad Dracula, and Vlad the Impaler. When he came to power, he was a cruel and vicious ruler, who for years tortured and murdered tens of thousands of people by the most cruel and inhuman means imaginable. It is said that he died on the battlefield, but we think now he did not. By some means, it seems he find a way to cheat death and became a vampire."

Mr. Morris whistled and shook his head, an uneasy look on his countenance. "So that's the Devil we're up against. I admit, it strikes more than a little fear into my heart."

"Forewarned is forearmed," said Dr. Van Helsing confidently, "and to-day is ours. Until the sun sets to-night, that monster must retain whatever form he now has. He is confined within the limitations of his earthly envelope. He cannot melt into thin air nor disappear through cracks or chinks or crannies. If he go through a doorway, he must open the door like a mortal. And so we have this day to hunt out all his lairs and sterilise them with Sacred Host—and should we find him sleeping within one of them, we will slay him."

A brief discussion followed as the group made their plans, deciding which tools and equipment would be needed to open all the heavy wooden boxes and to sterilise them, as well as which weapons were required to slay the vampire. Dr. Van Helsing suggested that they begin their quest with the house closest to hand, and then move on to Piccadilly, where they might be fortunate enough to find records regarding the purchase of other residences.

I sighed, staring out the window. It had begun to rain, and the dismal, grey outpouring which pattered against the eaves and window-panes only served to reinforce my deepening melancholia. I was overwhelmed with guilt regarding my actions over the past few nights. It mortified me to be keeping such a secret; yet at the same time, I was filled with despair; for I had truly thought myself to be in love with an extraordinary man. It was, I told myself, not a dream I had been living but a nightmare. I must put it all behind me and dedicate myself to the task at hand.

"You will have to go without me," I heard Jonathan saying anxiously. "I want to trap this demon; but I cannot leave Mina. I must stay and protect her."

"No, Jonathan," I replied. "You must go. There is strength in numbers. The Count has extraordinary powers, and you will need every hand to defeat him."

The men agreed. "Besides, if there are legal papers to be found, your expertise may prove invaluable," said Lord Godalming.

"But can we truly leave her?" Jonathan said, appealing now to Dr. Van Helsing. "Will she be safe?"

"The worst already has happen, my friend," the professor replied with a frown.

"It is true," I said. "Things are as bad as they can be. But please: do not worry about me. The important thing is that you find this Devil and finish this thing to-day."

"Then let us go at once, for we have no time to lose!" Jonathan cried.

"Not so," said Dr. Van Helsing. "Do you forget? Last night our foe banqueted heavily and will sleep late."

I paled at this, and the men let out a collective gasp at hearing such a thoughtless remark at my expense. Dr. Van Helsing's face fell as he became aware of what he had said, and taking my hands in his, he cried: "Oh, dear, dear Madam Mina, alas! That I of all who so reverence you should have said anything so stupid and forgetful. You do not deserve so. You will forget I said it, please?"

"I will," I answered quietly.

A little silence fell; then the professor pursed his lips and said: "There is one thing more I am concerned about. Madam Mina: have you received any thoughts yet from this creature?"

"Thoughts?" I repeated.

"As I said, by this blood exchange you are, I believe, connected now. He may send thoughts to your mind in an attempt to influence your actions."

"Oh!" I shivered at this frightening concept. "No; there has been nothing yet."

"Then I was right," Dr. Van Helsing replied, nodding. "With the sun's rays, he loses all his power. You will be safe from him till dark—and we will return by then."

As they finalised their campaign, I wracked my brain trying to recall anything I had learned which might prove useful in their pursuit; but Dracula had divulged nothing of his own intent to me. The only real secret in my possession was the knowledge that Dracula had a secret, top-floor lair at Carfax, full of books and art supplies; but there had been no earth-box there. I could, in any case, think of no way to suggest the fact without incriminating myself—and I was loath to do that.

Dr. Van Helsing insisted that we all required nourishment if we were to perform at our best. Breakfast was an awkward affair. We tried to be cheerful and encouraging to each other, but it felt false and strange. When it was over, Dr. Van Helsing stood up and said:

"Now, my dear friends, we go forth to our terrible enterprise. Are we all armed against ghostly as well as carnal attack?" The men assured him that they were.

The professor then turned to me and said, "Madam Mina, you are quite safe here until the sunset. I have myself prepared your chamber by the placing of protective things of which we know, so that He may not enter. Now let me guard yourself." From an envelope, he removed a small wafer. "On your forehead, I touch this piece of sacred wafer in the name of the Father, the Son, and—"

As the holy wafer touched my forehead, I felt a searing pain, as if my flesh had been burned by a piece of red-hot metal. I screamed in agony. The professor dropped the Host and recoiled in shock. The men froze, with horrified looks on their faces. As the scorching pain continued, I reached up and touched the spot, where I felt a welt rising beneath my fingertips.

"God help me!" I cried, sinking to my knees on the floor, and pulling my hair over my face to shroud it.

"This is truly the work of the Devil," Dr. Van Helsing whispered in horror.

Had I needed further proof that I had aligned myself with Satan, this surely confirmed it. "Even the Almighty shuns my polluted flesh," I cried, sobbing. "Must I bear this mark of shame upon my forehead until the Judgment Day?"

Jonathan threw himself down beside me in an agony of helpless grief. For a few sorrowful minutes, we held each other, while our friends turned away to hide their own silent tears. At length, Dr. Van Helsing said gravely:

"Dear Madam Mina, so surely as we live, that scar shall pass away when God sees right to lift the burden that is hard upon us. Let us pray that we can raise that veil of sorrow from your head to-day." There was hope and comfort in his words. We all stood and joined hands, praying for help and guidance, as we swore allegiance to each other.

Soon after, we gathered in the foyer, where the men brought their bags of tools and equipment as they prepared to leave. Without, the grey heavens continued their deluge, pelting the landscape with a driving downpour against a backdrop of lightning and thunder.

"Do you think the Count called up this storm to try to thwart us?" Dr. Seward asked anxiously, as he stared outside.

"He have not the power to control the weather by day," Dr. Van Helsing replied. "Only in darkness can he thus torment us."

"A little rain is not going to stand in our way," Jonathan insisted, kissing me good-bye at the door. "We shall prevail." At the sight of my angry red scar, he quickly averted his eyes.

"Be careful, will you?" I said.

He assured me that he would. Then the men all opened their umbrellas and hastened out into the elements. I returned to my bedroom, where I paced anxiously for some time, continually glancing out the window for their return. Each sonorous boom of thunder made me jump in alarm, as if a portent of impending doom.

When nearly an hour had passed without a sign of them, I began to grow worried. Perhaps I should have told them about the secret room upstairs, I thought—no matter how sorely it tarnished my image and reputation! What if Dracula was hiding there? What if he had made his way down to the chapel and attacked them? For all I knew, all five men could be lying dead at that very moment!

At last, from my window, I glimpsed a parade of five black umbrellas crossing the lawn below. I breathed a sigh of relief. One umbrella tipped back, and from beneath it, Jonathan waved to me, signalling with a nod that their work next door had been successfully accomplished. I waved in reply, watching the five departing forms as they turned down the byroad and disappeared from view, on their way to the village to catch a train into town.

That is when the messages began.

Mina! Dracula's voice intoned within my mind. *I must see you.*

The voice so startled me that I leapt to my feet. Dr. Van Helsing had said with certainty that the vampire was powerless to contact me during the day. How wrong he was!

Van Helsing is wrong about many things.

Oh! The fiend was reading my thoughts! *Go away, you monster!* I thought with all my might. *Leave me alone. I never want to see you again.*

You must hear me. You must let me explain.

No! I am through with your excuses and explanations! You are the Devil incarnate! Be gone! Be gone!

I am no Devil. I love you.

You cannot love me! You never did! You are a murderer and a liar! I hate you! I hate you!

His entreaties continued. I tried to render them unintelligible by frantically reciting a poem aloud. Then I began to sing. Still, his thoughts continued hammering away like a great, ceaseless noise inside my brain.

Unable to bear it any longer, I raced out of the room and down the stairs. Throwing open the front door to a blast of cold, wet air, I darted hatless out of the house into the pouring rain. I dashed down the drive and the densely tree-lined lane, mindless of the freezing elements which drenched me, or the mud which clung to my shoes and splattered against my skirts. My only thought was to put as much distance as possible between myself and Carfax, as if it might somehow stop the endless verbal barrage which threatened my very sanity.

As I rounded a bend in the road, a bolt of lightning flashed across the dark sky, illuminating it to a brilliant whiteness. I heard a sudden, loud crack and saw a burst of sparks overhead. Looking up, I saw to my horror that an immense branch, as large as a mature tree, had been severed from a giant, towering oak—and said limb was hurtling down with deadly speed directly at me.

SEVENTEEN

I HAD NO TIME TO SCREAM; NO WAY TO EVADE THE BRANCH'S deadly fall.

Suddenly, Dracula was there, his long, black cloak swirling about him. He scooped me up in his arms, and with an uncanny whoosh of sound, light, and speed, I was out of harm's way, transported deep within the cover of the wooded grove. My heart pounded in terror, not only from my close brush with death but to find myself alone again in this monster's arms, so far from the help of any other eye or ear. And, to my dismay, it pounded in excitement as well.

"Put me down!" I screamed, beating at him with my fists.

He set me on my feet, still holding me firmly by both arms as he looked down at me. His gaze fell upon the angry red scar upon my forehead, and he winced with what appeared to be genuine remorse. For an instant I believe he was actually deprived of the power of speech. Although the dense thicket of oaks sheltered us from the greatest power of the deluge, rain still sprinkled down upon our drenched forms through the leafy branches overhead and spattered against the dense undergrowth at our feet.

"You caused that branch to break on purpose, so you could

stage a rescue!" I cried accusingly as I struggled vainly to free myself from his tight grip.

"Hardly."

"Let me go, you fiend, you murderer!" I spit at him. "Or should I call you Vlad?"

His face darkened as he stared at me. "How can you think that of me? I was not Vlad the Impaler. I despised him and everything he did."

"The professor said—"

"The professor is wrong."

"You are lying. You are a monster!"

"Am I?" he asked quietly.

"Yes! I saw the real you last night. The perfect face you show to me is only a mask, to hide the Devil within!"

"The real me stands before you: the being I was before the Devil changed me. Anger tends to drive me to actions beyond my control. Something dark within me rises up and takes over—as it did last night with Renfield."

"You murdered him!"

"To protect you."

"Another lie!"

Still holding me tightly, he said: "Renfield was one of those, like Lucy, whose thoughts are so vivid that I could read them whether I wished to or not. Last night, I heard him raving that he wanted your blood. He had a plan to escape, to slash your throat, and to drink every drop that spilled from your body."

I hesitated. Could it be true? I had been warned that Mr. Renfield was a homicidal maniac. I recalled that he had escaped many times, and had once viciously stabbed Dr. Seward; and I could not forget the way he had looked at me on my last visit, or the brazen, rude remark he had made. "*If* that is so, you heard the ravings of a very sick man. You did not have to kill him."

"What would you have preferred? That I left a note for Dr.

Seward about the lunatic's intent? Mina: *he was going to kill you*—if not last night, then sometime soon. I could not take that chance."

I felt my resolve slipping slightly and struggled to hold tight to it even as I struggled to free myself from his grip. "Murdering a man on my behalf does not make it right. Murder is a sin—and not the only sin you have committed. You have befouled me!"

"How?"

"You made me drink your blood! What kind of depraved creature are you, that you would seduce me like that, with my own husband asleep in the bed next to me? Did you put me under a spell?"

"No. I put a spell on Jonathan, but not on you. You drank my blood of your own free will."

"You did not warn me of the consequences!" Tears stung my eyes now, mingling with the moisture from the rain. "You have damned me upon my death to an accursed existence as a vampire!"

"I have not."

I froze in astonishment. "You have not?"

"No. It is as I said: when you drank my blood, you created a telepathic connection between us. That is all."

"But then—why did Dr. Van Helsing say—"

"Van Helsing is a pompous, self-important man who fancies himself an expert in matters about which he knows little. To become a vampire, you would have had to drink a great deal more blood from my body than you did. Or I would have to drink *your* blood in a significant enough quantity that my essence pervades and changes yours. I have taken care not to do so. You are still human, Mina—as mortal as you were before."

I paused, dashing away my tears: confused, uncertain, and filled with sudden hope. Could it be true? Was I not really damned? Then a thought occurred to me, and I shook my head. "No. Whether or not you *fed* on me *sufficiently* to make me a vampire . . . your blood has still infected me. Do you not see this mark upon my forehead? You put it there! It proves I am unclean, rejected by the Almighty, and that you are aligned with the Devil himself!"

"It proves only that the evil monster who made me—the animal that I struggle daily to overcome—still lives on in my blood. I regret that I passed on some of that to you. But it was not enough to infect you permanently. Unlike mine, your human blood will repair and replace itself in time, and this kind of mark should never occur again."

I wept with fresh relief at this pronouncement. "Oh! If only that is true! But who else would believe it? For the rest of my life, everyone who looks at me will know that I was branded—for ever scarred—by a piece of holy wafer!"

He winced again. "I could remove that mark; but if I do it now, I fear it will only cause Van Helsing to suspect us of some further collusion."

"Collusion? Us? There is no *us*!"

"There is, Mina: and you know it as well as I do." His blue eyes penetrated mine. "I have made no secret of it: I love you. You are all I want. I do not want you for a day, or a decade, or a lifetime. I want to be with you *for all time.* But I want you freely, or not at all. The choice is still yours. Live your full, human life, if you so choose. Grow old with the husband you love. Have all the children you desire. I will not stand in your way. But when at your natural time you die, if you wish to be reborn into another life—a life of power and immortality with me—you have only to ask. And then, you and I can be together for ever."

"No. No. No!" I cried, determined to hold on to my anger despite the earnest emotion displayed on the perfect face before me. "I will not listen to your endless, devious attempts to persuade. Cannot you understand? I could never be a vampire! I have no wish to be immortal! Nor do I wish to be with you *at any time*—ever! I hate you. I hate you!"

To my astonishment, at this pronouncement, his resolve seemed to crumble. A tortured look crossed his face, and he let go of me and turned away. I stood still for a moment and then took a few steps back. Was I free to go? It seemed there was no invisible shield preventing my escape. And yet—if he was not holding me here by his powers—why did I suddenly have no will to leave?

"So this is where you stand. I had hoped, if I could control my desires, and court you in the old-fashioned manner, that I might . . ." He paused. "But it does not matter now." He turned back to me with a broken smile and said: "You need not worry, Mina. You will not be accursed with my presence any more."

"What do you mean?" I said warily.

"I have lived a very long time, and waited all my existence to find you. You are now my reason for being. I have no desire to continue if I cannot have you. Your men are determined to kill me. I will simply let them do it. You have only to say the word."

I stared at him, fully aware that he was a crafty Devil and a supremely powerful being. Surely he had no intention of dying at *any one's* hand! But as I looked into his eyes, it was suddenly as if I was looking through a window into Dracula's mind and heart. All at once, without words, I felt the weight of the lonely centuries he had lived through; the joy he had experienced during all the times we had shared; the intensity of his love for me; and the anguish and despair that now wracked his heart. This amalgam of feeling was so powerful that I gasped aloud.

I tried to remind myself that he was sending me these thoughts on purpose; that he had fixed on me as his eternal companion and would no doubt say anything to get what he wanted. But even if that was true, I could no longer deny the truth:

I still loved him.

I had never stopped loving him.

I could not bear the thought of life without him, or of his dying for any reason, much less because of me. I choked back a sob. He must have read my thoughts, for he instantly stepped forward and took me in his arms.

"Mina, Mina. I love you so."

"I love you, too."

He kissed me deeply. My arms wrapped around his shoulders, and I returned his kiss in a fervent expression of all the tangled emotions that had been building up inside me for months. When the kiss ended, his mouth moved to caress my cheeks, wiping away the tears and the rain; then he kissed his way down to my throat. Suddenly he paused, as if fighting some powerful inner struggle; with a ragged groan, he pushed me from him and turned away.

"What is it?" I asked.

"I cannot drink your blood any more."

"Why not?"

"I have already done so three times. Every human has different tolerances and immunities; but should I take any more of your blood, you might indeed become like me—but not, as Van Helsing thinks, some distant day after you die. The change may happen—and take your life—far sooner than you wish."

"Oh," I replied in a small voice, as I tried to rein in my fear.

He sighed and shook his head wryly. "Since the moment we met, it has been a test of strength and will to keep my hands and teeth off you; but it must end. To be in your company—even if I cannot taste your blood again, or make love to you—*yet*—it is reward enough for now."

My cheeks reddened at his mention of love-making. In truth, I had indulged in fantasies many times about that very subject, from the time I had first met him as Mr. Wagner, when I was a single woman. The notion had been shocking enough even then; but I was married now. I could *never* . . . it was inconceivable.

Nicolae looked at me sharply, apparently reading my thoughts, which made me blush even more deeply. He took my hand in his, brought it to his lips, and kissed it, saying:

"Relax, Mina. I understand that your desires conflict with your curious Victorian sense of propriety and morality. If I have your heart—"

"You have it."

"Then I am willing to forgo the rest at present."

The rain continued to spatter down from the trees. I was wet clear through, and I shivered. Dracula looked at me, as if suddenly conscious of how very cold I was. He glanced upwards, then slowly waved his hand with a deep concentration that I felt in my mind like a small tremor. Suddenly, an invisible, protective dome seemed to form above and around us. Although the rain continued elsewhere, within our immediate vicinity it stopped, and the air grew warm. Within seconds, he and I and our respective clothing were completely dry.

He gestured towards a fallen log near-by. I sat down beside him, overwhelmed and speechless for a long moment. At length, I said:

"What are we going to do? I cannot leave my husband; but I cannot give you up. I have tried, and it is not within my power. Neither can I stand by and watch the others destroy you."

"That will never happen."

"But they are visiting your houses as we speak. They intend to render all of your boxes of earth useless."

"I know. I should have stayed behind to protect my property—but it might have meant killing one or all of them, and I had promised you I would not."

"Thank you."

"Fortunately, I am not so vulnerable as they think. Many of the boxes they will find are decoys. I have other resting-places they have not discovered, where I have transferred my good Transylvanian earth."

"What happens if they find them?"

"They must not." Taking my hand in his, he said: "This is war,

Mina. To win a war, you must know and understand your enemy's weaknesses. To that end, I have spent numerous hours in the copper-domed Round Reading Room of the British Museum, reading up on Dr. Van Helsing. He has published a multitude of articles on a variety of subjects. I was fascinated to note that he proclaims himself to be a master hypnotist. Let us put that to our advantage."

"How?"

"I have a plan: a way we can convince your men to call off their hunt. A way that you can stay with your husband if you wish, and I will still be safe: we must deceive them into thinking that I have fled the country."

"Fled the country?"

Dracula told me the particulars of the plan he had in mind, a simple but rather ingenious plot which involved, among other things, my asking the professor to use his hypnotic powers to put me in a trance.

"Won't that be dangerous?" I said dubiously. "If I allow Dr. Van Helsing to hypnotise me, I might reveal the truth about my feelings for you, as well as your entire plan."

"You might—if Van Helsing actually proved himself to be a competent hypnotist—which I think highly unlikely. I have a great deal of experience in this art, Mina, and I can teach you some safeguards. In any case, I will be there in your mind the entire time should there be even the slightest danger of your falling under—and I will tell you what to say."

"I have little experience at play-acting, other than school dramatics."

"I have faith in you. I heard your acting skills at work last night, after I left the room, when you spun that remarkable story about our encounter." With a twinkle in his eyes, he mimicked my impression of him as a repulsive monster: " 'You have been my bountiful wine-press for a while, and shall be later on my companion and my helper. When my brain says Come! to you, you shall cross land and sea to do my bidding!' "

I covered my face with my hands. "Oh! I blush to recall what I told them. I think that tale only increased their thirst for revenge."

"It was quite imaginative—if a bit melodramatic."

I looked away, thinking over what he had proposed. Could I—should I—try to help him?

How could I not?

I knew how much Jonathan and the others feared and despised him. If I did not fight to save Nicolae, he might perish. Not only would that break my heart; but who could say which one of the others, if any, would come out of such an altercation alive? I felt like Helen of Troy, caught between two lovers, on the brink of war. I loved Jonathan; I wanted my sweet life with him and the family that we envisioned. Yet I also loved Nicolae. I could not be true to both men at the same time. I could only be true to myself and follow my heart: and my heart told me to do whatever was necessary to keep them both safe. Perhaps I was blind; perhaps I was too much in love to think straight; but I could not see any other course of action to follow.

"Nicolae: I will do whatever I can to help you. But the others all believe I am doomed to become a vampire when I die. Even if they think you have left England, I fear they would follow you and will never give up searching for you, as long as they think you are alive."

"You must convince them otherwise: that I will never return; that they should simply let you live out the span of your mortal life; and that when you die, you will not pose a threat to any one."

"How shall I convince them of that?"

"By telling them to stake you if you rise."

"You cannot be serious!"

"That group should have no compunction about promising to complete the act; they did it willingly enough for Lucy. But it is a safe promise, for *you will never rise*—not unless you wish to. Unless you decide to become mine of your own free will. And if that happens, I promise you: whether it is nine years from now or ninety-nine, I will come for you, Mina. I will take you away the moment you reach the grave."

I marvelled at the thought; the whole thing still seemed entirely fantastical to me. Could it be true? Was it possible that I *could* be true to both of the men I loved? Could I live first one life, and then the other?

What other solution was there to the riddle in which I found myself?

Then the image from my dream came to mind—the grotesque vision of Lucy whirling to face me as a hideous, hissing, vampire—and I recalled Dr. Seward's anguished voice on his phonographic diary as he recounted the story of the horrific Thing that Lucy became. I could not repress a shudder. Did I truly want to become a *vampire,* even if it meant spending eternity in Dracula's arms?

"It would be an eternity of bliss," he said, although I had not spoken aloud. "I will not lie to you. It comes at a heavy price. But I would be giving you a gift, Mina; a gift which few people can ever hope to possess."

"Is it a gift?" I said uncertainly.

"Yes. With immortality comes great power. You love learning, Mina. Think of the possibilities. Think of all that you can learn and do, with infinity before you."

"I admit: it *is* a thrilling notion: the idea of time without end. I could read every book in your library. I could read every single book in the British Museum!"

"You can become as accomplished a pianist as Beethoven, Mozart, and Chopin."

"I could live to see all the marvellous things that will be invented in the future. I could meet and know my great-great-grandchildren."

"And you can choose your form. You can be that great-great-grandmother, or you can be as young and beautiful for ever as you are to-day. You will never sicken, and never die."

"But that is not true. You *are* dead."

"Not dead," he insisted. "*Un-Dead.* An entirely different thing. It is Darwin's theory of evolution at work: only the fittest survive, and form new species."

I looked at him. "A new species that does not die."

"Exactly."

"But . . . you said you have been lonely for centuries."

"I would be lonely no longer if I had you."

"You are feared and hunted."

"We will live where we are unknown."

"What if I turned out like Lucy and your sisters? I would never wish to hurt any one."

"You will not. You will be the sweetest, loveliest, most benevolent vampire who ever graced the earth."

"How can you know that?"

"Because I will guide you every step of the way, my darling, and teach you everything I know. In time, you will become as powerful as I."

I studied his face, so beautiful, so perfect in every detail. Until a week ago, I did not even believe that vampires existed. Now I understood that they were not only very real, but they were not all the vile, evil, remorseless creatures the professor had described. Dracula had evil within him, but he struggled against it; he had a heart and a conscience. Was that really so different from many of the human beings I knew? He required blood to exist, but he had found a way to take his nourishment without killing any one—and in most cases, without the person even remembering it. Would it be such a bad thing, I wondered, to live for ever in such a manner? Particularly if I had such a man at my side?

"Would you really wait ninety-nine years for me?" I asked.

"What are nine decades when you have eternity?"

"If I die an old woman—will you still want me?"

"You forget: I am an old man. I will always want you."

"If I become Un-Dead, would it be safe to share each other's blood again?"

"Perfectly safe. We could indulge any time we liked, just for the pleasure of it."

That was an enticement I could not ignore.

"You said, before, that the Devil changed you. What did you mean? How old are you? Who were you before you became a vampire?"

"Ah. Now *that* is a very long story, which I will reserve for another time." He kissed me and said with reluctance: "I must go. I have work to do."

He helped me to my feet and, with a flick of his hand, removed the invisible dome that had been protecting us. The rain had stopped, although the moisture from the overlying trees spit at us as we hurried through the woods, taking a short-cut which he said led directly to the village. Knowing that he planned to make an appearance before the men that very afternoon, I expressed my concern for his safety and for the safety of my husband and the others. Dracula reassured me that no harm would come to any one.

"Will the others see you as I do?" I asked.

"No. It is vital that they recognise me as the old man they saw last night and the one your husband knew in Transylvania."

"Jonathan has already seen you looking younger—although not this young, perhaps: once in the chapel of your castle, when you had grey hair instead of white. And again two weeks ago in Piccadilly. We saw you outside a jewellery shop."

"What was I doing?"

"You were staring very intently at a beautiful woman who was sitting in an open carriage, and wearing a cart-wheel hat."

"Ah—yes. The woman in the cart-wheel hat. She was indeed

very beautiful. Had I known you were there, however, I would have been staring intently at you."

"I did not think it was you. You looked fifty, at least. And your face—it frightened me."

"I was not so particular that day about the form I took. I was steeped in bitterness. I thought I had lost you for ever."

We had reached the edge of the trees by then. He touched my face, gazing at me with such affection, I could not imagine that he could ever be cruel.

"*A tout a l'heure,*[4] my love. I must return to Carfax to prepare for my train ride into London." He kissed me good-bye. "I will see you as soon as it is safe; and I will always be close in thought."

At the village telegraph office, I sent the wire Dracula had requested, addressed to Dr. Van Helsing at the Piccadilly house, where I knew the group to be:

PURFLEET 3 OCTOBER 1890

VAN HELSING ET AL.

LOOK OUT FOR D. HE HAS JUST NOW, 12:45, COME FROM CARFAX HURRIEDLY AND HASTENED TOWARDS THE SOUTH. HE SEEMS TO BE GOING THE ROUND.

MINA

I then returned to the asylum. I knew I must keep occupied or go mad with worry. All afternoon, I busied myself transcribing

4 See you later.

the latest contents of Jonathan's and Dr. Seward's journals, which proved to be voluminous.

It gave me pause to listen to Dr. Seward's horrified phonographic rendition of the previous night's events, when the men had broken into my chamber and found me with Dracula. I blanched with dismay as he recounted my fabricated tale of what had occurred between us, which depicted Nicolae as such a horrendous monster. It was all untrue; yet I'd had no choice but to type it all up for the record.

Before I knew it, the clock in the hall was striking four. The men had promised to return from their quest before sunset, which would be in an hour or two. I got up and began to pace anxiously, wondering what had happened. Just then, I heard Dracula's voice in my mind:

Rest easy, Mina. Phase One went precisely as planned.

Is everyone all right? I thought in reply.

Not a scratch on me or any one. Your telegram did the trick. The group was at my house at Piccadilly, lying in wait. May I always meet such ill-trained enemies! I made quite a show for them before I fled.

Where are you now?

I am off to take care of Phase Two. Be well. I love you.

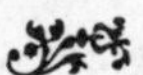

THE MEN FILED BACK INTO THE HOUSE JUST AS THE SUN WAS making its final descent. As I met them at the front door, I saw in their faces a mix of emotions. Dr. Van Helsing appeared the most upbeat of all, but Jonathan looked positively broken down. It pained me to see it. Just the night before, he had been a happy man with a strong, optimistic, youthful face. To-day Jonathan looked drawn, old, and haggard, his eyes hollow, and his face lined with grief. His energy remained intact, however; I felt as if he were a flint or cannon, barely containing his inner force, ready to explode into action at the slightest provocation.

"What happened?" I asked, my heartfelt concern for him overwhelming the innocence that I endeavoured to convey.

"He came, but he got away," Jonathan replied with a defeated frown. Upon catching sight of the scar on my forehead, he looked quickly away. I understood why: it was a visible reminder of what he deemed to be my unclean state and his failure to protect me.

"The villain flee, yes," Dr. Van Helsing said, "but we learn much to-day and have great success: we find and destroy all his boxes but one."

"You must tell me everything," I said.

Over dinner, the men regaled me with the story of their adventure that afternoon.

"We took care of all the boxes in the Carfax chapel," said Dr. Seward. "They're full of Host, and useless to him now."

"I employed a locksmith to get us into the Count's house at Piccadilly," Lord Godalming explained, "pretending it was mine and that I had lost my key. We found eight boxes of earth there. Quincey and I found six more boxes each at his places at Mile End and Bermondsey, and destroyed them all. That is—we destroyed them for *him*."

"Then we rushed back to Piccadilly and learned of the telegram you had sent, Mrs. Harker," put in Mr. Morris.

"You said the Count go south from Carfax," explained Dr. Van Helsing, "so we believe he visit his other houses first, to check their status. We lie in wait. At last he come."

"Count Dracula seemed to be prepared for some surprise—at least he feared it," Jonathan said. "It was a pity we had not organised some better plan of attack—but I went right at him with my kukri knife."

"Oh!" I cried, alarmed, for I had seen that knife, which he had inherited from his father. It had a long, curved blade that could function equally as a knife or an axe, and it would be a fearsome weapon of war.

"Only the Count's diabolical quickness saved him," said Dr. Seward. "A second less, and that trenchant blade would have shorn through his heart."

"As it was, it slashed the fiend's coat-pocket," said Mr. Morris, "and a great stream of bank-notes and gold coins scattered to the floor."

"We advanced on him with crucifixes and holy wafers," said Lord Godalming. "The Count cowered back and threw himself straight through a window, then hurled some choice words at us from below."

"We took off after him, but lost sight of him," Jonathan cried angrily, stabbing the meat on his plate with his fork. "He was gone. Gone! And the earth-boxes did not total up. There is still one remaining somewhere. If the Count chooses to lie hidden, he may baffle us for years!"

"He will not baffle us, my friend," said Dr. Van Helsing firmly. "We will find that missing box, and all will be well. I tell you: this was a good day. We have made all of the Count's lairs uninhabitable to him, but one; and we have learned something—much, in fact! He fears us! Let us now wait and see what he does next."

THAT NIGHT, THE PROFESSOR FIXED UP MY BEDROOM WITH garlic—as he put it—"to guard against any coming of the vampire," and assured me that I might enjoy a peaceful sleep. He also placed a bell at my disposal, which I was to sound in case of emergency. As a further precaution, Lord Godalming, Mr. Morris, and Dr. Seward took turns keeping watch outside our chamber door, despite my insistence that this seemed unnecessary.

The moment my head touched my pillow, I heard Nicolae in my mind:

So: my little theatricals were well received?

You made an excellent impression, I replied in thought, with a little smile.

I feel you smiling. I wish I was there to see it.

I stifled a surprised gasp. *How does this bond work between us? Can you read my thoughts at any time, or only if I send them to you?*

I can read your mind at any time now, my darling.

I was taken aback by this. Did I really want all of my thoughts known by another? And yet . . . did I now have any other choice? *Why do I not hear everything you are thinking?*

You are new at this. It takes time. You will hear me when you need to, I promise. Now I must go. I have much to arrange. You know what to do?

Yes.

Until later, then. Sleep well. I shall wake you when the time comes.

AT THREE O'CLOCK IN THE MORNING, NICOLAE'S THOUGHTS AWAKened me from a deep slumber. I sat up in bed, wiping sleep from my eyes as I recalled the task at hand. Heart pounding with anticipation, I touched my husband on the shoulder, then whispered hurriedly in his ear:

"Jonathan: wake up."

"What is it?" He sat up, groggy yet alarmed. "Is something wrong?"

"No. But I need you to call the professor. I have an idea. I want to see him at once."

Jonathan gave the message to Dr. Seward, who was sitting sentry. A few minutes later, the doctor returned with the entire party, all clad in their dressing-gowns. While the men waited in the doorway, filled with curiosity, the professor said, "What am I to do for you, Madam Mina?"

"You said I have a mental connection to Count Dracula. Let us see if that is so. I want you to hypnotise me."

EIGHTEEN

"Hypnotise you?" Jonathan repeated with concern.

"Yes. Perhaps I can help us by learning something of his whereabouts."

Dr. Van Helsing's face lit up. "Excellent, Madam Mina. Excellent." He motioned for Jonathan and the others to stay back and for me to sit up on the edge of the bed. Without another word, he stared down fixedly at me and began to make slow passes in front of my eyes with his hands. He looked so comical, standing there in his dark purple satin dressing-gown, and waving his hands about like some crazed medium, that it was all I could do not to laugh. I reminded myself of the seriousness of my mission, however, and gazed at him steadily, as I listened to Dracula's reassuring thoughts in my mind. I then closed my eyes and sat very still, pretending to be under the professor's influence.

"You may open your eyes now, Madam Mina," I heard him say gently.

I did so, feigning a far-away look which I hoped was credible.

Dr. Van Helsing indicated to the other men to come in. They silently gathered at the foot of the bed.

"Where are you?" Dr. Van Helsing asked in a low tone.

"I do not know," I replied, in a voice as dreamy as I could make it. "It is all strange to me."

"What do you see?"

"I see nothing; it is all dark."

Dr. Van Helsing nodded to Jonathan to pull up the blind. The day was just upon us, and a rosy light diffused itself through the room.

"What do you hear?" the professor asked very patiently.

"The lapping of water. It is gurgling by, and little waves leap. I can hear them on the outside."

"Then you are on a ship?" he said in surprise.

"Oh, yes!"

The men all gasped. Even as I stared forward with glazed, unfocused eyes, I could see the eager glances they exchanged.

"What else do you hear?" the professor prodded.

"I hear the sound of men stamping overhead as they run about," I replied, drawing on the memories of my recent sea-voyage to the Continent. "There is the creaking of a chain, and the loud tinkle as the check of the capstan falls into the ratchet."

"What are you doing?"

"I am still—oh, so still. It is like death!" I noticed that the sun had now fully risen—the moment when Dr. Van Helsing supposed my mental connection with Dracula would end—and so I stopped, closed my eyes, and began to breathe softly and deeply, as if I were asleep.

Dr. Van Helsing placed his hands on my shoulders and gently guided me down onto the bed, until my head lay upon my pillow. I pretended to sleep for a few moments; and then, with a long sigh, I stretched and sat up, as if awakening in wonder at finding the others all gathered around me. "Have I been talking in my sleep?" I said innocently.

"You were hypnotised, my dear," Jonathan said, "just as you suggested. And it worked wonderfully well."

"Oh! What did I say?"

The professor quickly repeated the conversation; then the men all started to speak excitedly at once.

"He's on a ship!" Mr. Morris cried.

"He is getting away!" added Lord Godalming, and the two men immediately started for the door; but the professor's calm voice called them back.

"Stay, my friends. That ship, wherever it was, was weighing anchor whilst she spoke. There are many ships weighing anchor at this moment in your great Port of London, and we know not yet which one to seek. But God be thanked that we now have a clue! It is as I suspect: he meant escape! With one earth-box left, and a pack of men following like dogs after a fox, he saw that London was no place for him, and he leave the land. He have prepare for it in some way, and that last earth-box of his was ready to ship somewhere. For this he took all that money, which we saw spill from his pockets! For this he hurry so the last time we see him, lest we catch him in his weakness before the sun go down! Our enemy have gone back to his castle in Transylvania. Of this I am as certain as if a great hand of fire wrote it on the wall!"

I hid a little smile of satisfaction at hearing this, for it was precisely what Nicolae and I wanted them to think. However, Jonathan immediately cried:

"We cannot let him escape! We must go after him!"

"Indeed we must," said Dr. Van Helsing, "but our old fox is wily, and we must follow him with wile. There is no rush at present. There are waters between us, which I believe he cannot pass even if he would, unless the ship were to touch the land—for the

Vampire cannot cross moving water on his own, or so it is said. Therefore, he remain on this ship until it reach safe harbour. This give us time to find out the name of the ship and by what route it takes. Then we can make our plan and follow him."

I had anticipated this reaction, and had prepared my appeal. "But why need we seek him further, when he is gone away from us?" I said sweetly. "He has fled to the Continent. He is gone. Cannot we just let him go?"

"Never!" returned Dr. Van Helsing.

"But why? He is finished here. There is nothing more to fear."

"There is much to fear, my dear Madam Mina. He can live for centuries, and you are but mortal woman. Do you not see the stain upon your forehead? He has marked you. Time is now to be dreaded, for you drank his blood."

This I knew to be untrue. Unconsciously, my hand went up to touch my scar, which was still red and tender. "Perhaps your theory is wrong, Professor."

"It is not wrong."

I had more to say, but was cut off when Dr. Van Helsing rang for breakfast, and then launched into a discussion with the men about the best means to seek information about Dracula's embarkation, which they intended to confirm that very morning. I would have to wait, I realised, and seek an opportunity to discuss the topic further.

AFTER BREAKFAST, THE PROFESSOR SET OUT FOR THE PORT OF London, accompanied by the others—all except Jonathan, who insisted on staying home to watch over me and keep me company. I felt a bit awkward at first in my husband's presence, concerned that I might make some remark which would give away my complicity in the affair with Dracula. Yet at the same time, I was most grateful for this opportunity to be together. It was the first time—other than a few moments in the privacy of our bedroom—that we had been alone to really talk, since the day we had left Exeter.

The two of us spent the morning going over the papers again. While I typed up the most recent journal entries and reports, he placed everything in order, reviewing them to make certain that we had not missed anything. When this was accomplished, we agreed that we needed some diversion and decided to take a walk into the village.

As we walked down the wooded lane, the crisp autumn air seemed to revive us. With the birds singing in the trees, and the distant bleating of the sheep, it seemed impossible to believe that we were embroiled in the strange, unearthly drama which had so altered our lives. From Jonathan's easy gait and relaxed features, I saw that he too was appreciating this moment of reprieve from our collective anxiety.

"The Count's departure has bought us some time," he said with a little smile. "Knowing that this horrible danger is no longer face to face with us every moment—that is a comfort."

"Yes."

His glance touched my forehead, and his smile disappeared. "I am so sorry for what has happened to you, Mina. If ever there was a woman who was all perfection, it is you, my poor wronged darling."

My cheeks reddened. "I am no saint, Jonathan. I am as far from perfection as a woman can be."

"Nonsense. You are an angel. Surely God will not permit the world to be the poorer by the loss of one so fair and good as you. This is my hope; and I will cling to it to sustain me through the dark times ahead." He reached out and took my hand. "At least we have something of a guiding purpose now. Perhaps we are the instruments of ultimate good."

My blush deepened at his words. Oh! If Jonathan only knew

what I had done, and what I still meant to do—could he but be privy to the feelings within my breast, for his very rival—he would surely recoil from me in horror and disdain and hate the very ground I walked upon. *Tell him,* my mind cried. *Tell him everything. He is your husband. He deserves to know the truth.* But with a rush of despair, I knew that I could not. Were I to do so, all would be lost: for war would ensue, and one of my two loves was sure to die, if not both of them. I allowed my guilt to subside, stuffing it into a tiny box in my mind, determined not to think of it, to concentrate on the here and now, and to enjoy Jonathan and this day.

When we reached the main street of the village, we were assailed by the aroma of sizzling fresh fish from the Royal Hotel, and we could not resist its advertisement for "World Famous Fish Dinners." We were quickly seated at a cozy table by the fire, where we enjoyed the best fish and chips that either of us had ever tasted.

"I should never have allowed you to come to London," Jonathan said, as we ate, "knowing that that creature was here."

"You could never have guessed what would happen. And I am glad I came."

"How can you be glad?"

"Had I stayed in Exeter, I would have been paralysed by worry. At least this way, we are together, and I can try to be of help. But there is another reason. There is something I have been wanting to tell you for several days, but I have not had the opportunity: I found my mother and father."

Jonathan stared at me in astonishment. "You found them? When? How?"

I told him about my excursion on my first evening in town, apprising him of all that I had seen and learned—with the exception, of course, of any mention of the man who had accompanied me.

"Well, that does beat all!" Jonathan said with a laugh when I had finished my tale. "What an exceptional and interesting heritage. You always said you were descended from royalty, Mina. It seems you were very close indeed, for you are the daughter of a lord. Do you intend to contact him?"

"No. The simple knowledge of who I am and where I came from has answered so many questions that I am quite content."

"It is a shame that your mother and father could not marry, and very sad that she died. It would have been wonderful to meet her."

"To know her—to have her in my life—that would have been beyond anything."

"A gipsy for a mother! Just think of it! I wonder who her people were."

"I suppose I shall never know."

"No wonder you dream so often, Mina, and seem to sense things before they happen."

"It does seem to explain a lot, doesn't it?"

We both laughed. As I wiped my hands on my serviette, my eyes fell upon my gold wedding band, and my thoughts catapulted in an entirely different direction. "Jonathan: where did you get the money to purchase my wedding ring?"

"Remember the horde of gold coins I found at Dracula's castle? I took some. I decided it was my due, after all he had put me through."

"I assumed as much," I nodded, thinking how ironic it was that Dracula himself had financed the very band which had wed me to the man he despised as his rival.

"Whenever I think about our wedding," Jonathan said, "I am so ashamed. I was such a wreck, barely able to lift a finger. You were so brave, you never complained. I am still determined, you know, when all this is over, when you—when you are not—" His gaze darted to my forehead, and he went on firmly: "When our lives are ours once again, we will have a proper wedding in a proper church, with bridesmaids and flowers and music, everything you could want."

"I have everything I could want right here," I assured him. "A big wedding is really only to please others. We have no family and so few friends. Just being together and moving forward with our lives: that is all I require to make me happy."

Jonathan smiled warmly as he reached across the table and covered his hand with mine. "You are a treasure, Mina. I am so lucky to have you."

"It is I who am lucky."

After luncheon, we strolled down the main street of the village in a light-hearted mood. When Jonathan saw that the baker's shop was selling miniature plum tarts (my life-long favourite), he insisted on purchasing some. We consumed the delicious treats on a bench in a little park overlooking the river, where we tossed morsels of crust to the ducks and geese that gathered at our feet on the grassy bank. When we resumed our walk, Jonathan paused outside the door to the small general shop, where a stand held walking-sticks for sale. He picked one up.

"What do you think, Mina? These are all the rage. Do I need one of these to look proper and important?" He posed with the stick in a ridiculously pompous, comical manner.

A laugh bubbled up from deep within me. "Perhaps you do. You are an important solicitor now."

"But more importantly: you are an important solicitor's wife."

A display of old books in the shop-window caught my eye. "Look." I pointed to a slim, attractive volume, which I instantly coveted. "It is *The Complete Sonnets of William Shakespeare.* I have always wanted my own copy."

"Let us go in and take a look at it." Jonathan put back the walking-stick, pushed open the door to the shop, and held it ajar for me.

"It is probably expensive."

"I don't care." We entered the shop, and Jonathan had the clerk retrieve the book from the window.

"It is quite an old book, and magnificently bound," the clerk said, naming a price which I thought quite excessive; but Jonathan did not even blink, simply indicating with a silent nod of his head that the clerk should give the book to me.

I took the book in my hands, running my fingers over the cover of smooth, bottle-green leather, and the letters of the title embossed in gold. I carefully turned the gilt-edged pages, admiring the fine quality of the paper, the skill of the typesetter, and the familiar and beloved poetry within.

"Do you like it?" Jonathan asked.

"I love it."

"We'll take it," Jonathan said.

As the clerk went to wrap it up, I smiled. "Thank you, dearest. I will cherish this book always."

"I am glad you pointed it out. It is so nice to see you smiling again."

❧

WE CONVENED A GENERAL MEETING IN DR. SEWARD'S STUDY EARLY that evening, where the scouting party revealed all that they had learned that day.

It had been a surprisingly easy task, Dr. Van Helsing explained, to find the ship upon which the Count had sailed. The Lloyd's Register listed only one Black-Sea-bound ship that went out with the tide: the *Czarina Catherine.* Certain enquiries at the wharf, which involved plying rough men with drink and coin, turned up the following facts: that a tall, thin man, dressed all in black except for a conspicuous straw hat, had paid the captain of the *Czarina Catherine* to accept as freight a large, rectangular box, big enough to hold a coffin. The same man had delivered the box himself, lifting it down from the cart entirely unassisted, although it was so heavy that it took several men to load it onto the ship.

The man asked the captain to wait to set sail until he had completed a few other arrangements, a request which caused a loud row between them.

"You'd better be bloody quick," the captain cried, "for my ship leaves this bloody place before the turn of the bloody tide."

A thin mist soon began to creep up from the river, growing into a dense fog, which entirely enveloped the *Czarina Catherine*. It became apparent that the ship would not sail as expected. The water rose and rose; the captain was in a frenzy; then, just at full tide, the man clad in black came up the gang-plank with the necessary papers for his box to be unloaded in Varna, and to be given over to a particular agent there. After standing a while on deck, he disappeared. The fog melted away, and the ship set sail on the ebb tide.

I had to smile at Nicolae's tactics. He had called attention to himself in every possible way: by wearing a hat that was slightly out of season; by causing an argument with the captain in full view of the stevedores; by lifting a box that was far too heavy for one pair of human hands; and by calling in the fog which had so dramatically delayed the ship's departure. In so doing, he had made certain that his "departure" would be noticed and remembered.

"And so, my dear Madam Mina," Dr. Van Helsing concluded, "we may all rest for a time, for our enemy is inside that box of his, far out upon the sea. When we start after him, we will go on land, which is more quick, and meet him when the ship docks at Varna."

"Are you certain that the Count remained on board the ship?" Jonathan enquired.

"He would never leave his only remaining box of earth," the professor replied. "And we have even better proof of that: your wife's own evidence, when in the hypnotic trance this morning."

"In that case," I put in, "since he has been driven from England, will not the Count take his rebuff wisely? Will he not avoid this country for ever, as a tiger does the village from which he has been hunted?"

"Aha!" Dr. Van Helsing replied, "your simile of the tiger is good. I shall adopt him. A tiger who has once tasted blood of the human, he care no more for other prey. He prowl unceasingly till he get more. This beast we now hunt from our village is a tiger, too. Look at his history! In his living life, Dracula was a ruler and a warrior, who go over the Turkey frontier and attack his enemy on his own ground. He be beaten back time and again, but always he return, with persistence and endurance. He work for decades, maybe centuries, to migrate to this city which hold such promise for him. Mark my words: we may have driven him off to-day, but he will be back!"

"I think that highly unlikely," I persisted, "and it seems unnecessary now to pursue him."

"Unnecessary?" Dr. Van Helsing cried. "Unnecessary? But it is of the greatest necessity that we follow him! Think of all the people this monster will kill, even in his own land! And he have so infect you, Madam Mina, that in time, in death, you shall become like him. This must not be!"

"What if you are mistaken? You said, Professor, that even though I drank Count Dracula's blood, I can live out my life in peace. Only when I die will we know if I present a danger to myself and to humanity. Isn't that right?"

"This is correct, yes."

"Then why not simply let my life run its course, and—if indeed I become a vampire as you fear—you can dispatch me as you did Lucy."

The men all regarded me with horror. "You are asking us to wait for your death, and then haunt your tomb?" Dr. Seward cried. "To stab you in the heart and cut off your head?"

"If that is what is required to free my soul, then yes. But it may not happen."

"Never!" Jonathan cried.

"Unthinkable!" cried Dr. Van Helsing. "We cannot know how long the rest of us will live, Madam Mina. We may not even be here to do this horrible deed."

"We must end this *now,* once and for all," Lord Godalming insisted.

"We must utterly stamp him out!" Dr. Van Helsing concurred. "For if we fail, this Dracula may be the father or furtherer of a new order of beings, whose road must lead through Death. We must go out like the old knights of the Cross, to redeem your soul, and to avenge the death of the so sweet woman he murder: Miss Lucy!"

"Dracula did not murder Lucy!" I blurted vehemently, leaping to my feet. "*You* did that! Lucy died because you *transfused* her too many times!"

A hush fell over the room. Five pairs of eyes stared at me in stunned consternation.

"It is true. You gave her the blood of four different men! There are different types of blood, and that is what killed her."

"Do not be absurd," Dr. Van Helsing said impatiently. "Blood is blood with humans: it is all the same."

"That monster turned her into a vampire," Dr. Seward declared fiercely. "We saw the horror of her resurrection with our own eyes."

"I understand," I went on hastily, "but if you continue on this terrible road, I fear that some great harm might befall one or all of you. Please! For my sake, I beg of you: call off your hunt."

The men's glances were all now drawn as one to the mark on my forehead. As they exchanged silent looks across the table, I sensed their doubt and mistrust and realised I had betrayed myself. In speaking thus, I had given them cause to suspect me. Not of being in love with Dracula, perhaps, but of being *in league* with him; that the monster, as they called him, had so poisoned my blood that I could not help but champion his cause despite myself, even if it spelled my doom.

"I think it best that nothing be definitely settled to-night," Dr. Seward said quietly.

"Yes; yes. Let us all sleep on it," Dr. Van Helsing replied in an off-hand manner. "To-morrow we shall meet again, and try to think out the proper conclusions."

THE PLAN WAS NOT WORKING, I THOUGHT, AS I LAY IN BED DIStraught that night.

It succeeded in part, Dracula's voice announced in my mind. *They think I have left the country.*

Yes, but what good is it if they insist on following that ship? When they intercept that box and find it empty, they'll know you tricked them, and they will redouble their efforts to find you.

Undoubtedly.

They no longer trust me.

I know. I am sorry.

What shall we do?

Re-think. Replan.

His thoughts went quiet for a moment. Although the windows were shut, I could hear the sounds of the night without: the faint chirp of crickets. The wind in the trees. The distant baying of a hound. With my eyes closed, I saw Dracula in my mind: his handsome face smiled at me with such intimate affection, I felt as if he could see into my very soul. And yet he was still an enigma to me. There was so much I had yet to understand, so many things I wanted to ask him, I barely knew where to begin.

Begin anywhere.

I smothered a self-conscious laugh, glancing guiltily at Jonathan's sleeping form beside me. Would I ever get used to Nicolae's ability to read my mind so unconditionally, while I had such limited access to his? *All right. When were you born?*

In 1447.

With wonder, I did the mental calculation. *That makes you . . . 443 years old.*

I told you I was an old man.

You also promised to tell me who you were in your human life, and how you became a vampire. Will you tell me now?

I will tell you presently. I will come for you at midnight.

Midnight? But is that safe?

I heard the amusement in his reply: *Fear not, my dearest love. No one sees me unless I wish to be seen.*

Midnight was not far off. I lay in the darkness for a little while, listening to Jonathan's even breathing—torn between my love for him and my love for Nicolae—and the constant, painful feelings of self-reproach engendered by this immoral duality. At length, I rose silently. By the aid of the moonlight filtering through the blinds, I got dressed; then I sat in the armchair in our sitting area and waited.

Suddenly, around the edges of my bedroom door rushed in a trail of dust motes which assembled into Dracula's form. As he waved a hand in Jonathan's direction, I moved into my lover's embrace. He kissed me, then removed his long, black cloak and enveloped me in it.

Where are we going? I asked in thought.

Carfax. It is safe again, since they think I am gone.

Sweeping me up into his arms, he carried me out onto the balcony and shut the casement windows behind us. I felt the now-familiar blast of cold wind, whirr of sound, and flash of images and light, and we were once more ensconced in Dracula's secret parlour.

All was as warm and welcoming as before. Most of his books had been unpacked and stowed on the shelves. The portrait of me still stood prominently on the easel in the corner. Nicolae led me to an open spot before the smokeless fire, where—to my astonishment—I saw a brand-new phonograph sitting upon a low table, with a wax cylinder on the spindle. He had fashioned a cone of tin, much like a megaphone, around the forked listening device.

"You bought a phonograph?" I said in surprise. "What is that cone for?"

"To amplify the sound. It is a fascinating machine, but I devised a better use for it than to simply record the voice. Listen." He put the instrument in play. After a few scratchy moments, the faint sound of a violin began to emanate from the cone, playing a song which held great meaning for me: *Tales from the Vienna Woods.*

I gasped in wonder. "How on earth did you . . ."

He nodded wordlessly towards a violin, which rested in a case near-by.

"I did not know you played the violin."

"There is a great deal about me that you do not know." With a smile, he took me into his arms and assumed the waltz position. We began to dance to the familiar tune.

"What a thrilling concept: recorded music," I enthused. "Think what could be done with it!"

"The quality and volume of the sound—that is a problem which must be perfected. I am certain others are working on it as we speak."

He whirled me about the floor. Although the space was far more confined than the pavilion where we had last waltzed together, it was such a pleasure to dance with him that I found myself laughing with delight. All at once, to my intense amazement, the walls of the room seemed to move outward. The room grew in size until it became a magnificent, brilliantly lit dance hall, in which we were the only dancers. Was I imagining it? Was

I dreaming? No . . . I knew it was Dracula's magic, a trick of the mind . . . and I loved every minute of it. My senses reeled. For a time, I quite forgot where I was. There was nothing but the music and the man and his eyes holding mine, and the sublime sensation of waltzing in his arms.

When the song ended, I caught my breath, smiling up at him. "Thank you for making that recording. It was wonderful. I could dance with you for ever, and be very happy."

He beamed. It was the most brilliant, purely happy smile I had ever seen cross his face. "I will hold you to that," he said, as he kissed me.

LATER, AS WE SAT ON THE SOFA BEFORE THE HEARTH (THE ROOM had returned to its normal size), my thoughts returned to the situation at hand. The festive mood fled, replaced by a wave of despondency. "Nicolae: I did as you requested," I said with a sigh. "I let the professor hypnotise me, and I tried to call the men off. But I am afraid I have failed you."

"You performed brilliantly, my love. It is I who have failed. I underestimated my enemy. My plan was faulty. But it is no matter. This has bought us a little time. The hunting party does not intend to leave the country just yet, am I right?"

The term *hunting party* made me cringe. "Not for a week or two. They said it will take three weeks at least for the *Czarina Catherine* to reach Varna. The four of them mean to take the speedier route overland, which they said should only take five or six days."

"Four of them?"

"The professor insists that Jonathan stay here to watch over me—an idea which seems to torment Jonathan. He wishes to protect me, but he is equally eager to seek his own revenge."

"I do not blame him—given his feelings for you and what he perceives me to be." We sat looking at each other for a long moment in the glow of the fire-light; then he said: "You asked me a question earlier: you wanted to know who I was, and how I became a vampire."

"Yes."

"I said I would answer. It is not a pretty story, I am afraid—and it was so long ago, it seems almost meaningless to me now. Are you certain you wish to hear it?"

"I do. You said you were not Vlad Tepes, or Vlad the Impaler, as many called him."

"That is true." He paused, then looked at me. "Vlad was my brother."

"Your brother?" I said, astonished.

"Other than Vlad, I can look back on my family heritage with pride. I am descended from a long line of kings. Our father was the ruler of Wallachia."

"Then you are a prince?"

"I am—or was. In 1859, Wallachia united with Moldavia to form the state of Romania. In the era when my father was king, our homeland lay directly between the two powerful forces of Hungary and the Ottoman Empire. The rulers of Wallachia were forced to appease both empires to ensure their survival, forging alliances with whichever one served their best interest at the time. I was the youngest of seven children—I had three older brothers and three sisters—and I came late in my mother's life, born just a few months after my father and my oldest brother Mircea were assassinated."

"Oh!"

"So you see, I never knew my father—just as you never knew yours. My brothers and sisters were all so much older than I, it was as if I were an only child. I was sixteen years younger than Vlad, and when I was born, he and my brother Radu were both still being held hostage in Adrianople, where my father had sent them to appease the Turkish sultan."

"Your father sent your brothers away as hostages?" I was appalled.

"He did. Radu remained there for years. Vlad was released, but I rarely saw him. I spent the better part of my childhood alone, educated by my mother, an intelligent and good-hearted Transylvanian noblewoman. In 1453, when I was six years old, the Christian world was shocked by the fall of Constantinople to the Ottomans. The entire region was at war. In the midst of this chaos, Vlad seized the Wallachian throne and began his reign of terror."

"Is it true that he murdered tens of thousands of people?"

"Perhaps more than a hundred thousand before he was through," Nicolae said bitterly. "Vlad enjoyed recounting the stories of his inhuman cruelty in every gory detail. One morning, when I was still a boy, he awakened me early and made me ride with him for hours, so that I might witness his latest victory. I fell asleep during the ride; and when I awoke, to my horrified eyes, I saw before me an entire city of residents impaled on stakes on the outskirts of a town—thousands and thousands of them."

"Dear God," I cried, horrified.

"Impalement was not my brother's only method of torture, although it was his favourite. From burning and burying alive to strangulation and every kind of mutilation—suffice it to say that the list of tortures he employed was like an inventory of the tools of Hell. He claimed to be wreaking vengeance for the deaths of my father and brother, but the majority of his victims included our own people—women, children, peasants, and great lords alike—any one whose behaviour did not fit within his own rigid moral code, or whom he saw as a threat to the throne."

I felt sickened. Nicolae glanced at me in hesitation. "I warned you that it was not a pretty story. Do you wish me to go on?"

"Yes."

He stood and paced as he resumed: "I hated my brother more and more with each passing day; but I was young, and my mother and sisters and I were all under his protection and his power. In time, he insisted that I be trained in the manner of a son of European nobility—which meant working with a tutor to learn all the skills of war that were deemed necessary for a Christian knight. It was against my nature to kill. Whenever Vlad stopped by to watch, he made fun of me, taunting me to strike back with the sword, calling me weak: the useless Dracula who would never amount to anything. I applied myself to my training with one aim in mind: that one day, I would be able to fight my brother and kill him.

"Then chance intervened. The Turks invaded Wallachia. I was fifteen years old at the time. Vlad abandoned us and fled to Transylvania, where he was arrested and imprisoned. Rather than surrender to the Turks, I helped my mother and sisters to escape. I got them safely across the mountains into Transylvania, to the duchies formerly governed by our father, and appealed to the king for aid. My mother and sisters found a haven there, and I went off to war. For fourteen years I struggled against the Turks on one bloody battle-field after another, fighting for the freedom of our homeland.

"One day I heard that my brother had been released from prison and had regained his throne. His reign of terror began all over again. When I was twenty-nine, Vlad led an army against the Turks near Bucharest, and called for me to join him. I went with murder in my heart; but it seemed that someone else had killed him before I got there. Some reports claimed he was assassinated by disloyal Wallachians just as he was about to sweep the Turks from the field. Other accounts have him falling in defeat, surrounded by the ranks of his loyal Moldavian body-guard. I even heard that the Turks sent his head to Constantinople, where the sultan had it displayed on a stake to prove that the evil Impaler at last was dead. But my brother did not die on that battlefield at all—although it was several years before I discovered the truth."

"What truth?"

"He faked his death, to escape the many assassins intent on killing him after he regained his throne."

"Where did he go?"

"I am getting to that." There was a fevered look on Nicolae's face. Red flames smoldered behind the blue of his eyes, and his voice was so filled with bitterness that it made me cringe. "We lost that battle and retreated. I had had enough of war. Believing my brother to be dead, I hung up my sword and returned to Transylvania, determined never to fight again. My mother had died, but my sisters were now living in the castle of a Transylvanian *boyar*—a member of the privileged class—two of them married to the boyar's sons. The nobleman—a count—had two lovely daughters, identical twins named Celestina and Sabina. I fell in love with Sabina, and we were married."

"Married?"

He nodded, and went on in a wistful tone: "We soon welcomed our first child: a boy we called Matthias, after her father. Sabina's sister also married and had a child. The two women were radiant in motherhood. We were all very close, and for five years we were very happy. But then our fortunes turned. One day, Celestina's daughter disappeared from the yard where she was playing—stolen, we thought, by gipsies. Shortly thereafter, a strange man appeared in the village."

"A strange man?" A sense of dark foreboding overcame me.

"I never saw him, but heard reports of him. Suddenly, people in the village and outlying farms were dying. They were always found pale and lifeless, as if all the blood had been drained from their bodies, and there were angry red marks on their necks where they had been bitten."

"Oh!" I cried, understanding precisely where he was heading.

"One night, my brother Vlad appeared to me. I was in shock. I had long thought him dead and buried. When I recovered my wits, I asked him where he had been for the past five years. With a chilling laugh, he said that he had been travelling. When he was in prison years earlier, he had learned from an old monk that there existed a secret school called the Scholomance, high in the mountains of Transylvania, where the Devil taught his evil arts in person to a select few. After Vlad feigned his death, he followed the old monk's clues and searched for the Scholomance. At last he found it. However, it was not run by the Devil at all, but by a very old, wise, and skilled vampire—whose name was Solomon."

"Solomon? Like in the Bible?"

"I believe he was the very same man."

I stared at him. "You are saying that King Solomon was a vampire?"

"He became one."

I knew the story of Solomon. He was the wisest king of his time—but he had dark, perverse, insatiable appetites. Against God's orders, he collected enormous amounts of gold from his people, built up his army of horses and chariots, practiced idolatry, married foreign women, and kept a thousand wives and concubines. "God turned his back on Solomon for his sins and tore his kingdom in two."

"Yes. So Solomon looked to other means for his eternal salvation. He had been given a magic ring from heaven, which gave him power over the good genii as well as demons. He now used that ring to help him practice the art of sorcery, determined to find a way to make himself immortal. And he succeeded—but his experiment went wrong. He gave himself eternal life, but at a very high price."

"Was he the first vampire, then?"

"Perhaps; it is hard to say. All I know is, he adapted to his new form and travelled the globe for more than a thousand years, giving rise to legends everywhere of a strange creature who slept in the cold loam of the earth and fed off the blood of the living. He learned all the secrets of nature and the weather, the language of animals, and every imaginable magic spell, finally settling on a mountain-top in Transylvania, where he has been teaching his secrets ever since to a few scholars at a time—men who become wandering vampire wizards called Solomonarii, or sons of Solomon."

"I have read about the Solomonarii! I thought they were a myth, a product of Romanian folklore."

"They are very real."

"Did Solomon take your brother as a student?"

"No. He saw that Vlad was truly evil, and would only use any skills he learned for wickedness. But Vlad was determined to become immortal. Vlad killed one of the young Solomonarii, drank all of his blood, and became a vampire himself. As a vampire, his innate blood-lust only continued. In time, he decided to come home."

"So it was your own brother who changed you and your sisters?" I said, horrified.

"Yes. They were lovely young women before Vlad got his hands on them—two were mothers with young children. One night I walked into a room to find my brother's teeth clamped upon my sister Luiza's throat. She was pale and lifeless, his eyes were blazing red, and both of their mouths dripped with blood. I sprang at Vlad, trying to save her, but it was too late. He dropped her, and with a roar, he sank his teeth into my own throat. He was as strong as twenty men; I never had a chance. I felt the life being drained from me. When I was on the brink of death, Vlad toyed with me. He asked me if I wished to join him in Un-Death. I could become immortal, he said. It was that, or die. I had no idea what kind of choice I was making. I only knew that I did not want to leave this earth, or leave my wife and child.

With the last breath in my body, I said: Yes. Please. Save me. Do not let me die."

"Oh!" I cried in anguish.

Nicolae's eyes flashed, alternating between blue and red, and his entire posture seemed to vibrate with barely contained hatred as he continued: "My brother slashed his own wrist and made me drink his blood. Then he finished the job he had started: he drained me until I could breathe no longer. Two days later, I awoke to find myself in the family tomb . . . with the bodies of my sisters beside me. I rose, confused. What had I become? I felt different: a strange anger welled within me.

"I left the tomb and returned to the castle to find my wife. I passed a servant who recoiled with dread. I could smell his blood. I craved it. I looked in a mirror and saw that I had no reflection! I went mad with fear and horror. I was transforming into something hideous and evil, but it was a self I could not see. I found Sabina. She screamed in terror at the sight of me, cradling our shrieking son to her breast."

Suddenly, to my horror, Nicolae transformed before me into the pale, monstrous, red-eyed creature I had seen a few nights before in my chamber, as he said in a ghastly tone: "She called me a ghost, a demon, a monster!"

I screamed, leapt to my feet, and recoiled. Nicolae glanced at me, as if surprised to find me there. There was a dreadful pause. I remembered what he had said: that in times of great anger, an evil side of him emerged. With what looked to be a Herculean effort, he mastered that anger and reverted to himself, to the form that I knew and loved, except that his blue eyes were still cold and hard. He made no comment about this extraordinary transformation, only went on, in a voice that was deadly calm:

"And so I killed them."

I stared at him in disbelief. "You . . . killed your wife and child?"

He nodded. "I went mad. I not only killed them, but I slaughtered every other living thing in the castle, from the children and the servants to the elders and the live-stock, until there was nothing left but a river of blood in every passage and stairwell—and myself and my sisters—who I soon discovered had been changed, exactly as I was."

I was speechless. Dracula paced before me, scowling.

"When I came back to myself, when I saw what I had done, I was overcome with revulsion, regret, and horror. Vlad found me and laughed. Laughed! Then he welcomed me to the fold, and said: 'You have outdone yourself, brother. At last, you understand the thrill of taking life, the passion that has driven me for so long.' I looked at him. My sword was still in my hand. I believe it was not until that moment that Vlad realised what a terrible blunder he had made: for I had become just as powerful as he. Vlad was a superlative swordsman, but I was a newly made vampire filled with hate and rage. And so . . . I went at him, and sent him to Hell where he belonged. I later discovered that the streets of the village were littered with the dead—my brother's final murdering spree. All the deaths there and at the castle were attributed to a plague."

A shudder ran through me, and I swallowed hard. I was so shocked and repelled, I could think of no words to say. At length, I murmured quietly: "I am so very, very sorry."

"So am I." Nicolae looked at me now, his eyes and face haunted by deep, piercing remorse. "I have spent four centuries attempting to atone for my crimes that night. But I can never forgive myself. The pain, the guilt . . . it never goes away."

"Oh, Nicolae."

He met my gaze, open, wounded, vulnerable. "Do you hate me now?"

The look on his countenance wrenched my soul. I fought back my fear and horror, telling myself that the evil being he had been that night was gone forevermore. It was an aberration, the product of his brother's blood, four hundred years past. Trembling, I went to where he stood by the hearth and took him in my arms. "I could never hate you."

He sighed with intense relief and held me tightly, as if drawing comfort from our embrace. We stood thus in silence for some moments. Then he murmured against my hair:

"I fell into a state of great self-pity and despair after that. I missed my wife and son with an ache that would not mend. I despised myself for what I had done. I was horrified by my insatiable appetite for blood. My sisters were carrying on in the most wanton manner—but I vowed that I would never kill again. I wanted to end my life, but I did not know how. I finally realised that there was only one place in the world where I could find out what had really happened to me, and learn how to live with it. I went in search of the Scholomance myself."

"Did you find it?" I asked, breathless.

He took a few steps away and said: "I did. It was a magical, healing place. I remained there for fifty years."

"Fifty years!"

"Solomon could not make me mortal again, but he was—and still is, I can only assume—a great teacher. It was an education I needed if I was to live for ever."

"So it is true, then . . . not all vampires have the same powers as you?"

"No. Although I have not met many others; just a handful of Solomonarii, and—during my travels—a few dozen or so of the vampires they had apparently made."

"What was Solomon like?"

"He was a fascinating, wise, complicated old man—a wizard with uncanny abilities and a good heart. I mended under his tutelage and followed his advice, determined to use the eternity before me to better myself."

"What happened after you left the Scholomance?"

"I went home and lived—or should I say existed—in that damned castle with my accursed sisters and watched the centuries fall away. Feudalism died out with the plague, but Castle Dracula and all its holdings belonged to me. I earned my income from the peasants who worked my land. My sisters and I aged very slowly. We took on new identities for each succeeding generation. I travelled whenever I could. But I was gone for too many years. My sisters grew strong in their own right and became more intolerable every day. They were not discreet in their activities. The locals soon feared and shunned us."

"My God. It is all so incredible. Is there nothing in the history books about what happened to you? Anything I could cite, to clear your name?"

"Not even a footnote. I am the forgotten son. The atrocities that Vlad Tepes committed are well-documented, however. He is the Dracula that history remembers."

NINETEEN

THAT NIGHT, AFTER DRACULA TOOK ME BACK TO THE asylum, my mind was so full of all that I had learned, I could barely close my eyes. I believe I had just started to drift off when I was awakened by Jonathan, who was eager to get on with the day's proceedings.

Despite my attempts to engage in the early-morning banter at the breakfast table, I was obliged to stifle several yawns, and I nearly nodded off a few times. More than once, I saw the men's gazes fix upon the scar on my forehead with troubled frowns. Dr. Van Helsing insisted that I return to bed, promising that my health was more important than anything they might discuss that day. I did so, although I slept fitfully, beset by frightening dreams of war, vampires, murder, blood, and demons.

When I awoke, it was nearly four o'clock in the afternoon. I went down-stairs, and heard voices from within the study. Dr. Van Helsing was saying: "Jack: there is something that you and I must talk of alone, just at the first at any rate. Madam Mina, our poor dear Madam Mina is changing."

I paused outside the door, listening.

"I have noticed that myself," came Dr. Seward's voice.

"You heard how Madam Mina defended the Count with such passion yesterday?"

"I suppose it is some of that horrid poison which has got into her veins, beginning to work?" Dr. Seward answered.

"Yes," was Dr. Van Helsing's reply. "With the sad experience of Miss Lucy, we must this time be warned before things go too far. I can see the characteristics of the vampire coming into Madam Mina's face. It is now but very, very slight; but it is to be seen if we have eyes to notice. Her teeth are some sharper, and at times her eyes are more hard."

Oh! I thought indignantly. What rubbish! I had tried to dissuade them from pursuing Dracula, yes—but my teeth were quite as usual! I had not changed physically at all—there was no reason why I should have!—but of course they did not know that.

"There is more," the professor was saying. "There is to her the silence now, as it was with Miss Lucy."

"I saw that too, at breakfast," Dr. Seward replied. "Mrs. Harker barely said a word. It is as if her tongue is tied in some mysterious way. I hate to think of dishonouring such a noble woman; but I *know* that she forms conclusions of her own about all that is going on. From our past experience, I can only guess how brilliant and true her thoughts must be. Yet for some reason, she now will not, or cannot, give them utterance."

Idiots, I thought. I did not speak at breakfast because I was exhausted!

"My fear is this," Dr. Van Helsing replied in an anguished voice. "That if she can, by our hypnotic trance, tell us what the Count see and hear—is it not true that he, so powerful a being, can compel her mind to disclose to him what she know?"

"You mean he might be able to read her mind?"

"Precisely."

"If that is true, he would be privy to everything we are thinking and planning."

"We must prevent this. We must keep her ignorant of our intent. This is a painful task. Oh! So painful that it heart-break me to think of it; but it must be. When to-day we meet, I must tell her that for reason of which we will not speak, she must be no more of our council, but be simply guarded by us."

"We will have to tell Harker. He will not be happy about it."

I did not stay to hear more. The whole thing was too absurd. I might as well beat them to the punch, I decided.

After dinner, as Jonathan and I freshened up in our chamber, I told him that I would not be joining him at the meeting that evening.

"But why?" he said, with surprise and concern. "Are you not feeling well?"

"I am fine, I assure you," I replied as I straightened his tie and collar. "But I see the way everyone looks at me now. I think it better that you should all be free to discuss your movements without my presence to embarrass you."

Jonathan nodded silently and went off. When he returned some hours later, to my dismay, his manner was very different. He was silent and removed, and he could not meet my eyes. Obviously, he had been indoctrinated by the others.

He stayed up past midnight, writing in his journal. When I bent to kiss his dark head before going to bed, I felt him flinch at my touch. He did not even bid me good-night.

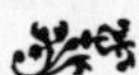

"It is ridiculous," I told Dracula later, as we strolled through the trees in his moonlit garden, hidden behind his great wall. "My husband treats me like a leper. They all think I have changed—but it is my scar that has prejudiced their minds and allowed their fears to infect their imagination."

"They see what they want to see," Dracula agreed with a frown. He took my hand, adding, "I heard your dreams last night. I was afraid my story would frighten you. I am sorry that it did."

"I am glad you told me."

He glanced at me in the white light of the moon as we walked along. "I have been listening to your thoughts all afternoon. I see that there is still a great deal more about me that you wish to know."

"I admit, Nicolae: I am curious about many things."

"Shall I tell you now?"

"Please do."

"All right, then. First: you wonder how I transform myself into mist or dust."

"Yes!" I cried, fascinated. "How is that possible?"

"It is corporeal displacement, a matter of controlling the mind and certain forces of nature—not easy to explain."

"Physics again."

"Yes. Even the new vampire can vanish through cracks no wider than a knife-blade. The mist and dust is something I learned much later."

"What does it feel like to move as a mist?"

"It is a bit like being a ghost. I can see and hear, but I cannot touch or feel."

"What about animal forms? Can all vampires do them?"

"No. It took me 130 years to master the wolf. Another eighty to perfect the bat."

For some reason, that made me laugh. "Show me one. Become a bat!"

"No."

"Why not? I have already seen you as a bat before, several times in fact—although I did not know it was you."

"Then that will have to suffice."

"Why?"

"Bats have their uses, but they are ugly little creatures. Seeing such a transformation—it would only repulse you. I do not wish to leave that image in your mind."

"All right then. Become a wolf."

He shook his head, amused. "I will not."

"You cannot do it, can you?" I teased. "That is why you refuse. You can only become the lowly bat."

"I can become a wolf, I assure you," he bristled. "It is the primary form I take when I wish to feed undisturbed on animal life."

"Oh. I see. Can you become any other animals?"

"Yes."

"Which ones?"

He hesitated, then pulled me to him. "I think we should leave this subject at present."

"Why?"

"Because," he said softly, "I prefer that you think of me as a man." He kissed me. My arms wound around him. Desire rose within me; my heart began to race; but suddenly he was pushing me away. His eyes grew hard and his entire body shook, as if he was struggling with every ounce of will-power against some powerful inner force that threatened to overcome him.

"You wanted to see a wolf," he said, when at last he regained control of himself. "If we are not careful, you will."

We stood in silence for a minute, as I willed my heart to return to its normal pace. I noticed that we had wandered to a side of his great house that I had not seen before. In the moonlit darkness, I perceived an adjacent building of ancient grey stone that looked like a small church. It had a row of tall, arched windows that were inset with stained glass, and a great, iron-bound, oaken door.

"Is that your chapel?" I asked.

"It is."

"Will you permit me to go within? I have heard so much about these earth-boxes of yours. I would very much like to see one."

Nicolae frowned. He seemed unhappy about taking me there, but at my insistence, he pulled a ring of keys from his pocket and unlocked the chapel door. We entered. A musty, earthy smell pervaded the place, and it was very cold inside. He quickly found and lit several candles. In the flickering darkness, I could see that it was a good-sized chapel, perhaps as large as some old country churches. The high stone walls and beamed ceiling were thick with dust and cobwebs which hung down like tattered, fluffy rags, as was the altar and the carved stone figurines which adorned it.

As Nicolae raised a candle, I could see that the room was filled with great rectangular chests, more than two dozen of them. The boxes looked to be sturdily made of some unfinished hardwood—the type of crate that might be used to deliver large goods or furniture, or a coffin—but they were plain and rather ugly. The lids of all the boxes had been pried off and were scattered haphazardly across the floor. Nicolae took my hand, and we moved together towards one of the wooden boxes. I gazed down at it, taking in the layer of earth which lined the bottom with a sense of repugnance.

"Do you really *sleep* in a box like this?"

I felt him flinch and sensed his discomfiture at my reaction. "I do not actually sleep. It is more of a trance. And I only resort to a bed of this kind when I must: when I am away from home."

Now I noticed the pieces of crumbled wafer—the Holy Host—which were sprinkled about inside the box. I recoiled, remembering the excruciating pain when a similar wafer had touched my forehead. Nicolae glanced at me in sympathy and silently squeezed my hand.

"Does the Host affect you the same way?" I asked.

"Yes."

"What about the crucifix?"

"I avoid them, the way I avoid the direct rays of the sun. They both make me feel nauseous, sap my strength, and have the power to burn my skin."

"And garlic?"

"I was averse to garlic in the early days, when I was first changed; but I think it had more to do with the smell than to any uncanny powers the plant possessed. It seems to be an enduring superstition, however." Abruptly, he added: "Have you seen enough?"

I nodded. We left the way we had entered and strolled out onto his grounds. He led me to a path of sorts that meandered through the high grass and weeds among the trees. We walked in silence for a while, as I tried to envision a distant future in which I might be required to sleep in one of those boxes of earth—an idea which filled me with mild disgust. A sudden thought occurred to me, and I said:

"If I was Un-Dead, would I need to rest by day on English soil?"

"It depends on where you die. A vampire needs to rest on the soil native to the region where he was made."

"Doesn't that present a problem?"

"How so?"

"You said we would be together for ever. If you must rest on Transylvanian soil, and I die here—"

"A mere technicality, my love, and one which is easily resolved—as long as no one is hunting us. I still have enough soil of my own here, safely hidden. Or we could take a shipload of English dirt to Transylvania."

"I see you have it all planned out."

"I do."

The wind rushed by in a sudden gust, and I began to shiver. Nicolae removed his cloak and wrapped it around my shoulders. "Thank you." As I drew comfort from the cloak's warmth, I glanced at him and noticed something small and white, like a scroll of paper, peeking out from his shirt pocket. "What is that?"

He touched the scroll self-consciously. "This? It is nothing. Just—a sketch I have been working on."

"May I see it? Please?"

Reluctantly, he withdrew the scroll from his pocket and gave it to me. I stopped and opened it, studying it in the moonlight. It was a pencil sketch of me, which had clearly been done from memory. It portrayed me in a romantic posture, standing on a high bluff overlooking a dramatic coast line and the sea.

"It is the cliffs at Whitby," I said, with a little smile.

"It is not finished. It is imperfect."

"It is beautiful." I carefully rolled up the paper and returned it to him. "Has any one but me ever seen your art?"

"A few people, over the years. I once gave a painting to Haydn."

"Joseph Haydn?" I laughed. "You mean you really did know him?"

"I travelled a bit on the Continent in the previous century. It was an entrancing chapter of history. The music and dancing were dazzling. The fashions were magnificent, with the exception of the wigs and that detestable hair powder. Men and women alike wore brightly coloured silks and satins, and were bedecked in jewels. People attended lively parties all night long and slept by day, a schedule which, as you can imagine, fit in very well with my own habits."

"How did you travel if you were obliged to sleep on Transylvanian soil?"

"A man can carry most anything with him, when he owns a carriage and cart." Nicolae shared a story about Mozart which had me laughing into stitches. We talked on for a long while as we strolled his grounds, sharing anecdotes and past experiences, a subject which seemed inexhaustible, particularly in his case. I could have talked on in this way for hours; everything about him fascinated me. But there was a topic which had been worrying me for many days now, and at length I brought it up.

"Nicolae: there is something we must discuss. This double existence I am leading—it weighs heavily on my conscience."

"I know."

"I love you. Yet I also love my husband. I feel sick with guilt and shame about the way I have been deceiving him. You said I have a lifetime to decide whether or not to join you in Un-Death; but the truth is, there is a choice I must make now; and that choice fills me with such pain—"

"You do not have to make that choice yet, my darling."

I sighed and shook my head. "But I do. I cannot go on meeting you behind his back like this any longer."

"You will not have to."

"What do you mean?"

"I have been waiting to tell you, fearing it might cause you grief or worry; but I have formed a new plan."

"What plan?"

"We both know how much your husband hates me; and the professor's thirst for my blood is as deep and unrelenting as my brother's demonic need. I see now that the only way I will ever be able to survive in peace is if those madmen think that I am truly dead."

I took that in. "What do you intend to do? Fake your own death, as your brother did on the battlefield?"

"Yes. Nothing else will satisfy them. I must give them the opportunity to kill me, and they must see me die—or think they have slain me—with their own eyes."

"How will you accomplish that? Do you mean to stage some kind of battle here?"

"No. They think I have fled the country on a ship, and this suits me very well. I will let them follow that box of mine to Varna—and beyond."

"Beyond?"

"I will have the greater advantage close to my home ground, where I know the geography intimately and can enlist the assistance that I require. I will leave ahead of you and the others. I have booked passage on a ship to Paris for myself and one large crate of earth. From there, I will travel by the Orient Express. There is much that I must arrange before your hunting party arrives. And there is something I must ask you to do, Mina, in the meantime."

"What is that?"

"Continue to let Dr. Van Helsing 'hypnotise' you. Convince him that I am aboard the *Czarina Catherine.* Tell him the same thing every day: that you see lapping water, that I am in the dark hold of a ship. Can you do that?"

"Yes."

He stopped in an open patch of wild grass between two large elms and turned to me, the moonlight caressing his face as he touched my cheek with his cool fingers. "One more thing: you must insist that they take you with them."

"Take me with them?"

"If you are in their company, I can use your mind to track your progress and your whereabouts. And I want you to be there with me, at the end."

"The end!" I cried. "I do not wish to see them kill you!"

"They will not kill me, my love, I promise you." He placed an affectionate kiss upon my lips. "Trust me. Just do as I have said, and all will be well. They will think they have dispatched me for good. After that, you can return to Exeter with your husband. We can see each other every now and then; and one day, if you wish it . . . we can be reunited."

The cold wind rustled through the leafy branches of the trees surrounding us, and I glanced away, drawing Nicolae's cloak more tightly about me. I tried to imagine the days and weeks ahead of me, and the role that he wanted me to play. How right Scott was when he wrote: *Oh, what a tangled web we weave, when first we practice to deceive!* It seemed that this charade I was involved in would never end. If only I could tell Jonathan and the others everything that I knew! But they would never believe it. I had already tried to convince them to call off the hunt, and that had proven hopeless. Perhaps Nicolae was right: only by creating the false impression of his death would he ever be safe. And he must be safe.

I shoved away all thoughts of guilt. I was doing the right thing, I told myself. I would do what I had to do, to help Nicolae implement his plan. When the hunt was over—when the day came that Nicolae was free—*then,* I decided, I would (somehow) summon the strength to say good-bye to him for the rest of my mortal life. I would be Jonathan's loyal wife, the wife he deserved, and I would remain faithful to him until the day I died. And then . . . And then . . .

Nicolae was looking down at me, a beam from the moon illuminating his handsome face and compelling eyes. *And then,* I thought, *I will be his for ever!*

He bent his head and kissed me: a deep and passionate kiss. As I returned his embrace, I sensed from him that the moment of our parting was near at hand. A sudden sadness welled up inside me. "When will you leave?" I whispered against his lips.

"To-day."

"To-day!" Tears sprang into my eyes; I was suddenly too choked up to speak.

"Do not be sad, my love." He tenderly brushed a tear from my cheek. "We will not be apart for long."

"But we will. Anything could go wrong. Even if your plan succeeds, it will be decades before we can be together again."

"But we *will* be together, Mina. It is our fate, as inevitable as the sunset that follows the dawn. You are the blood of my blood; and even if we were not bound by blood, we are bound by mind and thought, and by the love that we share."

Urgently, he brought his mouth back to mine. As his kiss deepened, and his body pressed closely against mine, it seemed to me as if we were two halves making up a perfect whole. We caressed each other with our hands. All at once, I felt frustrated by the clothing which separated us, overwhelmed with a yearning to touch his bare flesh and feel his flesh against mine. I heard his thoughts; they mirrored my own. With his lips on mine, he swept the cloak I was wearing from my shoulders. His hand caressed my waist, my back, my arms, and then swept up to settle on my breast. My eyes closed, and I gave a little gasp. I heard his heavy breath in my ear and felt him pressed hard against me.

"Ah, my love," he murmured against my lips. "I ache for you."

I knew that he wanted me—and not just my blood. He wanted to make love to me. I could not deny that I wanted him that way as well. The very thought assaulted me with guilt. It could not be! It could not be! Not until—*until I was Un-Dead.* Just kissing and touching him this way was a deep enough sin, for I knew I was committing adultery in my heart.

From behind my closed eyelids, I felt an intense, penetrating heat. Now his warm, insistent mouth was moving down to passionately kiss my throat. I gasped again, and my body tingled in anticipation. I knew that Dracula must not take any more of my blood; he had said it could prove dangerous—even deadly—for me. This was my last chance to stop him. My last chance . . .

But I did not want to stop him. It was the last time in this mortal life that we would be together. The last time, for so many long years! *Let me have this to remember him by,* I thought, as I insistently pulled him closer. I heard an animal-like roar; then Dracula sank his teeth into my throat, and all rational thinking ceased.

At first, as I felt my blood flowing outward from my body into his, I experienced the same delirious, languid ecstasy that I had come to take such pleasure in. There was another sensation too, a kind of dark, blissful tingling that seemed to pervade my every pore. But after a few moments, the feeling changed. His hands, which had been holding me to him with urgent gentleness, now gripped me with such fierce possessiveness that they hurt me; and his teeth clamped down with a renewed ferocity that caused me to cry out in pain.

If he heard my cry, he paid no heed. Panic rose within me. I struggled in vain to push him away. What had always felt like an act of love now became akin to a violent attack. I felt myself growing weaker as Dracula continued to feed with a savage intensity that I had never experienced before.

"Nicolae," I whispered. "Please—stop—"

My mind began to swim. Terrified, I thought: *this is the end. I am going to die.*

And then I knew no more.

❧

When I came to, I was back on the balcony outside my bedroom window, in Dracula's arms. The sky was still pitch-black. I could discern anguish, self-loathing, and regret in his voice as he whispered, "My love, I am so sorry. I did not mean to hurt you."

He set me on my feet and gazed down at me. "My God. You're still bleeding." Before I could blink, he was pressing a handkerchief firmly against the wounds on my throat. "I am so sorry," he said again. "If I harmed you to-night, Mina, I will never forgive myself."

We moved into each other's arms and clung there. I shivered, unable to forget the pure terror I had felt when the animal in him had attacked me so brutally. "I should have tried to stop you before you began. But I did not wish to."

"I fear there may be consequences."

I looked at him, my heart pounding with trepidation. He had insisted that I would only become a vampire after I was old and grey, *if* I chose to become immortal. Did I still have that choice? "How will I know if I—"

"When it happened to me, it was an immediate change. I died and was reborn. If it happens to you, this way, it will be different. It may take a while. From what others tell me, you will feel yourself slowly changing. You may become very tired. You will find it more natural to sleep during the day. You might feel chilled or light-headed. It might seem as if your senses are growing sharper. You will find food distasteful, and it will become increasingly difficult to eat or drink."

"If I feel those changes," I asked, fear spiralling through me, "will it mean that I am going to die?"

"Let us not conjecture. Let us hope you will be all right."

I nodded. The notion was too terrifying to contemplate. *I will be fine,* I told myself. *I will be fine.*

He cradled my face with his hand. His fingers, I noticed, were warm. "I must go. The sun will be up soon."

"I shall miss you," I replied, my voice breaking.

"And I you. But we will be in each other's arms again, I promise. And during this time apart, we will be together every day in thought." He kissed me once more, and I closed my eyes, savouring it. "I love you, Mina."

I opened my eyes to return the sentiment, but he was already gone.

I CREPT INTO BED IN THE DARKNESS, STEEPED IN SADNESS. I WILLED myself to think of something else, to relax and fall asleep.

No sooner had I closed my eyes, than I began to dream.

I dreamt that Dracula made love to me.

IN MY DREAM, I FELT THE PRESSURE OF WARM HANDS AGAINST MY body, caressing my breasts through the thin fabric of my nightdress. The touch set my very flesh afire. Now lips were on my lips, hot and hungry, tasting and kissing me with fevered need. I did not need to open my eyes to know who my dream lover was: I was in Dracula's arms again.

Suddenly, there was no barrier of clothing between us. My nightdress had magically disappeared. I felt the weight of his long, hard, naked body pressed against mine. My skin felt searing hot against the warmth of his flesh. As his hands roved tenderly across my body, every nerve ending seemed to tingle at his touch. I recognised the guilt of my passion but I surrendered to it, straining to hold him closer to me.

His warm, insistent mouth now travelled down to caress my naked breasts. I gasped with pleasure at his kiss and touch. Slowly, expertly, he moved lower, paying tribute with his lips, tongue, and fingers to every part of my body, parts which had never before been touched in such a manner, and seemed to come alive as if for the very first time. My senses began to reel, and then to mingle one with the other, so that it seemed as if I could *hear* the passion of his touch and *feel* the deep blue of his eyes. With every sharp gasp of ecstasy, I felt as if I were tasting air instead of breathing it.

He never spoke a word; yet my entire body was aflame. With shameful joy in my heart, I trembled as I moved against his hands, seeking more of the delicious rapture he was giving me.

He played me like a stringed instrument, awakening within me a harmony that I had never known existed, producing profound and unimagined tunes.

When I felt him enter me I clung to him, pressing him ever closer, our two bodies fused as one. As he moved with me towards the brink of ecstasy, I was overwhelmed by an intense need that until that moment had never been recognised. All at once, just as I heard his own fevered exclamation, I felt the core of my womanhood explode with pleasure, as if my body had splintered into a thousand brilliant fragments of sensation and light.

I awoke with a great gasp to find myself lying in a tangle of bed-clothes, my heart racing, my body still tingling with intense and wondrous sensation. I saw my husband's sleeping form across the bed from me, and my cheeks burned with shame. I was naked! My nightdress lay on the floor beside me! I quickly sat up; and after I put the garment back on, my eyes were drawn to the window, where, in a shaft of light from the waning moon, I thought I detected the flickering remnants of a trail of dust seep out through the joinings; but no. It was just specks of dust; or perhaps I imagined it.

My God, I thought, as a flush suffused my body, what manner of woman was I, that I had allowed my mind and body to betray me so? At the same time, I wondered: is *that* what love-making was *supposed* to feel like?

Even though it had all been a dream—a shameful, magnificent dream—I could not prevent the secret smile which curved my lips. I felt reborn. Renewed. Alive. For the very first time, I felt as if I understood what it meant to be a woman.

TWENTY

As the first rays of dawn crept over the horizon, I called for Dr. Van Helsing. He had evidently expected such a call, for he arrived moments later, fully dressed.

"Do you wish me to hypnotise you again, Madam Mina?"

"If you wish; but I have called you for another reason." I launched into the dialogue that I had carefully prepared. "I know that you will leave soon for the Continent, and that you intend for me to remain here with Jonathan. But I must go with you on your journey."

The professor and Jonathan both looked startled. Dr. Van Helsing said: "But why?"

"I will be safer with you, and you shall all be safer, too."

"How can that be, Madam Mina? We go into great danger, and great unknowns."

"That is why I must go. The Count has control of my mind. If he wills me, I must try to go to him—by any means, and by any device, even if it puts me or those I love in mortal danger—even you, Jonathan." The guilt which rose to my face as I spoke was not the product of any play-acting. "You men are brave, and strong in your numbers. Together you can defy me, but should

Jonathan be obliged to guard me alone, I fear I would break down his endurance. Besides, I may be of valued service in tracking the Count. You can hypnotise me while we are en route, and learn that which even I myself do not know."

"I have been saying the same thing for days!" Jonathan cried eagerly. "Professor, I hate the thought of sticking it out here while you four share all the danger—and Mina will be better off with us."

"Madam Mina, you are as always most wise. You have convinced me. You shall come with us."

THE WEEK PASSED IN A KIND OF BLUR. THE MEN MET SECRETLY ALL day long, making their arrangements for our trip overseas. Although I was now to come with them, they shared almost nothing of their plans, treating me with cordiality but a decided wariness. Dr. Seward arranged for his friend Dr. Hennessey (who had watched over his patients earlier, while Dr. Seward tended Lucy in London) to take charge of the asylum while he was gone. Jonathan's work schedule had been very slight when we left Exeter; still, he wrote to his assistant at the law firm, spelling out all the necessary arrangements that must be undertaken in light of his delayed return.

Every day, Nicolae came to me in my mind, informing me of his progress as he journeyed back to his homeland. Every night as I lay in bed, I relived in my mind the magical dream of love that I had shared with him. Oh! I thought. If only Jonathan would touch me in that way! But Jonathan kept his distance.

The evening before we were scheduled to leave England, as I was preparing to go down to dinner, Jonathan burst into our room, smiling and carrying a large box which looked like it had come from an exclusive London shop.

"Mina, I have something for you."

It had been a long time since I had seen such an expression of exhilaration and eager anticipation on Jonathan's face. I crossed to him. "Have you been to town?"

"Yes. I saw this in a shop window, and I thought of you." He laid the box on the bed. "Go ahead, open it."

I opened the box—and gasped in delight. Lying within was a long, white, wool cloak, trimmed in speckled white ermine, with a matching ermine hat. "Oh!" I cried. I instantly wrapped myself in the cloak's sumptuous folds and ran my fingers through the soft fur collar. "Jonathan! It is gorgeous! But it must have cost a fortune."

"I care nothing for the cost. If I am right, this is something that you have been wishing for ever since you were a little girl."

I did not yet comprehend his meaning, but I donned the ermine hat and moved before the looking-glass, where I stared at my reflection. "I look like a queen." As soon as I spoke the words, I recalled the childish wish to which Jonathan had just referred. My eyes caught his in the mirror, and I saw in his smile that we were sharing the same memory.

"You were six years old, seven perhaps," Jonathan said softly, "and I was just a couple of years older."

"We were playing dress-up in your mother's sitting-room at the orphanage."

"You were the Queen. You were wearing a ratty old white tablecloth as a cape. And I was your subject." With a grin, he re-created the scene: He picked up his umbrella, handed it to me, and then solemnly knelt before me. "Your Majesty," he said, bowing his head.

With a smile, I touched first his right and then his left shoulder with the umbrella, and declared in an imperious tone, "I dub thee knight. Arise, Sir Jonathan. You may kiss my hand."

He rose and kissed my hand, then bowed with a courtly flou

ish. "I swear allegiance to you, Your Highness, and will defend your honour all the days of my life."

Our eyes met, and we burst out laughing. "I had forgotten that."

"You made a wish that day that your parents would find you, and that you would be recognised as a princess. And you vowed that one day, you would wear a long, white cloak trimmed with the finest ermine."

"How do you remember?" I said in wonder.

"I remember everything about you. You have always been a princess to me." As he spoke, he gazed down at me with warmth and affection—the way he used to look at me, before I had been branded.

"Oh, Jonathan."

He stepped forward now and took my hands in his. "Mina: these past months have been a living Hell for me. I know they have been for you as well. And I know that I have been—aloof—this past week. I feel bad about that, and I want to say I am sorry."

"Jonathan: hush," I said quickly. "It is I who have been aloof. You need not apologise."

"Yes I must. I know why *you* are silent. It is the poison in your blood that is doing it to you. And I have allowed the very poison which has infected you to pollute my own mind. All week, I have looked at you as if you were something tainted or evil. I have been afraid to touch you or talk to you. I let the others convince me that I should tell you nothing of our plans—nothing! Not by word, or inference, or implication!"

"They are right to say so!" I interjected. "You should not trust me. For if the Count can read my mind—"

"Damn the Count and his accursed tricks! I do not care if he can hear every word I am saying. I hate keeping anything from you. I hate being obliged to censor everything I say. You are my wife, Mina. I love you. I have loved you all my life. There should be no secrets between us."

I felt a great blush rise to my cheeks, and I could not look at him. "No; there should not."

"If I continue shielding my thoughts with you," he went on earnestly, "I fear we will grow even further apart. It will be as if a door is closing between us. I do not want that—and I refuse to do it any more." He took me in his arms. "We leave to-morrow. We have a long journey ahead of us. But we will be together. And in as little as a week or two, this will all be over."

"Will it?"

"I hope so. But if it should take longer, or God forbid, if we should fail at this attempt, I want you to know that I will not forsake you, Mina. I will follow that vile monster to the ends of the earth if need be, to set you free! I swear to do whatever it takes, to send him for ever and ever to burning Hell!"

He kissed me then, and held me tightly. Oh! I thought, as I returned my husband's embrace; what was I to do with such fierce, undeserved loyalty? How could Jonathan know that his loving, selfless offer was the last thing on earth that I could have wished for?

JONATHAN MADE LOVE TO ME THAT NIGHT. IT WAS THE FIRST TIME we had been intimate in nearly two weeks, since we had left Exeter. As he took me in his arms, I was so eager to express my affection for him that I suppose I must have responded to his advances a bit more avidly and creatively than usual.

"Mrs. Harker, what are you doing?" Jonathan asked at one point, a little taken aback.

"I don't know," I responded softly. "Don't you like it?"

"I do, I do," he said. As I glanced up at him through the darkness, I could see that his face was lit with a splendid grin. Soon, he pounced on me. I made a few suggestions of my own, which he was surprised but happy to follow.

I believe we shared a very mutually satisfying connection.

Afterwards, as I lay glowing within his embrace, he turned to me and said with a wicked little smile: "I suppose there *are* some benefits, after all, to that vampire blood in your veins."

We could not help but laugh.

❧

We left Charing Cross six days after Dracula's departure, on the morning of 12th October. We brought only one change of clothes with us; and as we crossed the Channel on the steamer, I was grateful for the beautiful, white wool cloak Jonathan had given me, which protected me from the brisk sea air. We arrived in Paris that same night, and took the places secured for us on the Orient Express. Travelling by train night and day, we arrived on the evening of the 15th at Varna, a port city in eastern Bulgaria on the Black Sea, and checked into the Odessus Hotel.

I encouraged Dr. Van Helsing to hypnotise me every day just before sunrise or sunset, times which he seemed to think were crucial to the telepathic process. Each occasion was a repetition of a similar theme:

"What do you see and hear?" he would ask me, after passing his hands before my eyes as if casting a spell.

I now yielded at once, giving him the impression that he could simply will me into speaking and that my thoughts would obey him. "All is dark," I replied on the first occasion. "I can hear waves lapping against the ship, and the water rushing by." The next day, I added: "Canvas and cordage strain and masts and yards creak. The wind is high—I can hear it in the shrouds, and the bow throws back the foam."

My performance seemed to satisfy everyone. "It is evident that the *Czarina Catherine* is still at sea, hastening her way to Varna," Jonathan said.

Lord Godalming had arranged before leaving London that his agent should send him a daily telegram saying if the ship had been sighted. The *Czarina Catherine* had to pass by the Dardanelles, the strait between European and Asian Turkey connecting the Aegean Sea with the Sea of Marmara, and which was only a day's sail away from Varna. So far, there had been no sign of her. When we arrived in Varna, Dr. Van Helsing met with the vice-consul to get permission to board the ship as soon as she arrived. Lord Godalming told the shippers that the box contained goods stolen from a friend of his and received consent to open it at his own risk.

"The Count, even if he takes the form of a bat, cannot cross the running water of his own volition," the professor said as we sat over dinner in the hotel's dining-room that first night, "so he cannot leave the ship. If we come on board after sunrise, he is at our mercy."

I alone knew that this plan would come to naught. Nicolae had told me that the professor's theory about vampires crossing running water was entirely untrue; and more to the point, he was not aboard that ship at all.

"I will rip open the box and destroy the monster before he wakes!" Jonathan cried.

"Will we not be suspected of murder if we take such an action?" Dr. Seward worried.

"No," Dr. Van Helsing replied, "for if we cut off his head and drive a stake through his heart, his body should fall into dust, leaving no evidence against us."

"Why dust?" Mr. Morris asked. "Miss Lucy's body did not turn to dust when we did the same to her."

"She was a brand-new vampire, so her body had not yet decayed. Count Dracula is centuries old. To dust he must now return."

Nicolae had been in daily mental contact with me ever since he left England. He had taken the identical route to ours six days earlier, also riding the Orient Express, secretly taking his rest by day in the freight car, in a box of earth disguised as cargo. At this moment, he informed me, he was already at Castle Dracula, making certain necessary arrangements for the action to follow.

What about the Czarina Catherine*?* I asked him in my mind. *What happens when the ship docks at Varna?*

Wait and see, he replied.

A WEEK PASSED IN VARNA, WHILE WE AWAITED WORD OF ANY sighting of the *Czarina Catherine.* During this time, I began to feel very tired and slept a great deal, often well into the afternoon. My appetite diminished, I was often chilled, and I noticed that I looked a bit more pale than usual, which made the red scar on my forehead stand out even more prominently.

I could see that the men noticed these changes and worried about them privately, even if they did not remark upon them openly to me. They all still believed that I had been tainted on the night that I drank Dracula's blood. I reassured myself that these symptoms were merely due to the stress of my sleep-deprived nights and days of travel.

A telegram arrived on the 24th of October, informing us that the *Czarina Catherine* had been sighted passing the Dardanelles—implying that it would dock in Varna within twenty-four hours. The men erupted in a sort of wild, happy excitement. To everyone's disappointment, however, the *Czarina Catherine* did not dock at Varna the next day, or the day after. Four tense days passed without a word about the ship or any reason for its delay. All the men were in a fever of anxiety, except for Jonathan, who I found every morning sitting very calmly by himself in our hotel room, whetting the edge of the great Ghoorka knife which he now always carried with him. The sight of that razor-sharp kukri made my blood run cold as ice, for I could not help but imagine with horror what might occur if that blade ever touched Nicolae's throat, driven by Jonathan's stern and unflinching hand.

Jonathan kept his pledge to keep me in his confidence, and soon convinced the others to do the same. I continued to allow Dr. Van Helsing to "hypnotise" me twice a day, on each occasion repeating the same information. One day at sunrise, whilst I was in my feigned trance, he did something which greatly dismayed me: he opened my mouth to inspect my teeth.

"So far, no change," the professor said.

"What change are you looking for?" asked Mr. Morris.

"Do you remember how Miss Lucy's canine teeth grew longer and more sharp in the last days before she died?" Dr. Van Helsing said. The others nodded with quiet gravity. "There are other things too, which I look for. Did you not see? Already, Madam Mina loses her appetite. If she should start to crave blood—"

"What then?" Lord Godalming asked in a worried tone.

"We would be obliged to take . . . steps," the professor replied regretfully.

"What steps?" Jonathan cried, appalled.

A silence fell. Dr. Seward answered quietly: "*Euthanasia* is an excellent and a comforting word."

"Are you out of your senses?" Jonathan cried. "You would put my Mina to death before her time? I will not hear of it!"

"You do not understand, friend John, because you were not there," Dr. Van Helsing said. "We all saw the horror of Miss Lucy's resurrection."

"It was not like a flesh and blood woman at all," Mr. Morris insisted, "but a Thing of wanton lust and terror. Believe me, Harker, you'd rather have your wife dead than roaming the fields in such a monstrous form."

My heart pounded in alarm. Dear God! If these men were to become convinced that I was irrevocably becoming a vampire, they meant to kill me! I tried not to think about the fact that it *could* happen; that Nicolae might have drunk from me one too many times, and that . . .

Rest easy, his voice proclaimed in my mind. *Whatever happens, those butchers will never harm you. I will be there, my love; I am watching over you even now.*

Where? I thought in reply. *Where are you?*

Near-by. I am moving the ship forward. It is a tricky business, commanding the weather.

I smiled inwardly. Such a casual remark, for such an incredible task. Quickly, I opened my eyes and produced the sweetest smile I could muster. "Oh, Professor! What have I said? I can remember nothing."

Jonathan and the others all looked away with guilty faces. "You only tell us what we already know, Madam Mina," Dr. Van Helsing replied hastily. "The ship, she is still somewhere en route."

"She must be held up by the fog," Lord Godalming observed. "Some of the steamers which came in last night reported patches of fog both to the north and south of port."

"We must continue waiting and watching," the professor said. "The ship may appear at any moment."

That morning, a telegram came. We all gathered in the hotel's sitting-room to read it:

LONDON 28 OCTOBER, 1890

LORD GODALMING
CARE OF H.B.M. VICE-CONSUL, VARNA.

CZARINA CATHERINE REPORTED ENTERING GALATZ AT ONE O'CLOCK TODAY.

LLOYD'S LONDON

"Galatz? No! This cannot be!" Dr. Van Helsing cried in shock, raising one hand over his head for a moment, as though in remonstrance with the Almighty.

"Where is Galatz?" Lord Godalming asked, growing very pale.

"In Moldavia," Dr. Seward replied, shaking his head in stunned frustration. "It is their chief port of entry, about 150 miles north of us."

"I knew something strange would happen when that ship was so delayed," Mr. Morris said tensely.

Jonathan's hand went to the hilt of his great kukri knife, and his lips turned up in a dark and bitter smile. "The Count is toying with us. He used Mina's mind; he knows we are waiting here, so he called in the fog so he could bypass us and outrun us."

"I wonder when the next train starts for Galatz?" the professor mused.

"At six thirty to-morrow morning," I answered, without thinking.

Everyone stared at me. "How on earth do you know that?" asked Lord Godalming.

I blushed. I knew because I had looked it up; because I knew that Dracula was not on that ship at all, and he had said we would be obliged to proceed beyond Varna. "I—I have always been something of a train fiend," I said quickly. There was truth in the statement, thank goodness; Jonathan could vouch for it. "At home in Exeter, I used to make up the time-tables so as to be helpful to my husband. I have been studying the maps and time-tables all week. I knew that if anything went wrong and we were obliged to go on to Transylvania, we should probably go by Galatz. There is only one train, and it leaves to-morrow as I say."

"Wonderful woman!" murmured the professor.

"What will we find in Galatz?" Dr. Seward asked. "No doubt the Count has already disembarked and is well on his way somewhere."

"Then we will follow him," Jonathan asserted with new-found determination.

Dr. Van Helsing spurred the men into action, delegating the work that needed to be done. Train tickets were bought; letters were obtained; authority was granted from the proper channels to provide access to the ship in Galatz; and early the next morning, we all boarded the train which carried us onward on our journey.

As I sat in my window-seat on the locomotive, gazing out at the passing pasture-lands which rose to distant hills and then green mountains, my anxiety and anticipation grew—for every movement of the train brought me closer to Nicolae.

When we get to Galatz, what then? I asked him in my mind. His answer came sure and swift:

You must get them to keep following the box. I will keep it moving ahead of them.

Why?

I need to control the time and place where they kill me.

Then he told me what he wanted me to do.

We took rooms in Galatz at the Metropole Hotel. The others immediately dispersed to see the vice-consul and to make enquiries at the docks and the shipping agent's. When they returned that evening, we gathered in the professor's sitting-room and they told me all that they had learned:

"The *Czarina Catherine* is indeed in harbour," Jonathan explained. "The box was taken off the ship by an agent with an order from a Mr. de Ville of London, who had paid him well to remove it before sunrise so as to avoid customs."

"De Ville!" Mr. Morris repeated with a shake of his head. "There's that name again—the sly Devil."

Dr. Seward said: "The agent, following his instructions, delivered the box to a man who deals with the Slovaks who trade down the river to the port. But the trader was just found dead in a churchyard with his throat slashed, and the box is gone."

"The locals swear he was murdered by a Slovak," Jonathan said bitterly, "but we know it was the Count who murdered him, to cover his tracks."

It was not I, Nicolae said in my mind. *I am trying to leave a trail to follow! I have no wish to cover my tracks! That trader was a thief. He tried to swindle my good Szgany partners. But naturally, your men attribute this foul deed to me.*

"What do we do now?" Dr. Seward said.

"We must think," Dr. Van Helsing said, sinking into a chair, his brow furrowed in concentration. "We know, from what Madam Mina tell us in her hypnotic trance this morning, that the creature is still inside that box—which I feel certain is now on its way back to Dracula's castle."

"Why does the Count remain in the box, now that he is on land again?" asked Lord Godalming. "Could he not travel apart from his box if he wished, retiring to its comforts only as needed?"

"Perhaps he fears discovery," Jonathan said.

"Yes," Dr. Seward agreed. "He needed to get away from the city unknown and unseen. And those Slovaks—the locals said they are murdering fools. Should they discover what the box truly contains, it might be the end of him."

Hardly. The Slovaks I employed are my friends. They have worked for me for generations.

"Remember, he doesn't like bright daylight," Mr. Morris added, "and by all reports, the weather's been fair recently."

"That is true," said Dr. Van Helsing.

Tell them I need to be taken back to my own place by someone.

"It seems to me," I put in, "that if the Count is still inside that box, he must need to be *taken back* to his own place by someone. Otherwise, had he the power to move himself as he wished, he would have gone either as man, or wolf, or bat, or in some other way."

"I agree," said Dr. Van Helsing. "Our problem is this: the box left that ship two days ago in the hands of the Slovak. There are many routes they could have taken. Where is it now?"

"Why don't we just go straight up to the castle and wait for it?" Jonathan said.

The professor shook his head. "The Count may choose to emerge from that box under cover of cloud or darkness, the moment it reach Transylvanian soil. We cannot be certain when or where that will take place. No; we must intercept it en route. But where? How?"

The men all fell silent, apparently too tired and dispirited to offer any further suggestions.

Now.

I said: "May I share my own theory?"

"Please do, Madam Mina."

"We are all agreed, I think, that the box carrying the Count is on its way to his castle in Transylvania. The question is: how is he to be taken? I have given the matter some thought."

"Go on," the professor said.

"If he goes by road, there are endless difficulties: curious people might interfere, there are customs and tax collectors to satisfy, and there is the added danger that we, his pursuers, might easily follow. Alternatively, he might go by rail; but a train is a closed environment, offering little chance for escape. I think his safest and most secret bet is to go by water."

"By water?" Jonathan repeated, sitting up with eager interest. "Do you mean by river?"

"Yes. Which also fits in with the theory that he needs to be 'taken back' by someone. You said that, in my trance this morning, I heard cows lowing and the creaking of wood. These sounds would be consistent if the Count's box was on the river in an open boat. I have examined the map." I opened up a map of the region and spread it out on the low table before them. "There are two rivers that lead from Galatz in the direction of Castle Dracula: the Pruth and the Sereth. The Sereth is, at the village of Fundu, joined by the Bistritza River, which runs up around the Borgo Pass. The loop it makes is as close to Dracula's castle as can be reached by water."

These words had no sooner left my mouth than Jonathan leapt up, took me in his arms, and kissed me. "Marvellous!" he cried.

"Our dear Madam Mina is once more our teacher," the professor said, elated, as all the men shook me by the hand. "We are on the track again. Our enemy has a head-start, but we will catch him. If we can come on him by day, beneath the sun and on the water, which he cannot cross unaided, our task will be over. And now, men, to our Council of War! We must plan what each and all will do."

Men? Dracula's voice called out indignantly. *What, are you not part of this Council of War? What imbeciles these creatures are.*

I struggled to hide my smile. *At least they are well-intentioned imbeciles.* It was interesting, I thought, that no one had made the connection that my mental link to the Count—which they found so helpful while I was under hypnosis—might also serve to work against them. It seemed a bit ludicrous to me that Count Dracula, whether it was day or night, should need or choose to remain inside a box all the way up-river to his castle; but no one else appeared to suspect a thing. They believed implicitly in the mission they were undertaking.

A rapid conversation followed. Lord Godalming offered to hire a steam-launch and head up the Sereth River. Mr. Morris said he would buy some good horses and follow along the river-bank, lest by some chance the Count should disembark somewhere.

No, Dracula's voice said suddenly. *Do not let them split up. The party must stay together, or it will be too difficult for me to control.*

"I think it far better if we all stay together," I interjected quickly. "There is safety in numbers. The Slovak will no doubt be armed and ready to fight."

"Yes," said Dr. Van Helsing, "which is why neither man must go alone."

"But if we keep to one party—"

"No, I think it a better plan to divide into factions," the professor insisted.

Damnation. I did not anticipate this.

Dr. Seward immediately offered to go with Quincey. "We have been accustomed to hunt together, and we two, well-armed, will be a match for whatever may come along."

"I have brought some Winchesters," said Mr. Morris. "They're pretty handy in a crowd, and there may be wolves."

"But who will go with Art?" Dr. Seward looked at Jonathan as he spoke, and Jonathan glanced at me. I could see that he was torn with indecision; for as much as he wanted to join the fight, he also wanted to stay with me.

"Friend Jonathan," the professor said, "you must do this. First, because you are young and brave and can fight. My legs are not so quick as once, and I am not used to fight with lethal weapons. Second: because it is your right to destroy this monster which has wrought such woe to you and yours."

The man is eloquent, is he not? Dracula intoned in my mind.

"And we can take no chances, John," Dr. Seward interjected. "We must be certain that the Count's head and body are separated, so that he cannot reincarnate. Your kukri might be needed at the last."

That sounds unpleasant.

Jonathan nodded quietly as the professor continued: "To sum up, then: while Lord Godalming and Mr. Harker go up-river in a steamboat, Dr. Seward and friend Quincey will guard the bank on horseback. Whoever come upon the Count first, in daylight, will kill him in his box. Then we all meet in Transylvania at Castle Dracula."

"Why at the castle?" Mr. Morris asked.

"Because I go there myself," Dr. Van Helsing said, "to obliterate the remaining occupants of that nest of vipers. And I take Madam Mina with me."

Good God!

Jonathan leapt to his feet, crying hotly: "Do you mean to say, Professor, that you would take Mina into the jaws of that Devil's death-trap? Not for the world! You do not know what that place is! It is a den of hellish infamy, the very moonlight alive with grisly shapes that would devour you—and her!"

"Oh, my friend, it is because I would save Madam Mina from that awful place that I would go. And who but she can lead me there? When you arrived at the castle, you were taken by a roundabout route in the dark, you said; and you leave in a state of great mental anguish. Could you find your way there again?"

"Probably not," Jonathan admitted with a frown.

"With Madam Mina's hypnotic powers, surely we shall find our way. I will not take her into the castle itself; no, never; but there is grisly work to be done, and I am pledged to do it, friend Jonathan. I would give my very life to destroy those gloating vampires whose lips you felt upon your throat!"

Jonathan sank back into his chair in defeat as a small sob escaped his throat. "Do as you will," he said softly. Taking my hand in his, he kissed it fervently. "But I will not let Mina go into that enemy's territory unarmed. The place is crawling with wolves. We will give her a gun of her choosing—and teach her how to use it."

That is the first sensible thing he has said.

I am sorry, Nicolae. I tried to encourage them to stay together.

Do not worry. This will certainly complicate things—I will be obliged to keep track of all four parties now en route—your factions as well as the Szgany's boat—and I refuse to stage my death until Van Helsing is there to witness it. But somehow, I will make it work.

Where are you now?

In the vicinity. Mina: I will not be able to stay in contact as often now. I can only communicate via thought when in human guise, and there may be entire days and nights when I must take another shape. But I promise I will be watching over you.

WITH LIGHTNING SPEED, THE ARRANGEMENTS WERE MADE. IT IS A wonder what can be done with the power of money, properly applied! The men carried among them a small arsenal. Jonathan saw to it that I was given a large-bore revolver, which Mr. Morris instructed me how to load and operate in a field behind the hotel.

"I have never held a gun in my life," I admitted.

"You'll get the hang of it, Mrs. Harker," Mr. Morris replied, "and believe me, you'll be glad you have it."

I mastered the weapon with surprising facility. Although I prayed that I would never be obliged to use it, I could not deny that I felt a little thrill when he placed the cold metal instrument in my hand—and an even greater thrill when I loaded, cocked, and fired the weapon several times in succession at a target nailed to a tree.

Good shot, I heard Nicolae intone approvingly in my head. *Perhaps you do not need my protection after all. One warning, however: take care before you shoot at bats or wolves. I do bleed—and you never know where you might see a friendly face.*

As there was no time to be lost, Mr. Morris and Dr. Seward set out that very evening on their long ride, planning to keep to the right bank of the Sereth and follow its curves. Lord Godalming hired an old steam-launch, which he was experienced at working, having had for years a similar launch of his own back home.

All at once, it was time for them to go. As we stood outside the door of the hotel, Jonathan gazed down at me affectionately. "Take good care of her, Professor."

I felt my courage failing me. This entire expedition was setting forth on my word. I had no real idea what Nicolae was planning for these men up-river, except the vague notion that he intended to somehow stage his own death. What if something went wrong? With a little gasp, I suddenly recalled the dream I had had some weeks before, in which my four Englishmen had swooped down upon a wagon carrying Dracula, dead in a box—and one of my men had died! Tears started in my eyes as I thought: what if Jonathan or one of the others should be hurt? What if Nicolae did not survive?

"There must be no tears now," Jonathan said as he tenderly wiped away the moisture from my cheeks and wrapped my white cloak more tightly about me. "Not until this is over, and only then if they fall in gladness."

"I love you, Jonathan," I said, kissing him. "Be careful."

"I will. You do the same. Do not be afraid to use that revolver." He kissed me again, then strode off with Lord Godalming in the direction of the river.

TWENTY-ONE

As there was no night train available which could take us directly to Bistritz, Dr. Van Helsing and I did the next best thing and took a train by way of Bucharest to Veresti, arriving late the following afternoon. We were to drive ourselves to the Borgo Pass, for the professor did not trust any one else in the matter. In Veresti, he bought an open carriage and horses, all the equipment and supplies required for our journey, and plenty of fur rugs to keep us warm. Fortunately, the professor knew something of a great many languages, so he got on all right in his transactions.

We started off that same night. For the sake of propriety, Dr. Van Helsing told the landlady at the inn where we dined that we were a father and daughter travelling together. She put up a huge basket of provisions for us that seemed enough for a company of soldiers.

For three days and nights we drove on, stopping only to take nourishment, and keeping up a good speed. We were in good spirits and did our best to cheer each other. The professor seemed tireless; at first he would not take any rest and did all the driving himself. I now felt so tired during the daylight hours that I could hardly keep my eyes open. At times I fell into a deep slumber from which it was difficult to wake. I could see that the professor was becoming very wary of this tendency in me. I suppose I was just in denial: but I insisted that it was only the rocking motion of the carriage along the rutted road that induced such lethargy. On the second night, exhaustion finally overcame the professor, and he was obliged to hand over the reins to me. I drove on through the night while he slept beside me.

We changed horses frequently with farmers along the way, who were willing to make the exchange for sufficient coin. The country-side was lovely: field, forest, and mountains as far as the eye could see, full of beauties of all imaginable kinds. The people we encountered were strong, simple, and kind, but appeared to be very superstitious. On the first day, when we stopped at a house for a hot meal, the woman who served us saw the scar on my forehead and cried out in alarm, making the sign of the cross. Then she thrust out her hand and pointed two fingers towards me, in a gesture that made her hand look like a little head with horns.

"What does that mean?" I whispered to the professor.

"It is a charm or guard to keep off the evil eye," he replied in a low tone.

I believe the woman put an extra amount of garlic into our food. I used to like garlic very much, but I suddenly found that I could not abide it. I left my meal untouched—which caused Dr. Van Helsing to send another wary look my way.

Every day, I gave the professor hypnotic reports, implying that Dracula was still inside his box on the river. Every night, Dracula came to me in my mind, informing me about the progress of the others.

Jonathan and Lord Godalming are stopping and inspecting every boat they pass on the river. They have taken to flying the Romanian flag, so as to pass as a government boat—very clever. But of course they find nothing.

What of Dr. Seward and Mr. Morris?

Still riding hard, without incident.

The country got wilder as we went. The great spurs of the Carpathian Mountains, which at Veresti had seemed so distant and so low on the horizon, now gathered round and towered before us. Several times I spied a bat circling in the sky above our carriage, before it took off into the distance. Twice I thought I spotted a wolf crouching low under the cover of the trees, staring fixedly at us. Was it Nicolae, keeping his eye on me?

Houses now became few and far between. At night, we could hear the howling of wolves. The diligence from Bukovina to Bistritz passed by us twice on the dirt road, but we saw no horsemen, and only encountered a few peasants along the way. The weather grew colder by the hour. Snow flurries came and went, then quickly melted away. I felt a strange heaviness in the air, or perhaps it was only a heaviness within me; for the further we progressed, the more the blood in my veins seemed to grow cold and sluggish. At times, I felt light-headed; at other times, I could not stop shivering, despite my warm wool cloak and the fur rugs Dr. Van Helsing had purchased, which I wrapped around me.

"We should get to the Borgo Pass by dawn," the professor said, as we drove on in the early-morning darkness of the third day. "The last two horses we got will have to go on with us. We may not be able to get another change."

His maps, I knew, would soon be of little use. Jonathan had written in his journal that once he left the diligence at the Borgo Pass, it had taken but a few hours in Dracula's rapidly moving coach to reach his castle. Unless we could see the castle from the pass, however, we would have no idea which direction to turn—

and I was growing a little uneasy, for the professor was relying on me, and my mental connection to the Count, to lead the way. But I could offer little assistance, since I had not heard from Dracula all day.

JUST AFTER SUNRISE, WE SAW SMOKE FROM A CAMP-FIRE, AND detected a band of gipsies camped in a thicket not far from the roadside, an event which proved to be most remarkable.

"Let us ask those gipsies for directions to Castle Dracula," said the professor, as he brought our horses to a stop. He clambered down from our carriage, and I joined him.

As we approached the group, I admired the gipsy wagon. It was painted a deep red and embellished with gold scroll-work, with a curved, barrel-like roof-top and yellow curtains at the windows. Dr. Van Helsing hailed the travellers, who were gathered around the camp-fire. A sturdy-looking gipsy man with shoulder-length black hair and a black moustache returned the greeting with an aloof, unsmiling nod. The women—who were beautiful, wrapped in long cloaks against the cold, their dark heads covered by colourful cloths which descended down their backs—gave us suspicious glances and stuck to their work, cooking breakfast over the fire.

"They do not look very friendly," I whispered to the professor.

"Yet they may be of help." He made his request in what appeared to be the gipsies' own tongue. As soon as the words left his lips, every one of the gipsies looked absolutely terrified and crossed themselves. The man who had so calmly greeted us now leapt to his feet, shaking his head vehemently and shouting a string of forceful proclamations that I did not understand.

"What is the matter?" I asked Dr. Van Helsing.

"From what I can gather, he is refusing to share that information—if in fact he knows it—and he warns us most strenuously to stay far away from that castle if we value our lives, for it is populated by demons."

Just then, the door at the back end of the gipsy wagon flew open. An elderly gipsy woman wearing a dark purple head-covering descended the ladder and began hobbling straight towards us, her dark eyes fixed on me. The look on the old woman's face was so full of concentrated interest that I found myself frozen to the spot. Why was she looking at me thus? Was it, again, because of the scar on my forehead? But no; her attention seemed to be drawn to my whole being, as if she was deciphering something extraordinary about me. She stopped before me, grabbed my hand, and held it tightly in her wrinkled grasp, as she stared into my eyes. Then she gave a little gasp; her face lit up with delight, and she spoke in an animated, gravelly voice. I did not understand the words; but from her gestures, as she pointed to me, to herself, and to the other gipsies by the fire, her meaning instantly became clear to me.

She was saying that I was one of them!

The other gipsies now rose and gathered around me in a state of happy excitement, touching me, hugging me, shaking my hand, shouting, and smiling. I was so overwhelmed, I hardly knew what to say or think. Dr. Van Helsing conducted a brief conversation with them, which he quickly translated for my benefit.

"They say the old woman knows things. She says you are of their family. I explain that you are from England, but she insist that their blood runs in your veins from very far back."

I was speechless with wonder. Was it possible? Was my own mother—*was I*—descended from these very people?

The gipsies invited us to share their camp-fire and their breakfast, and the professor agreed that we might make a brief stop.

We spent a half-hour in their company, during which time they treated us with generosity and kindness and regaled us with their stories, which Dr. Van Helsing did his best to translate. They said they were members of the Konoria tribe, one of many thousands of nomadic gipsy tribes in Romania. The old woman was their seer; the greater part of their income came from the fortunes she told. The most spine-tingling moment came when the old woman took my hand again and said in a voice heavy with meaning:

"You face great danger, and will be forced to make an important choice. Listen to what your body tells you. It is changing. Let it be your guide." (At least, that is how Dr. Van Helsing translated it for me, with a grave, worried frown.)

This prediction about danger, choices, and my body changing filled me with silent dread; but I pushed it quickly from my mind, refusing to believe it. Even gipsy fortune-tellers could be wrong, couldn't they?

The old woman also warned us to stay away from "the dreaded castle," an admonition which the rest of the group repeated most emphatically. The thirty minutes passed as in the blink of an eye, and it was with great reluctance that I rose to leave the group. As we hugged and shook hands in parting, I knew it was most unlikely that I would ever see these people again, for the gipsies' itinerary, by nature, was uncertain.

"Well, that was most interesting," Dr. Van Helsing said as the two of us once more got under way.

"I have never had a relative to call my own. I learned, only recently, that my mother may have had gipsy blood in her. To think that one of my distant ancestors might have been a member of that clan is truly thrilling."

"Yes. But it is a shame they could not, or would not, assist us in finding Count Dracula's castle. Although I suppose I should not be surprised." The professor fell silent for a moment, then glanced at me with an odd look. "What did the old woman mean, do you think, when she say you will be forced to make an important choice?"

"I have no idea," I said, as a little shiver ran through me.

A FEW MILES FURTHER DOWN THE ROAD, WE CRESTED THE SUMMIT of the Borgo Pass and stopped to look around us in wonder. In every direction were endless mountains and valleys covered by dense pine forest, interspersed with scattered deciduous trees ablaze in every shade of autumn colour from green to orange, gold, yellow, russet, and red. It was breath-takingly beautiful; but to my dismay, I saw no castle. Indeed, there was not a single sign of human existence anywhere.

There is a byroad about a mile up ahead.

Dracula's voice came to me so unexpectedly that I jumped.

I marked it with three boulders and a wooden cross, he continued, *a little amusement for Van Helsing's benefit. Turn right and follow it.*

Thank you, I thought, *but what then?*

Be patient. I will guide you. You are almost here. You are almost in my arms.

Aloud, I said: "We must continue on, Professor. This is the right way. There is a byroad up ahead."

"How do you know? I cannot see the castle."

"I just have a feeling."

The professor nodded and told the horses to move forward. We soon came to the byroad. "Aha!" he cried. "Do you see that cross? The locals must have put it there as a safeguard and a warning. We are indeed on the right track."

Dracula intoned with a chuckle: *I am glad he appreciated that, for in making it, I singed my fingers.*

It was slow going. The byroad joined with many other roads.

We were not sure that they were actually roads at all, they were so neglected and overgrown. To complicate matters further, a light snow began to fall; but Nicolae's voice continued to instruct me. It seemed to me that he was taking us on a rather circuitous route, for despite an entire day of driving, we still saw no sign of the castle. The professor, however, did not appear to be concerned.

We travelled on until dark, climbing up through a densely forested and rocky stretch of terrain. Since we were so near to our destination, the professor said that we should treat ourselves to a true rest; so we made camp that night in the forest. While Dr. Van Helsing tethered and fed the horses, I made a fire with some of the wood we had brought with us and prepared supper. The aroma from the cooking food, however, did not appeal to me at all.

When the professor joined me by the fire, I handed him his plate with a smile and said: "Forgive me; but I have already eaten. I was so hungry that I could not wait."

I saw that he doubted me; but he only looked away and ate in silence.

He had purchased several tarpaulins and a quantity of rope, with the intent of fashioning tents for our shelter; but neither of us had any experience in setting up such things. After three failed attempts, we gave up and made two simple beds by piling the fur rugs atop each other, side by side by the fire. Dr. Van Helsing urged me to go to sleep, while he kept watch for wolves or any other danger.

At the mention of wolves, I grew alarmed. "Please, Professor; do not shoot at any wolves unless you are certain they mean to attack us. They are God's creatures, too, and we have invaded their country, after all."

"I will respect your wishes, Madam Mina, and look on wolves with a kind eye if I can," said the professor with a smile.

I stretched out on my makeshift bed, pulling one of the fur

rugs over me. The clouds had shifted, revealing the starry heavens in all their glory. We were deep in the wilderness, miles and miles from anywhere, enveloped by a profound sense of quiet. As I listened to the rush of the wind in the trees, the night chirp of the insects, and the distant howling of the wolves, every sound seemed louder and more distinct than I had ever heard it before.

I was not tired. I missed Jonathan. I wondered how he was and tried to imagine what he was doing at that very moment. I tried to hypnotise myself into falling asleep by counting the stars above, but it did not work. I wondered at this strange, new nocturnal tendency in me. Surely it was nothing to worry about; surely, I told myself, it was just because I had napped part of the day, because my sleeping schedule had become topsy-turvy.

I saw that Dr. Van Helsing was nodding off, and told him that I would be happy to stand guard in his stead since I was not sleepy. My pronouncement seemed to make him sad; but he acquiesced with grace, lay down on the bed beside me, and fell instantly asleep.

I sat up on my bed of furs and kept watch far into the night. At length, however, despite my best intentions, I must have fallen asleep . . . because I had a dream.

In the dream, I was lying on my rug by the fire, with Dr. Van Helsing slumbering just a foot or two away from me. Only the top of his silvery head was visible above the fur rug in which he was wrapped. As I gazed at his sleeping form, I was overwhelmed by an urge to be closer to him, to run my fingers through that silvery hair, which shimmered so softly in the fire's glow. Silently, I scooted my body next to his. When I pulled the edge of the fur blanket back to reveal his face, however, to my shock it was not the professor at all: it was Jonathan—a Jonathan who looked decades older, with silvery hair! He looked so dear and peaceful in repose. My heart overflowed with love for him. I felt compelled to kiss him. As I slowly bent my head to him, intending to touch my lips to his stubble-covered cheek, I felt a sudden, gnawing ache in my jaw, along with an insatiable thirst.

I craved his blood.

With a roar, I lunged for Jonathan's throat.

Mina.

I awoke with a start to find myself hovering over the sleeping professor, my lips just inches from his throat. I recoiled in horror and mortification. What on earth was I doing? What had prompted such a depraved dream? And why, oh why, had I acted it out in real life? I had never been prone to sleep-walking, as Lucy had. Yet—had I not awakened—I might have actually bitten Dr. Van Helsing!

What was happening to me? In a panic, I felt my teeth, relieved to discover that they were still their normal size and shape.

Mina.

It was Dracula's voice, breaking into my thoughts. Heart pounding in confusion, I turned away from the professor—only to come face to face with a pair of tall black boots. I looked up, and saw Dracula in the flesh, towering above me.

❧

I LEAPT TO MY FEET AND THREW MYSELF INTO DRACULA'S ARMS, SO happy to see him, I thought my heart might burst.

Thank God you are here! I thought.

"We can speak aloud. He will not waken." Dracula kissed me soundly, then studied me in the flickering light of the fire. "You look well, if a bit thin. The outdoors seems to agree with you."

"I just had the most wicked dream."

"I heard."

"What kind of animal am I, to have such a dream? I am no

better than the three harpies who descended on Jonathan at your castle!"

He seemed a bit taken aback by that, but said: "I suppose *harpies* is as good as any other word for my sisters." He kissed me again, then said: "I have missed you, my darling. To see you from afar, and be unable to take you in my arms—I cannot tell you how many times I have come this close to risking everything, by appearing in front of you."

"Did my dream not appall you?"

"Why should it? It was only a dream."

"No. It was a premonition." I shivered as a dark, foreboding feeling came over me. "You said there would be consequences, Nicolae, and I think you may be right. So was the old gipsy woman we just met. I have tried to deny it; but I believe I am changing."

"Changing how?"

"I am cold so often. Food has become repulsive to me. I have to force myself to eat and drink. Lately I am tired all day long, and I lie awake much of the night."

He studied me. "I thought I detected something."

"What does it mean? Am I . . ." I could hardly bring myself to say it: "Am I becoming a vampire? Am I really going to die, and soon?"

"I surely hope not. But I do not know." He shook his head, deeply troubled, as he held me to him. "That last night before I left England, if only I had not—"

Tears started in my eyes. "I wanted you to kiss me, to drink of me," I said—although I admitted to myself that he had gone too far, taken too much.

"I should have restrained myself."

"Is there not anything we can do?"

"Sadly, no. I am so very, very sorry. If I have poisoned your blood, there is no antidote. We must wait and see if your body succumbs to it."

"Oh! How foolish we have been!" I cried in anguish. "We have been playing a dangerous game—a game with my very life!" I began to weep.

He drew back to look at me and said softly, "Mina: it does no good to worry. Your fears may never come to pass. But if they do—if you *are* to be a vampire—it is not the terrible fate that you imagine. Trust me, there are great wonders beyond this life that you know. And whatever happens, my darling, I promise you: I will be with you, every step of the way."

I wiped away my tears. "You had better stay close, then. Dr. Van Helsing checks me every day. Should he find any sign that I am irrevocably changing—if it looks as if I am going to die before you do—I am certain that he intends to kill me."

"Idiot! This man calls himself your friend?" More calmly, he added: "I would not worry about him either, my darling. In a matter of days, this hunt will be over. You can hide your symptoms for that long if they persist. If your blood has indeed been altered, we should know it by then." Cradling my face gently, he said in a loving, reassuring tone: "And then you and I can decide what to do, my love."

I nodded. As I struggled to calm myself, I suddenly remembered something. "Why have we not come upon your castle yet? By my reckoning, we should have reached it to-day."

"I have been delaying your arrival by deliberately sending you in an alternate direction."

"I thought so! Why?"

"I do not want you to encounter my sisters. In my absence, they terrorised the local peasants and murdered several farm-boys. I warned them that you and your Englishmen might be coming, and that if they touched a hair on your heads, I would destroy them with my own hands—but I cannot guarantee your safety, nor can I stay and guard them every minute."

I frowned. "The professor is determined to go up to your castle at his first opportunity and slay your three sisters."

"I am aware. He is a fool. One man alone, against those three—he does not stand a chance, even if he comes upon them in their daytime trance. We are not like the new-born, Mina. We can awaken at will."

"Oh!" I cried, desperately worried.

"I do not want either of you going up to the castle, under any circumstances."

"All right. What of the others? Do you have news of Jonathan?"

"The boatmen have been delayed by engine trouble. Lord Godalming seems to be an amateur fitter, but it is taking him some time to fix the thing. The horsemen took a wrong turn at one of the river's tributaries and lost an entire day going in the wrong direction. It is enough to drive one mad. But I am determined not to show my face until all are assembled in one place. Those four must be the ones who dispatch me; and it is imperative that the professor, more than all the rest, be there to witness my apparent death."

"Are you certain, wherever this dreadful meeting occurs, that you can escape unharmed?"

"Yes: as long as it occurs at night—a condition I will take great pains to assure."

"And no one will be hurt?"

"No one will be harmed by my hand, I promise you that." He paused, then said: "Dawn approaches. I must go while I still can."

"Go where?"

"Back to the river, to see how they are getting on with that steam-launch. I have a lot of ground to cover, so I must take another form. For the next day or two I will not be able to share my thoughts."

"How will I know which direction to go?"

"The horses will know. I have spoken with them. They will keep you in the vicinity, but out of sight of the castle."

"When will I see you again?"

He smiled and kissed me. "When they think I am dead."

When Dr. Van Helsing awoke, I forced myself to eat breakfast to keep up appearances. It made me so nauseous that it was all I could do to hold down the food. We packed up our belongings and travelled on, following a rough road all day. I was extremely tired and slept all the way, leaving the driving to the professor, secure in the knowledge that the horses knew the route. Just before sunset, however, I was awakened by Dr. Van Helsing's exultant cry:

"There it is!"

I opened my eyes to find us on a roadway at the crest of a hill. The sky was grey and cloudy, feebly lit by the descending sun, and a cold wind promised the advent of snow. Immediately before us were green and gold undulating hills and valleys, interrupted only by the narrow white ribbon of road, which crisscrossed it here and there. In the far distance, the silvery thread of a river wound among deep gorges, between great, jagged, green mountains, which rose sharply to meet the sky. My heart leapt in surprise, however, at the sight just a few miles beyond us: for in the very centre of this heavily forested landscape rose a very steep hill; and perched majestically on a rocky crag at its summit was an old castle of very dramatic appearance.

"All day, the horses keep trying to head down a different path," said the professor, "which would have taken us far out of the way. It take all my strength to get them to follow my lead. And I am right! For as sure as I am born, that is Dracula's castle, just as your Jonathan describe in his diary."

I stared at the castle in wonder and alarm—aware that Dracula did not want us there—but thrilled to see it with my own eyes.

Even from that distance, and in the dim light of late afternoon, the edifice was far larger and more magnificent than I had expected. It was ancient and many storeys high, built of pale grey stone with a smattering of red brick, and outfitted with countless small windows and a multitude of red-roofed, turreted towers in varying sizes, shapes, and heights.

Other than the castle on its precipice, the scene was unmarked by any other sign of habitation. I knew from Jonathan's diary that the few scattered farms in the region were many miles distant, and that the closest hamlet was a day's ride away.

"The castle is so close, we can reach it now on foot, if we wish," the professor said.

"We had best not go up there, Professor," I replied quickly. "It is too dangerous."

"We shall see."

We made camp again on the hill-side in view of the castle. There was something wild and uncanny about the place. I could hear the distant howling of wolves, which set my nerves on edge. Darkness soon fell: a pure, black darkness, for the heavy clouds now blanketed the stars. The wind blew harsh and cold, and despite my warm wool cloak, I shivered as I sat on our fur rugs by the fire, unable to get warm. Try as I might, I could not get myself to eat more than a few bites of dinner.

"Where do you suppose the others are?" I said, by way of making conversation.

"It is hard to say. But one thing we know for certain. They have not yet found and killed Count Dracula true dead, for if they had, your soul would be free—your appetite would return—and your scar would be gone."

A sudden scream from the horses broke the stillness. I glanced over at them, alarmed. They were whinnying and tearing at their tethers, as if possessed by some unknown terror. I stared into the darkness apprehensively, but I could see nothing. Then the professor did a strange thing. He rose and, with a long stick, he drew a line in the ground all around me. Over this dirt ring he dropped pieces of crumbled holy wafer, until they encircled me entirely.

"What are you doing?" I asked.

"I fear—I fear," was his only reply. He then moved several feet away and said, "Will you not come closer to the fire, and get warm?"

I rose obediently, intending to take a step in his direction; but as I stared at the Host on the ground, it seemed as if some invisible force was holding me back, filling me with dread. I was terrified that if I crossed that holy barrier, my entire body would burst into flame. "I cannot do it," I whispered in anguish.

"Good," he replied softly.

"How can it be good?" I cried. "I am afraid to pass; afraid for my life!"

"What you cannot pass, dear Madam Mina, neither can any of those we dread."

I understood his meaning, and—with a horrified gasp—I sank down to the ground. A great heat of sorrow rose within my chest, and tears spilled from my eyes. My darkest fears had come true! I could not hide the truth from him—or myself—any longer.

"Oh Professor! Am I really becoming a vampire?"

"I regret, but it is so, Madam Mina." His eyes filled with compassion, he came to sit with me on the rug within my protective circle.

I sobbed as if my heart would break. What a bitter, bitter pill to swallow! If only I could go back in time, I thought: to Dracula's last night in England, to that moment when he held me in his embrace, and passion was overtaking us both. It was clearly that last bite which had proven fatal. Oh! What I would not give to have my life back; to be allowed to live a normal span, without the fear of rising in Un-Death! That, however, could never be. At some point, perhaps quite soon, I would be obliged to say good-bye to Jonathan for ever. I would never have the children that I yearned for—the children I would have so deeply loved and cherished.

"How long do I have, Professor?" I whispered brokenly. "A year? A month? A week? When will the final change happen?"

"*It will not happen,* Madam Mina! This I swear to you. It is why we are here. I will slay this foul Dracula true dead and free your soul, if it cost me my life to do it!"

These words, which I knew Dr. Van Helsing intended to comfort me, only served to compound my sorrow. I did not wish any harm to come to Dracula. There was no acceptable solution to the terrible dilemma in which I found myself; only this one dreadful, inescapable conclusion: I was going to die, and I had no one to blame but myself.

I wept openly for some time. At length, I dried my eyes and sat in miserable silence. The horses were still restless; and as the professor and I were both too anxious and upset to sleep, we kept a grim watch together. The night wore on, dark and very cold, the silence broken only by the infrequent, distant howling of wolves. Presently, a light snow began to fall. The professor got up and returned with several thick wooden sticks, the ends of which he began sharpening with his knife. The sight of those wooden stakes filled me with dread, for I knew their deadly purpose. He had killed the Un-Dead Lucy with a similar implement, before severing her head with a blade. With a surge of fear, I wondered: would he one day be compelled to use one of those stakes on me?

"Do you intend those for the women at the castle?" I enquired, as I shivered beneath my fur rug.

"Yes."

"Please do not go up there, Professor," I implored earnestly. "You may have found it a simple matter to slay Lucy while she lay asleep in her tomb, but there is no guarantee that those predators will be asleep. Even if they are, they are age-old vampires who might easily awaken."

"How do you know this?"

"I . . . cannot say. I just do. You cannot succeed against three vampires."

"I must try. I must slay the vile women who inhabit there."

"You must not! Would you leave me here on my own, completely defenceless? If something happened to you, how would I get home? No! Promise me you will not do this thing."

The professor frowned and looked at me. "For all the world, I would not wish you harm, Madam Mina, but I have not come all this way not to finish the deed. Perhaps we can wait until—"

Suddenly the horses began to scream anew. At the same time, there came a change in the lightly falling snow and mist before us. It began to circle round like a great wheel, and in its white depths, about ten yards away, I caught a shadowy glimpse of three beautiful women.

"Mijn God," the professor said under his breath, staring in amazement.

The sight, I think, did not astonish me quite as much as it did him, for I had seen Dracula appear in a similar manner many times before. The wheeling figures of mist and snow came closer, keeping ever without the holy circle. At last they materialised before us into three beautiful, voluptuous young women, dressed in clothing from a bygone century, with bright, hard eyes, white teeth, and ruby-red lips.

"It is them, just as Jonathan describe!" the professor murmured.

Without a doubt, it had to be Dracula's sisters. They were all stunningly lovely, with features and figures so perfect, they nearly took my breath away. Two had black hair, like Dracula; one—the most beautiful of them all—was blonde; and they all bore a striking resemblance to their brother. They all smiled and pointed at me, laughing, as they spoke in some foreign language, their voices sweet and low as music. My hand moved instinctively towards the revolver which I wore in a holster at my hip, but had never used. The professor said:

"Bullets are useless against the vampire, Madam Mina."

"What should we do?"

"Nothing. We can have no hope against them while they are in possession of their full powers. We must wait for day."

The women continued to speak in their foreign tongue in strange, soothing, seductive tones, which seemed to be aimed at me. "What are they saying, professor?"

"They are saying: 'Come, sister. Come to us. Come!' "

I cringed at this. For reply, one of the vampires said in haughty, heavily accented English: "Do you prefer that we speak your tongue, English girl?"

"Do come, English girl!" laughed another.

"Why do you stay with this old man?" sneered the blonde. "We know many young and beautiful boys. We will share them all with you." She made wanton, sexual gestures with her hands and body.

My heart pounded in fear, horror, and repulsion, but I was unable to tear my gaze away. Is this the kind of creature that I was destined to become? Oh, God forgive me! *Nicolae, come quickly,* I thought in desperation. *They are here. They have come for me.*

Dracula made no reply. I remembered, then, his warning that he would be far away to-night, in another form, and unable to communicate.

Dr. Van Helsing rose and made as if to leave the circle, but I grabbed his hand and stopped him. "No! Do not go without. The Host protects us. You are safe here."

"It is for you I fear," he replied.

"Why fear for me, Professor?" I replied ruefully. "I am almost one of them already. No one in all the world is safer from them than I. Oh! How horrible they are! I wish they would go away!"

Dr. Van Helsing seized some of the wafer and stood. "They cannot approach me while I am so armed." He advanced on them. The three women drew back a bit but continued to hover, licking their lips at him and laughing their low, horrid laughs, taunting us menacingly.

Suddenly I heard a loud screech and the fluttering of wings. A large black bat appeared out of the snow-gloom and bore down on the intruders, flapping and screaming. The three harpies hissed and roared at the bat in frustration. Then they hurled sticks and stones at it, but the great bat dodged every missile with unrelenting skill and speed, circling ever closer to them. At last they gave up. In unison, the three women transformed back into phantom shapes, then melted into the mist and snow and whirled away in the direction of the castle. The bat hovered in the night air, and for a long moment seemed to be staring at me with its beady red eyes.

Then it flew off, disappearing into the mist.

When I awoke, I was lying in a warm cocoon beneath one of the fur rugs. I sat up to find the sun high in the sky, hidden by deep clouds. Although it was cold, most of the previous night's snowfall had melted, clinging only in patches beneath the trees. Shivering, I pulled my cloak tightly about me. I saw that I was still encircled by the pieces of holy wafer. Our cooking gear and other supplies were in their usual places, but there was no sign of the professor.

I called out to him, but received no reply. To my astonishment, I noticed that the horses and carriage were also gone. I was alone!

All around me, the forest was still and silent, the only sound the rush of the wind through the trees. Where was Dr. Van Helsing? Why had he left me thus, alone and vulnerable? Although the holy circle had worked against the female vampires, he knew it would not serve to protect me from wolves!

The terrible events of the previous night came back to me in a rush. Surely it was Dracula who had flown in as a bat and frightened off those awful vampire women. Looking up through the trees, I could see Dracula's castle on an eminence a few miles away.

Suddenly, I understood where Dr. Van Helsing was. He had gone up to the castle, to complete his deadly purpose!

TWENTY-TWO

I LEAPT TO MY FEET, DEEPLY WORRIED, FIGHTING BACK A BRIEF wave of dizziness. Dracula had expressly forbidden us to go up to his castle. I had seen how beautiful and seductive those women were. I could not forget how they had once descended on Jonathan, eager for his blood, or how—by his own admission—he had been overcome by lust and had lacked the will to fend them off. I had been similarly overwhelmed by desire, I realised, every time I had been in Dracula's presence. In my dream the other night, I had felt the innate sexual urge of the vampire within myself!

Dr. Van Helsing seemed to believe that vampires were entirely powerless during the day, but I knew better. Despite his stalwart beliefs and his bag of tools, he could become their easy prey. I must go to him, I realised, without delay. It might yet be too late! But how? I was encircled by the Holy Host, a barrier I dared not cross!

I heard a chattering in the near-by trees. Among the waving branches, I spied two squirrels involved in a merry chase. An idea came to me. I called to the animals, making little kissing sounds in the air. The small creatures darted down the tree-trunk and dropped to the forest floor, where they froze, staring at me. I continued my entreaties, pointing to the crumbs of Host on the ground before me. The squirrels approached, a few halting feet at a time. I stood stock-still, not wishing to frighten them. They each pounced upon a crumb of wafer and gobbled it up. They quickly ate several additional crumbs, then stuffed their cheeks with more and dashed off into the trees.

With a smile, I saw that a small opening had been cleared for me in the circle, just wide enough for me to pass through. I cautiously stepped out, then paused. If the professor was in danger, I would surely need a weapon. I spotted one of his discarded carving attempts on the ground near-by: a thick wooden stake, about eighteen inches long, with an end point that was imperfect. A defective weapon, I thought, was better than none; and so I grabbed it up and hastened down the hill.

I moved as fast as my feet could carry me, taking a short-cut across the forested hills and valleys, crunching through the undergrowth in the direction of the castle. At length I caught up to the dirt road, which was narrow and very rough, and wet with mud from the newly melted snow. I followed the road as it wound up a steep incline towards the castle. The ancient edifice sat perched in all its grandeur on the summit of a sheer rocky precipice, its lofty stone walls and red-roofed towers looming high above me, topped by tall, narrow windows here and there where sling, arrow, cannon, or musket could not reach.

The way was very steep and muddy. My skirts and, to my distress, my once-beautiful white wool cloak became sodden and filthy at the hem. Snow clung in shady spots along the roadside. The rocky face that I passed was studded with mountain ash and thorn, whose roots clung in cracks and crannies of the stone. I was obliged to stop repeatedly to catch my breath, but I toiled on.

Looking up, the castle appeared to be an immense grey monolith, its red-roofed towers pointing towards the heavens. Looking down and outward, I could see nothing but a vast sea of tree tops capped by distant, jagged mountains.

At last I reached the object of my journey. Breathing hard, I stopped outside the castle in an ancient, moss-covered, cobblestone courtyard of considerable size. My heart quickened as I saw our horse and carriage tied and waiting out front. A quick visual survey of the vehicle confirmed that the professor's bag of tools did not lie within. Evidently he was somewhere inside the building. But where? The castle was vast. With a sinking heart, I realised that he—and *they*—could be anywhere.

The main front entrance was set in a projecting doorway of massive, carved stone, much worn by time and weather. To my surprise, the doorway stood wide open. The ancient, nail-studded, oaken door had been broken off its hinges and lay flat on the paving stones. I remembered that Dr. Van Helsing had bought a blacksmith hammer in Veresti. He must have put it to good use here, I thought, taking this precaution to ensure that no matter what happened, he could not be held a prisoner in the castle, as Jonathan believed *he* had been.

I hesitated for an instant. What would I find inside this lonely old castle? Was I going to my death? Perhaps; for if those vampire harpies were truly awake, I knew I did not possess the strength or skill to combat them. However, the professor might be in mortal danger. I had to at least make the attempt.

I crossed the threshold. The large, circular foyer had four arched doorways in the high stone walls. My eye was drawn to several fresh, muddy footprints on the stone floor: tracks that could well have been made by the professor.

I removed my cloak and laid it over a chair, then followed the shoeprints through one of the arches and along a passageway. I soon found myself in an immense chamber. The only source of light came from several narrow, undraped apertures high up near the ceiling. The room was very cold. I paused, shivering, to let my eyes adjust to the low light. I soon perceived that the walls were filled from floor to ceiling with shelves of books: hundreds of thousands of volumes. My heart pounded. So this was Count Dracula's library! This was where he had spent so many long, contented hours, for so many centuries! And no wonder. It was a fabulous room. The windows were curtained with draperies of richest velvet, and the furnishings seemed to be upholstered in the costliest and most beautiful of fabrics. A half-dozen marvellous, gilt-framed paintings hung here and there, canvases depicting European landscapes which, I noticed with astonishment, were similar in style to some that I had seen in the National Gallery in London.

All was silent. I noticed more bits of muddy residue on the stone floor and pressed on, leaving the great chamber and moving down another long passage. I tried every door that I passed, but found all of them locked. At length, I came to a door that stood open. It was a sparsely furnished bedroom that was very dusty from disuse. Traces of mud led towards another open door at the far corner of the room. Hoping that I was following in the professor's footsteps, I made my way through, proceeding into a passage which led to a circular, stone stairway that went steeply down.

As I descended, I had the strangest sense that I had traversed this path before, although I knew that could not be so. In a flash of understanding, I knew why: Jonathan had described the room above and that very staircase in his diary! I recalled that it led to a chapel in the lower reaches of the castle, where Jonathan had twice encountered Dracula asleep.

As I reached the bottom of the steps, I heard the now-familiar, uncanny laughter of the female vampires. My breath caught in my throat as I hurried down a dimly lit, tunnel-like passage. The voices were whispering softly now, amidst their wanton laughter:

"Relax, my lovely one."

"We know what you want, Englishman, and we will give it to you."

"There is no escaping us now."

My heart pounded in terror. I stopped before a heavy, oaken door which stood ajar. Gripping the wooden stake tightly in my hands, I peered cautiously around the door-jamb. The angle of my first glimpse confirmed my suppositions: it was indeed an old chapel. I caught sight of an open-beamed ceiling and high, stone walls flanked by ancient, magnificent, stained-glass windows which flooded the room with multiple hues of light. As I widened my view, I saw three coffins standing against the far wall, their lids removed.

Then my eyes fell upon a sight which filled me with such shock, horror, and revulsion, that I believe I will never forget it as long as I live.

Not a dozen feet distant from where I stood, Dr. Van Helsing lay sprawled on his back on the stone floor, wide-eyed and unmoving, as if stunned into paralysis. His bag of tools lay beside him, its contents—stakes, hammers, knives—spilled out across the floor. He was stripped to the waist, and his shoes and socks were missing; and all three female vampires, their eyes flaming red, were assaulting him in a state of wanton sexuality. One dark-haired harpy was slowly and languorously licking his feet and sucking his toes. The other was kneeling beside his head, pressing her bountiful, exposed cleavage against his mouth while running her fingers through his hair; and the third—the blonde beauty—was straddling him, her long dark skirts billowing about her as she rocked her lower body against his pelvis while seductively massaging her hands along his naked chest en route to his throat.

The intensity of their lust must have so consumed their focus as to make them unaware of my presence. The blonde vampire's mouth opened wide as she laughed, revealing two sharp fangs.

Now she pushed her sister aside and poised herself to pounce on the professor's neck.

There was no time to think or plan. I dashed into the chamber. With the weight of my body behind me, and all the force I could muster, I threw myself at the blonde vampire, ramming my wooden stake down at her upper left back, where I believed her heart to be. My hands stung from the pain of contact—I heard a cracking of bone as the stake sank several inches into her flesh—(did it go in far enough to paralyse her?)—blood spurted from the wound, splattering me in the face—she screeched in agony! She let go of her victim and sank to the floor, writhing and cursing.

The other two vampires reared up, the stunned surprise in their red eyes vanishing as their faces contorted in fury like beasts from Hell. One of the professor's stakes lay at my feet—I grabbed it and rushed at the closest harpy—the one who had been tantalising him with her cleavage. But the third vampire lunged at me, shrieking and cursing as she dashed the stake from my hands.

The ensuing confrontation occurred in such a blur of terror that I cannot accurately recall it; nor could I make sense of it at the time. I only know that I found myself fighting back against both of the dark-haired, snarling vampire women at once. Had it been night, I would have been dead in an instant, for their strength would have been tenfold what it was by day; as it was, I was no match for their combined force. I strained with every fibre of my being to avoid contact with their awful teeth, knowing that if they did not succeed in killing me with their hands, they could drain me of my blood in minutes if they so chose.

Suddenly, there came a great crash. From the corner of my eye, I saw fragments of coloured, splintered glass flying in all directions. I heard a ferocious snarl. To my astonishment, one of the arms that gripped me was ripped from its very body in a gush of blood. The vampire screamed and fell back; I saw a flash of grey fur, angry fangs, torn flesh, a fountain of gore. Now a heavy wooden stake came out of nowhere and plunged into the third vampire's heart. As she screeched and sank to the floor, I realised the implement had been wielded by Dr. Van Helsing.

My eyes fell upon the beast that was viciously attacking the other dark-haired vampire. It was a great, grey wolf! As the animal ripped at her limbs and throat, the professor pounded the stake into his own victim with a hammer. She writhed and screamed, her lips foaming with blood.

Seconds later, all was silent. The two dark-haired vampires lay motionless on the ground, where, to my astonishment, they aged before me into wrinkled, hideous old crones. There was blood everywhere. I saw that one of the stained-glass windows had been shattered. As the professor and I caught our collective breath, the wolf paused in regal beauty, staring at me with deep blue eyes—eyes which I suddenly recognised.

"Oh!" I cried. But before I could act, the blonde vampire staggered to her feet, still young and beautiful, the stake still lodged in her back. She lunged at me with a roar of fury. Just before her teeth could sink into my throat, the wolf leapt upon her with an enraged growl, threw her to the floor, and tore out her throat with such force that her head was nearly severed from her body. Both head and body withered to reveal the ancient being within.

The wolf then darted for the doorway, where it paused for one long backwards look, and then disappeared.

My knees gave way, and I sank to the stone floor, trembling. My face, hands, and clothes were all splattered with blood, and the professor was equally covered in gore.

"Minj God!" Dr. Van Helsing cried, wild-eyed. "Madam Mina! How on earth did you find me? But you will tell me later. I thank God you have come. I thank you a thousand times over. That wolf: *that* is a mystery. Where did it come from?"

"I have no idea," I lied.

"Who could believe it . . . who could believe it. To think that

I, Van Helsing, should fall prey to those vixens . . . it is inconceivable!"

"What happened, Professor?"

He found his bloodied shirt and put it on, shaking his head in chagrin as he spoke. "I found them here sleeping, as I expect. I stand over the blonde's coffin with the stake, ready to plunge it into her breast; but I am so struck by her beauty, I cannot do it. She look so fair and radiant and full of life that I shudder as though I had come to do murder. And so I pause. I delay." His cheeks burned crimson as he finished buttoning his shirt and donned his coat. "I stare at her in captive fascination, as if under a spell. Suddenly, her eyes blink open, and she gaze at me—oh! Such a gaze! Such beauty! So full of love! My head, it whirl with new emotion. The very instinct of man in me call out to love and protect her."

He retrieved his socks and shoes and sank down on a bench to put them on, sighing heavily. "Then she rise from her tomb and take me in her arms. She kiss me. Never have I known such a kiss! I feel such ecstasy, I cannot describe. My mind, it is all in a cloud. Then suddenly, there are two of them embracing me, not one. And then—" He shook his head, mortified. "Never, never have I been so ashamed."

Oh! How well I understood the sensations which he had just experienced! How many times had I felt just such ecstasy, when Nicolae held me in his arms?

"Do not berate yourself, Professor. You are not to blame. And it is over now. They are all dead."

"No; not dead yet, Madam Mina. Even this one, whose head the wolf nearly took off—even she may not be full dead. Do we not completely severe the head of each, they may reincarnate."

I paled at this. "I will help you."

"No. This is bloody work; the work of butchers. I would not wish for you to have that memory in your brain, Madam Mina, to trouble you in years after. I will do it."

"I have come this far, Professor. I wish to see how it is done."

Dubiously, he consented. He found his saws and other knives; and we completed the terrible, bloody deed, three times in succession. It was truly a thing of horror, and I shudder to recall it. The only consolation came at the last moment, when the blade made its final cut through each vampire's throat; for at that brief instant, I thought I perceived a look of sweet peace cross each wizened face, as if the soul of her former, benevolent, human self had been freed to take its place among the angels. Then, before our very eyes, each body melted away and crumbled into dust, as embers in a spent fire, as though the death that should have come centuries before had at last asserted itself.

As we drove back to camp, the professor asked me how I had managed to get away from the holy circle in which he had left me. When I had finished my explanation, he again thanked me for coming to his rescue, and said, shamefaced:

"May I ask a favour of you, Madam Mina?"

"Of course, Professor."

"Will you be so good as to not breathe a word of this to any one? I could not hold up my head, were the others to know how I so weakly fall under the vampire's spell."

I agreed, and said that he might write the events in his journal as he wished, leaving out my part in it.

Dark clouds had gathered in the late-afternoon sky, and the professor predicted that it would snow again. When we reached camp, I realised that I was starving, and got myself to eat a decent portion of the food I made. Dr. Van Helsing built a crude sort of lean-to with one of the tarpaulins to protect us while we slept. I lay awake most of the night, however, shivering beneath my fur rug until just before dawn. Over and over, I relived in my mind the horrors of that awful afternoon, and the dreadful women who had attacked us.

Was that the fate to which I was doomed as a vampire?

Nicolae had said he would train me to become like him; but what if he failed? What if I became a wanton, preying vixen like those seductive harpies, with no conscience or soul?

❦

THE NEXT DAY—THE 6TH OF NOVEMBER—I WAS STARTLED AWAKE by the sound of Dracula's voice in my mind.

Mina. Awake.

I opened my eyes groggily as I wiped sleep from my eyes. From my bed of furs beneath the lean-to, I could see that the ground was encrusted with a light covering of snow. I glanced out briefly. From the position of the sun, I sensed that it was late afternoon. The sky was filled with scattered dark clouds, and it was very cold, with the promise of more snow in the air.

I am here, I replied as I lay down again. *The wolf: it was you?*

It was. I wish I could have been there sooner—but it was day. I crossed a very great distance to reach you.

Thank you. I am sorry.

Sorry about what? My wretched sisters? It was their time. They were not growing with the world but against it. I would have done the deed myself centuries ago, but I could not bring myself to kill my kin and only company. My only regret is that it put you in such danger.

I am safe now. Except—

Except what?

I am becoming like you. There is no longer any doubt.

A small silence fell. Then he said, with regret in his voice: *I am sorry, my love.*

I have tried to think what to do. But not knowing how much time I have—

We will decide together. But it will have to wait a day, at least. The moment of truth is at last at hand.

Do you mean to-day—?

Yes. Jonathan and Godalming made it up-river to the Bistritza—at last. The other two are not far behind. Both parties now approach on horseback. The Szgany will soon reach the vantage-point and will unload my box from their boat. That is when I mean to climb inside it.

When will—it—happen?

An hour or two from now. Just after sunset. The timing is critical. I must be in full possession of my powers, yet there still must be light enough for them to see.

What do you mean to do?

This you will soon discover. Mina: this is important. The professor must be a witness. You must bring him there.

My pulse skittered. I glanced out of the lean-to at the professor, who was sitting on a log near-by, cleaning his Winchester rifle. *Where?*

Cut across the forest for about a mile. I will direct you. You will come to a road. Follow it eastward for another half mile. There is a perfect viewing spot on a hill-side overlooking a stretch of the road.

"Madam Mina: are you up?"

I crawled out from beneath the lean-to. "Yes, Professor."

"You were sleeping so peacefully, I did not wish to wake you. I made coffee, and there is some bread and cheese. Would you like some?"

The smell of the coffee made me feel ill, and the idea of eating was again so repulsive to me that, as much as I would have liked to please him, I could not bring myself to the attempt. "No thank you," I replied, to which he frowned.

Leave now.

"Professor," I said, crossing to where he sat, "I have a strong sensation that Jonathan is drawing near and that the event we have all been anticipating is about to occur. We must go to him at once."

We started off almost immediately. We looked like a pair of tattered soldiers, I thought, wrapped in furs to guard against the bitter cold, our clothing muddied and encrusted with the dried blood of the vampire women, and toting our arms: Dr. Van Helsing his Winchester rifle, and I my revolver. We made our way on foot, following the mental instructions which Nicolae was sending me. Our progress was rather slow, as the forest floor was thick with undergrowth and blanketed in a thin layer of snow, and inclined steeply downhill through the woods.

We soon came upon a sight that made me recoil in horror: a young woman's body lay at the base of a tree, her red blood drenching the surrounding snow. "Oh!" I gasped. She was fair-skinned and fair-haired, and looked to be about my age. From what was left of her clothing, I guessed she was a peasant. Her face had been mutilated beyond recognition, and her limbs were half-eaten.

"Wolves," Dr. Van Helsing said grimly.

As if on cue, there came the distant howling of wolves, a sound which made me shiver with fear. I saw now why Dracula had been reluctant to show me his wolf-form. He had been a most beautiful animal indeed, and I was filled with gratitude to him for saving our lives the day before; but it was disquieting to contemplate the extraordinary fact that the wild creature I had seen was the man I loved—and this poor woman's body was a terrifying reminder of the vicious calibre of his deadly attack.

We came to a rough road and followed it eastward. We had gone about a half mile when I became very tired and had to sit down on a rock to rest. Nicolae's voice came to me, pointing out a high rocky ledge on the hill-side above the road where we would be less exposed, and where he wanted us to watch and wait. I issued a subtle suggestion to Dr. Van Helsing, giving him the impression that he had chosen the spot himself: a sort of natural hollow in the rock, with an entrance like a doorway between two boulders.

"See!" the professor said, leading me in by the hand. "Here you will be somewhat in shelter, and I can protect you if the wolves should come."

"More importantly, it is an excellent vantage-point," I replied, gazing at the magnificent valley below us. "We can see for miles."

The view was spectacular. The road below us snaked back and forth down the steeply wooded hill-side and then crossed a wide, undulating, wooded valley. Far beyond, the river wound its way into the distance like a dark ribbon; beyond that, the tall mountains which encircled us rose towards the setting sun. When I glanced back, I could see Dracula's castle on the peak behind us, cutting a clear line against the sky.

Promise me you will not leave that spot, Mina, Dracula commanded in my mind.

I will; if you promise that no one will be hurt.

I told you: no harm will come to your men at my hand, but this is all I can swear to.

What do you mean? I thought, alarmed.

The Szgany have agreed to leave your Englishmen alive, unless obliged to defend themselves—but they are gipsies, and everyone is armed. I cannot predict the actions of so many.

This news filled me with unspoken dread. *Where are you now? Where is Jonathan?*

Look and see.

In the distance, I thought I detected movement in the gaps between the trees. "Professor: where are the field-glasses?"

Dr. Van Helsing took his glasses from the case and searched the horizon. "Look! Madam Mina, look!" he cried suddenly as he handed me his glasses and pointed.

With the aid of the field-glasses, I was able to perceive a group of mounted men rounding a bend in the road not far below us, and heading in our direction. From the men's clothing, I ascertained that they were gipsies; they must be the Szgany to whom

Dracula had referred. In the midst of them was a four-wheeled cart—a long leiter-wagon which swept from side to side like a wagging dog's tail with each inequality of the rough road. Atop the cart was a great, long, wooden chest, similar to the ones I had seen in Dracula's chapel at Carfax.

The professor said excitedly: "Do you see it, Madam Mina? It is the very box we have been chasing since the day it left London harbour. The awful Thing that we seek is imprisoned there!"

Dr. Van Helsing could have no idea that the encounter we were about to witness was being staged for his benefit. However, he was right about one thing: Dracula *was* inside that chest. My pulse raced as I glanced at the setting but still-visible sun. Nicolae said that he must be in full possession of his powers or his ruse would not work—and it was yet day!

Now the hair rose on the back of my neck, as I experienced a sudden, overwhelming sense of déjà vu. The scene bore an uncannily similarity to the dream I had had some weeks previously—the dream in which a terrible battle had ensued, and one of my men had died. "Oh no!" I cried under my breath.

In fear I turned to the professor, only to discover that he had made another circle around me on the rock where I stood, by scattering it with Holy Host.

"Is that necessary?" I cried.

"Yes. No matter what happens, you shall be safe here from *him!*" Dr. Van Helsing took the glasses from me and swept the whole space before us, adding in a worried tone: "Where are our friends? If they do not come quickly, all is lost! The sun is sinking fast. At sunset, that monster can take his freedom in any of his many forms and elude all pursuit."

I hoped against hope that this very thing *would* come to pass. After a pause, however, the professor gave a great cry and said: "I see two horsemen coming up from the south, cutting through the woods towards the wagon. Look! Who is it, do you think?"

He quickly gave me back the field-glasses. At that distance, it was impossible to tell who the horsemen were, but I said I thought it might be Dr. Seward and Mr. Morris. The howling of the wolves came louder now, filling me with trepidation. Sweeping the field-glasses all around us, I could see dark grey dots moving singly and in twos and threes and larger groups, converging towards the centre of activity.

"Wolves!" I cried in terror.

Friends, came Dracula's mental reply.

"They gather to attack their prey," responded Dr. Van Helsing grimly.

I now caught sight of two other men riding at break-neck speed through the woods on the north side of the road, heading towards the gipsies and their rumbling cart. The first man I recognised; it was my husband. *Please God,* I prayed, *do not let Jonathan or any one else get hurt.*

Leave God out of this.

"Jonathan and Lord Godalming are approaching from the north," I said quietly.

The professor let out a gleeful shout as he picked up his Winchester. "Wonderful. They are all converging. Make ready your weapon, Madam Mina, in case of need."

I removed the revolver from my holster, my heart pounding in fear and dread, for I knew the end was coming. The sun was low in the sky; but until that moment when it finally and completely sank beneath the mountain-tops, Dracula's powers were severely weakened. Should the men catch up to him and attack him before sunset, they might well succeed in truly killing him.

How far off are they? came Dracula's voice in my mind.

Not far, and closing fast! I replied anxiously.

Instantly, as if someone had opened a heavenly tap in the grey clouds above, it began to snow. This was immediately followed by a high wind, which caused the snow to swirl about fiercely;

within seconds, the landscape below was entirely blotted out by a sea of white.

Did you do that? I thought.

As if with great effort, he responded: *Just—buying time—until the sun sets.*

It was strange to see the snow falling in such heavy flakes so close to us and to where I knew the cart and approaching horsemen must be, while in the far distance behind us, the sun still shone as brightly as ever, as it sank closer towards the mountain-tops.

"Curse this ill-timed storm!" the professor cried. "I can see nothing!"

Down came another blinding rush of snow. The wind came in fierce bursts, driving the snow with fury all around us in circling eddies. For several long minutes, I could not see an arm's length before us.

All at once, the hollow-sounding wind roared by with a great rush, sweeping away every last flake of snow so that we could view all before us with perfect clarity. The gipsies and their cart rumbled into view on the road immediately below. Moments later, the four horsemen darted out of the trees.

"Halt!" shouted Jonathan and Mr. Morris in unison, coming at the cart from two opposite directions, their strong voices ringing with passion and command. The gipsies might not have known the language, but there was no mistaking the men's intent from their tone. The Szgany reined in as Lord Godalming and Jonathan dashed up on one side, and Dr. Seward and Mr. Morris closed in on the other.

Panicked, my eyes darted towards the mountain-tops, for the evening was drawing near—every second, the sun descended lower and lower—but it had not yet set.

The leader of the gipsies, a splendid-looking fellow who sat astride his horse like a centaur, fiercely shouted something to his companions, who lashed their horses and began to spring forwards; but the four Englishmen all raised their Winchester rifles in unison.

"Halt or we fire!" Jonathan shouted.

"Cover the rear," Dr. Van Helsing commanded me quietly, "and do not fear to fire if necessary." As he pointed his rifle at the leader below, I aimed my revolver at the party of gipsies behind the wagon, anxiety coursing through me.

The Szgany, seeing that they were surrounded, tightened their reins and stopped. Each man then quickly drew whatever weapon he carried, be it knife or pistol, and held himself in readiness to attack.

There was a brief standoff. I waited and watched in an agony of suspense. The wolves drew closer. I alone knew that this encounter, from the gipsies' side, was being staged; I alone knew that the Szgany had been ordered by Dracula not to attack unless it was a matter of life or death; yet there were far too many weapons drawn for my comfort. It seemed to me that every man on that road was in mortal danger. Suddenly, the leader of the Szgany, with a quick movement of his reins, threw his horse out in front and, pointing to the sun and then to the castle, said something which I did not understand. In response, his men surged around the cart as if to protect it.

"Now, Quincey!" Jonathan cried urgently. "Before the sun sets!"

While Dr. Seward and Lord Godalming kept their rifles trained on the gipsies, Jonathan and Mr. Morris threw themselves from their horses, drew their kukri and bowie-knives, and began forcing their way through the ring of men towards the cart.

As I watched breathlessly, I felt not only fear now but a wild, surging desire to be a part of the action; *to do something.* I suddenly realised that the barrier of Holy Host surrounding me was obscured by a thin layer of snow. Ignoring the professor's protests, I darted out of the now-defunct circle to a more advantageous spot down the hill-side, where I trained my revolver on the crowd of gipsies surrounding Jonathan, looking for any man who might mean him harm.

The majority of the Szgany lowered their pistols and knives and stepped aside to let Jonathan and Mr. Morris pass. No doubt my men attributed this acquiescence to their awe-inducing impetuosity and singleness of purpose—but I knew the truth.

Not all of the gipsies were so compliant, however. With the corner of my eye, I saw one of their knives flash and cut at Mr. Morris. Dear God! Had he been wounded? To my relief, he continued to move forward unimpeded. Now Jonathan reached the cart and leapt upon it, where, with desperate energy, he attacked one end of the chest, attempting to pry off the lid with his kukri knife. Seconds later, Mr. Morris sprang up beside him and attacked the other end of the chest with his bowie.

In seconds, the sun would set. The shadows of the whole group fell upon the snow. Under the efforts of both men, the nails of the lid drew back with a screech. The top of the box was thrown back. Inside, I spied Nicolae lying upon a bed of earth. With a start, I saw that it was not the Nicolae I knew and loved, but the old, pale monster the men expected to find, his eyes glaring with a vindictive look. What did he intend to do? I wondered. Was this part of his plan?

Now I shrieked in horror. For just as the sun disappeared below the mountain-tops, Mr. Morris's bowie-knife plunged into Dracula's heart; at the same instant, Jonathan's hand came down with a sweep and a flash, his great kukri knife shearing through the Count's throat. Before I could even draw a breath, Dracula's entire body crumbled into dust and passed from sight.

All was silent but for the echo of my scream in the wind.

TWENTY-THREE

I SCREAMED AGAIN IN TERROR AND BEWILDERMENT. NICOLAE had said he was only going to stage his death! Did his ruse not succeed? Was he truly dead? Could it be that this was part of his plan all along—to free me from his "curse"?

Lord Godalming and Dr. Seward let out shouts of victory. Dr. Van Helsing stood cheering on the hill-side just above me. Jonathan and Mr. Morris leapt down from the wagon, whooping with joy. No sooner had their feet touched the ground than, to my horror, a Szgany darted up in fury, shouting as he aimed a deadly blow of his dagger at Jonathan's back.

I raised my revolver and fired, the thrust of the gun jerking against my hands as the explosion echoed forcefully in my ears. The attacking gipsy cried out, clutching his shoulder and dropping to the ground, his weapon falling from his grasp. Jonathan whipped around, his astonished glance finding me on the hill-side. And then chaos reigned.

The gipsies cantered about in an atmosphere of surprise and confusion, and then started riding away as if for their lives. The injured gipsy and those who were unmounted jumped upon the leiter-wagon and followed in haste, shouting to their departing horsemen in their native tongue as if afraid of being deserted. Even the wolves took part in the communal upheaval, loping off into the woods.

Through the ensuing tumult I watched and waited, filled with dread. Where was Dracula? Was he safe? At last, I heard his voice in my mind:

You are worried. (He spoke with delight.)

Yes! I thought, immensely relieved.

I vanished before their knives could do lasting harm.

Are you hurt?

I am already healed. Go now. Let the men enjoy their victory. Play the vanquishing heroes. I will come for you when it is safe.

When?

Soon.

His voice was gone.

What was I to do when he came? I wondered. Earlier, I had promised myself that when Nicolae was safe, I would see him one last time and say good-bye. But I was becoming a vampire. Everything had changed.

As the professor trudged down the hill-side towards me, I saw that our party below was left entirely alone, with no sounds but the wind blowing through the trees. My gaze fell upon Mr. Morris. To my dismay, I saw him sink to the ground, holding his hand pressed to his side, blood gushing through his fingers.

"Mr. Morris has been injured!" I cried. Dr. Van Helsing and I flew down the hill, joining the others as we gathered around our wounded friend.

"Hold on, Mr. Morris," I said in anguish, kneeling beside him. "We have two doctors here. They will tend you."

With a feeble sigh, Mr. Morris took one of my hands in his. "I think my time is up, little lady. But don't grieve for me. I am only too happy to have been of service." Mr. Morris's eyes suddenly widened, and he struggled up to a sitting posture, pointing to my forehead. "Look! It was worth it, to die for this! Look!"

As all the men turned to look at me, my hand flew to my forehead. To my consternation, my skin was smooth and untarnished. My scar was gone! Nicolae must have removed it somehow, I thought, to reinforce the illusion of his demise.

With great effort, Mr. Morris whispered with a smile: "God be thanked that all has not been in vain. The curse has passed away."

In unison, the men all sank to their knees as they spoke a deep and earnest "Amen."

Mr. Morris's hand fell from mine. He took one last breath, and his eyes glazed over. "He is dead," Dr. Seward pronounced sadly.

Tears spilled from my eyes. Oh! I thought, this was my fault. My fault! I had silently collaborated with Dracula to stage his "death." I had deluded myself into believing that no one would be hurt. These men had bravely tried to save me from the vampire's curse—a curse from which, unbeknownst to them, I still continued to suffer—and now this gallant gentleman was dead. How could I ever forgive myself?

I saw moisture in the eyes of all the others, and I wept bitterly as we knelt by Mr. Morris's body in grief and respect. At length, my gaze met Jonathan's. We both stood and fell into each other's arms.

"Thank God you are safe," Jonathan said, his voice breaking with emotion as he held me tightly.

"I missed you," I said with deep sincerity, returning his embrace.

"All this time without word of you, it nearly drove me to distraction." He pulled back and kissed me, then studied my face intently. "Have you been well? Are you all right?"

"I am fine," I whispered.

He studied me and the professor. "What happened to you? Why are you both covered in blood?"

I darted a look at Dr. Van Helsing, who answered: "I slew the vampire women at the castle. It was a bloody business. And Madam Mina—" He seemed at a loss.

"I shot a rabbit last night and cooked it for supper," I interjected. "I had never butchered an animal before. I was not very good at it."

"Well, I saw that shot you took," Jonathan said, proud and grateful. "You were good at *that*. I believe you saved my life."

"As Mr. Morris said: I was happy to have been of service." Another sob escaped me, and Jonathan pressed me closely to him.

The wind picked up suddenly, rushing past us in a frigid blast laced through with flurries of snow. "We had best get back to camp at once, while there is still light enough to see the way," said Dr. Van Helsing, "and lay a fire before we all freeze."

The men placed Mr. Morris's body over the back of Dr. Seward's horse. The professor then took Mr. Morris's horse, I rode with Jonathan, and we all sadly and silently made our way up the hillside. At the camp, the ground was hard and frozen; and as we had no implements for digging in any case, the men respectfully laid Mr. Morris's body in a shallow snow-bank beneath the trees. All agreed that we would take him back with us to a churchyard in the nearest town where he could have a proper burial.

Lord Godalming and Dr. Seward, having roughed it together many times in the past, went to work fashioning excellent tents with the tarpaulins and rope we had brought, and long sticks we gathered. Jonathan and I built a good-sized camp-fire with the supply of wood we still had in the carriage, and we all soon gathered round it.

Snow covered the ground and nestled on the branches of the evergreens like icing on a cake. I shivered, pulling my filthy cloak more tightly about me as we stared into the fire. Jonathan sat beside me on a log, resting his hand on my knee as if to reassure himself that I was really there. The mood was grim and solemn, like a wake—which indeed it was. The satisfaction the men felt in their perceived victory over their enemy was greatly diminished by the terrible fact that one of our party had lost his life in the battle—and I, more than most, felt the weight of this burden.

DR. SEWARD AND LORD GODALMING TOLD ANECDOTES ABOUT the many places they had travelled with Mr. Morris, and the adventures they had shared. Everyone spoke from the heart about the good and kind gentleman whom we had all admired.

In time, a silence fell. In the distance came the occasional howling of the wolves. With a little gasp, I noticed two gleaming blue eyes staring out at us from the undergrowth beneath a nearby tree. A wolf! Or was it Nicolae? Jonathan, following my gaze, quickly grabbed for his rifle—but I reached out and stopped him.

"No!" I cried, heart pounding. "Do not shoot it. It poses no threat. Just wait, it will go away."

Indeed, no sooner had I spoken than the wolf turned and disappeared into the woods. Jonathan relaxed his grip on his weapon but shook his head. "I should have shot it. It may come back while we are sleeping."

"I am starving," said Lord Godalming. "Do you have any food in that carriage of yours?"

I cooked up a supper of sorts for the party, but as I bent over the bubbling pot, the smell of the food made me feel ill—a reaction I was determined to hide. To reinforce the illusion that Dracula was dead, I must give the appearance that all my vampire symptoms had gone away. I served up a plate for each of the men, who dug in hungrily.

"Is that all you are eating, Mina?" Jonathan asked, when he saw the tiny portion I had taken for myself.

"I am not very hungry," I said truthfully. "I am just tired and very sad."

Jonathan studied me quietly for a moment, with such a perceptive look that I worried he might suspect the true reason behind my lack of appetite; but he said nothing and turned back to his meal.

As they ate, the men fell into a long conversation, congratulating themselves for a job well done.

"It will take centuries before another Un-Dead can hope to gain the kind of knowledge and power that Count Dracula possess," said Dr. Van Helsing.

"We have made the world a safer place," agreed Dr. Seward with satisfaction.

Jonathan, who had been staring quietly into the fire, said: "I wonder. Have we?"

"Have we what?" said Lord Godalming.

"I wonder if we truly achieved our aim to-day."

My pulse quickened in alarm at this. Dr. Van Helsing said: "What do you mean, friend John?"

"Do you remember that night in my chamber at the asylum, when we all saw Dracula vanish into a wisp of vapour? You said, Professor, that he could come and go like a mist. In Lucy's diary, she said he once appeared from dust. Just because we saw Dracula *crumble to dust*, does that mean he is truly dead?"

This line of enquiry made me very anxious, particularly when Dr. Seward added, with a puzzled look: "Yes. What about that?"

Dr. Van Helsing replied emphatically: "He is dead, my friends. The Count's body crumble to its native dust because he is more than three hundred years old, just as his brides did when I slay them earlier."

"But Quincey was supposed to stab the Count with a wooden stake to the heart," Jonathan persisted. "In the fray of battle he must have lost the stake, for he delivered that blow with his bowie-knife."

"The stake does not kill, friend John; it only paralyses. To kill the vampire true dead, you must severe the head—and this you did. With our own eyes, we saw you slit Dracula's throat. We saw the mark which vanish from Madam Mina's forehead. By her own admission, her telepathic connection to Count Dracula is no more. This is our proof that he is dead."

"I see." Jonathan nodded with a weary but grateful sigh.

I sighed in silent relief. A lively discussion then ensued, in which the men shared the details of their separate adventures over the past few days. As they talked on, my mind began to drift. As far as the men knew, our quest was over, and I was "freed."

But I knew very differently.

I was grateful, oh so grateful, that Dracula's plan had worked and that he lived. I was equally conscious that as long as he existed, I was destined to die and become a vampire. I suddenly recalled a line from the rhyme Lucy had told me all those months ago at Whitby:

Married in black, you will wish yourself back.

We had thought it meant I would travel far away from home and wish to return to England. This had indeed come true; yet I now saw an additional meaning in the phrase. I truly did wish *myself* back: a return to *my own human, mortal self.*

I was taking on more and more vampire-like characteristics every day. Could I return to England, knowing that I was poisoned by Dracula's blood? How long would it be before the others discovered that my symptoms had not gone away?

And what would they do when they found out?

It was well after midnight when we retired to our makeshift tents. Jonathan had made a bed for us from a pile of fur rugs. I joined him there, wrapping my cloak about me as he drew a warm cover over us. He then took me in his arms.

"It is over, Mina. Over! At last, your soul is free!"

I was glad Jonathan could not see my face in the darkness. "Yes," I returned quietly.

"I love you so much," he whispered. "You are everything to me. Let us stop in Paris on the way home and celebrate. We will revisit all the places we enjoyed so much on our honeymoon. Only this time, we will stay at the finest hotel and dine at the best restaurants. Would you like that?"

"Yes," I said again, my voice breaking.

"When we get home, I want to start our family right away. We will have a houseful of little Harkers to fill our lives with joy. How many children should we have? Five or six?"

Tears stung my eyes. I could barely speak. "Six," I managed.

"Six it is, then," he said, kissing me. "Why are you crying, dearest?"

"Because I am happy," I lied.

"So am I." His voice began to fade as exhaustion overcame him. "We have a long, wonderful life ahead of us, Mrs. Harker, and we are going to make the most of it. Are you warm enough?"

Incapable of speech by then, I could only nod.

"Sleep well, my dear." Holding me in his arms, he drifted off to sleep.

I lay awake for a long while, steeped in misery, struggling to hold tears at bay.

At last, I slept.

And dreamt.

I dreamt I was home in Exeter, sitting in our garden on a bright, sunny day. A breeze softly rustled the leafy branches of the near-by trees. Birds chirped. Everything was lovely and serene.

I was reading the book Jonathan had bought me. It was Shakespeare's Sonnet 71:

No longer mourn for me when I am dead
Then you shall hear the surly sullen bell
Give warning to the world that I am fled
From this vile world, with vilest worms to dwell . . .

Suddenly, the sun which warmed my head and shoulders began to feel as if it were searing my flesh. I was overwhelmed by a terrible, growing thirst. I poured myself a glass of lemonade and took a sip, only to spit it out in disgust.

My attention was drawn to the twittering of birds in the nearby trees. The sound seemed heightened somehow: it was as if I could both hear and feel the bird-song ringing continuously throughout my body, like the hum of an engine or the purr of a cat. I rose, drawn to the sound like a magnet. I stopped and stared up into the branches of the nearest tree, waiting for—I knew not what. At the same time, my jaw began to ache fiercely. As I touched my teeth, wondering at this sudden pain, I discovered to my surprise that my four canines had grown long and sharp, like fangs.

Suddenly, a small bird flitted down from a limb towards me. As if by instinct, my hand shot out and grabbed the tiny creature in the air. In the space of a frenzied instant, I yanked the feathers from the bird's body and sank my teeth into its denuded flesh, sucking its blood urgently into my mouth, swallowing the delicious nectar as if my life depended on it. Only when the blood supply was finished did I pause and stare at the limp, mangled body of the bird clutched in my hand—whereupon I gasped in horror.

Good God! What vile act had I just committed? I had just killed one of the world's sweet and innocent creatures—and had drunk its blood! Worse yet, *I had enjoyed it.* Filled with self-loathing, I hurled the bird away into the trees.

I awoke with a start, overcome by a wave of nausea and disgust. I darted out of the tent and raced into the cover of the woods, where I retched violently. When I had emptied my stomach of its meagre contents, I took a few steps away, dropped to my knees in the snow-encrusted dirt, and burst into tears. I had long believed that dreams could be portents. Had I not dreamt of Dracula, on the night before he first arrived in Whitby? Had I not heard his voice calling to me, telling me that he was coming? Had I not dreamt about the very battle I had witnessed to-day, and seen that one of my brave men was going to die?

I knew what my mind was trying to tell me now: it was offering me a glimpse of my future. The woman in my dream: that is who—or what—I was becoming! "You will be forced to make an important choice," the old gipsy woman had said. "Listen to what your body tells you. It is changing. Let it be your guide."

Tears ran down my cheeks as I then recalled the words Jonathan had spoken before he fell asleep: "We have a long, wonderful life ahead of us, Mrs. Harker, and we are going to make the most of it."

I had promised Jonathan, once, that I would never leave him. But I could not return to England with Jonathan now. One night, desperate for blood, I might lunge for his throat and kill him. It was doubtful that I would make it as far as England, in any case. The way I was changing, it might be a matter of days before Jonathan and the others recognised the signs. Then Dr. Van Helsing—no doubt enlisting my husband's help—would surely slay me as they had slain Lucy, before I even reached the grave. Or worse: upon seeing me still infected, they would deduce that Dracula was still alive and renew their efforts to find and kill him—which would put each of the men in harm's way again.

No, I decided, overwhelmed with bitterness and regret. I could not risk putting them in such danger. Better that I left *now*, before they could learn the truth of what had happened to me. Did I dare take one last look at my husband? Should I leave a note for him? No. What would I even say?

I continued to weep silently for some minutes: for the family I would never have and the human life with my sweet husband that I would never lead. It was all lost to me—a loss that I deserved: it was God's punishment for all that I had done. I had betrayed Jonathan, and now I must pay the price.

At length, I dried my eyes and glanced about me, noting thankfully that the rest of our party were still in their tents, asleep. Quietly, I retrieved my water-flask, then rinsed my mouth and cleaned my teeth. When I had finished with these ablutions, I sat down on a log by the embers of the camp-fire.

Enough of this self-pity, I reprimanded myself. I supposed I ought to be relieved that things had turned out this way. I was no longer obliged to choose between my two loves. The choice had been taken from me. There must be countless people who would be thrilled to trade places with me. I was going to be a vampire with uncanny powers! I would be able to shift my shape to nothingness. I would have time to learn all there was to know. Had I not longed to be a princess? Was not Nicolae a prince? I would exist for ever with a man I deeply loved—and I could be with him immediately!

At that moment, I saw a trail of white mist emerging from the trees and moving towards me. My heart lurched. I felt a little thrill mingled with a wave of apprehension. It was happening! I was about to leave my life behind, to die and begin a new life as an Un-Dead, immortal being. The white mist swirled upwards, contracting into a man's shape; and suddenly Nicolae was standing beside me.

"Come home with me, my love," he said, holding out a hand to me.

TWENTY-FOUR

In a whirl of sound and wind and midnight air, Nicolae took me to his castle.

As he set me down on my feet in his great library, he kissed me passionately. "At last: you are here."

"I can never go back."

The room was lit by a myriad of antique lamps which threw long, quivering shadows on the dark stone walls and floor. Nicolae nodded, then said softly: "I know this is happening many decades sooner than you would have wished, my darling, but I cannot pretend to feel regret."

"I cannot just disappear, with no explanation or good-bye—but I have thought about how to manage it."

He read my thoughts. "The dead peasant woman in the forest?"

I nodded, breaking from his embrace. "She was about my size and colouring. Her face was completely gone. If we dress the body in my clothes and move it to a different spot, close to our encampment, the men will think I was killed by wolves during the night." As I spoke the words, I shivered, trying to imagine what it would be like for Jonathan to discover my mangled body. Would he blame himself? I thought, devastated. Would he spend his entire lifetime grieving? How could I subject him to such suffering? But what other alternative did I have?

"You must put the past behind you now, and move forward."

"That is easier said than done."

"You only say that because you have no conception of the kind of life you have before you." Nicolae took me into his arms again and looked down at me lovingly. "I will make you my wife, and we will share everything together, into eternity."

"How can you make me your wife? I am already married."

"You are married in this life. When you die, you will be reborn into a new life, as a new being—and you will be my bride. We will know a kind of happiness that until now we have both only dreamt of; for no two people were ever more suited to one another than you and I."

I nodded, falling under his spell. "I cannot quite grasp that this is all real."

"It is very real, my darling. And it was meant to be. If ever you doubted it before, you may doubt no longer. I have been thinking over what that old gipsy woman said—about you being connected by blood to their clan. It proves a theory I have held since the first time I beheld your picture and your letters, and was desperate to find you. Do you remember I told you that my wife had a twin sister?"

"Celestina."

"Celestina's daughter was stolen by gipsies and never seen again."

I caught my breath. "Do you mean—do you think that I was descended from—"

"I do. So you see: you and I were destined to be together, my love. You are my reward for centuries of loneliness." He kissed me again, then grabbed my hand, adding with enthusiasm: "Come. I have much to show you."

He led me up a wide, circular stone staircase and then down a long passage. The way was lit by lamps with open flames which hung on brackets on the walls. He unlocked a heavy oaken door. Inside was a comfortably furnished bedroom and sitting-room, much like the guest-room which Jonathan had described in his journal. Several lamps were already lit within. Now I gave a little gasp; for lying upon the bed was the beautiful emerald green silk gown which Dracula had presented me in his parlour at Carfax. Beside it were a pair of matching silk slippers.

"I brought them with me in the hopes that you might wear them one day. I see that they will prove useful immediately."

I understood his meaning: that my own clothes and shoes would be required to outfit the body in the woods. "I will put them on."

He courteously left the room with a bow. I was glad to be rid of my filthy, blood-splattered dress and boots, but deeply saddened to be obliged to part with my beloved white cloak, even though it was equally dirty. The emerald evening gown and slippers were a perfect fit. There was no looking-glass, of course; but from the admiring reaction I received from Dracula when I opened the door to admit him, I felt as if I were Cinderella, transformed and ready to attend the ball.

"You are stunning." Eyes shining, he took my hand and twirled me as he had done on the dance floor, then drew me to him. From his pocket, he withdrew a small jewellery box, which he offered me. "I had something else made for you. I hope you like it."

I opened the box to discover a beautiful gold brooch in the shape of a bird, its tail and plumage encrusted with rubies, sapphires, emeralds, and pearls. "Oh!" I cried, recognising the mythical creature it depicted. "It is a phoenix."

"It is said that the phoenix lives a thousand years, is consumed by fire, and then rises from the ashes, reborn anew, to live again."

"Immortal," I whispered.

He pinned the brooch to the bodice of my gown. "And mine, for ever." He gazed at me intently with his fascinating eyes, then kissed me fiercely.

Before I could thank him, he grabbed my hand again; and with undisguised excitement, he led me on a tour of his castle, showing me what lay behind all those locked doors. One of his favourite rooms was his well-outfitted art studio, where he both painted and sculpted. Dozens of canvases were stacked up against the walls. There were portraits of his sisters and romantic studies of lovers dressed in clothing from a bygone era, as well as expertly rendered landscapes of European scenes: majestic, snow-capped mountains, fields and valleys covered with flowers, verdant forests, and sparkling lakes and rivers, each painting adorned with small figures either picnicking, wandering alone, or journeying in a group.

"These are wonderful. Did you paint all these?"

"I did."

I was touched by what the paintings said about his loneliness, his romantic disposition, his love of nature, and his desire to travel and connect with others. "And the ones in the library?"

"Mostly mine. A few are by Jan Brueghel the elder and Peter Paul Rubens."

No wonder they had looked familiar! "You own works by Brueghel and Rubens?" I said, astounded.

"I studied with them in Antwerp in the early seventeenth century. We were good friends for a time—that is, until they discovered what I was and asked me rather emphatically to leave."

I shook my head in awe and wonder. "What a fascinating life you have led."

"It has had its moments. And yours, my darling, is only just beginning."

Taking my hand again, he led me down the passage to another chamber. Upon entering, I caught my breath. It was a comfortably furnished music room, hung with elegant tapestries and lit by many lamps and stately candelabra. A blazing, smokeless fire burned in the hearth. There were a harpsichord, a grand piano, and more than half a dozen other fine musical instruments.

I moved instinctively to the grand piano. "May I?"

"Be my guest."

I sat down on the bench and began to play a piece by Mendelssohn that I knew by heart. Dracula picked up a violin and played in harmony with me, a performance that was superb and deeply felt. When we finished, I could not hold back a delighted laugh.

"Do you play all these other instruments as well as you do the violin?"

"Some better than others."

"How very accomplished you are."

"With all the time in the world, one can achieve a great many things."

I fell silent at that, reminded again of my own imminent future. Is this what my life would be like? Days and nights spent with Dracula, filled with beautiful music, reading, conversation, and art—far into eternity? It was a thrilling thought; but as anticipation shivered through me, I could not help but feel a twinge of fear in my stomach. It all still seemed so fantastical, improbable, and . . . frightening.

I looked up at him from my seat on the piano bench. "After we . . . feign my death . . . what will happen next?"

He shrugged. "You will stay here with me, of course. I will take care of you until you die."

"Which will happen . . . when?"

"It is difficult to say. Everyone's path is different."

Apprehension rose within me. "Will it hurt when I die?"

"No. You will feel no pain."

"What will it be like, when I—"

"When you rise?"

I nodded, my heart pounding.

"I cannot really remember, it was so long ago; but others tell me that it is akin to waking up from a very deep sleep."

"Will I—will I be like your sisters, and like Lucy?"

"What do you mean?"

"You know what I mean."

He hesitated, avoiding my gaze. "At first, perhaps. A young vampire has yearnings and impulses that are difficult to ignore. But in time you will master them, as I have."

I was flooded with sudden panic. I could not forget the despicable, lustful actions of the vampire women we had slain, or my lascivious nightmare when I had almost preyed upon the professor. And what about the terrible crimes Dracula committed when he was first made? He killed his own wife and child, and all those people!

"My brother made me," he replied quickly to my unspoken thoughts. "*I* will make you. You will be different, and you will have me to govern you."

"What if you do not succeed?"

"I will succeed."

I could not feel his assurance. "Where will we live?"

"Here, there, anywhere you like."

"Anywhere except England. We could never go back to England."

"That would be unwise."

"I suppose we would have to avoid sunny countries."

"I generally do."

"And anywhere we go, we would have to cart along two giant crates of dirt to—to sleep upon—and guard them with our lives."

"Yes, and now that you will become a vampire in my own native land, it is far easier. We can sleep together on the soil of Transylvania."

Somehow, the notion did not appeal to me the way it did to him. "Tell me about . . . nourishment. How will we feed ourselves?"

"There are plenty of people to choose from when we travel. While at home, there are the animals in the woods, and the occasional stranger who passes through."

I thought of my dream earlier that night, the aching thirst, and the disgust I had felt after I sucked the life from a bird. Could I ever truly bring myself to feed from a live animal? What would it be like to attack a human being and suck his blood? I shuddered at the thought.

"It will become like second nature to you," Dracula said.

A great heat of confusion came over me. Did I truly want to live for all eternity as a creature who craved and required the blood of others to exist? What if I could not learn to stop before my victim was dead? I remembered, too, the fear that the professor and I had seen in the eyes of the gipsies and other people we had met on our journey into Transylvania: the way they had crossed themselves and protected themselves against me with charms to ward off the evil eye. What would it be like to be shunned and feared by all the world, for the rest of time? What would it be like never to eat food again? Never again to enjoy the warmth of bright sunlight on my face and shoulders? Never to see my own reflection? Could I be happy living in this lonely castle for ever? If we left Transylvania, would we spend an eternity running and hiding?

I loved Dracula; but did I want to become his Un-Dead bride for ever?

From the wary look on Dracula's face, I knew he was reading my mind.

"Mina," he said quietly, "these thoughts are only sparked by fear. They will not trouble you after you rise."

"That is the part which frightens me the most. The idea of becoming a being without any sense of conscience—I could not bear that."

"Are you saying that I have no conscience?"

"No. But you said yourself, it took years—centuries—to gain the kind of self-control that you now possess. You could not control your own sisters! What proof do you have that you can teach and control me?"

"I will *make* it happen."

I rose from the bench and stood before him, heaving a tremulous sigh. "Nicolae, I cannot pretend with you. You know every thought and feeling I have. You know how much I love you; and you also know how much I have struggled with this from the very first. I thought that I could embrace the idea of an eternal future with you, but now that it is here and real—" I shook my head. "I cannot do this."

Dracula let out a surprised, rueful laugh. "You cannot do this?"

"No. I cannot become a vampire."

"I am afraid you have no alternative, my love. Unless," he added, with a flash of danger in his eyes, "you intend to try to kill me."

"I would never wish you any harm, Nicolae."

"Then your fate is set, Mina. You have no other choice."

"But I *do* have a choice."

"Oh? What is that?"

Calmly, I replied: "I will simply go back to the others and convince them that—although Dracula is truly dead—despite the professor's theories about freeing souls, the vampire poison still lives on in my veins. And I will instruct the men to slay me."

"Slay you?" Dracula slammed down his fist on the piano with such violence that the instrument rang out like a mighty death knell, and the polished, black, wooden top crushed and splintered into dozens of flying fragments. "Are you out of your mind?"

"Do you not see? This will free us both."

"No!" he roared. "I will not allow those butchers to lay a hand on you!"

"It is my decision. My choice. It is what I want."

He grabbed me now, glaring at me in fury. "Mina: do you have any idea what I have gone through on your behalf? If you die, it will only be at *my hand,* to be reborn. I have waited four hundred years to find you! I will not give you up now!" As his eyes penetrated mine, I heard the next thought which flashed like lightning in his mind:

That weakling of a husband will never have her, or the child she carries in her womb!

I froze.

I stared at him.

Had I heard his thoughts correctly?

Did he just say . . . that I carried a child in my womb?

A child . . . ?

All at once, understanding came to me in a great rush. Is that what the old gipsy woman had meant, when she said my body was changing? All the symptoms which I had been experiencing over the past two weeks—the extreme tiredness, the chills and light-headedness, the lack of appetite, the nausea—had I been feeling this way, not because I was changing into a vampire—*but because I was with child?*

I saw the answer in his eyes, heard the truth in his thoughts, as a look of guilt and intense frustration crossed his face. He let go of my arms and backed away.

But wait, I thought: what about the holy circle I had been unable to breach? What did that mean? With a gasp, I suddenly remembered that I had never even tried to step outside either of the professor's holy circles until they had been cleared. I had been too afraid.

My hands dropped to my womb in sudden wonder and consternation. "You knew?" I cried, aghast. "*You knew, yet you said nothing?* You meant to *murder me,* turn me into a monster, and keep me here as your bride—*when I was not infected at all*—but was carrying an innocent child inside of me?"

He hesitated, glancing back at me. "Mina: my blood still runs in your veins. You may become a vampire yet—only time will tell—and if so, that child will never live to take its first breath. I was only protecting you."

"Protecting me from what?" I cried in anguished fury. "From the possibility of becoming a mother? From the joy of living the life that I have craved ever since I was a motherless child? My God! How could you? You say you love me; but you never did!"

"It is *because* I love you, Mina, that—"

"No! You love no one but yourself. You think only of what *you* want! That is not love; it is selfishness. And what you have done is pure evil!"

"Mina—"

Another thought occurred to me: "My God! My God . . . was any of it true?"

"Was any of what true?"

"Everything you told me: your sad life story, all those explanations and excuses for every charge that was laid against you—for what happened to Lucy—to Jonathan—to the men on the *Demeter*—was it true? Or did you just make it all up in an attempt to redeem yourself, and to appease me?"

"Now you doubt everything?" he cried with renewed ferocity. "Of course it was true!"

"How can I know? You lied about this. You lied to me about who you were from the first day we met. What else have you lied about? Oh! This whole charade—the chase after that box of yours—across the sea and up the river—it was all just a ruse *to bring me here,* wasn't it?"

"No—" he said, but his thoughts said *Yes.*

"Oh! It doesn't matter what is true! You are still the monster that everyone said you were! How could I have allowed myself to be so deceived? How could I have ever thought I loved you?"

I turned and bolted towards the open doorway. In a flash of speed, Dracula was suddenly standing just before me. "Where do you think you are going?" he demanded.

"Home. To my husband. Back to England, where I belong."

"I would like to see you try."

I darted around him and out the door, then started down the stone passage—whereupon I skidded to a halt. For he was now standing thirty feet ahead of me, at the far end of the corridor, blocking my exit, smiling at me mockingly.

"You forgot to say good-bye," he sneered.

I spun and fled in terror, only to find him waiting for me in *that* direction, just twenty feet beyond! I gasped in dismay. Ahead, there was an opening to a circular stairway. I lunged for it and raced up the steps, only to freeze in consternation. He was waiting there above me, arms crossed, and laughing wickedly.

I turned and fled back down the stairs, but he was there again, one floor below me! I burst into the passage in between, returning whence I came, my feet echoing loudly against the stone floor as I gasped for breath. I had just reached the music-room doorway when he suddenly materialised in front of me and grabbed me tightly by both arms.

"You will never go back to England, Mina," he hissed, his eyes flaming red, his teeth and fingernails long and sharp. "You will never see your husband again. You *will* be mine, even if I must kill you here and now, this very moment, and keep you by force. You are my destiny! We are bound by blood!"

His mouth lunged for my throat. I screamed and tried to pull away. Was that pounding footsteps I heard on the stairs or the sound of my own heart drumming in my ears? Just as I felt his teeth begin to puncture my flesh, to my astonishment, I heard a voice—*Jonathan's voice*—cry:

"Let her go, you fiend!"

Dracula looked up in surprise. Suddenly Jonathan was there—I saw the glinting flash of his kukri knife—there was a struggle and a clatter—then Dracula was lifting Jonathan bodily in the air and hurling him against the passage wall, where he slid, stunned and motionless, to the floor.

I stared in horror. Then instinct took over. In the music room just beyond, I spied the long, sharp pieces of wood from the shattered piano top scattered across the floor. I darted in, snatched one up, and raised it as a weapon. Dracula followed. As he hurled himself at me with a hideous roar, his own violent momentum helped drive the wooden shard straight into his heart.

Dracula cried out in shock, astonishment, and pain and dropped to his knees, bleeding, clutching at the wooden stake as if he meant to pull it out, but he seemed to lack the strength. He slowly sank to the floor and lay there, paralysed. For a moment I stood paralysed as well; for before my eyes, as he lay on the floor, his blood spreading out beneath him in an ever-widening pool, he slowly began to age into a gnarled, wrinkled, waxen-faced old man.

I heard a scream of anguish, and realised that it had issued from the depths of my own throat.

My God! My God! What have I done? He was dying, and I had killed him! I was suffused with the heat of sudden remorse, and tears spilled from my eyes. Then my gaze fell on Jonathan, lying senseless—perhaps dead!—in the hall, the victim of this man's hand; I thought of the innocent child growing within me, who deserved a chance to live; and I knew that I had done right. And I was not yet finished. I had one last, grisly deed to perform.

The kukri knife lay in the open doorway. Blinded by tears, I grabbed it and knelt over Dracula's prone body, holding the terrifying blade over his throat. He stared up at me, unable to move, now an ancient, withered man whose only recognisable features were his piercing blue eyes. As my gaze met his, I saw deep regret and anguish in those eyes, as if his own humanity had at last resurfaced.

"Forgive me, Mina," he whispered with great effort. "I loved you too much."

I faltered. He was himself again. Anger had turned him into the monster who made him; yet there was so much good in him. I had loved him. I *still* loved him. How could I kill the man I loved?

I sobbed and lowered the knife, my heart breaking. "I cannot."

"Do it!" Dracula whispered insistently. "I do not belong in this world. You do. Feel no remorse. Live the life that I was never allowed to have. Live it for the both of us!"

Tears coursed down my cheeks as I shook my head. "No. No."

With what seemed to be a supernatural effort, he raised his hand and firmly covered my own hand with his, so that we clutched the knife together. " 'Our revels now are ended,' " he quoted softly, haltingly, looking into my eyes. " 'These our actors . . . were all spirits and are melted into air, into thin air . . . and, like the baseless fabric of this vision . . . shall dissolve . . . and leave not a rack behind.' "

With sudden force, he rammed the great knife down across his throat. The blade slashed into his flesh; a ribbon of crimson blood arched into the air; and in a fraction of a blink, his entire body crumbled into dust and vanished from my sight.

My knees buckled, and I collapsed to the floor, staring at the bloody, empty space before me in stunned disbelief.

Dracula was dead.

I wept; but there was no time for grieving. I forced myself up and raced to Jonathan's side, where I knelt and took him anxiously in my arms. To my intense relief, I ascertained that he still breathed. I kissed him repeatedly, calling his name as I gently stroked his face. He soon opened his eyes. Stunned confusion quickly gave way to alarm as he struggled to rise.

"Where is he?" he cried.

"He is gone," I said, holding Jonathan tightly in my embrace, my cheeks still wet with tears. "I killed him."

"You killed him?" He was both astonished and relieved.

"Yes." I told him all that I had done, leaving out only the detail of Dracula's last, impassioned message. "I never could have done it without you. How did you come to be here?"

"I was uneasy all evening. Something about you was different, Mina. I was not certain I believed the Count was dead, and if not, he might still have you in his power. When I awoke and found you gone, I was afraid he had taken you. I rode up immediately. The door was open, but the castle seemed to be deserted. I looked everywhere. I raced upstairs, and then I heard his voice. He was threatening to kill you. I rushed in at him with my knife, but—" Jonathan flushed a deep red. "That is the last thing I remember." Quickly, he added: "I did not recognise him. Are you certain it was he? He looked so young."

I chose my words carefully. "He has appeared to me that way in the past."

He stared at me. "Did he give you that dress?" At my nod, he asked: "Did he hurt you?"

I paused. My heart felt as if it had been broken in two, a rent that could never be repaired. Dracula had inflicted that deep wound; but I could never share this truth with Jonathan. "No," I whispered. "Nothing that will not heal in time."

"And he is truly dead now?"

"Yes. And thank God you came when you did, my husband, or *I* would be dead—and so would our child."

Jonathan sat up now, looking at me in wonder. "Our . . . ?"

I nodded, unable to hold back a tearful smile as I took his hand and placed it over my womb. A look of such pure happiness crossed my husband's face, that I thought my heart would melt. In one breath, I both laughed and sobbed; then Jonathan took me in his arms and kissed me.

We returned to camp before the others awakened. Jonathan and I agreed that it was best not to mention the events that had occurred at the castle. Better to let the men go on thinking that Dracula had perished at their own hands the evening before, and that Mr. Morris had died a hero. And so it was that in all the journals we kept at the time, it was written that Dracula died at sunset on the 6th of November, dispatched by the blades of Jonathan and Mr. Quincey Morris.

The next morning we all began the long journey back to England, stopping to bury Mr. Morris in a quiet, respectful ceremony in a churchyard in Bistritz. I had become so accustomed to hearing Dracula's voice in my mind that its absence left a hollow, aching void. At times I wept unceasingly, and nothing Jonathan or the others said could comfort me. They attributed this dearth of emotion to what they called "my delicate condition." But I could not stop thinking about him, about everything he had meant to me, about the final words he had spoken.

Did he choose to die as a penance for his last evil act? Did he force my blade because he wished me to live on, unencumbered by what he saw as his unhealthy obsession? Oh! If only I had possessed the strength to stop his hand! For in spite of what he had done, and what he meant to do, I had not wanted him to die. I was steeped in guilt, and I knew that I would grieve for him every day for the rest of my life.

NOT LONG AFTER WE ARRIVED HOME IN EXETER, A SMALL PARCEL was delivered for me. To my astonishment, it contained a letter with the Sterling family seal:

Belgravia, London–16 November 1890

My dear Mrs. Harker,

Please forgive my delay in writing to you. Since the evening when I encountered you so unexpectedly in my entry hall, you have never been far from my thoughts. I believe I was speechless at the time, so taken aback was I at seeing you. My housemaid, Hornsby, shared the purpose of your visit and gave me your address. I can only imagine what you must think of me. Lest you harbour any misconceptions, I wish to acquaint you with the truth.

Many years ago, when I was a young man at University, I fell in love with a maid who worked at our house. Her name was Anna Murray. I loved her to distraction, and I believe that she felt the same way about me. I wanted her to be my wife. Unfortunately, love is not always enough in this world. We cannot always have what we want; other factors intervene. My mother learned of the relationship, and the next time I returned home to visit, I discovered to my grief that Anna had been dismissed. My mother said nothing about Anna being with child; she only impressed upon me the importance of duty, and that I must forget her.

In time, I married. I never heard from Anna again, but she was never far from my thoughts. Years later, when my mother lay dying, she admitted that she had sent Anna away because she was with child–my child! I made a determined effort to find her, and you. By then, Anna was dead; but my enquiries led me to the orphanage where you resided. I made an anonymous bequest, with the stipulation that the funds be used to finance your education. When you appeared before me a few months ago, I could not doubt who you were. Your mother was a beautiful woman, and your likeness to her is uncanny.

Needless to say, propriety forbids me from acknowledging you openly. But should you ever require my assistance in the future, you may contact me with discretion. Please know that in my deepest heart, I am proud to be your father.

I remain, yours truly,
Sir Cuthbert Sterling, Bt.

P.S. Hornsby asked me to enclose this book, which was a gift from your mother. She said it was one of her favourites.

I read this letter in silent amazement. It had been my own father who had financed my education! How strange and surprising life often turned out to be! Although I would never know my father, I owed him a great deal, and I would always be grateful.

For the first time in my life, I also felt a sense of peace with regard to the circumstances of my birth. My father said he had loved my mother to distraction, and this gave me great comfort. Had I not felt the same kind of burning, illicit passion that had driven my mother and father into each other's arms? At last, I could forgive them, even as I struggled to forgive myself.

So engrossed was I in these thoughts that I almost forgot to look at the other item which the parcel contained. I removed the brown paper wrapping to find a slim book, cheaply bound, which was inscribed inside with my mother's signature. I gave a little gasp.

It was *The Complete Sonnets of William Shakespeare.*

EPILOGUE

IT IS NOW THE SUMMER OF 1897, NEARLY SEVEN YEARS SINCE the events of which I have written here. It is time to bring my story to a close, time to return this journal once and for all to its eternal hiding place.

Our darling son, who was born eight months after our return from Transylvania, just celebrated his sixth birthday. We named him Quincey John Abraham Harker, in honour of all the men who participated in our perilous adventure all those years ago—but we call him Quincey. Lord Godalming and Dr. Seward are now both happily married to lovely young women, and from Dr. Van Helsing's correspondence, he seems to be as crusty and energetic as ever.

I think of Lucy and her mother often, and with affection. Every summer, Jonathan and I go to London and put fresh flowers on their graves in Hampstead.

My husband and I love each other more with each passing day.

Jonathan devotes himself to his work. He returned all those years ago from our trip to Transylvania in fighting form, and he has gained great respect as a solicitor. At the same time, with his encouragement, I have spread my wings. I am active in our community. I teach piano and dance. I belong to several ladies' auxiliaries. On occasion, I write articles for the local newspaper. It is fulfilling work, and it makes me happy.

So far, my husband and I have not been blessed with other children, but we hope that will change. Our son Quincey is a good lad: sweet, curious, and remarkably intelligent. He seems to be stronger and brighter than other children his age, but perhaps that is a mother's prejudice. Like his parents, his greatest pleasure is reading, and even at his young age, he has a talent for music and art. His hair is much darker than Jonathan's, and he has deep blue eyes, which I suppose must come from Jonathan's mother. Sometimes, however, when I look into their blue depths, I imagine that I see someone else—but I know that is impossible . . .

We spend our evenings with Quincey, playing music, reading aloud to each other from books on every possible subject, and quoting poetry. When Jonathan and I are alone, our intimacy has blossomed into something wondrously fulfilling.

"I am the happiest man in England," Jonathan commented last night, as he took me in his arms. "I have all that a man could wish for."

I returned the sentiment with heartfelt sincerity.

I love Jonathan dearly. He is my soulmate. How comforting it is to be with someone where everything is on an even keel! I am content, and very grateful for all I have.

At the same time, every now and then, I cannot help looking back. I cannot help asking myself: was it wrong to have loved Dracula? I do not know. But it happened, and I cannot alter it. I can only treasure what was, understand that it was never meant to be . . . and try to learn from it. Some relationships, no matter how real and vital, are too extreme, too dangerous, too exhausting to survive.

On occasion, against my will, I still dream of him—erotic dreams in which Dracula comes to me in my sleep and makes love to me. I sense his presence in every mote of dust and every appearance of mist. At the oddest moments, I have been startled by the certainty that I spotted Dracula's face in a crowd. I cannot shake the feeling that he still exists, that he is out there somewhere, watching over me; but I know that that is impossible, too . . .

I do believe one thing: that whatever destiny man may possess, my life was meant to be one thing up until him, and then radically, magnificently another—and now that he is gone—another still. All three versions of me (before, during, and after him) are different beings, each as unlike the other as the root differs from the blossom when the seed is sown. If all the days and nights in the world were to cease to be, I still hold that we were meant to meet and to love and to know the pain of violent disillusion.

I will always love him. I will never forget him. He changed me for ever, and I will be for ever grateful. My life is filled with infinite sweetness both because I knew him, and because he let me go. My life is now my own, and I know that it is better this way.

FROM

SYRIE
JAMES

AND

AVON A

Q & A with Author Syrie James

What inspired you to write *Dracula, My Love?*
I loved Bram Stoker's brilliant novel, and the unforgettable characters he had created. And yet, the story left me unsatisfied. His Dracula—one of the earliest literary depictions of a vampire—is an evil, ghoulish old man, endlessly discussed and feared, but rarely seen after the first few chapters. The two female characters in the book are sweet, feminine, and sexless, and their encounters with Dracula are almost entirely off-stage and shrouded in mystery. We know nothing of Mina's courtship or early life, other than a single, vague reference that she never knew her parents, and the fact that she and Lucy are close friends. We get theories about Dracula's origins, but never hear the true story from Dracula himself.

The book also leaves many unanswered questions. Who *is* Dracula? How did he acquire his uncanny powers? Who are the three vampire women at his castle, and what are they doing there? Why does Dracula choose Whitby as his port of entry into England, if Purfleet is his intended destination? After encountering Lucy in Whitby, why does he seek her out again in distant London, a city of "teeming millions"? Why doesn't Lucy's body crumble to dust when she is slain? And why does Mina become Dracula's prey?

The fact that Dracula's residence in Purfleet is next door to Dr. Seward's asylum is highly convenient and never explained. If Dracula can move about by day like any man, why does he need to be taken all the way back to Transylvania in a wooden box? Does he really die at the end, even though his attackers don't wield a wooden stake? Why does it take so long for Mina and Dr. Van Helsing to reach Castle Dracula? And what about the mental connection that's established when Mina drinks Dracula's blood? Stoker never uses that connection other than to give us Mina's repeated, hypnotic sightings of "lapping waves." Why don't Mina and Dracula ever utter a single syllable to each other telepathically? This seemed like a missed opportunity to me. What fun it would be, I thought, to imagine the telepathic bond between those two, and see how it played out!

As I re-read *Dracula*, I saw that there existed a wonderful opportunity to fill in the voids that Stoker had created—a way that I could answer all the unanswered questions, explain away all the inconsistencies, and bring a fresh perspective to this timeless work. Stoker's novel is told entirely through a series of letters, telegrams, newspaper clippings, and journal entries, which I could dramatize and bring to life. Instead of five different narrators, I could employ just one. I envisioned a new and more romantic interpretation of the story, told entirely from Mina's point of view, which would stick closely to the facts of Stoker's novel, but open it up to include the *untold story*: the secret account of Mina's passionate love affair with Dracula which occurred off the page, and was too scandalous to reveal.

***Dracula, My Love* is very romantic, but there is little or no romance in Bram Stoker's *Dracula*. How do the main characters in your novel compare to—or differ from—Stoker's characters?**

Stoker's Mina is smart, strong, logical, sensitive, and well-read—a woman with a "man's brain," as Van Helsing so ineloquently puts it. I strove to retain all these lovely, essential qualities, while at the same time fleshing out Mina's character arc, and reflecting her evolution as a woman. To that end, I focused on two major elements: the invention and exploration of her personal history, and her inner struggle between her affection for and loyalty to her husband, and her intense desire for that powerful being, Dracula, to whom she is drawn despite herself.

I wanted Dracula to be a central character and love interest—which meant he could not be Stoker's hideous, selfish, elderly recluse, whose sole purpose seems to be to feed on the living. Neither did I envision him as the suave but evil charmer so often portrayed in the movies. I envisioned Count Dracula not only as an attractive, charismatic, and highly intelligent supernatural being, but a sympathetic one: a man who had a very different explanation for every terrible act attributed to him. A man who'd been completely misunderstood. A man who'd taken full advantage of his gift of immortality to expand his mind and talents, and who would do anything to win the heart of the woman he loved. Stoker's Dracula can vanish at will, morph into a bat or wolf, and appear decades younger. Given these abilities, I reasoned, he would surely appear in his most attractive form to the woman he wished to woo—just as the female vampires at his castle (who are presumably as old as he) appear to Jonathan as ravishing beauties.

Your previous novels are critically acclaimed memoirs, written as if from the pens of Jane Austen and Charlotte Brontë. Was it something of a departure for you, to write a romantic thriller about vampires?

My last two books were indeed about real-life, beloved authors. But although this novel is an offshoot of a fictional story instead of a true story, it still shares many similarities to my past work. All three novels take place in nineteenth century England—a place with which, after many years of research, I've become very familiar. They are all passionate love stories featuring a strong, intelligent heroine and a man who, due to circumstance, is forced to disguise or withhold his feelings for the woman he deeply loves until a defining, culminating moment. As with Jane and Charlotte, I was working with an established story or set of facts which was riddled with gaps, and which I had the pleasure of bringing to life through imagined scenes and dialogue.

And as for vampires—I've been interested in them for years, ever since my son Ryan asked me to coauthor a screenplay that included vampires. Today's vampires are good-looking, powerful, immortal, and eternally young. They're the "forbidden fruit"—a combination of sex and danger that's a powerful aphrodisiac for many. A vampire who's lived for centuries should be incredibly good at everything, don't you think? Especially sex. Vampire sex should be the best sex a woman has ever had. After all, they've had centuries to practice.

Book Club/Reading Group Study Guide

1. Who are your favorite characters in *Dracula, My Love*, and why? Who is your least favorite character? How is Count Dracula similar to or different from the Dracula portrayed in Bram Stoker's novel, and/or in any of the film versions you've seen?

2. Compare and contrast the characters of Lucy and Mina in *Dracula, My Love*. How do the differences between them ultimately affect their fates?

3. Discuss Mina's character arc. At the beginning of the story, what are her viewpoints regarding love, marriage, a woman's role in society, and the need to follow that society's rules? Is Mina an example of traditional Victorian mores? How does Mina grow and change over the course of the story?

4. Early in the novel, Mina admits that she's always told Lucy everything, and that she and Jonathan made a solemn pact to be completely honest with each other. Yet Mina conceals her relationship with Mr. Wagner/Dracula from both Lucy and Jonathan. Why? How does the burden of carrying that secret affect her and influence the choices she makes?

5. What are Jonathan's and Dracula's respective strengths and weaknesses? Why is Mina attracted to them both? Do you think she loves one more than the other, or just loves them in a different way? Do you empathize and connect with

her feelings for Dracula? Who do you think is Mina's ideal mate?

6. A long list of evils is attributed to Dracula, most which he refutes. How plausible are his explanations? Do you think he was telling the truth? After hearing Dracula's version of events, did you feel sympathy for him?

7. When does Dracula begin to have feelings for Mina, and why? How does he go about pursuing her? Knowing that she is already engaged, what do you think he hopes and expects? How does their relationship build and grow over the course of the novel?

8. How does the telepathic bond between Mina and Dracula enhance the story and move the plot forward?

9. Discuss the scenes which explore the truth of Mina's parentage and personal history. How does her back story add to her character and to the novel as a whole? How does Mina and Jonathan's shared history influence their present and future?

10. Discuss Dracula's origin story as revealed in the novel. How did his personal misfortunes shape the being he becomes? Do you admire him for the choices he's made? Why or why not?

11. If you had an eternity before you, how would you spend it?

12. Mina reminds Jonathan that her dreams often come true. Did this fact affect your expectations while reading the novel? How does Mina's dream imagery serve the story? When Mina dreams that Dracula makes love to her, do you think it was really just a dream?

13. There are many unanswered questions in Bram Stoker's novel, such as Dracula's origin, his motivation for coming to Whitby and London, and the truth behind all that occurs at his castle. How does the author address these and other unanswered questions in *Dracula, My Love?* Did you find the answers believable and satisfying?

14. Did reading Mina's story in the first person enhance the experience for you? What are the benefits of telling a story from the main character's perspective, rather than the third person? What are the limitations?

15. Discuss the pros and cons of a vampire's existence as explained in the novel. Do you think Mina made the right choice at the end? Given her options, would you have made the same choice? Why or why not?

16. What physical and psychological changes does Mina experience when she is certain she is becoming a vampire? Were you surprised by the final revelation?

17. Discuss the book's climax and resolution. Do you think the ending was appropriate? What caused Dracula to react and behave the way he did? At the final moment, do you think he did the right thing?

18. Examine the Epilogue. Seven years have passed. What is Mina's perception of events? Is she right? What do you think happened to Dracula? In what ways has Mina's relationship with Dracula changed her forever?

BOOKS BY SYRIE JAMES

THE LOST MEMOIRS OF JANE AUSTEN
A Novel

ISBN 978-0-06-134142-7 (paperback)
$13.95/$17.99 Can.

"The reader blindly pulls for the heroine and her dreams of love, hoping against history that Austen might yet enjoy the satisfactions of romance.... [This book] offers a deeper understanding of what Austen's life might have been like."

—*Los Angeles Times*

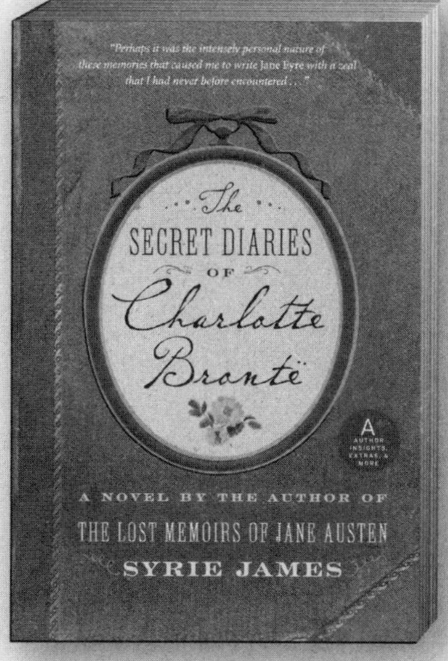

THE SECRET DIARIES OF CHARLOTTE BRONTË
A Novel

ISBN 978-0-06-164837-3 (paperback)
$14.99/$18.99 Can.

"James adapts Brontë's voice, telling Brontë's story as though it came straight from the great writer...a satisfying—if partly imagined—history of the real-life experiences that inspired Brontë's classic novels."

—*BookPage*

Visit Syrie James online today at www.SyrieJames.com!